ENDURANCE

ENDURANCE

Elaine Burnes

Mindancer Press
Bedazzled Ink Publishing Company • Fairfield, California

paperback 978-1-949290-85-1

Cover Design
by

An earlier version of this story was published in *Haunting Muses* (GusGus Press,
Bedazzled Ink, 2016)

Mindancer Press
a division of
Bedazzled Ink Publishing, LLC
Fairfield, California
http://www.bedazzledink.com

For Beth

Chapter 1

CAPTAIN LYN RANDALL entered the packed Observation Lounge. Soft piano music dampened the clink of glasses and bursts of laughter, voices breaking through. A bar bot moved among the small tables and upholstered chairs, delivering drinks. Her guests jostled for seats like the music might stop and the chairs run out. An energy of high expectation buzzed through the crowd. They'd spent the last month and a half speeding through space pretending to enjoy the stops along the way when what they came for was right here, right now. Given what happened the last time Lyn had been here, it was only natural that a completely opposite energy coursed through her. So instead of sitting front and center, the captain's prerogative, she slid along the back toward an empty chair by the map table.

The lights dimmed, showtime. Stragglers found seats. The crowd quieted and looked up. As their eyes adjusted, points of light popped against the black background. A river of stars, the Milky Way, spanned the clear dome overhead. A teaser. From the left, dull gray rings slowly crossed their view. The Keeler Gap followed, then more rings, brighter and brighter against the dark edge of space beyond.

"There," someone called out.

They turned and leaned. Like the sun rising from a vertical horizon, brilliant Saturn slid into view, growing, glowing with sand-colored bands of cream, yellow, and almost pink. Wavy storm clouds swirled near the southern pole. The mood of the room rubbed off on Lyn. An unexpected awe thrilled her. This was what she had hoped for when she requested this orbit. To feel with her guests a pleasant shiver tingling the toes and scalp.

Once the planet filled the dome, the ship, which had been turning to create this spectacle, stilled. The room went quiet.

"Welcome to Saturn," Natalie Okeke, the expedition leader, said in her soft Yoruba-accented English.

She stood before them, her eyes sweeping the room, holding each person for a fraction of a second, making each feel graced by her presence. Tonight she wore a bright batik head tie, a *gele* matching Omara Tours' gold and green. It fanned out from her head like a halo, no, like rings. Over her flight suit, she wore a matching *ibo* skirt and *buba* blouse.

"As you can see, Saturn's glow is not faked." She paused. "Go ahead, you wondered, didn't you." Low chuckles spread through the room. "In fact,

Saturn doesn't only reflect light. The sun is too far away. No, he also radiates from within. He is *hot*." She smiled seductively.

This was Natalie's first trip to space, and her early nervousness had settled into an ease as part storyteller, part scientist. She regaled her audiences with interesting details about Mars, Jupiter, Ganymede. She knew this stuff cold, how Saturn formed, how many moons. Lyn's thoughts drifted during that part of the talk. She scanned the crowd. A hundred passengers with the means to spend three months touring the solar system on the Grand Tour, a once-in-a-lifetime alignment of Earth, Mars, Jupiter, and Saturn.

"Enceladus . . ." Some things couldn't be blocked out. Natalie said the word reverently, drawing out the syllables. En-*cel*-a-dus. One of the more charismatic moons and with good reason. Natalie pointed to the tiny dot with her laser. Too small to see the bright pearl coloring or the plumes of water and ice. So small yet so dangerous.

A bright speck caught Lyn's peripheral vision, unrecognizable to the guests but a glowing, annoying intruder to her. That wasn't Enceladus. She opened a mind link.

Randall to Con. Ani, are you seeing this?

Second Officer Anilina Rodriguez responded from the bridge, *Yes, Captain.*

Is it the Aphrodite?

I think so. I've asked them twice to move, but they haven't responded. Should I turn us?

Please.

Lyn relaxed back into her chair. Slowly, the view through the dome shifted, removing the offending competitor's ship.

Thank you, Ani. Everything okay?

Yes, Captain. Enjoy the show.

Lyn acknowledged and closed the link. Enjoy the show. Why not? Halfway through her last tour. After twenty years chasing a dream of space exploration, or maybe running from ghosts, she was ready to head home. Not to her house in Bodega Bay, California, but her childhood home in the eastern Montana desert. Back to flying a plane. In air. One of her mom's open-cockpit replicas, perhaps. She could almost feel the wind on her face.

She returned her attention to her guests, noting that not everyone wore their Omara Tours flight suit. She'd ask Sharyn Wang, the hotel manager, to remind the guests that suits were a safety precaution and to be worn at all times.

That speck caught Lyn's eye again, the *Aphrodite* intruding on her guests' view of Saturn's E ring, right as Natalie pointed out how it formed from icy jet plumes in Enceladus's south polar region.

Ani opened a mind link. *Capt—*

No. Lyn cut her off. *We're not moving again. I'm on my way. Let's have a little chat with our* Aphrodite *friend. Randall out.*

This was her sector of the orbit. No one was going to mess with her last tour. She rose from her seat, nodding politely to Natalie. She slipped out the door and descended the stairway that circled the elevator one flight to the Bridge Deck. Holograms from past tours lined the walls. Smiling guests ogling Venus, excursion pods zipping toward Earth's moon. Everything on *Endurance* was geared toward making the guests comfortable and inviting them to explore, with large windows and the domed top deck. Yet the ship had an intimate feel. Cozy hallways, carpeted and quiet. Discreet handrails and polished fixtures. She crossed the landing and short corridor past her quarters and conference room. A small, beetle-shaped house bot ducked into its compartment in the wall. Housekeeping, Sharyn's realm, kept a low profile and bots hid when people approached to avoid tripping hazards and to add to the illusion that on an Omara Tour you never had to see the cleaning.

She entered the bridge and steadied herself against the railing. The tourists loved this amenity, getting to watch the crew, but it was like staring down a steep balcony. When Omara renovated the ship for tourism, she spared no expense, adding holographic screens to the walls and ceiling. The room lacked windows, but the screens could display any view outside, filling nearly 180 degrees. Dramatic didn't begin to describe it. Slightly nauseating did. Lyn always got a little vertigo when first entering, like standing on the edge of the Grand Canyon. And she knew Ani liked to pump up the drama.

She squinted at bright Saturn filling her entire field of vision from floor to ceiling. Layered rings slashed diagonally across the front screen and overhead to the wall behind her. Yep, Ani went all out tonight. The view from the lounge had nothing on this. The two crew were silhouettes, the young pilot in the command seat and Ghez, the navigation officer, one level below her. Purple sidelights guided Lyn down three steps to the command level.

"Could you ease back a smidge on the projection," Lyn said as Ani moved to the first officer's chair and she took the commander's seat.

"Squeamish?" Ani asked.

"A bit."

"How does someone who's afraid of heights go to space?"

"Space isn't about heights. And how about letting me see my hand in front of my face."

"Projection, 100 percent," Ani commanded. "Lights up 30 percent."

The planet shrank to a life-size view. And the lights revealed empty seats next to Ghez. One for helm, Ani's usual seat, another auxiliary, and one to the right of the command chair. *Endurance* kept Earth–Baker Island time, so it was night and since they were in orbit for the next week, down to a skeleton crew.

Ghez swiveled in nir seat. "Good evening, Captain. I've spotted another ship in our sector."

"Where?"

"Too small for visual. A research vessel." Ne swung back to nir console. "ID is RV *Mars Jedica*, out of the Lavenza Institute."

"Not our problem. Especially if we can't see it. Research vessels have a separate contract. So where's our big, annoying friend?"

"You sure you want me zooming in?" Ani asked.

Lyn met the tease with a half-smile. "Let's get some evidence. Zoom and capture."

Ani gave the voice commands, and the glowing dot grew. Soon the luxury space cruiser sat before them, Saturn's surface glowing in the background. Lyn had seen the ship in orbit above Clarke Terminal at Baker Island, Earth Control's main launch site in the Pacific. With nineteen decks—compared to *Endurance*'s five—and eight thousand passengers and crew, the Jupiter-class cruiser was too big to dock at the space elevator or maintain low orbit, so its passengers were ferried from the terminal.

"Right in our line of sight to the planet," Lyn said. "Ghez, can you document that for me, please?"

"Yes, Captain. Positioning is two sectors off contract."

"Figures." Lyn opened a voice link. "*Endurance* captain to the *Aphrodite*. Please respond."

"*Aphrodite* here," a low, possibly masculine, voice answered. "What can I do for you, Captain?"

"This is Captain Evelyn Randall. I hope you're having a nice evening. I noticed you drifting into our sector. Please correct that." Manners mattered, but she wasn't going to ask, like it was a favor. Their ship was in violation.

"Good evening, Captain Randall. Third Officer Thomas Philbrick here. I'll look into your request."

The link went silent. Lyn drummed her fingers on the armrest, waiting, watching for any movement by the enormous ship. Anticipating her query, Ani shook her head. No movement detected.

"*Endurance* to *Aphrodite*. Please update your status."

"One moment, *Endurance*," Philbrick called back. "I'm seeking authorization to acknowledge the request."

Lyn's eyebrows rose. Ani also showed surprise. Who was in charge over there? Minutes ticked by.

"Visual requested," Ani said.

The screen filled with the enormous face of a woman. Lyn startled at the intense dark eyes boring into her, angled brows and deep furrows setting Lyn on edge. Instantly, she knew she didn't want to anger this woman.

"Ani."

"On it."

The image shrank to normal and far less threatening. Now her eyes showed boredom more than annoyance. Fine lines from the corners matched the small, but sincere, smile. She had wavy black hair and light brown skin. A beaded evening gown and dangling sparkly earrings meant she was not on duty.

"This is Captain Celeste Bratt. What can I do for you, Captain Randall?"

Lyn reflexively pulled smooth the front of her flight suit. *Don't apologize for ruining her fun.*

"There was no need to interrupt your evening, Captain Bratt. I simply pointed out your ship has drifted into our sector. All you need do is return to your contracted orbit. With my thanks."

Captain Bratt barely controlled a peeved eye roll. Whether directed at Lyn or her nincompoop third officer wasn't clear.

"Of course." She glanced to the side, nodded, then faced Lyn with a wider, though still genuine smile. "We haven't had the pleasure of meeting, Captain, but I've heard good things about you."

"Likewise," Lyn lied. She'd never heard of Celeste Bratt, but she didn't know most of the other tour captains.

"Your ship is adorable," Celeste said. "I'm quite jealous."

Ani gasped. Did she imagine Captain Bratt wanted *Endurance* as a shuttle, her private chariot to carry her from one end of the behemoth to the other?

"Yours is . . . impressive," Lyn said.

"That it is."

Lyn sensed Captain Bratt wasn't completely buying the "bigger is better" superiority of the opulent *Aphrodite*. She was beginning to like this woman.

"We should get together for drinks some time," Celeste continued. "After this Grand Tour." A hint of annoyance with those last two words. Definitely liking this woman.

Lyn could empathize. The Grand Tour was pure marketing. Anyone with the time and money could take the tour whenever they wanted. Her boss, Omara, for example. But the alignment was ripe for the masses. A tour could be squeezed into less than three months, and companies had rushed ships through production to be ready.

"Will you be stopping at any of the moons?" Lyn asked.

"Alas, we have too many passengers for surface excursions. Strictly observing from afar, I'm afraid."

"I'll bring you a souvenir," Lyn said impulsively. Did she really intend to take her up on the offer? Why not? Ani was quiet beside her, watching. Was that a bemused grin? Ghez, ever the professional, pretended to ignore them and inset a view of the *Aphrodite* moving back to its own orbit.

"Please give my regards to Omara when you see her next," Celeste said.

"You're acquainted?"

Celeste smiled warmly. "Oh, yes. We go way back."

"Well, then, we'll have stories to share."

"We will." Celeste rested her chin on her hand, her intense gaze unsettling, but not in a bad way. Then she took in a deep, perhaps regretful breath. "I wish I could chat, but I need to go judge a dance-off."

"Enjoy," Lyn said, her mouth suddenly dry. "It was nice meeting you."

"Likewise."

The screen blinked off. Ani switched to the view of the *Aphrodite*, continuing to move slowly out of visual range.

"*That* was interesting," Ani said.

"I'll say."

"I think she was flirting with you."

"I highly doubt that." Lyn's hot cheeks made her grateful for the room's dim lighting.

"Why not? You're flirtable." Ani nudged her. "*Qué linda*."

"Watch your boundaries, Second." She said it with a smile. Ani was like the kid sister she never had. Oh, to be twenty-five again.

She eyed the engagement ring on Ani's left hand. "How are you adjusting?" she asked as a diversion.

Ani blushed, and her wide smile warmed Lyn. Oh, to feel *that* again.

"The concept is great, but it feels funny. Kind of in the way." She twirled it. "Rob wasn't happy I was wearing it on a chain around my neck. Too symbolic, he said."

"You'll get used to it." She didn't add it was harder to get used to *not* wearing a ring. Instead, they chatted about wedding plans, venues. "Saturn would be nice," Lyn said.

"Yeah, I should have booked us on the *Aphrodite*," Ani deadpanned. "Captain Bratt could have performed the ceremony."

Lyn slapped her gently on the arm. They sat quietly then Lyn gave her hand a gentle squeeze. "I'll miss you, you know."

"I might not quit. Not yet."

"Really? Being away from each other for weeks at a time isn't a healthy way to start a marriage."

"I can do shorter Mars tours. I like flying. Rob knows that." She added quietly, "I might switch to a cargo carrier."

Lyn knew Ani loved piloting and had no interest in being a captain who also had to play host and judge dance-offs. "Then I still get to say I'll miss you, but whatever you decide, I know you'll be good at it." She hadn't told her crew this would be her last tour. It was a relief to know Ani had plans of her own, so she didn't have to feel like she was abandoning her. One of the parts of her job she enjoyed most was mentoring younger staff.

"Well, with this crisis averted, I'll return Control to you, Second." She stood and Ani rose to switch seats.

Once off the bridge, Lyn's mood settled. Rather than return to the Obs Lounge, she decided to make her rounds and turn in. She roamed the quiet hallways, deck by deck, making sure everything was shipshape. While she walked, she whispered, "Tara." A woman appeared, visible only to Lyn. Not suited for space, she wore casual clothes, like she did back when they shared a home on brief leaves. Lyn mentally chatted, told her about her day, how it felt to be back near Enceladus. Not as terrifying as she'd thought. Tara didn't say anything, her quiet presence was all Lyn needed.

In her quarters, she dashed off a note to her parents then opened a com link to the ship's central computer. "How are you feeling tonight, Petra?" Lyn asked.

The computer responded, "Good evening, Lyn. All systems are functioning well. And yourself?"

Lyn appreciated Petra's personal approach. "Very well, thank you." She listened while the computer ran through the various departments, noting topics to bring up at the next staff meeting. Lyn could mentally link with any system and perform her own diagnostic, but she enjoyed the conversational interaction.

When Petra finished, they wished each other a good night, and Lyn changed into a fresh suit, remembering to check the pockets before putting the old one in the Recyc-All. The downside of space travel was not being able to sleep nude, to feel the soft sheets. Her thoughts returned to Celeste Bratt. Maybe she would get in touch. Just drinks. Then again, if she returned to Earth permanently, a long-distance relationship wouldn't make sense. But even thinking the word relationship was a hopeful sign. She switched off the light and fell asleep to Saturn's glow through the window.

IT BEGAN WITH a low rumble intruding on a dream. Lyn stood at the edge of a high cliff as vibrations rattled her body before the ground suddenly fell away. She jolted awake to a brilliant flash filling her cabin and the pressure of her blanket snapping tight. The bed shook her like a carnival ride. Not the bed, the room. Not the room, *Endurance*. Darkness, then the dim glow of emergency lights. Her lamp, toiletries, tablets, everything not locked down spun and swirled like leaves in a gale. A shriek of metal tearing, glass shattering. A high-pitched whine, metal under stress. It sounded like the ship was being torn open. A memory rushed of a tornado ripping the roof off the barn. Alarms whooped the shrill warning of hull breaches. She was immobilized by the bedding, facing the ceiling. It buckled and bent then sprang back into place. Instinctively she activated her suit and squirmed a hand out to flip the hood on. The soft faceplate stiffened and the suit sealed her in, applying pressure against any potential decompression. Gloves deployed from her cuffs. Red lights flashed, life support failing.

She opened a com link. "Captain to the bridge. What's going on?" There was no response.

The room spun. Her stomach heaved. She wiggled out of the tight bedding, a safety measure for just such circumstances, only to be flung across the room, slamming into her dresser. She grabbed for the railing circling the room and steadied herself. The ship shuddered. Her teeth chattered.

Lights streaked by outside the window. Stars spinning. No, *Endurance* spinning.

"Captain to Engineering. Respond, Chief."

Nothing.

"Captain to Medical! Activate!"

Lyn lost her grip and somersaulted, bouncing off walls and furniture. Photos swirled past her head. That family gathering two summers ago with her parents and four remaining brothers smiling into the camera. Tara and her by their tent in the Bitterroots. Books thunked against the clear front of the case, matching her heart pounding against her ribs. She fought to grab the railing. The force pulled on her shoulders then slammed her into the wall. Inch by flinging inch, she made her way out of her bedroom, through her suite and office to the door to the bridge.

"Medical to the Captain," Dr. Amos replied, calm. "Do you have an emergency?"

"Sure sounds like it from the alarms I'm hearing. What's going on?"

"I'm waiting for status updates," he said.

"Go to Code Red, and remain active until I release the order. Assist any injured."

"Acknowledged."

She crashed into the ceiling, like a vicious version of her brothers' crack the whip. Or when her dad would twirl her in circles by her hands. Screaming with joy and mock fear. This was not fun. She'd trained for this, but it had been a long time and under controlled conditions. She pressed the door switch. It didn't budge. She flipped the manual release.

"Petra," she said, connecting to the ship itself. "Status report."

"Forces from an unknown source are altering our momentum and trajectory," Petra answered. "We have lost attitudinal control. I'm sorry, but I can't be more specific at this time. I'm not able to access the required systems."

That was disturbing. Lyn braced her feet against the wall and heaved on the door. The ship vibrated up her legs. The door slid in a stutter, wide enough for her to squeeze through. The bridge was dark except for lights from the walkways and instrument panels. Ani, suspended and tumbling, flailed to corral an unconscious Ghez. Lyn joined her, batting away loose debris. Together they zipped nir helmet into place and strapped nem to the navigator's seat. She opened a link. "Are you okay?"

"Yes," Ani responded. She dodged a flying chunk of metal. "Controls are down."

That left manual backups, or Lyn's mind link. Last resort, but with shipwide failures, it might not work anyway. She pulled herself along railings to the command seat and strapped in. The vibrations had stopped but she could feel every whip and lash as the ship yawed and spun. She lifted the manual console from beside the seat. She hadn't used this since the systems check before they left Earth over a month ago. Simple joystick and buttons. It powered up smoothly from the battery backup. Thrusters responded, thankfully, but with no visual, she couldn't tell if they were heading straight for Saturn's surface or a moon. Even the rings posed a hazard if they hit ice chunks.

"Ghez," she called.

"Ne's out cold, Captain," Ani said.

"I can't get a position on this thing. I don't know what direction we're heading in."

Ani yanked up the navigator's console. "Neither can I."

"Petra," Lyn called to the ship's computer. "Can you help here?"

"I'm unable to access the controls," Petra replied.

What good was a ship's AI if it couldn't help in an emergency?

"Ani, go into my office and let me know what you see out the window. We'll do this the old-fashioned way."

"On my way."

As Lyn waited for Ani to get to the window, she heard from her first officer.

"Franklin to the bridge."

"Randall here, Marc. Where are you?"

"In my quarters." His cabin was the farthest aft on the Bridge Deck, next to the muster area known as the Paddock.

A loud thunk came through the link followed by a groan. "I can't get out."

"Don't try," she said. "It's not safe. Ani and I are working to regain helm control."

"Acknowledged." He sounded disappointed.

"Captain," Ani called in.

"What have you got?"

"Give the forward starboard thruster 20 percent for fifteen seconds."

Lyn entered the command. The yaw lessened.

"Now tap the port ascent thruster."

"Tap? That's not very precise."

"It's a feeling, not a number. Want me to do it?"

"I can handle it." She tapped the button.

"Once more."

Lyn tapped again. She felt a little less like dice tossing in a cup.

"Good," Ani said. "Now we're just pitching ass over teakettle."

"That a technical term?" Rather than be annoyed by Ani's flippant remark, Lyn was relieved. If she could stress-joke, she wasn't freaking out.

"Yep. I need you to toggle the forward ventral thrusters, maybe ten seconds, followed by the aft dorsal by five seconds."

Ten seconds, five seconds. Sweat beaded Lyn's face, the faceplate fogging slightly. "Why both?"

"*Endurance* is fussy," Ani replied. "The manual buttons are clunky and imprecise. Best to be ready to work both."

"You might be the only person who knows these controls better than I do," Lyn said.

She worked the buttons, responding as Ani called out instructions. The ship slowed then stilled. Random items continued to ricochet around the bridge. Gravity was off. The red flashing lights switched to yellow. Whatever had breached was sealing itself. The life support siren quieted but echoed in Lyn's head as she caught her breath, frustrated by the darkness and no visibility to the outside.

"Where are we? I can't tell," Lyn said.

"I can't either," Ani replied. "I'm on the other side now, in the conference room. I don't see Saturn, so unless it's dead ahead, we're okay."

"Small comfort." How hard would it have been to put a window in the front of this bucket, she lamented to herself. "What can you see out there?"

"A whole lot of stars," Ani said quietly. "But, Captain, everything seems . . . off. I can't see any moons or rings."

She hadn't said it like they were simply turned away from the planet. What the hell were they dealing with?

Chapter 2

THE RIDE WAS over. Time for Lyn to laugh and pretend she hadn't been scared shitless. Her heart still pounded, beating against the harness, throbbing in her neck. And this had been no carnival ride. Her brother Duncan wasn't going to ruffle her hair and tell her to stop being a baby. She had a sudden, surprising urge to cry. Everything started to hurt. Her shoulder where she hit the wall, the floor, the door. Her neck from being whipped about. Even her hands from gripping the railing, then her armrest. She took several deep breaths, waiting for her medical nanobots to kick in and take care of the pain.

Ani returned to the bridge and strapped herself in next to Ghez.

"Petra, what's the ship's status?" Lyn struggled to keep her voice calm. This was beyond unprecedented.

"The dome around the Observation Deck has detached, emergency hatches have sealed the breach," Petra said.

Shite. "Was anyone up there?" Lyn asked.

"Unknown at this time," Petra said. "No other catastrophic hull damage. Fire suppression initiated in Engineering and the Galley. Systems throughout the ship are shutting down to prevent further damage. For example, water has been cut off to Laundry—"

"That's enough, Petra, as long as we aren't at risk of imminent destruction," Lyn said. She undid her harness and went down to check on Ghez.

"Air and pressure are stable and normal," Ani read. "It's safe to breathe, Captain."

They unzipped their helmets and Lyn undid Ghez's. Ne sputtered and spit out one of nir front teeth. She grabbed it as it floated by and tucked it into nir chest pocket. "Hang onto this. Doc will want it. How are you feeling?"

"I'm okay. A little dizzy."

"Concussion, at the least."

She checked her navigator carefully for other injuries. Blobs of blood floated from nir nose and mouth. Lyn went to the first-aid cabinet and grabbed a pressure bandage. She handed it to Ani. "Hold this tight over nir face. Zero G messes with blood flow." She turned to Ghez. "Let's get you to Medical."

"I'm fine, Captain. Let me help."

"You two can help by going to Medical and assisting anyone along the way. That's your order."

Ani helped Ghez out of nir harness. They pushed off toward the doorway.

Lyn strapped back into her seat. The chronometer read 0300, and she guessed maybe a half hour had passed since she first woke to the emergency. There was no response to her SOS. She put out a call to the *Aphrodite* but, again, no response. What was that other ship Ghez mentioned? The *Mars Jedica*. She opened a link but heard nothing, nor any answer to her hail. That didn't happen unless there was damage to communications in general. She'd never heard of an SOS or mayday going unanswered. There were simply too many ships out there. Especially now, with the Grand Tour. She left the mayday beacon on repeat. If nothing else, Mars or Earth would get the signal in an hour or so.

What the feck happened? Adrenaline slowly drained from her muscles, leaving tingles. Of all her training scenarios, this most resembled an engine malfunction or a fuel explosion with hull ruptures. But *Endurance* rarely used its massive liftoff engines. The beauty of the space elevator meant they needed a small amount of fuel for the engines to break orbit. Then the thrusters took over. The Recyc-All could make fuel on demand, so they didn't store any, especially since they were going to be in orbit for a week.

Could it have been a bomb? A terrorist attack? There were few conflicts left on Earth since the Revolution ended forty years ago. The Grand Tour, however, was a massive marketing operation. If someone wanted to send a message, it would be a newsworthy opportunity. Space tourism was still limited to the elite, despite recycling technology reshaping the global economy. The new governments were set up to eliminate overt poverty, but it didn't mean everyone was equal. Lyn sighed in resignation. Could this be a more personal attack, a ghost from her past, revenge? She shook away the thought this had anything to do with her whistle-blowing. That was years ago now.

With no answers in sight, it was time everyone heard from and saw their captain. She unhooked her harness and let herself drift away from her seat. She set Petra to monitor helm and sent Marc down to Engineering. Making sure the engines were safe was the next priority.

She opened a shipwide com line as she made her way to the hallway. "This is Captain Randall." She paused. What should she say? She had no idea what had happened, what danger remained outside the ship. "This is Captain Randall," she repeated, forcing herself to speak calmly. "All crew, note we remain in Code Red. All passengers, if you are in a safe place, please remain there." *And if not?* "A crewmember will be by to help. Although this is *not* a drill, we are regaining control and the ship is intact." A slight lie. She hoped no one had been on the Obs Deck. "If you are injured, the Advanced Medical Officer System has been activated and is available to respond. I'll follow up with more information soon." She clicked off the link.

Outside the bridge, all seemed normal except for the lack of gravity. And the voices. Shouts down the hallway, clattering objects, banging, like fists against walls or doors. Beyond the stairs and elevator were the luxurious bridge-deck suites. She glanced out the window of the conference room as she went by. Ani was right, of course. Nothing but a mass of stars, not a planet in sight. At the stairwell, she passed a hand over the door to the stairs going up to the now-missing Obs Deck, sealed shut and creating an airlock. Such a close call.

As she rounded the landing and entered the corridor, the scope clarified. Guests and objects spilled into the hallway, upside down, floating. Shouts from inside rooms. A half dozen crew were already moving in and out of cabins. Lyn checked the first suite. Nikoleta and Dae Canno from Texas. She had connected with them over dinner the second week. They ran a geoengineering company, reclaiming the Texas desert. Lyn's dad was doing the same in Montana. Nikoleta, hair puffed out in zero G, clung to her bedding, dodging small flying objects. A crablike house bot floated near the ceiling, catching items with its six arms and stowing them in a bag.

"How are you?" Lyn called from the doorway.

Nikoleta's tense expression relaxed. "Thank god, you're okay. We're okay, I guess. Dae, well, he's in the bathroom. Feeling a bit queasy."

"Stay put for now," Lyn said. "We'll let you know when it's safe to move around."

"What happened?"

"I don't know yet. First priority is making sure everyone is safe and the ship is secure. So far, so good." Lyn smiled confidently, if deceptively. She had no idea if all was good.

She made her way through the hallway, dodging debris, helping to pull people from the wreckage of their rooms. The air stank from a mix of vomit and blood. In one room, she ripped a sheet to bandage a man with a gaping scalp wound and in another held a woman while a crew member wrenched free her foot. All the while she had her mind on the Paddock, where the lifepods were stored. Would they need them, and were they damaged? She tried to keep up with progress on other decks through her com link, but there was too much background noise. Everything not locked down swarmed like the clattering, noisy flocks of starlings over the fields back home. Swarms. That's what it looked and felt like. But as her team left each room, the calls and shouts quieted a bit more. With ship's sensors offline, her mind link was useless, but she knew this ship, and her gut told her this was a human emergency, like when that transport skim she took home from the Aerospace Academy got hit by a microburst. They dropped two hundred feet in a matter of seconds and rolled as well. Humans might not be built to withstand a microburst, or whatever this was, but ships were. Though the lost Obs Deck. That was bad.

Anyone not crying out for help fired questions at her and her crew. Her team calmly answered with reassurances. "Everything will be fine." Fact was, there'd never been this level of emergency on an Omara Tour, but their training taught them enough to know that if the ship hadn't decompressed and they were still alive, that, yes, everything probably would be fine. If only someone would answer her damn SOS. Her link to the ship's external communications relay remained silent.

Finally, she was in the Paddock, an oasis of calm. She moved along the walls on each side, checking the pods. They sat in bays inside the outer hull. Luckily, otherwise they might have been stripped away like the Obs Deck. Eight in total, three on each side, two at the back on either side of the airlock where supply ships docked. Everything was secure. She continued around the Paddock. Zero G felt like swimming and she kicked her feet occasionally, futilely, forgetting. One of the perks for the passengers was zero G time, carefully controlled, perfectly safe. A swinging cabinet door banged her head. "Damn!" She rubbed the spot.

She floated down the back stairway and into the fitness center. A chaotic scene greeted her. House bots scrambled about, corralling free weights that were a little too free. Yoga mats drifted through the air. Rather than risk colliding with a dumbbell, she went back up to the Bridge Deck and took the midship stairs down to the Main Deck's guest section. More of the same, but of a less frantic tenor. Crew were helping guests and collecting debris. In Room 409, she steadied a stretcher as two crew positioned an elderly woman with what looked like a broken leg. An older man hovered, batting away items that might hit the woman. Probably her husband. He followed the stretcher as it left for the Medical Suite on the lowest deck.

Lyn continued along the corridor. In the reception area near the main docking door, she met up with Sharyn Wang, her hotel manager. Sharyn's white hair flowed outward as she clung to the railing.

"Have you been able to account for everyone yet?" Lyn asked, in a low voice. She told her about the lost top deck. If anyone had been up there . . .

Sharyn's shocked expression told Lyn she hadn't known. "Everyone has moved about so much, I won't be able to till we can muster them."

"Can't do that till we clear this mess."

"I'll start a room-by-room. The bots can keep track."

The chief engineer, Edward Sawyer, called to Lyn and said he could restore gravity.

"Let's make sure everything is secured first," she said. "I don't want anyone falling down the stairwell." She nodded to Sharyn. "That will help."

Sharyn stayed on Deck 3 while Lyn went down to Deck 2. More guest cabins and the dining room and galley. At the front of the ship, a waste pipe had split open, adding more stink to the air. Bots had shut off the flow and were slurping up the mess. Guests had formed a line along the hallway and were stowing debris in bags. Things were calming down. She let the group know they'd soon have gravity back.

At the doorway to the dining room, she stopped. The tables and seating were securely attached, but everything set up for breakfast—cloths, centerpieces, dishes, silverware—formed a dense cloud.

"Miriam!" she shouted for her executive chef.

"In here," came her voice from the kitchen. "Don't try to come through."

"You okay?"

"Ever try to navigate a room full of floating knives?"

"Edward can get gravity back, but we can't if it's not safe."

"Just do it slowly. I'm under the work bench."

"Understood."

Lyn sent a shipwide message that they'd restore gravity and for everyone to find a place to stabilize safely. Crew would know what to do. She hadn't seen Marc, so he was probably down the next level in Engineering. She gave the okay for Edward to reboot the system, slowly dialing up to one G. While he did, she watched dishes land and kept a link open to Miriam as the knives drifted down. When her feet hit the floor, she had to consciously engage her leg muscles, like after a long swim. It always surprised her how quickly the body acclimated to weightlessness.

Was the worst over? She wouldn't know till they'd accounted for everyone. She loved her crew, she'd handpicked each of them, but none had more training than commercial flight school. Omara Tours' safety record was admirable but also meant no one had experience dealing with a dire emergency. She hoped they could handle whatever lay before them.

On the bottom deck, the acrid smell of burned synthetics assaulted her before she got to the Engineering suite. Through dense smoke, a row of dim emergency lights outlined the room and spots hit key control panels. Marc and Edward were reattaching a panel in the wall, and Isabel Roig, assistant engineer, was sliding shut a hatch in the ceiling to the bay between decks where the retractable wings were stored. Edward flipped a switch, and the suite's lights came on revealing the toll the event had taken. A fan whirred to life and the air began to clear.

"Wings are undamaged and secure," Isabel said. Her sooty mustache alarmed Lyn.

"You've breathed in too much smoke," Lyn said. "You should go to Medical."

"I'm fine. Medbots are handling it." Isabel wiped her sleeve across her mouth.

"Still, please go once we have a quiet moment and get checked out."

"I'll be fine," Isabel said.

If Lyn was going to lose her patience with anyone in this mess, it would be Isabel Roig. You simply didn't argue with a request from your captain. Isabel always presented very professionally, then that façade could suddenly slip. That she worked well with Edward usually made up for the aggravation.

"That's an order, Roig," Lyn said.

"Yes, Captain."

Edward said the engines were offline but life safety systems were coming back. No loss of atmosphere, so no breaches other than the Observation Deck, which, because of the dome, had the weakest framing. It was designed to protect the rest of the ship in case of a failure, hence the sealing of the shaft and stairway. Damages were limited to unsecured objects and physical injuries, none of which was life threatening.

"A pipe broke in Laundry," Marc said. "There's a floating flood there, but bots are vacuuming it up."

Isabel reported Dr. Amos had a dozen patients, the four most critical in Medical, the rest in their rooms. He was monitoring the medbots in another two dozen guests. Lyn let out a relieved breath when Sharyn called down that all passengers and crew were accounted for. She searched the faces of her staff. Nothing had sunk in yet other than a preliminary relief they were still alive.

"Do we know—?" Isabel asked.

Lyn shook her head. "We'll have to review the logs to see what it was, but for now, I'm getting reports that bots have started repairs."

"Engines aren't damaged," Edward said, "only offline as a precaution."

"What do we do now?" Marc asked.

"I thought we'd all meet in the dining room," Lyn said. "The sooner guests can see us operating normally, the better."

"What do we tell them?" he asked.

"The truth. We don't know, but we're working on finding answers," Lyn said. "I sent an SOS two hours ago. We've heard nothing from anyone."

Any ship within range should have responded. Worst-case, the signal would have reached Mars and Earth Control, the two agencies that oversaw all space operations.

"If we were on an ocean," Isabel said, "I'd think we were hit by a rogue wave, which would hit everyone else as well. But out here?"

"Could it have been a swarm of microdebris?" Edward said.

"An asteroid? Aliens?" Marc added.

Lyn raised her hands to stop them. "Let's get the outside sensors rebooted. In the meantime," she said to Marc, "I think we should go see for ourselves."

Leaving Edward in Engineering, and seeing Isabel over to Medical, Lyn and Marc then made their way up the central stairway to the Bridge Deck. From a storage closet, they donned lifepacks and flipped on their helmets and gloves. Inside what was now an airlock around the last set of steps to the Obs Deck, they tethered to the wall and waited while the pressure equalized.

At the top of the steps, Marc released the Obs hatch and peered up through what had once been the floor of a luxurious lounge but was now the outer hull. They floated out into space. All the furnishings had been stripped away, the carpet shredded. Walls rose to knee height, and where durapanes and frames would take over to allow an almost unfettered view, nothing remained. Nothing between them and infinity. As relieved as Lyn was that no one had been up here, a little of her died to see her beloved ship so violated. She spun to take in their surroundings, noting dismally no sign of Saturn.

All around, stars and the Milky Way filled their view. Without bright Saturn, the stars popped with a surreal brightness. They'd seen this on their trip out, in the long empty stretches between planets. So where was Saturn? She focused on one bright star, maybe the sun, but larger than it would be from Saturn. To its right sat an even larger object. If that was Saturn, they were no longer in orbit, or anywhere near it. She called up Petra's star chart. "Locate Saturn."

"Saturn is not in this solar system," Petra replied.

She tapped Marc on the shoulder to get his attention. "Did you hear that?"

"Saturn can't just vanish. Computer malfunction?"

She selected the bright star. "Identify object."

"Object is Toliman. Designation HR 5460."

"That doesn't make sense," she said to Marc. "We shouldn't be able to distinguish it from Rigil Kent. But if that's Toliman, is the other Uranus?"

"Seems too bright." Marc selected the bigger object. "Identify."

"Object is Rigil Kentaurus. Designation HR 5459."

"That's not possible," Lyn said. "Petra, are you experiencing a malfunction?"

"Not that I'm aware of, Captain."

"Then where are we?"

"We are in the Rigil Kentaurus system. Formerly known as Alpha Centauri, the binary system is the closest to Earth—"

"Petra! Stop! How did we get here?"

"Unknown at this time."

What the—? They each turned, taking in the stars around them. Lyn made out constellations, blurs within the Milky Way but definitely recognizable. She knew this sky, but didn't. She floated, turning slowly, staring at the glittery blanket above and all around them. Rigil Kent?

"Where is our sun?" Marc asked Petra.

Petra gave them the coordinates. Lyn turned but couldn't find it among the billions of stars. Too small. Too far away. This simply wasn't possible. She pulled on her tether till her feet set firmly against the hull, longing to lie down, to hug the ship. She closed her eyes and became keenly aware of the hiss of her breath inside the helmet and her pulse pounding in her ears. This wasn't an unfamiliar feeling, that realization after she'd stepped off the trail in the woods, gotten turned around, and then couldn't find her way back. It's a stone in your gut that grows, pressing on the diaphragm, making it hard to breathe. Your scalp tingles and you know—you are lost.

She switched off her mic then arched back, opened her eyes to take in the stars, familiar and not, and howled loud and long, like the last wolf crying to be heard, to be found.

Chapter 3

"I WISH WE hadn't gone out there," Lyn said when they were back in the airlock.

"What do we say?" Marc asked. He hit the button to repressurize.

"Nothing. For now, at least. We didn't come up here. If anyone asks, we say we'll look into it." She groaned. "Frak! Petra, our previous conversation about our location is to remain confidential pending authorization from me. If you are asked what happened, please say you are investigating."

"Acknowledged," Petra said.

When the pressure equalized, they removed their lifepacks and stowed them back in the closet.

"It's physically impossible to be in Rigil Kentaurus, so where are we?" Marc asked.

"Until we know otherwise, we're right where we were, that's what we tell them."

"I wasn't pretending to be a guest."

Lyn yanked off her gloves and stuffed them back in the cuffs. "Well then, shit and damn, hell if I know."

They descended the stairs and went to Lyn's office. For the first time since the event, she relaxed enough to realize she hadn't peed since she'd gone to bed how many hours ago? She retreated to her bathroom, hoping the waste system was repaired. The dark color of her urine also reminded her she hadn't taken in any liquids. It flushed without incident and she was relieved on both fronts.

Back in her office, she poured them both cups of water. "Be sure to keep hydrated." She also made coffee.

"Isn't coffee counterproductive?" he asked, but he didn't turn it down.

"I consider it vital."

Lyn downloaded updates from Petra and the doctor while Marc checked with Miriam on the status of breakfast and sent out an announcement that everyone would meet in the dining room at 0700.

THOSE CLOSEST TO the door quieted when Lyn and Marc entered the dining room. She was still learning their names. Arbaza, the Norrgards, that person with the great laugh—Moyle. She forced a reassuring smile and eye contact, asking how they were. I'm here for you, she hoped to convey.

Round banquette tables lined the two long walls, one filled with windows. She stopped at the end of her table, the large oval near the door. With no Saturn throwing light into the dining room, the windows reflected back, so she was relieved to see no evidence of the mystery outside. Service bots laden with trays of eggs, sausages, fruit, breads, cereals, and beverages scooted from the kitchen and lined up, forming a buffet table. Guests gathered in groups, some dressed, others in bathrobes, buzzing with questions, relaying tales of their harrowing night. Still innocent and ignorant and best left that way until answers were found.

They didn't know anything more than we hit some turbulence, Lyn reassured herself. Some might wonder how that's possible, but most will just be glad it's over.

She spotted the day's itinerary projected on a screen by the door.

> *Day 42:*
> *A half day's sightseeing on Titan is included in the package: Excursion vehicles will depart from the Paddock beginning at 0800. Here, you will enjoy an up-close look at the icy surface and take a turn at the controls of the Sampler. Back on board, we'll examine our finds.*

She made a mental note to disable that thing. Regardless of where they were, this trip was over. Marc whistled the room to quiet.

The cowboy hat marked the Cannos. The Betero family clustered up front. Four generations, nineteen members. They were on the tour to celebrate a reunion and the elders' hundredth anniversary. The matriarch, Zoya, had worked at the original NASA. She'd regaled them at dinner with stories of settling Mars.

Where should Lyn start? Some small joke? What a ride, eh? They stared at her like a schoolyard of frightened children. Someone called out, "What happened?" Another, "Were we attacked?"

She raised her hands, they quieted. "Please, I'll do my best to answer your questions, but it's still early and we're still assessing—" *Don't say damage. Don't let on how serious this is. Not yet.* "Here's what I know." She clasped her hands behind her back. "As you are well aware, early this morning we experienced a rough ride." She tried a smile, hoping to convey the insignificance of it all. Their tense expressions told her no one was buying it. "Yes, it was serious, but the ship is safe and sound. A lot of you were injured, and I'm happy to report only a few are still in Medical for observation by Doctor Amos. Engines are offline as a precaution. There's nothing wrong with them, and the fuel supply is secure."

Murmurs buzzed like a current around the room.

"Thank you all for helping each other and for following instructions and doing the things we rehearsed." She eyed those in robes. "Please remember to always wear your flight suit." It wasn't required, by Earth Control or Omara, but these were tourists, she always argued, not trained astronauts. "As for why this happened, which I know is your main question, we're not sure yet. We know it was not caused by any malfunction on *Endurance*. The Observation Deck sustained damage and the emergency hatches closed automatically. Thankfully, no one was up there."

She couldn't inhale before the questions flew.

"What happens now?"

"Are we going to be rescued?"

"Can we still go down to Titan today?"

"Were we attacked?" An angry shout.

Lyn searched the crowd. A woman, at the back.

"Well?" the woman said.

"No. There is no sign of an attack." *Why would she even think that?* Lyn didn't recognize her but didn't bother to access the manifest for her name.

More questions peppered her. She raised her hands for quiet. "Please. We don't know yet whether we need rescue. There is no sign any propulsion systems were affected, but we'll examine everything carefully. As soon as I know more, I'll let you know. For now, have some breakfast. We still have a lot of cleanup to do to your rooms and the common areas. My staff are working to gather information. As for today's excursions," she glanced at Marc, "we need to inspect the landers, so we're canceling those for today." A few groans. "We will resume classes as soon as we have those rooms cleaned up. The fitness center is also a mess. In the meantime, enjoy your breakfast, and I'll keep you informed of our progress."

The guests resumed their buzz of conversation, but it was of a gentler, less frantic tenor. A line formed at the buffet table.

She turned to Marc and said softly, "I want all senior staff in the conference room as soon as Miriam can get away."

"Can we eat?"

Right. Breakfast. "Yes, of course."

"You should too."

"I will."

She grabbed a pastry and ate it on her way to Medical. The Medical Suite barely qualified as one. Four beds, each taking a corner, left a narrow path between them. Dr. Amos was the sole medical personnel. To the right, a door led to his office and charging station and the so far never-used refrigerated cadaver cupboard. Lyn was relieved to see little damage from the event. Doc was good about stowing his gear. The big things were bolted to the floor.

She spotted Ghez, sitting up in the far left bed, chatting with Dr. Amos. The doctor, though humanoid in structure, would never be mistaken for a human. His smooth composite face had an immobile mouth, but his expressive eyebrows, almost realistic eyes, and common gestures, were enough to put people at ease without being creepy.

Ghez grinned on seeing Lyn, showing a newly implanted tooth. "Like new," ne said. A purple bruise spread over nir nose and under each eye. The blood had been cleaned from nir dark, shoulder-length hair. They chatted, Lyn relieved when the doctor said the concussion was minor and he'd cleared Ghez for limited duty. She suspected the navigator would play an important role in the foreseeable future.

"Do we know what happened?" Ghez said.

"We're still trying to figure that out," she said, "which is why I'm here. I'd like you to get some breakfast then meet me and the rest of the senior staff in the conference room."

She accompanied nem to the dining room then continued up to the bridge. She found Ani alone in the command seat. A house bot sat on the second step, slurping. When Lyn moved, it ducked into its slot in the wall. Ani rose to relinquish command, but Lyn waved her down and sat next to her.

"What was that doing?" she asked, indicating the aisle.

"Ghez's blood landed on the stairs."

"Ah. How's system restoration coming?"

"Up to 90 percent complete," Ani said.

Lyn told her about the meeting. "It's going to be a long day. Go eat. I'll stay here."

"I'm not hungry." Ani stilled then shifted to face Lyn. "Where are we?"

Ani's question could not be dodged. She was too savvy for that to work. "That's what we need to find out. That or what happened to Saturn."

"I can't reach anyone," Ani said. "Not Mars Control, not the *Aphrodite*. There's no chatter out there. Just static."

"We'll figure this out, but you need to eat. That's an order. I've got the Con."

Ani hesitated but then rose and left in silence. Poor kid, Lyn thought. She stared at the viewscreen, back online but showing only stars and a swath of Milky Way. Ani had set it to the front wall only. No dramatic views today. Lyn sensed it would be simply too disturbing to feel like you were sitting out in the middle of nothing. Which they probably were. The bot resumed carpet cleaning. Such a normal sound, except for the reason.

"Petra," Lyn said then stopped. What could she even ask the ship?

"Yes, Captain? How can I help?"

Lyn gave a rueful chuckle. *Help. If only you could.* "Can you take us home?"

The ship was silent for a few seconds. "I can, but it will take so long, you won't survive the trip."

"Gee, thanks. You're sure you know where we are."

"Yes. Should I proceed?"

"No. Go to autopilot for now, please, and hold position."

"Yes, Captain."

She rose, stiff and with great effort. Did Edward set gravity too strong? She stretched and moved toward the aisle away from the cleaning bot. If they really were in Rigil Kentaurus, the SOS she'd sent earlier, traveling at light speed, wouldn't reach Earth for four years.

BY ONES AND twos her staff arrived in the conference room. Marc Franklin, first officer. He appeared none the worse for it other than a scruffy shadow of a beard. Over their five years together, Lyn had come to rely on his knack for bonding with the crew while maintaining authority. He was young and impulsive, though, so she'd have to watch that. He'd never been in a crisis. Nothing like this.

Edward Sawyer, chief engineer. Never Ed or Eddie. "My parents named me Edward," he'd told her when they'd met, and he'd refused her handshake. Nothing personal, she'd come to learn. He was just more comfortable around the powerful engines of a spaceship than the warm touch of a human.

Isabel Roig, assistant engineer. Socially, she was Edward's opposite. Outgoing, adaptable, full of self-confidence. Maybe too much. Their expressions were grim.

Then Sharyn Wang. Her role included housekeeping and all entertainment. She was Lyn's trusted eyes and ears into the social dynamic among both guests and staff. Executive Chef Miriam Kapoor thrived on crisis, though more of the culinary kind than the existential lost-in-space kind. A white bandanna wrapped her short-cropped hair, standing in for the chef's toque. Lyn could relax around Miriam and Sharyn like no other crew members. Miriam ruled the kitchen in a way Lyn never could and that made them a kind of equal. It would be interesting to see how that played out. Case in point, Miriam set a plate and utensils in front of Lyn. She didn't say anything, just raised one eyebrow and sat. Fried protein strips—Miriam's famous bacon—grapes, and a lemon poppy seed muffin, Lyn's favorite. Her stomach grumbled, followed by a wave of nausea. So much for that.

Dr. Amos arrived next. State of the art, he'd come with the ship and knew things about it no one else did. Lyn often confided in him and forgot he wasn't human.

Natalie slid into a seat almost unnoticed. No dramatic *gele* this morning. Her short, natural hair and unembellished flight suit signaled stress. Her first time in space and look what happened. Ghez, on nir second tour. Shy, ne had yet to bond with the rest of the crew. An unknown. Ani arrived last. A born pilot, inwardly focused, an introvert. Now, with Rob back on Earth, with so very much to lose. Though no more than anyone else, really.

They took their seats quietly. This was Lyn's tribe, usually informal and chatty with each other. Easygoing, friendly. Edward stared at the table, but everyone avoided eye contact. If this was not a simple computer malfunction, they were grossly inexperienced for what they were about to face.

"How are you all holding up?" Lyn asked. One by one, they admitted while concerned, they were okay. She relayed what she and Marc saw outside the ship and what the computer told them they were seeing. "Rigil Kent and Toliman."

All eyes turned to Lyn. Expressions ranged from fear to disbelief.

"At this point, you know about as much as I do. Saturn is not visible, and the charts are either misaligned, malfunctioning, or—"

"We're screwed," Ani said.

"Let's not start there," Lyn said. "Ghez, Natalie, I need you to pore over the charts for any malfunction and confirm where we are. Then we'll be able to focus on what we need to do."

Ghez called up the charts, which filled the side wall with a 3-D image. Current Earth–Baker Island time displayed 0900. The chart showed a bright dot larger than the sun as seen from Saturn but with a smaller twin off to the left. Just what she and Marc had seen from outside.

No one spoke.

Lyn broke the silence. "Natalie. Can you confirm those?"

Natalie rubbed her face as if to clear her vision. "I don't need a computer to tell me those are in fact Rigil Kent and Toliman. See Proxima?" She stood and pointed to a small dot. "Much smaller but distinctively red."

"So the magnification is off?" Ani asked.

"No," Ghez said. "That's a hundred percent. You'd see the same thing out a window."

Ani's eyes widened, her brow furrowing. "*Puñeta!*" She turned to Lyn. "We're in Centaurus?"

"It appears so," Lyn said.

She leaned back and waited while the news seeped in. However independent the ship had seemed, it was always tethered by a communications thread. The grapes on the plate in front of her had arrived on a resupply ship two days ago. Other ships served as beacons and emergency way stations. Planets, moons, and asteroids dotted the solar system like islands in the ocean. They were never truly alone or cut off. Until now.

"There has to be some explanation," Ani said. "We all know it's physically impossible for us to be here in the span of a few hours."

"More like a few minutes." Lyn thought about all the stories she'd read, all the movies about castaways, people stranded, even science fiction stories about being lost in space. She'd been stranded before, alone in space. But not really. All she had to do was set a course for the rescue ship heading to meet her. That was not going to happen here. Nothing compared to the quiet washing over her, blanking her mind. Theirs too? The first stage of shock. How long would it last and what came next? Panic? Depended on their training.

Lyn cleared her throat. "A diagnostic of the ship's computer shows no malfunction, but Edward, I'll want you to tear it apart and make sure."

"I saw Orion out there," Sharyn said. She would bear the brunt of easing the guests' growing anxiety that could bloom to panic once they learned the truth.

"The angle is wrong," Edward muttered. "The angle is wrong."

"Both true," Natalie said. She shifted the image. "You see Orion much the same. And Cassiopeia? Look to the left." She pointed to a tiny speck of light. "That's . . ." Her hand trembled. "Our sun."

Here it comes, Lyn thought, the wave broke. The shake spread up Natalie's arm. She sank back into her seat, her shoulders shuddering from quiet gasps that grew into sobs. Miriam, closest, went to her. As Natalie quietly keened, Lyn closed her eyes. *What if the guests all do this? Crux, Ani's right. We're screwed.*

When she was a child, Lyn used to spend hours studying anthills in her back yard. Columns of the tiny creatures roamed the dusty yard, following invisible markers leading back and forth to their home. Away for food, back with a load to share. She delighted in messing with their orderliness, wiping away the scent trails, flattening the hill itself, placing her hand in their path and when they climbed aboard, swinging them away and dropping them in the dry brown grass. Far from home. Yet they found their way back, redug their cone entrance. Did the ants know or care what happened to them or who this interfering giant was? Now, what hand had swung them across the galaxy?

Natalie hiccoughed. Lyn opened her eyes. Miriam held Natalie. Doc started to rise but she touched his arm. He could do a quick scan, inject a mild sedative, restore peace and quiet to the room. Instead, she went to kneel by Natalie. Together they waited as this young woman on her first trip to space let out the grief and horror they all held within, whether by training or temperament.

Eventually Natalie quieted. Lyn asked her if she wanted to go to her quarters. She shook her head.

"I'm sorry, Captain."

"Nothing to be sorry about," Lyn said. "This is a lot to take in and we're not done yet."

Sharyn had found tissues. Natalie blew her nose, and Lyn returned to her seat.

"We all remember our high school astronomy, right?" Lyn said in an even tone, leveling her gaze on Natalie. "Roughly, four light years, correct?"

One quick nod and blink.

"Our maximum speed is 1.6 million kph. Anyone care to do the math?"

Silence.

"I didn't think so. We're talking a good three thousand years."

A number not even comprehensible in terms of their existence, their lifespans. This doesn't happen, not to her, not on an Omara Tour, not to anyone. This can't be how it all ends. Lyn noted the expressions on her crew. Some, Marc and Miriam, had worked together for the five years since Lyn became captain of *Endurance*, ferrying tourists around the solar system, a fine-tuned machine, with not so much as a space-sick passenger, never mind a major malfunction or crisis. Sharyn had four years. Lyn knew Dr. Amos from her time training on *Endurance* when she was with Pulsar. Others were newer. Isabel, Ani, Ghez.

Now Ani stared straight ahead, stricken, no doubt thinking of Rob. Marc closed his eyes and let out a breath. Lyn relied on him for so much—adviser, friend, almost a brother. Miriam covered her face with her hands. She didn't need this. None of them did.

"How is that possible?" Sharyn said, her voice hollow and thin.

"Not possible," Edward muttered. He rubbed a hand across his salt and pepper buzz cut. A sign of stress or concentration. Stress, Lyn thought.

"No, it's not," Lyn said. "And yet, here we are."

Panic rose like slow waters. To the knees, to the hips. It had already engulfed Natalie. Soon none of them would be able to breathe. As captain, it was Lyn's job to bail. To keep them so busy they didn't have time to panic. Keep them breathing.

"Edward," she said, "I want you to help Natalie and Ghez go over these charts with a nanocomb. Rewrite the entire program if you have to." She turned to the others. "I don't want any rumors swirling. We'll tell the passengers everything we know as soon as we are absolutely sure. *And* when we know what we're going to do about it."

"But what *can* we do?" Miriam asked.

Lying could do more damage than good, but did she have to lie? "If, in fact, something threw us across the galaxy, which we know is impossible with current technology, then that something can get us back."

"You think it's aliens?" Sharyn asked.

"Oh, let's not go there."

"The Chinese?" Isabel asked, her tone accusing, her eyes darting to Sharyn.

Lyn knew the story all too well, the rumor that China wanted to militarize space by claiming Saturn's moon Enceladus. Lyn herself had helped prove otherwise, and it was years ago now. No, the Chinese never weaponized the moon. Instead, the solar system became a tourist trap. But old feelings die hard. Never mind Sharyn had never set foot in China. She'd grown up on Maryland's Eastern Shore until, like millions of others, she evacuated inland, fleeing rising seas and an irradiated exclusion zone.

Lyn braced herself, hands on the table. "Okay, this is exactly what the guests will spend their time doing—speculating—if we don't keep a lid on this. Until we know otherwise—say little green people knock on our door— this is a natural occurrence, albeit an extraordinary phenomenon." For all she'd been through, she was by nature an optimistic person. She could use that. Moods were contagious, after all. "Look, until a few decades ago, we didn't know what half the universe was even made of. We didn't think there was any way to fix the climate. Now we have recycling technology. We never thought we'd break the speed barrier for interplanetary travel, then a woman named Vera invented the Geller Drive." She thought, but did not say out loud, *I've got a chip in my brain that gives me the computing power of a machine that filled a room just a century ago.*

"So someone invented interstellar travel, and we're the guinea pigs," Marc said.

"Maybe. Maybe not." She waved her hand toward the wall. "But we are proof it is possible if that chart over there is accurate. Personally, I think it's kind of exciting. We might have stumbled on a wormhole."

The mood of the room ticked up slightly.

"Natalie, Ghez, I'd like you to look for any signals. Maybe other ships were affected." She dismissed them and addressed Sharyn. "We should get the classes back online as soon as possible. Keep people busy."

"What do I tell them?"

"That we're working on it and, let's see . . ." Lyn checked the chronometer embedded in her cuff. "Tell them I'll give a full briefing at dinner. Oh, and turn off that itinerary." She turned to Miriam. "How are we for supplies?"

"Pretty full. We didn't lose power long enough to affect the fresh food." She touched a finger to her lips. "Was it just the day before yesterday we met the supply ship?"

"I trust you'll use up the fresh food before it spoils."

"That's my MO," Miriam said.

"I know. And thank you."

"For that?"

"No. For everything I'm going to need you for."

Miriam rose to leave but turned back. "I need something from you, too."

Miriam rarely asked for favors. "Name it."

"Don't isolate yourself. Come to the dining room for meals. It will go a long way toward easing the guests' anxiety."

"I'll try to do that." Crisis of the century and she needed to stop and schmooze?

"You can start with lunch, and with that." She indicated the untouched plate.

"Understood," Lyn said, resigned. She picked up a grape.

Dr. Amos returned to Medical. Ani to the bridge. Lyn and Marc sat alone. She tossed the grape back on the plate, then, reconsidering, popped it in her mouth and pushed the plate toward Marc. The ship's ventilation system purred low in the background. A reassuring, common sound.

"Three thousand years, huh." Marc broke the silence between them. He grabbed some bacon and pushed the plate back.

"Give or take." She scrutinized her first officer while he munched the bacon. His suit was crisp, he'd shaved. When did he have time for that? Some people's resting faces were too frowny or too smiley. Marc's soft features formed a perfect blank mask. Then if he was unhappy, you knew it. Likewise when he was pleased. That might be what helped him connect with the staff.

"This is it, then?" he asked. His features revealed only concern, not defeat yet or disbelief.

"What do you mean?"

"We're never getting home."

"Why do you say that? For all we know we could pop back just as suddenly."

"Or pop another four light years farther away." He clasped his hands in his lap. "Is there something I should know?"

"Like?" She suspected where this was headed.

"Like anything from your mysterious past with Pulsar Force?"

His tone dripped with suspicion. This was a side of Marc Lyn hadn't seen.

"That's over and done with. Besides, they never had the ability to do this."

"That you know of. I know *you* didn't have anything to do with it, and this ship isn't capable of anything remotely possible. But Pulsar? This was their ship and you made enemies there. Could they have done this?"

"If anyone wanted to get me, they had a decade to do it without endangering a hundred innocents. And this was a training vessel, not a secret weapon. Could this be a test gone bad? No idea. I wasn't that big a deal in the force."

"Big enough to reveal a huge scandal. They disbanded after that Enceladus . . . thing. Didn't they?"

That "thing." Tara and five crew members killed, Lyn the lone survivor. After graduating from the Aerospace Academy, Lyn had married Tara and followed her to Pulsar Industries, a top space-exploration company. Her first assignment after her cadetship on *Endurance* was led by none other than Captain Tara. A "trip beyond Mars," six months testing Pulsar's latest technology for long-distance space travel—a new engine, new recycler, improved gravity. Exactly what Lyn had hoped for to start her career. Bit by bit, though, it fell apart.

First was the food poisoning from the second supply cache. Two crew dead, the remaining four sick and weak. Another cache destroyed. They were too far from Earth to go back. No one close enough for rescue. No option but to continue to Saturn's moon. Tara hadn't told them the true mission. Not even Lyn. They were good at tucking their personal and professional selves into compartments. When they found a beacon on Enceladus from the Chinese, Tara, distraught and furious, admitted her orders were to get to the moon first, to claim it for Pulsar. Force, not Industries. A covert operation securing the outer planets for military outposts, something specifically prohibited in the treaties that ended the war, that enabled a New Era of peace on Earth.

They were all near death. Tara and the others went to the moon's surface for recycler material, Lyn left alone in the orbiter. Days later the lander returned on autopilot, the crew dead. Tara dead. Lyn stranded. They'd filled the hold, so Lyn fed that into the recycler for food, fuel, and air. She set a course for Earth.

It made no sense. Why send a bunch of green recruits on a cutting-edge mission with new technology? Because they were expendable. All they had to do was get there. They didn't have to get back. If they had all died, they would have been memorialized as heroes, the area closed off for as long as an investigation would take, which could be years, decades. In the meantime? Pulsar would have it to themselves. But Lyn survived and went public.

Did they really disband after that Enceladus . . . thing? "Who knows," Lyn said. "When something operates in the dark, how do you know when it's gone? This isn't worthy of speculation, given our current circumstances."

"Captain, we're receiving a mayday beacon," Ani called from the bridge. "There's another ship."

"We'll be right there," they said together.

Chapter 4

"A SHIP?" LYN didn't bother to hide her excitement as she hopped the steps to the command level. *We're not alone.* "A mayday, so nothing alien?"

Ani moved down to helm. Marc took his seat beside Lyn.

"Correct," Ani said. "It's the *Mars Jedica*—we saw it . . . last night. That seems so long ago. Registered to the Lavenza Institute for Advanced Study. No one's responding though, just the automatic beacon."

Lyn's excitement tempered. Would have been nice if it had been a bigger ship, say the *Aphrodite*. Able to take them all on board. Another captain to make decisions. Still, this changed everything. "Let's go. What are we waiting for? Engage. Set a course. Whatever you need."

"It's at least a day away with thrusters," Ani said. "Can we power up the main engines?"

"Right. Good idea." Lyn called down to Engineering. "Edward, are we safe to power up engines and move this bucket of bolts?"

"Is it necessary?"

"We've found another ship."

"Then it is. I'll monitor from here."

Once they were under way, Marc asked Petra what she knew about the Lavenza Institute.

Petra responded, "The Lavenza Institute for Advanced Study—a consortium of universities working to understand human existence, from philosophy to art to cosmology. It runs programs on the moon and Mars and has seven campuses on Earth, one on each continent."

"Sounds innocent enough," Lyn said.

The ship's image grew as they closed in over the next hour. It was a small vessel, but not small enough to fit in one of *Endurance*'s pod bays, not that they had one available. They'd have to connect via the aft docking station, like they did with supply ships. Lyn had seen others like it out of Mars. Probably typical university stock—durable, unbreakable. It could be full of terrified students.

Ani slowed *Endurance,* switching to thrusters. "Should I use the over-under maneuver?"

"Good thinking, yes," Lyn answered. "I'd rather we don't have an audience."

With no forward or ventral windows, *Endurance* could ride over the *Mars Jedica* then back up to dock. No one could see what was going on. Ani switched the camera angle, keeping the *Jedica* in view. There wasn't much obvious damage. Windows were intact, no scorch marks on the hull. An engine cowling was bent, the other one missing. The *Jedica*'s docking port filled the screen as Ani handled the connections.

"Docking complete," Ani announced.

"Let's go take a look," Lyn said to Marc. She called for the doctor to join them.

As they walked the hallway to the docking station in the Paddock, curious faces greeted them from rooms along the way.

"I felt the ship move, Captain," Mr. Kunis in Room 503 said. "Are we heading home?"

"Just testing the engines," Marc said.

In the Paddock, they donned lifepacks and helmets. Lyn opened a link to Ani. "Anything coming from inside?"

"No, Captain."

"Then we'll assume the worst—no atmosphere or gravity."

The doctor joined them and they stepped into the airlock. Lyn punched the controls to analyze the other ship's pressure. "Hmm," she muttered. "Appears to be 90 percent of *Endurance*'s."

Marc released the *Jedica*'s hatch and pushed it open. Lyn watched the gauges on her screen. Temperature hovered near minus 17 degrees C, oxygen 15 percent and dropping. They stepped through. Her stomach shifted as she rose. With no gravity on the stricken ship, it was like stepping off a cliff but rising, not falling. It was also pitch dark. They switched on their helmet lights. She braced against the ceiling and looked around.

They had entered a main cabin with five rows of double seats. No sign of any passengers. To their right, the command section; to their left, presumably living quarters and the engines. Through the windows they could see stars. They turned to the front, pushing aside floating chunks of debris. Blackened instrument panels were dusted with white fire suppressant. The air registered toxic from smoldering fires.

As they approached, they could see the command seat was empty but a charred mess, a hole burned through at chest height. They found a woman strapped in the copilot's seat, no helmet, suit not activated. Unconscious or dead, Lyn couldn't tell. Soot coated her face, fire suppressant whitened her short, dark hair.

Doc touched the woman's neck. "She's alive. Vitals uploading now."

Lyn read the numbers transferring to the doctor's database. Pulse weak, blood pressure low, temperature well below normal. His other hand moved over her body, scanning internal organs, bones. He withdrew a portable oxygen tank from his torso and placed the mask over her face. "She's safe to transport."

They discussed the logistics of moving her. Marc went to the airlock, and Lyn heard vents hissing as the pressure equalized so the hatch could remain open. Toxins would vent to space while fresh air streamed in from

Endurance. She scanned the cockpit. Blood smeared the front window, and her light caught a dark, frozen blob, likely blood, floating near the ceiling. Their victim, securely strapped in, appeared unscathed.

"There has to be someone else," she said to the others.

"Here." Marc called from the back of the main cabin. Lyn and the doctor joined him.

A woman was caught under a broken cabinet. Dr. Amos felt the woman's neck. "I'm afraid she's dead."

Marc and the doctor pulled her out, her body stiff from rigor mortis. Lyn noticed she was not burned. Her long blond hair was held in a single braid, her scalp darkened with dried blood from a wound on her right temple. One arm appeared broken. A ring on her left hand caught Lyn's eye.

"She has family," she said quietly. "But they all do, don't they?"

Both women wore flight suits with the logo from the Lavenza Institute. Neither suit had activated, so either they ignored basic safety precautions or whatever hit them was quick.

"Let's take the aft service stairs," she said to the doctor. "I don't want guests seeing this."

Marc retrieved hover-stretchers from the Paddock storage room, and Lyn and the doctor returned to their survivor. He unsnapped her harness and gently guided her out of the seat and to a stretcher.

"Ease her out slowly," Dr. Amos said as they neared the hatch to *Endurance*. "Our gravity could be painful compared to zero G or even Mars."

She moaned softly as they passed through the airlock, her breathing more labored. Lyn stayed with her while Marc and the Doc retrieved the body. They decked that stretcher under the first one, covering both with a cloth.

Marc stayed on the ship while Lyn and the doctor led the stretchers down to Medical. Ruby Fischer, the broken leg from Room 409, lay in the first bed by the door, her husband, Herschel, at her side. The other beds were empty. Dr. Amos shut the soundproof privacy screens. They transferred the survivor to the far left bed, her companion to the far right. The stretchers would find their way back to the Paddock storage room.

Dr. Amos ran his eyes along the survivor, scanning. His hands brushed lightly, pressing here and there, feeling organs.

"There are no internal injuries or broken bones, but she is suffering from mild hypoxia, smoke inhalation, and hypothermia," he said when he finished. "She should make a full recovery."

He wrapped her in a warming blanket.

"Can you wake her?" Lyn asked, impatient for answers.

"I'd like to wait, give her time to warm up, let the medbots get a handle on things."

They turned to the deceased. Death grayed her white skin. Doc ran his hands along her body. "The first injury appears to be the cause of death. A severe blow to the head. That bled profusely, indicating she was alive. These other injuries, broken arm, fractured vertebrae, had little bleeding and no swelling. They apparently occurred postmortem. Looks like she was thrown about quite violently."

"None of those injuries seem enough to kill her," Lyn said. "Couldn't the medbots stop the bleeding?"

He scanned some more. "She doesn't have any medbots."

Lyn looked puzzled. "No medbots?"

"Correct."

Certainly there were populations on Earth that didn't have access to nanobot inoculations, or refused them, but she'd never seen it in someone who went to space, let alone worked out of Mars.

"Thank you, Doctor," Lyn said, grimacing at the thought of the woman being tossed about like a rag doll.

She looked back to the still figure on the other bed. *Your peaceful repose is about to be severely disturbed,* she thought.

She noticed the doctor staring at her. "What?"

"Am I correct you have not eaten a meal since dinner last night?"

"Can't be." She paused to think. "Wait, I had a grape at the staff meeting."

"That's five hours, Captain."

"I can count, Doctor."

"Please go eat. We can awaken our patient in another hour."

Like she had time for this, though she had noticed a headache forming.

"It's that or I hook you up to a feeding tube."

"Fine. I'll be back in an hour."

"I can monitor your nutrition intake, you know."

"Yes, I am very much aware of that now."

Lyn stopped by the Fischers on her way out. *Now, Captain,* the doctor called through her mind link. No privacy screen for her, it seemed.

Since she had to pass the galley on her way back up to the *Jedica*, she stopped in.

"Didn't see you at lunch," Miriam said, motioning her to a stool by the work table.

"We had a . . . development. Do I need to write myself a permission slip?"

"What would you like?"

"A sandwich would be fine. I have to get upstairs."

Miriam sliced a fresh loaf of cricket bread and slathered spreads and piled slabs of her protein bacon, lettuce, tomatoes, Martian cheese. Lyn's stomach growled watching her.

Miriam handed Lyn the half-wrapped sandwich. "Can you share this development?"

"Love to, but later." Lyn took a bite and moaned with pleasure. "I'll definitely be at dinner."

Miriam waved a gesture that meant either goodbye or yeah, right.

Marc stood by the *Jedica*'s hatch, watching a holographic display. "How's our patient?"

"Still out," Lyn said. "Find anything?"

"Not yet. Petra's downloading the ship's logs. We'll need to repair the power supply before we can get a better look inside." His eyes dropped to her sandwich.

"You get any lunch?" she asked.

"I wasn't hungry, but now that I see that." He reached for it playfully.

Lyn pulled away. "Not on your life. I'm under doctor's orders, so you are too. Go see Miriam."

He chuckled and made a sad face.

She laughed and hopped back, waving the sandwich. When he reached for her again, she grabbed his arm, swung it up, twisted him around, and brought him over her leg to the floor in a roll.

He hooted with delight. "You've been practicing," he said, jumping to his feet.

She relaxed and he swiftly knocked her legs out but held her so she went down slowly, not even losing the sandwich. She shrieked a laugh. He playfully pressed his foot onto her stomach.

"Duncan!" she said between gasps.

Marc stepped back, releasing her. "I'm sorry."

Lyn remained on the floor, breathing hard. You don't mistake Marc Franklin for Duncan Randall. Living, breathing Marc for Duncan, a dim memory from a long-ago childhood. He knew the story, how her oldest brother had died, but she'd let her guard down. Get it together, Randall, she chided herself.

He gave her a hand and pulled her to her feet, facing the open door to the *Jedica*.

"Shite," she said. "A woman died on that ship and we're out here giggling like school kids. What if someone had seen us?"

He didn't say anything. She looked forlornly at the crushed remains of her lunch. Life goes on. Right? She considered tossing it, but remembered her suit would transmit how many calories she'd taken in. Why reckon with the doctor if she didn't have to?

They went down the stairs together. Lyn finished eating and tossed the wrapper in a recycling bin. Back to business. They parted at the landing for the kitchen and her mood lightened as she overheard, "Oh, lord, another one!"

It was good to smile again. Then she entered Medical and her newly filled stomach clenched. Now came the hard part.

Her nose wrinkled at the lingering smoke and chemicals. A sheet covered the dead woman. On the bed next to her, the survivor stirred, as though waking from a deep sleep. She looked about Lyn's age. Doc stood by her side. He had cleaned most of the soot from her face. Lyn pulled shut the curtain between the two beds. No need to see that upon first awakening. Everyone knew what a sheet over the face meant.

The woman blinked, trying to focus. Her eyes darted between Dr. Amos and Lyn. Her brow furrowed. She took a breath and looked down at the mask over her nose and mouth. She shifted, like she was testing, did everything work? The warming blanket was heavy and thick. She pulled it down.

Lyn leaned in and introduced herself and Dr. Amos. "You are safe. You are on board the *Endurance*."

"What happened?" she asked, her voice muffled by the mask.

"We're not sure. We were hoping you knew. The important thing is you're going to be all right," Lyn said. "What is your name?"

Her gaze roamed the small curtained area. "Diana Squires." A quick gasp. "Where's Rose?"

"Is that the woman who was with you?"

Here it comes.

A nod and intake of breath. "Yes, she's my wife."

Oh, feck.

Diana shifted up on an elbow. "Where is she?" She coughed violently and fell back.

"It's the smoke inhalation," Dr. Amos said. "This will help." He held his thumb to her neck and Lyn heard the hiss of a jetspray.

While she waited for Diana's coughing to subside, Lyn pulled a stool over and sat next to the bed. She didn't like towering over the poor woman.

"I'm very sorry to have to tell you this," she said. "Rose didn't make it."

At first, Diana didn't react. Lyn thought she might not have heard. Maybe there was hearing damage. Then, "I don't understand," Diana said, raising herself again. "Where is she? Where's our ship?"

"It's here, docked to *Endurance*. Diana, I'm so sorry, but Rose died."

Even Lyn felt the blow those words struck. Diana looked at her as if she had spoken gibberish. She pulled off the mask. "What? No. You must be mistaken. Where is she?"

"She's here." Lyn used all her might not to look over at the curtain shielding the bed holding Rose.

"I want to see her." Her voice was strong and defiant. Demanding. As if that alone could change the truth.

Lyn looked to the doctor. "Is she well enough?"

He nodded. While Lyn helped Diana stand, he pulled the curtain aside. Diana stared at the sheeted form on the next bed. She looked at Lyn questioningly. Lyn held onto her arm while the doctor slowly drew the sheet away.

Hope ricocheted off reality and hit Diana squarely in the chest, pushing her back, buckling her at the knees. Lyn braced to support her. She understood.

You couldn't look at Rose and believe she was asleep or unconscious. Her skin tone had progressed to a waxy yellow. Her eyes were half closed and her jaw slack, mouth open. Blood matted her hair. Her limbs askew from the rigor.

"You have to help her," Diana said to the doctor, her eyes locked on Rose. "Do something!"

"There's nothing I can do," Dr. Amos said. "She is past the point of—"

Lyn shushed him. A clinical analysis would hardly be helpful at this point.

"No," Diana whispered, her head moving in a shake of denial. She wrenched free from Lyn and backed away, glaring. "What did you do to her? Who are you?"

"Please." Lyn held her hands up. *Don't tell her to calm down. Don't say it'll be okay. It won't.* "Something damaged your ship. Mine too. This is the *Endurance*. We were on the Grand Tour. We saw your ship at Saturn. You probably saw ours. Do you remember anything?"

Diana shook her head. She raked her fingers through her hair then stared at the white powder coating them. Tears dropped onto her palms. She wiped her hands on her thighs and leaned back against the bed, her face crumpling with realization.

"No, no, no," she kept muttering. She touched Rose's face then pulled her hand back like she'd been burned. Lyn could only wait her out. Eventually, she hugged herself and cried softly. "What happened to her?" she asked between quiet sobs.

"She hit her head hard," Dr. Amos said. "She did not survive long after that and she certainly was not conscious."

With a trembling hand, she wiped tears from her cheek. "So she didn't suffer?"

"No."

Silent minutes ticked by. Lyn was about to speak when Diana turned, looked at each of them in turn, and asked for a moment alone. Her breath caught, like a hiccough.

"Of course," Lyn said. "Take all the time you need. We'll be in the doctor's office." She couldn't vouch for him, but she was relieved.

Lyn watched as the doctor removed the seal on the cadaver cupboard and turned on the refrigeration.

"Do you want to call me when she's ready?" she asked.

"That may be unnecessary. She's unlikely to spend more than twenty minutes."

"Really?"

"Studies show that's the average time loved ones spend with the deceased."

"I didn't realize that's something people would study." She checked her chronometer. It was 1700. Dinner would be in an hour and she'd promised Miriam she'd show for it. Plus, it was time to come clean with everyone about where they were and what they knew. "She'll need a room," she muttered to herself. She opened a mind link to Sharyn and filled her in. *Find one down here in crew quarters. For now, I want her away from the other guests. We need to keep an eye on her.*

Understood, Boss.

Lyn sat in the doctor's office, reviewing reports from Edward, Natalie, and Ghez. No malfunction in the computer or programs. They confirmed they were indeed near Rigil Kentaurus. She mind-linked to Marc. *Let's look around. Maybe the* Aphrodite *is out here too. Also, let staff know we'll fess up at dinner about where we are.*

Will you want Natalie to give a presentation?

I'll handle it. The view out the window is all the presentation we'll need.

Diana appeared in the doorway. Lyn checked the time. Dang, twenty minutes. She had no frame of reference to know whether Diana looked worse than usual, but her blank, defeated expression and slumped posture fit the current circumstances.

"What happens now?" Diana asked

Good question, Lyn thought. "We'll get her cleaned up, and—"

"May I do that?"

"Of course." She avoided looking at the cupboard. "Beyond that, I'm afraid I haven't thought it out. We're dealing with a crisis."

Diana stood with her arms crossed, staring at the floor. Her expression changed, like she was processing all this new information. "Does your crisis have anything to do with us? Our ship?" she asked, raising her gaze to Lyn's. She inhaled, as though steeling herself. "Did you kill Rose?"

"No. God, no," Lyn said quickly. She rose and offered her chair. "Please, sit. Your ship was sending out a mayday. We found it floating, disabled. We have no idea what happened." She refrained from explaining where they were. She needed to tread carefully. For all she knew, Diana should be considered a suspect. "Do you remember anything?"

Diana breathed deeply, coughed, then settled back in the chair. "No, I don't." She rubbed her head.

"It may come back," the doctor said. "Right now you need rest."

"We'll find quarters for you," Lyn said, "and I'll be sure your things are brought off your ship." A quiet pause followed.

"I need to contact the Lavenza Institute." Diana's voice broke. It took several breaths to say, "And—and her parents."

Now was not the time to tell her that was not possible, at least not for four years. "Our, ah, communications are down."

Diana nodded, but Lyn sensed it was less from understanding than being overwhelmed by emotions.

Dr. Amos got a basin of water and a sponge, and Diana went back to Rose. He stood quietly by his desk. Lyn sat in silence. Silence always seemed to accompany death. The refrigerant gurgled. Diana's acrid smell hung in the air. She checked the time. Dinner was in half an hour. What if she wasn't finished by then?

Sharyn arrived. "I have a room ready."

Lyn stood with a stretch. She motioned Sharyn to follow. Diana stood by Rose and hummed softly. She smoothed the sheet and held Rose's hand. For her part, Rose didn't look much improved other than the blood cleaned off, revealing a long, ugly gash beginning above her right eyebrow and disappearing into her hair. Lyn had noticed Diana was about her height, but now she looked shrunken, diminished by grief. If ghosts existed, surely they were the bereaved and not the dead. When Diana looked up and acknowledged their presence, Lyn introduced Sharyn.

"We can take you to your quarters if you are ready."

Diana's calm façade crumbled with a realized horror. "I don't—I don't want her to be alone."

Lyn put her arms around her. It was like holding a fragile, frightened bird. "She won't be. Someone will be there around the clock."

Diana held onto Lyn and cried.

"Do you want to leave first, or wait for her—?" Lyn couldn't bring herself to finish, to say the doctor would put Rose into the cadaver cupboard.

Diana gripped Lyn tighter and sobbed into her shoulder. Lyn nodded to the doctor. He handed her a jetspray. "It'll help her sleep."

"We'll take good care of her," Lyn said, pulling Diana gently away from her. "It's time."

The room Sharyn led them to was her own. Lyn asked the question with her raised eyebrows.

"Miriam said I could bunk with her," she said softly.

Diana ignored them or was too tired to pay attention. They sat her on the bed, and Lyn gave her the sedative. She slumped over. Sharyn pulled off her boots.

Sharyn indicated a house bot in the corner. It looked like a cassock. "We'll keep an eye on her," she said quietly. In the hallway, she added, "Poor kid. I can't imagine what she's going through."

Lyn could. "Yes, it's hard and it will be hard for a long time, but right now, I've got a ship full of people who need to know where they are."

Chapter 5

LYN PUT OFF her announcement till everyone had eaten. No need to waste Miriam's good food. Surely no one would have an appetite after what she had to say. She simply asked everyone to stay when they'd finished. That was enough to cause a nervous buzz of chatter.

Perhaps sensing the mood that would follow, Miriam had outdone herself. Lyn knew she used cooking as a stress reliever, so judging by the menu, she should be as relaxed as a kitten. She started them off with a creamy artichoke soup topped with Parmesan and a sticky tempeh, mango, and lime noodle salad. The main course was roast pumpkin and spinach lasagna. The meal finished with chocolate marquise. If they all died now, at least they'd be happy.

Lyn mind linked to her. *M, I might not get the chance later to thank you for this, but it was simply stunning. How'd you pull this together?*

I didn't. It was the menu all along. I just hope they don't all puke it up later.

Lyn's senior staff filled her table, no special guest privileges tonight. The meal was mostly quiet, with the occasional nervous glance from Ani or Ghez. Even Sharyn, the queen of small talk, struggled to come up with an appropriate topic. Ani pushed food around her plate, but a look from Lyn improved her appetite. Edward slurped and smacked, shoveling in the lasagna like it was his last meal, but he always ate that way.

Lyn wiped her mouth and stood. The already quiet room stilled further. No need for Marc to whistle. The windows behind her showed nothing like what they should be seeing. She purposely had Ani position the ship so the double suns were visible. She dimmed the lights to limit glare. Miriam and her staff watched from the kitchen doorway. The rest of *Endurance*'s crew sat at tables at the back.

"Can everyone hear me?" Murmurs and nods. "I know you have a lot of questions, and we'll be here until they are all answered to the best of our current knowledge." She inhaled a deep, settling breath. "Here's what we know."

She relayed the events of the previous night. "At approximately 0230 something happened. What, we don't yet know. As you are well aware, things got pretty shook up. Thankfully, no one died and medical nanobots activated as designed and the injured are healing." She nodded toward a couple sitting at a table across from her. His arm was in a sling and she had a bandage around her head.

"*Endurance* withstood the event well. She is a fine ship. Self-repair programs are already at work, and we expect to be fully operational in a week."

The mention of a timeframe caused a buzz of chatter and groans, a mix of relief and concern. A week was either good news or alarming.

"Why has there been no sign of rescue?" a woman called out from the back.

Lyn walked along the row of booths against the windows. *Here it comes.* "What you are seeing is a binary star, not our sun."

"Where the hell are we?" a man yelled from across the room.

Lyn ignored the outburst. "Those who live in the southern hemisphere know these as Rigil Kentaurus. That's the larger star. The smaller one is its pair, Toliman." She turned to point. "And here, much dimmer, is Proxima Centauri. As you can see, Rigil Kent is much like our own sun."

"Is this a joke?" Another voice.

"I wish it were."

"Why are they so big? Are they going nova?"

"Good question." Lyn took in a deep breath. She put her hands in her pockets to hide the shaking. "They are large because we are close to them. In the span of a few minutes, we traveled 4.3 light years away from our sun, our home."

A quiet clink of a fork or spoon on a plate. These people weren't dummies. They knew what this meant.

"How?" a weak voice from in front. Nikoleta Canno.

Lyn shook her head. "We don't know. Technically, it's not possible. And there's no easy way to say this, but right now, we have no way to get back."

The room erupted. Shouts, cries, gasps, all made it impossible to hear the questions being flung at her. Lyn raised her hands. "Please. One at a time. I'll stay until you've all been heard."

The noise grew. Some people stood.

"Listen up!" Marc shouted.

They quieted down and hands shot up. Lyn pointed to one.

"The ship moved a few hours ago. I heard it was to test the engines. Is that true?"

"Not quite," Lyn said. "We weren't sure what we would find, but it turned out another ship was affected."

More loud chatter.

"A small research vessel out of Mars," she continued. "It had been in orbit around Saturn at the same time as us. It is now docked to *Endurance*."

Please don't ask about who was on board.

"Who was on board? Are they okay?"

Damn.

"There were two women on board. I'm sorry to say, one was killed. The other is recovering and expected to be okay. She's resting in crew quarters now."

More hands. Lyn pointed.

"Does she know what happened?"

"We'll be asking her that, but right now she's suffered a terrible loss, one we thankfully dodged, so I'm letting her rest. We'll examine her ship and its logs to see if they can tell us anything."

"Is anyone else out there? Other ships?"

"Not that we know of yet, but we're looking."

For the next two hours, Lyn and her staff fielded questions. Other than some confusion caused by Edward's minute description of the anatomy of a rocket engine, it went as well as Lyn could expect. A few broke down but others comforted them. Most seemed dulled by the news. It hadn't sunk in fully. But it would. To keep them focused, she covered everything from how they could have traveled faster than light to how they would survive.

"Thanks to recycling technology," Lyn said, "we can sustain ourselves pretty much indefinitely." That was the important piece she wanted them to remember. "We are in no danger." She should have said immediate, but that wouldn't be helpful under the circumstances. "You came on this trip because of a particular interest in space travel and a curiosity about our universe. I expect we'll be able to use that curiosity. I feel confident that together we can figure out what happened and how we can get back. I just can't promise it will be any time soon."

THE NEXT MORNING Lyn dragged herself to the dining room as Miriam had requested. Problem was, 0600 was before most guests were up and about.

She poured a cup of coffee and stood still. The only others were two women at a booth near the back, under a window. They faced into the room like they couldn't bear to see what was out there. What wasn't out there. All the tables were large, Omara encouraged guests to mingle, and each could seat eight. They were dwarfed by the expanse of white tablecloth. She shouldn't sit by herself, but she didn't want to intrude either. A bot carrying a tray of muffins detoured around her. One of the women looked her way. *Shite. Now what?* The other woman turned. Quick, check the database. Jeanne and Suzanne Cormier, from Quebec. Right. They'd been among the first to join Lyn for dinner. Delightful couple as she recalled. Jeanne was some kind of life coach. Yes, you licensed her AI hologram to advise and inspire you to live your best life. Lyn had been smitten by Jeanne's warmth that made you feel you were the most important person in the world—at least that was how Lyn reacted. But she saw it with the others too. It was clear, though, how much she adored her wife. They shared shy smiles and looks throughout the meal, even though they'd been together almost twenty years.

Lyn went to their table. "How are you this morning?"

Jeanne stared at her plate. A muscle at the angle of her jaw bulged, teeth clenching.

"About as well as can be expected, I suppose," Suzanne said in a soft French accent. Her eyes were sad and red.

"If there's anything I can do—emphasis on the can—let me know."

Neither spoke.

"Well . . ." *Shite. What do you say? Enjoy your day?* "Well . . ."

"We have two children," Jeanne said, also with an accent.

"Jeanne." Suzanne placed a hand on her arm.

"No, she needs to hear this."

Lyn pulled out a chair and sat facing the dreaded window. She gripped her mug. "I'm listening."

"They are with my parents," Suzanne said. Pain arced across her face. It was one thing to be separated from family. They all were one way or another. But children?

"How old are they?"

"Eight and ten," Jeanne said. "Jacqueline and Eloise."

Lyn caught herself smiling. "Beautiful names."

"This was a belated honeymoon," Suzanne said. "We weren't sure about being away so long, but, really, the girls love my parents' farm and they are at the age where they won't like that sort of thing much longer." She fell silent. Her hand covered her mouth and her eyes squeezed shut as if blindness and silence could make it all go away.

"Trip of a lifetime," Jeanne said, flat. "*Merde.*" She gripped Suzanne's hand.

The Omara Tours contract plainly stated that space travel was hazardous. There hadn't been a single accident in the ten years she'd been in business, but Omara was clear to her guests that things can go wrong and when they go wrong in space, there's little you can do. She required guests to create a last message for family or a friend that she kept on file. They were always deleted at the end of the tour. Because the ships always returned. Until now. The Cormiers knew the risk. But did they understand it?

"I can't even begin to imagine what you're feeling," Lyn said. "But it's early yet. We will get answers and we will do everything we can to get back."

"They are probably already worried," Jeanne said. "We've sent messages every day. And now . . . there is no point?"

The message wouldn't arrive for four years.

"The silence, the not knowing," Lyn said.

The women nodded. Suzanne wiped her cheek.

More guests filtered into the dining room quietly, without the boisterousness of a day filled with the excitement of visiting Titan or taking a turn at the controls or sending back happy images to loved ones at home.

Lyn stood. "Thank you for telling me about your children. And please," she said quietly, "help each other." She glanced around the room. "We are in this together, and together we can make our way back. I'm sure there must be a way." She set her half-full mug on the return table and left for her staff meeting.

She sat, weary, at her usual place in the middle seat facing the door as her senior staff assembled. Over time, Lyn had come to appreciate one of the less charismatic classes at the Aerospace Academy. Buried in Professor James's lessons about command and leadership were three nuggets she retained: A captain is the servant of her crew, people are as important as operations and long-term planning, and no one is as smart as a group thinking together.

"Thanks for starting your day early," she said, "and let's do this each morning for the time being."

She went around the table, listening to updates. Repairs continued, the Observation Deck frame was self-repairing, Isabel said. "On track to finish in six days."

"It may be a mixed blessing to get that open again," Lyn said. She turned to Sharyn. "How's our newest guest doing?"

"Hasn't stirred. Which leads me to the difficult question—"

Lyn's mind went blank.

"What do we do with the body?" the doctor finished for Sharyn. "There isn't much point in keeping it in the cadaver cupboard."

Lyn blinked. "First, 'it' is a woman, and, second, she was the loved one of our guest. They were married."

"Oh," Sharyn said.

"Yes."

"What do we do?" Sharyn asked.

The room was remarkably quiet for being full of people. No one moved. It was like they weren't even breathing. A room of dead people, Lyn thought. No, people *were* talking. Listen. This is your job.

"Company protocol is we bring the body back," Marc said. "Clearly not an option."

"Would she want a service?" Sharyn asked. "Her wife, I mean."

"I'll have to ask her," Lyn said.

"I can if you want," Sharyn said.

"I should do it."

LYN HELD A boxed breakfast in one hand and tapped on Diana's door. No answer. Quietly she let herself in and set the box on the table. The smoky smell stung her throat. She presumed the lump under the covers was Diana. A small mountain of crumpled tissues rose from the floor. Sharyn might regret her generosity. On the wall next to the bed, a vintage photo showed a young Asian couple grinning on a boat, beside them a pile of shellfish. Oysters, Lyn remembered Sharyn mentioning. They'd have to be her great-grandparents for there to still be oysters in Chesapeake Bay. Another photo showed a beautiful sunset over the water with one of the bay's iconic lighthouses on stilts aglow. No one had been allowed back for more than forty years.

Lyn pulled up a chair, reintroduced herself to the lump, and sat down. "I wanted to see how you're doing."

Diana didn't move or say anything.

"We need to talk."

Nothing.

How do you tell someone the worst news possible, losing your spouse, isn't the worst news possible? She cleared her throat. "I need to tell you something."

The lump shifted. At least she was alive.

"I don't know if you recall my mentioning we were in a crisis."

Diana peeked out. "I do. Is it over?"

"No, I'm afraid it's not." Lyn paused, not finding the words.

"Does it have anything to do with that binary star out there?" Diana glanced toward the small rectangular window.

Lyn froze. "Yes." She scrutinized Diana's face for signs of understanding. She worked for the Lavenza Institute, on Mars, so she was no tourist. But her puffy red eyes weren't because of that double star. "That's Rigil Kentaurus."

Her expression didn't change. No confusion or shock. "That's not possible, unless I was unconscious for a really long time and aged very well."

"No, it's not possible. Nevertheless, it's true."

"How?" Almost not a question. Like she didn't really care.

"We don't know. Two days ago, we all went to bed. We keep Earth time from Baker Island, where we launched from. During the night, our ship—yours too it seems—was violently thrown out of our solar system and into another. We're trying to figure out how but don't have a lot to go on. I was hoping you might be able to help. You went through it too. Maybe your ship recorded something ours didn't. Are any memories coming back?"

"Not really. We were on Mars time. The last thing I remember is eating breakfast. When it began, we strapped in . . ."

"How did it begin?"

"We lost gravity," Diana said, after a long pause. "That wasn't so odd. Could have been a malfunction. It'd happened before. That's all I remember."

"Okay." Hardly. She couldn't bring herself to say what she came for.

"What happens now?" Diana asked.

"We're taking it one day at a time. We had quite a bit of damage, which we're repairing. Some passengers were injured, but none ki—" She stopped. Except for the wife of the woman in front of her. "I'm sorry."

Diana rolled toward the wall. Her shoulders shook with silent sobs.

Lyn waited. She moved the box of tissues within Diana's reach. She grabbed three, blew her nose, and wiped her eyes.

Lyn tried another tack. "You're out of the Lavenza Institute. What do you do there?"

Diana rolled onto her back, sat up, and leaned against the headboard. Her eyes and nose were red and raw. She wiped her nose on a tissue and held it in her lap, like it was precious and breakable. "I teach astrophysics. Cosmology to undergraduates for their junior year off-planet. Rose teaches the history of religion."

Lyn tucked away Diana's profession. Time for that later. "Religion's an unusual topic for a Mars campus."

"Lavenza takes a multidisciplinary approach to understanding our existence." She took a fresh tissue, flattened it then folded it in half and in half again, spreading and smoothing. Then she opened it and wiped her cheeks and blew her nose. She grimaced. "Do you know there's a very good chance we don't exist at all?" She didn't wait for Lyn to respond. "Reality, as we know it, could be a mathematical illusion. Or we might be a projection on the edge of a black hole."

"I am aware of those theories. Doesn't make the pain go away."

Diana pulled her knees up. "She always said she wanted to be shot into a star."

That's what Tara wanted. Don't we all.

"I can arrange that."

"I want it to be our sun."

"Can't help you there. I'm sorry, but I can give Rose a proper space burial."

Diana seemed to consider this. She blinked a few times, her chin pressed to her knees. "Can we do it soon? She's Johari. They bury their dead within twenty-four hours. And I don't like to think of her lying alone in a freezer. That's harder than losing her."

"I'll make the arrangements."

LYN, MARC, AND Sharyn entered the small room containing the launch tube at the front of the ship's lowest deck. How many times had Lyn watched scientific instruments switched in and out here? It had never been used for this. The high, stiff collar of her dress uniform cut into her throat. Omara's trademark Arabian sword squeaked in its scabbard at her side. Marc's banged the back of her knee.

Rose, in her cleaned Lavenza flight suit, lay on the tube's rack, ready for loading. Dr. Amos had done a fair job. He'd closed the wound and hidden it under her now-clean hair. Eyes and mouth closed. No, she didn't look like she was sleeping, but she wasn't as ghastly as she had been. Diana stood by her side. Lyn was relieved to see she'd showered and wore a fresh flight suit. Ani had positioned the ship to face Rigil Kent.

Omara Tours had no protocol for this. On the rare occasion someone wanted a space burial, Omara handled it herself. It was never done on a tour. It seemed important to Lyn, however, for her most senior staff to bear witness as a sign of respect. She let Diana take the lead, though, and had no idea what she would do. A quick research into Johari burial practices hadn't turned up a lot. Petra told her the custom was a quick burial directly in soil. Actual practice was left to the loved ones.

Now they stood silently. Diana bent over Rose and murmured too softly for Lyn to hear. She straightened and faced three strangers. Maybe this wasn't such a good idea, Lyn thought miserably.

Diana exhibited composure the bereaved are usually allowed to let slip. "Thank you for this, Captain Randall." She addressed them all. "I'm sorry you didn't get to meet Rose." She bit her lower lip then stoically continued. "The Johari aren't a religious sect, but Rose talked about God a lot. Not just because it was her job. If I could believe, I'd believe in hers, because her God is in nature, the cosmos, even in people. To the Johari, each of us *are* God. That's a power I'd love to have access to." She paused and rested a hand on Rose's arm. "If she's right, and she usually is, then she now knows all the whys she'd spent her life trying to answer. And if she's right, her spirit, her soul, has diffused like the star dust we all come from, and we can all share in her spirit." She closed her eyes and tipped her face upward as if greeting warm sunshine. "Her energy can never be destroyed. Her light will never dim. She was and always will be my guide star." She squeezed her eyes shut as if to hold back tears. Then she wiped her face and stepped back.

How do you follow that? Lyn had chosen William Penn, the founder of a state bearing his name in search of religious freedom. "'For death is no more than a turning of us over from time to eternity,'" she recited.

Diana gave a tiny, approving nod.

"We commend the spirit and bravery of Rose Squires as we commit her body to space."

She let Diana slide Rose into the tube. Marc stepped forward to close and secure the breech door. Diana waited, her hand shaking. Then she pushed the launch button. The surge of the vacuum propelled Rose toward the star.

Lyn and Sharyn accompanied Diana back to her quarters. Miriam had sent down a tray of food. Diana refused it but assured Lyn she'd eat later, that for now she was too exhausted. She lay back on Sharyn's bed and immediately fell asleep, or appeared to.

In her quarters, Lyn changed into a regular flight suit. She paused mid-zip and reached for the photo she kept on her bedside table. Tara, with the barest hint of a smile and her trademark downward gaze, like she was above it all. Her dark hair draped over her shoulder, arms crossed. Lush eyebrows framed her intense gaze. Then in her twenties, she was physically imposing and often paced with impatience and pent-up energy.

Marc called from the bridge, "Captain, we've found the *Aphrodite*. Issuing a mayday."

A shot of adrenaline jittered through her. "What's their status?" She set the photo back on the table and zip-sealed her suit.

"No answer to our hails."

"That's not good. How close are they?"

"A couple hours before we're in visual range."

She checked the time. An hour till Miriam's dinner call. "Let's go. And use this time to make sure everyone gets something to eat. I'm guessing it'll be another long night."

Chapter 6

ENDURANCE SPED TOWARD the *Aphrodite* on autopilot while her crew ate dinner. Lyn wished she could do the same—eat dinner on autopilot instead of pushing food around her plate. Miriam, perhaps anticipating the mood, went with a comfort-food menu, ravioli with squash and porcini mushrooms. At Sharyn's urging, Lyn had approved a return to custom, so she and Marc shared the captain's table with six guests. Marc was pushing food into his mouth. He reached for a roll, poured wine for the others.

She ran through scenarios while pretending to listen. Best case, the *Aphrodite* was undamaged. That presented several possibilities, including everyone on *Endurance* moving to the larger ship. It wouldn't get them home, but it would increase their chances of survival. No response to their hail didn't bode well.

Worst case, there was nothing but debris. No, maybe not worst case. Worst case would be a disabled ship full of people and *Endurance* incapable of helping. Whom do you save?

Marc nudged her. Mr. Abebe had said something, a napkin tucked under his chin.

"I was saying, Captain," Mr. Abebe continued, "that I awoke this morning forgetting what you had told us last night. Even about what happened. My first thought was, do not miss the trip to Titan. It was a second shock to remember."

Was he expecting an apology? "I know the feeling."

"Do you?"

"Yes, actually, I do." It was a lie. She hadn't slept long enough to forget anything.

"I apologize. I am sure you have family back home too."

"We all do," Lyn said.

"My son graduates from college next spring," Mrs. Ivey said. Her husband put down his fork.

"What is he studying?" Marc asked.

Her expression shifted, lips tightening. She swallowed, set her silverware down, and folded her napkin. She stood and left the table.

"I'm so sorry," Marc leaned toward Mr. Ivey. He shook his head, rose, and followed his wife.

A few people at other tables watched the couple leave then glanced at the captain's table. Some resumed eating, others sat quiet.

"It will take time," Mr. Abebe said. "To adjust." He picked at his food.

Petra sent Lyn a private message. *We're within visual range.*

Here we go. She acknowledged and set her napkin by her plate. "If you'll excuse me, I'm needed elsewhere. Please enjoy your dessert." Enjoy. What a stupid thing to say.

Do you need us all? Marc messaged.

Not yet. First visuals only. Still time before we're close enough to do anything.

Lyn entered the bridge, took her seat, and turned on the front view. They were approaching the *Aphrodite* head on. At this distance, it didn't look too bad. She could discern the outline of the ship, and the superstructure appeared intact, but the image was very small and pixelated. She pulled up Ghez's shots from the other night to compare. Those views were of the starboard side. It was hard to tell what she might be seeing.

She walked laps around the bridge, restless from too much sitting. Across the back, down nine steps, across the front, and back up. Each time the magnification of the live image increased, she picked up her pace. She squinted at the screen. Shouldn't there be more decks? Was it the angle?

The pixels gradually resolved into small dots. Asteroid debris?

"Autopilot disengaged," Petra announced. An alarm chirped. Lyn's balance shifted as the ship slowed to a stop. "Collision hazard ahead. I will halt forward movement and await instructions."

She took her seat, breathing deeply, and called for Marc, Ani, and Ghez. When they were settled, she said, "Let's circle and see if we can get a better view."

Slowly the *Aphrodite* rotated on the viewscreen. The lower decks were obscured by a cloud. Of what became clear as the ship turned broadside. The back half was missing. Lyn kept wanting to wipe the blur away so she could see the ship, but there was no ship to see. That's what the dots were. Not asteroid. Ship debris. Walls and lights and tables and beds and—

"Catastrophic failure," Marc said. A technical term. Hardly described what they saw.

"Anything other than the mayday coming from over there?" Lyn asked Ghez.

"No, Captain. Either they aren't communicating. Or they can't."

"Or there's no one alive," Marc said.

"Ani, how close can we get?" Lyn asked.

"This is it, Captain. Ten kilometers."

Their voices remained calm, professional. No trace of what they might be feeling.

"Initiate rescue protocol," Lyn ordered.

Marc mind linked to her. *Are you sure?* This was not a discussion to have in front of crew.

Of course I am. The Outer Space Treaty is clear. We render aid.

What was he suggesting? They leave? Pretend they never found the ship?

He indicated the screen, the wreckage. *What can we possibly do? We have twenty-five crew members. Total. There were eight thousand on that ship.*

If there is so much as one person alive over there, we need to help them. Though one would be better than eight thousand.

Marc had never questioned her orders before, but they'd never been in this situation. Ani and Ghez leaned back in their seats, no doubt wondering at the extended silence.

I'm in charge of crew operations, Marc said. *I think the risk is too great. The treaty allows for that.*

In our space, Lyn thought. When you can call for help and a dedicated rescue ship handles the messy details. *Not an option out here,* she messaged back. *We can send one pod, see what we're dealing with. I'll lead and ask for a volunteer to pilot.*

Why not send the doctor? He's expendable.

He was right, of course. If needed, they could build a new doctor from the Recyc-All and reinstall his programs. But she was the one who would have to make the tough decisions. Triaging injured was a mundane task compared to what awaited them. She needed to see for herself what she'd have to decide on. And time was of the essence. She overruled her first officer. *This is not up for discussion.*

I can't let you go, he said. *What if something happens to you?*

Then you get to play captain.

Marc leaned on his elbow and rubbed his eyes. *I want it on the record that I disagree.*

So recorded. "Ani," Lyn said. "I'll be taking one pod for a reconnaissance of the *Aphrodite*. Please ask the pilots for a volunteer."

"That won't be necessary, Captain. I'll do it."

THE DEBRIS MADE navigating arduous as Lyn and Ani circled the *Aphrodite*, assessing damage, looking for signs of life. All decks were exposed, layered like a sliced cake. If the ship had any self-sealing capabilities, whatever hit her did too much damage too fast for them to close off. Conduits, wiring, and insulation hung shredded. The few bodies floating past were in pajamas or nude, bloated by the vacuum of space. No one seemed to have been wearing a suit. *They aren't that uncomfortable. Did the company even provide them?*

She thought of Captain Bratt. Was she alive? If so, where? Or was she out here, in her beaded gown? "You okay?" she asked her quiet pilot.

"I'm fine, Captain."

A male torso floated by. Ani sucked in a breath and maneuvered around it. "Shite, Ani—"

"I believe you were my age on the Enceladus mission. You came through fine."

Disaster, not mission. "That's open to debate. Trauma is like a virus. It can flare up at any time. Just know that."

"Okay." Ani focused on finding a path toward the destroyed ship.

Lyn tried to comprehend the damage. All that luxury came with a price, and the *Aphrodite* was a fragile egg now cracked open and spilling its guts. A Humpty Dumpty that was not going back together again. They headed to the bridge, where command staff might be alive. Luckily, this bridge had windows. They peered through as they cruised by. Missing panes, however, signaled a sad reality. Then they saw a figure, helmeted, suited, strapped into the command seat.

"*Endurance* to *Aphrodite*," Lyn said into her mic.

"*Aphrodite* here," a faint voice gasped, adrenaline worn off, exhaustion remaining.

"What is your status?"

"Status? We're fucked."

Ani skillfully docked to the emergency port on the roof of *Aphrodite*'s bridge. The view aft revealed an empty swimming pool, its protective dome gone, shards of wall, a hole to an elevator shaft.

They brought aboard Thomas Philbrick, the third officer. Nearly catatonic with trauma, he could barely speak. They strapped him into a seat, removed his helmet, and gave him water. He drank like a dying man in the desert. So this was Thomas Philbrick. Was that just three nights ago?

Sweat matted his thin hair, a stubble of beard marked the time passing. His eyes, wide and terrified, scanned the small space then settled on Ani and Lyn. "You got hit too? Are you the only ones left?" He gasped for air.

"No," Lyn said. "I mean yes, we were hit too, but our ship survived. What happened?"

Captain Bratt had been sleeping, he said, when something hit the ship or something happened to the ship. He wasn't sure. It was the night shift, skeleton crew. They were parked below Saturn's rings so they could illuminate the observation lounges where parties were in full swing. A Solar System Soiree. He hadn't left the bridge since making a short exploration of the surrounding areas.

"The captain's gone, her quarters, everything voided to space." He spoke without emotion, in shock. "There might be people alive. I can feel vibrations through the superstructure. Some banging. Not random like a swinging bolt."

Survivors. How many? Decisions. What if there were too many to fit on board *Endurance*? Whom do you save? She adored her crew, but they were not survivalists. Not that she expected to find needed expertise on the *Aphrodite*. Any exobiologists in the house? How about a propulsion physicist? Anyone know how to open a wormhole?

"Where is everyone?" he asked. "Why are you the only ones who responded?"

He didn't know.

There was no easy way to break this news and no time to be gentle. She told him where they were. How far from Earth, from the solar system called home. He squinted as she spoke and tipped his head as though his hearing was off.

"Do you understand?" she asked.

He shook his head slowly. His eyes darted from Lyn to Ani then out the front window. "Rigil Kent?" he asked, his voice a whisper.

"Yes," Lyn answered.

He blinked. "We're stranded?"

"Yes."

She could see him shut down, as Diana had, as many of her guests had. The shallow breathing and unfocused eyes. If he was the senior surviving officer, this was now his ship. Lyn didn't know him, had no idea of his background or training. "Let's get you rested and fed. We have a lot of decisions to make."

BACK ON *ENDURANCE*, Dr. Amos checked out Philbrick and Miriam gave him a good meal. Then Lyn again gathered her senior staff. Philbrick told them where to find *Aphrodite*'s lifepods. They dotted the perimeter of each deck and were able to self-eject as needed. Like *Endurance*'s, they sat inside the hull so likely survived, at least where there was hull. Philbrick seemed to have perked up. Maybe the food did him good. Crew quarters were on Deck 2, he said, pointing to plans they downloaded from *Endurance*'s computer. That was gone. All environmental controls, engines, and support infrastructure like the kitchens, were on Decks 1 and 3. Gone. Most of the guests stayed in rooms on Decks 4 through 12—also gone. The upper decks, 14 and 15 were the apartments. High-end, high rollers stayed there. Sixteen through nineteen held the entertainment—pools, bars, restaurants, casinos, and shops. The Star Deck at the top was completely domed. All decks wrapped around an open center.

"There's an atrium, waterfalls, an amusement park. You can look straight up and down through the ship to the stars. Could," he corrected. Now you could look anywhere and see stars. "Deck thirteen, though it's not numbered, is—was—a transparent promenade circling the ship."

"That's why it broke apart there," Edward said. "Everything below that, and aft of the central atrium is gone. There are no environmental controls, no engine room." He paused. "No life support."

"Three quarters of the ship," Lyn said. "No redundant systems housed elsewhere?"

Philbrick shook his head. "If anyone is alive, it'll be because they are in suits and their rooms didn't breach. The closets double as survival cabinets and have emergency rations."

"Whatever hit us sent us spinning and reeling," Lyn said, "yet the *Aphrodite* sits still in space, surrounded by its debris. Why?"

"What difference does it make?" Philbrick asked.

"Not for rescue, I suppose," Lyn said, "but we're trying to figure out what happened. Your ship's computer might have recorded it."

"I hardly think that's our priority right now," Philbrick said.

Lyn pressed on. "You said your ship was parked?"

He nodded.

"We were moving," Ani said. "Toward Titan, for the morning excursions."

"That could explain it," Edward said. "Depending on what caused the event, it might have made a difference who was moving and who was still."

Lyn hadn't thought to ask Diana that, but now recalled the *Mars Jedica* had also been stationary in space. Philbrick was right, though. Topic for another day.

Well past midnight, she dismissed her staff and sent Philbrick off with Sharyn to find yet another room. Alone, she turned to stare out the window at the distant, fuzzy blur of the destroyed *Aphrodite*. How many people were there, banging away at their doors, screaming for help? Slowly dying.

Chapter 7

LYN ONLY HAD twenty-five human crew. Finding volunteers was easy since everyone offered to help. Guests also inquired, once she delivered the sad news at breakfast, but she couldn't risk them without knowing their skills, which, she realized, she'd better figure out in the coming weeks. She divided her crew into rotating teams and activated six of *Endurance*'s eight pods to head back to the *Aphrodite*.

Lyn monitored the teams from *Endurance*'s bridge. Ani led Team Alpha. They found a dozen functioning lifepods. Jupiter-class pods were designed so anyone could operate them, with simple pictograph instructions. Several of the pods were connected to intact hallways and passenger cabins. Ani led her team down those passageways, checking each cabin. Meanwhile Marc led Team Beta on search and rescue.

It had been two days since the event. Anyone who survived the initial destruction could die without access to water if they hadn't already suffocated. Ani's team was diverted to rescue once all the pods were released. With hallways exposed, the only way to extract survivors from intact rooms was from the outside—deploy the emergency airlock each pod came equipped with, equalize the pod's pressure to the cabin's, then release the emergency window and get the passengers out. Still, room after room revealed dead occupants. Most not in suits, but some were. As Lyn heard the reports, the scope of the tragedy crystallized.

Over the next four days, rescuers worked around the clock. After the first day, Lyn joined the rotation, commanding a pod. Marc argued against it, but she again overruled him. There simply weren't enough qualified crew available and she couldn't bear to ask others to do something she wasn't willing to do. On the third morning, after catching a few hours of sleep, she paused when she looked at her personal calendar. Sharyn had disconnected the infoscreen itinerary, but Lyn had not deleted it—11 December 2178. The day they should begin their return to Earth. They should have finished exploring Saturn's rings, she should have had her cathartic return to Enceladus. Had it been only six days? Four light years go by in a blink and six days feel like a lifetime.

A few crew members survived. Housekeeping, galley staff, engineering. They found more dead than alive, however. Of Lyn's crew, perhaps Miriam best understood such a massive scale of loss. She had grown up in a string of refugee camps. Lyn could see it in the quiet way she followed orders, volunteering to inventory food supplies and getting them to the lifepods. In the organized chaos of the rescue, Lyn didn't have time to pull anyone aside and ask how they were doing. That would have to wait. She hoped they could keep it together until the job was done.

In the end, they found 595 souls alive, of all genders, ranging in age from toddlers to elderly. Families, couples, friends. All were weakened by hunger and thirst. Many injured, and Dr. Amos set aside two pods for medical units. The joy of being rescued morphed into varied reactions to the news of what had happened and where they were, on a spectrum of shocked to horrified. Lyn was encouraged to see them rally to support each other and settle in their new home, one they no doubt viewed as temporary. She hoped they were too busy to dwell on that.

Lyn's crew filled *Aphrodite*'s dozen lifepods with survivors and any food they found, then docked them end to end, like a train, so people could move from pod to pod. The pods were designed to hold over a hundred each, so the sixty or so left a lot of room to move about and be comfortable. Miriam had done a masterful job divvying up the food supplies they'd found on the ship and programming the Recyc-All to make space rations. Lyn overheard groups discussing ways to set up entertainments and provide childcare for the kids. Some took to their bunks in a daze.

As a final check, Lyn and her crew went back to the *Aphrodite* and did another deck-by-deck, room-by-room search to make sure they got everyone. No one was going to be left behind. While her crew searched, she turned to the next problem. Now what? Almost six hundred survivors. Unimaginable. In the month and a half of the tour, Lyn barely knew the names of the hundred guests on her ship. What to do with all these people?

The question wrapped her like a shroud. In the privacy of her quarters, she turned to Tara, activating the hologram of her former commander and wife, for company and to bounce ideas around as much as anything. What were they dealing with? Long-term survival in flimsy lifepods and a small tour ship. How would that even be possible?

"You know what you have to do," Tara said.

"Last resort," Lyn replied. The memory of what happened at Enceladus stabbed her. "Could you try to be more helpful?"

"What would Tara do? Is that what you want to know?"

"I didn't sign up for this."

"You know what—"

Lyn turned her off. The problem with augmented reality was the infuriating lack of imagination. Projecting your own thoughts into the image of someone else wasn't much use.

She trusted her crew. Surely they could sort this out if they put their heads together. After dinner Lyn and her staff met to consider the options. Thomas

Philbrick joined them but sat quiet, stricken. He hadn't shaved. His hair stood out in thin tufts. Lips chapped. He was a wreck. The doctor had found the expected traumatic stress, but after almost a week, the medbots should be controlling it. Why, Lyn wondered, did he seem so paralyzed?

She reviewed what they knew then got to the point. What would they have to do to bring everyone aboard? The limited seating in the dining room prevented scheduled meals, so they'd have to offer round-the-clock food service, straining existing staff.

"I'm sure we can get you more staff," Lyn said to Miriam. "We need to throw out the idea we serve paying guests."

Where to put them loomed large. They could convert the Obs Deck into a dormitory once it was rebuilt, but that still wouldn't be enough room. Leaving them in the pods was risky. They were only designed to support life for a month. The time it would take for rescuers to come from Mars or Earth to Saturn or elsewhere in the solar system. That solar system. Not this one. They weren't built for long journeys or harsh conditions.

"We're talking the rest of their lives," Miriam said. She understood the complexities of keeping large groups of people contained. But that was on Earth. In space? She shook her head. Forever. That's what they were discussing. Not until rescue, not a short time. Talk moved on to the logistics of resupplying, given the pods couldn't land or take off themselves.

Natalie pointed out there were planets in the system. At the very least, they'd be a source of material for the Recyc-Alls. Maybe even habitable. It may not have to be forever in the pods, she said.

A squeak directed their attention to Thomas Philbrick. He cleared his throat and tried again. "You act like we're cargo. We're people. Just like you." He had barely moved throughout the discussion, his face blank with shock.

The room went silent.

"What do *you* suggest, then?" Miriam said leaning forward, clearly irritated.

"I don't know!" He gulped air like a fish.

"I'm sorry if we've been insensitive. We're all tired and running out of time." Lyn gestured around the table. "Everyone is trying their best."

Miriam settled back in her seat. Philbrick lowered his gaze.

Edward pointed out that they could scavenge the *Aphrodite* itself. The wreckage could supply material to build out the pods into a more viable station. At the very least, it could be converted to S rations and feed them for months. With modern recyclers, anything could be broken down into its subatomic particles and rebuilt into almost anything else—a case of wartime necessity mothering invention.

The energy around the table rose as Marc and Edward discussed logistics. The main issue was the *Aphrodite*'s recyclers were rudimentary, unable to form complex materials the way *Endurance*'s could. Even food would be limited to space rations, but it would be food. And water. They'd need engineering expertise to design plans and craft actual structures.

"Please remember this is also a graveyard," Isabel said, softly but firmly.

Philbrick jerked like he'd been slapped. Lyn cringed. More than seven thousand people had died. Bodies. Body parts. For all she knew, it was also a crime scene.

Philbrick closed his eyes and wiped sweat from his upper lip. "Do you know what it's like to grow up in a bone camp?"

Marc crossed his arms and leaned back. Edward sat, impassive. Natalie covered her face with her hands.

"Yes, pretty much," Isabel said, surprising Lyn. "My hometown is surrounded by graves."

Billions had died over the course of the war and famine that followed what had come to be called the Women's Revolution after years of a world-encompassing apocalypse. Forty years later, mass graves were still being uncovered. Lyn's dad had found several in the course of his reclamation work. Remains needed to be documented, every bone sampled in hopes of identifying family members who could mourn. Bone camps, filled with itinerant workers provided that labor. It had to be grueling.

Maybe that explained Philbrick's traumatized demeanor. You can overcome only so much. Yet Isabel understood. What different lives they'd lived from Lyn, surrounded by a loving family, the loss of a brother notwithstanding. That Philbrick was here at all meant he had some sort of inner reserve.

Lyn checked the time. Two a.m. This discussion could go on forever. The questions tightened with each passing hour. Stay or leave? Go for help or watch each other die?

"Let's take a break. Get some rest, be back in four hours." She dismissed her staff except for Marc. Miriam sent up a tray of food.

Fatigue settled like a weight. Lyn stood and stretched. She turned to the window that had been at her back. The wreckage of the *Aphrodite*. The graveyard. "We've heard the options. I can't make this decision by committee, but I also can't make it alone. What do you think?"

"I think Edward's right. There's a lot of material on that ship, even if they avoid the bodies."

She sat back down. "We'd have to stay here. Provide the Recyc-All and engineering expertise. Meanwhile there might be a habitable planet nearby."

"We could leave them here, or we could take the *Jedica* and go for supplies or a planet." Marc grabbed a grub muffin and poured a cup of coffee. He gestured to Lyn with the pot. She nodded. He poured another and set it in front of her.

She stared at the steaming liquid. "You saw Philbrick. Think he can handle the responsibility?"

"What's his training?"

Lyn called up his record. "Five years on *Aphrodite*, before that four on cargo runs."

"About the same as me."

"Yet you are first officer and he's only third."

"This is a rinky-dink outfit." Marc flashed a toothy grin. "It's easier to move up." He dished a bowl of steaming quinoa porridge.

Were those raisins? She spooned some for herself. "I don't think he can handle it."

"I think this is his chance to shine. Nothing prepares you for an emergency like an emergency."

"Who told you that?"

"You did." He stirred his porridge.

"I must have been joking. The only thing that prepares you for an emergency is preparation." She dipped her spoon but didn't eat any. "I'm not comfortable leaving him alone with six hundred terrified civilians."

"He's not the only staff. There are about a dozen others," Marc said between mouthfuls.

"No one senior to him or with more experience running a ship." Watching him eat made her hungry. She took a bite of muffin.

"Someone from here could go over." He chugged his coffee. He ate like a teenager. Where'd he put it all? Hollow legs?

"I can't ask that."

"I could volunteer."

"By contract, I can't let you."

"You really think the contract means anything now?"

"If you die, it'll mean a lot." She spooned in a mouthful of porridge. At least the doctor would be pleased.

"Sounds like you don't have a lot of confidence in their survival either way."

"My responsibility, regardless of contract, is to this ship and her passengers and crew. Top priority. I can't do anything that would jeopardize our chances. Even for others." She swiveled to face the crippled *Aphrodite*.

Marc stood and joined her at the window, arms crossed, biceps filling out his sleeves. Add a cape and he could be the African-Cree-Canadian Superman. "I've been thinking about going for captain. Get my own ship."

That didn't surprise her. Marc was young and eager, on a smooth path to his career goals, whatever they were. Or at least he had been. "You'd like to start now? With them?"

"I'm scheduled to take the exam in February." He relaxed and clasped his hands behind his back.

"When were you planning to tell me?"

He looked down at her. "Right about now."

"Ironic. Right about now I was going to announce my retirement. Once we were headed home. This was to be my last tour."

"You're a bit young for retirement."

"Job change then. Back to Montana. Fly a little lower in altitude."

The muscles in his jaw clenched and relaxed. "What about the *Jedica* option—leaving *Endurance* here?"

That could be Marc's chance to be captain.

"I'm not dismissing it completely," she said, "but the *Jedica* doesn't have the speed of *Endurance*, or the capacity. We don't even know if it's functional. Could it even bring back enough material for another month?" She nodded at the window. "There's almost six hundred people over there."

Marc returned to his seat and finished off his porridge. Lyn stared into her half-full bowl. Food shouldn't be wasted. Not the real stuff anyway.

"What do we do with them?" Lyn asked when she'd finished.

"I say leave them here, safe in their pods."

"I say bring them aboard, make room."

"Do we flip a coin?"

"If only it were that easy. This may be the hardest decision a captain can make."

"And you're on your way out. I'm on my way up. Maybe it's my turn."

Cheeky bastard. If she didn't like him so much, she'd consider a disciplinary warning. She kicked him gently instead. "It doesn't work like that."

This was the rapport she'd encouraged with her crew. More family than coworkers. Was that a mistake? Maybe it was time to listen to him, let him take on more responsibility. Factually, there was nothing to support either decision over the other. They were equally likely to die. Bringing the others on board could jeopardize everyone on *Endurance*. Then again, the pods were good for at least a month. Worst case, after a month, they could still take them aboard. Why not try Marc's way?

There was one choice to make and making it was Lyn's responsibility. She sent Marc away and headed to bed. She had no doubt he'd be asleep in minutes while she stared at the ceiling.

"YOU CAN'T LEAVE us," Philbrick said.

Lyn felt instant regret. Marc's only visible reaction to her decision, his recommendation, had been to stare at her. Now they both watched Philbrick crumble under the weight of their hopes.

"Of course we're not leaving you." Lyn leveled her gaze on him. "We'll go in search of a planet or asteroid or anything we can gather resources from. If we find a planet, and it's habitable, great. If we don't, we'll bring fresh supplies for your people. In the meantime, you can start scavenging the ship. We can give you an upgraded Recyc-All."

He went mute, shaking his head. She had carefully outlined her plan to him. While *Endurance* went in search of a planet, Philbrick would organize the survivors—find out what their areas of expertise were. If there were engineers, start drawing up plans to expand the pods. Keep them busy. Keep bailing.

"You are not helpless here," Lyn said. "You are an officer. You are a pilot. You can take a pod over to the ship and collect material. We know which docking ports are functional." This wasn't rocket science, she thought, but she had no idea if he was up to even these simple tasks. "In a month, we'll reassess next steps."

"How do we know a rescue isn't in the works?" he asked.

"Unless someone has perfected superluminal travel, it's not going to happen."

"Then how did we get here?"

Yeah, good question. She sighed. "If you see a wormhole open and a Red Cross ship arrive, do let me know."

ANI TOOK LYN and Third Officer, now Captain, Thomas Philbrick back to the *Aphrodite* pods. They weren't without amenities. Each had a kitchen, a common area, and bunks that could be closed for privacy. What they couldn't provide was artificial gravity, which meant an entire set of techniques and skills to learn. Going to the bathroom, washing up. Even eating presented challenges. Already some suffered from space sickness. Dr. Amos had reprogrammed the rudimentary first aid robot to perform more extensive diagnostics and procedures. "Let's hope no one bursts an appendix," he said to Lyn. He meant it as a joke, since medbots could handle infections, but to Lyn it signaled a more dire threat. If something catastrophic happened, they'd be ill equipped to handle it.

She made her way through each pod, introducing herself, explaining the plan—go for help, come back with supplies, find a planet for them to settle— and answering questions.

"Why can't we go home?" a boy, maybe five or six, in Pod 2 asked.

"We will," Lyn said. "But it's going to take a long time and we need to find a place for now."

Yu, he said his name was, seemed satisfied with her answer. His mother, however, felt differently.

"Can you take him with you?" she asked. She didn't even lower her voice. The child began to cry and clung to her.

Lyn never thought she had a maternal bone in her body, but even she was taken aback by how quickly the woman would give up her child. What desperation leads to that? Five days trapped in a room inside a ruined spaceship, not knowing what would happen or how they would die, but knowing they surely would.

"I'm afraid not," Lyn said.

"These are children," she said. "I counted. There are fifty-seven who are under eighteen. Surely you have room for them."

Lyn paused to consider how to answer the woman. It wasn't an unreasonable request. It was the kind of triaging most people considered acceptable. "Right now, we don't have the ability—even the room. We lost our top deck. It's repairing itself, but would need to be modified to hold even the children."

Judging by the noise she made as she turned from Lyn, she was not convinced.

"Let's see what we find in the next month. I'll consider it then."

Lyn addressed them carefully. "We are *not* abandoning you," she stressed. "We are going for help since help can't come to us. We'll be back. One month. We'll be back."

She chose to overlook the paucity of habitable planets back home. *We only need one. Endurance* was kitted out for exploration, but exploration of the already known, not this unknown. Back on her bridge, after she gave the order to depart, she disconnected the com link to the pods so she couldn't hear their pleas.

Chapter 8

LYN'S CREW WERE exhausted, traumatized, but reporting for duty. Natalie kept herself together, setting up a planet-finding lab on the newly restored Obs Deck. Many guests had asked for the housekeeping bots to be put to use elsewhere, that they'd clean their own rooms. Everyone was pitching in. Except one. Sharyn had mentioned that Diana took food back to her room, not otherwise engaging with the others. Lyn could hardly blame her but realized she might be their best hope for finding a way home. When she'd asked Petra for Diana's Lavenza Institute bio, she learned her newest guest came with some real bona fides.

There was no answer to her knock, so Lyn let herself in. Once again, Diana was in bed, the covers over her head. Nine days had passed since Lyn last sat here. Nine horrific days and so far things had only gotten worse. The lump under the covers held little promise, but nothing did these days.

The air was stale and rank, like something had died in a corner, or on the bed. Dishes caked with food scraps covered Sharyn's table. Clothes spilled from a duffle bag on the floor.

"I need your help," Lyn said, pushing down the irritation of seeing her friend's quarters essentially trashed.

No movement.

"Diana."

Still nothing. Lyn collected the dishes, dropped them into the recycling bin, and pressed the process button. She reminded herself this was grief, not laziness, though she didn't know the woman and it could well be. The Recyc-All hummed quietly, sending pulverized dishes to the main plant in Engineering where they'd be broken down further and remade into new, useful objects.

Lyn pulled up a chair. Don't judge, she told herself. She'd been here too, but she'd had her mother to drag her out of the miasma of grief. Diana had no one. "I know you hope that if you lie here long enough, maybe you'll wake up to find out it was all a bad dream."

Muffled crying.

"The only thing that happens is time still moves forward. You'll wake up older. Maybe gray."

A loud, wet sniff. "So?"

"Like I said, I need your help, *Doctor* Squires. Your résumé is impressive. Physics at Yale, mathematics at Stanford, Ph.D. in theoretical physics from Harvard. Your specialty is wormholes. We could sure use one now."

Diana pulled down the covers. Her eyes were red, hair greasy. "How do you know all that?"

"Your ship's files. I was hoping they had some insight into what happened."

"Did they?"

"No." All Lyn had learned was that the *Jedica* was what she suspected all along—a bare-bones vessel with no unique capabilities.

"What is it you want me to do?"

"Are you aware another ship was affected? The *Aphrodite*?"

"Yes. I haven't been in a coma."

No, you've been wrapped in this cocoon of grief while others, also grieving, put their lives at risk to save others, but Lyn didn't say that. "We need to find a planet, we need skilled scientists. You fit the bill."

"What about Natalie? She says she's the expedition leader."

"So you haven't been in a coma. She's great, mind you, and I'd want you to work together, but she only has a master's and this is her first trip to space."

"I'll think about it."

Lyn knew she shouldn't be frayed by this. Diana wasn't staff. She wasn't even a guest. She'd suffered a great loss. It wasn't Diana's job to make decisions that affected the lives of others, or to follow orders. Still, her jaw clenched.

"This isn't a request. You have to do something. It's this or cleaning rooms, but we have robots for that." She glared at the silent house bot in the corner. Had Diana disabled it or was the room cleaner than it might have been?

Diana didn't move or say anything. Crux, Lyn thought, do I have to rip her out of bed?

"I won't be much help," she finally said.

"What makes you say that?"

"I'm not nearly as impressive as my résumé."

"Did you lie on it?" It wouldn't be the first time Lyn had encountered a faked résumé.

"No, but I'd never have gotten into those schools except for my parents' connections."

"They might get you in, but only you can get yourself out with a degree. I fail to see your point."

"You can't trust me. I'll only screw up." Diana rolled onto her back. Her face reddened and tears welled. She put her hands over her face and blurted, "It's my fault Rose died!"

Lyn leaned forward, her tone softened. "How so?"

Diana wiped her nose on her sleeve and cleared her throat. "I do remember what happened. At least some. We lost artificial gravity. We had to get strapped in. I couldn't get my harness buckled." She hiccoughed. "I'd never practiced it. Rose got out of her seat to help me. That's when whatever it was hit us. And killed her." A couple of deep breaths, like she was screwing up her courage. "I might as well have killed her myself."

This was serious, though perhaps not surprising. "Have you been back to your ship since you've been here? It's docked and accessible."

"No. I couldn't."

"Come with me." She pulled the covers down and took Diana's hand.

To avoid running into guests, Lyn wended their way up the back stairs, Diana following quiet and sullen. In the Paddock, Lyn led her through the *Jedica*'s hatch, cautioning her about the shift to weightlessness. It was dark.

"Do you know where the lights are?" Lyn asked.

Diana opened a panel by the door. Lights flicked on, revealing the ruins. A sharp intake of breath. Lyn took her hand. "You need to see this."

Together they floated to the front of the ship and paused before the bloodied window. A small cry from Diana. Lyn turned her toward the pilot's seat.

"What happened?" Diana asked. She touched the charred remains then flinched like it was still hot.

"A fuel line to the forward thrusters ruptured and ignited, exploding straight into it. If Rose had been sitting there, she would have been killed."

Diana stared at the two seats, one ruined, the other intact.

"She didn't have medbots," Lyn said. "Did you know that?"

Diana nodded. "Joharis reject most modern technology. She was conceived naturally, no genetic modification or nanobot injections."

"Pretty dangerous profession to be so unprotected."

"I had to learn some pretty sophisticated first aid. I'd never needed to know about tourniquets or infections before I met her. But she loved flying, and nothing would stop her."

Lyn was rethinking her opinion of Diana. She spoke of Rose with such care and love. "She could have added them at any time."

"Rose didn't give up her religion entirely. It's not exactly a religion. More a philosophy. She rebelled by embracing technology but truly believed the human body was sacred and should not be tampered with. Her parents—" She sucked in a sharp breath and curled into a ball, as if cramped with psychic pain. "Oh, god, how can I tell them? This is all my fault."

Lyn held her arm. "No. It's not. The fact is, if she hadn't helped you, she certainly would have died. Not even medbots could have saved her. The only difference is you might have died too."

Diana wrenched away with an animal-like growl. "I wish I *had*." She pushed off toward the hatch.

Lyn grabbed her hand. "Diana, don't—"

Diana pulled free. Lyn followed but kept her distance. She didn't speak until they were back in Diana's room. "I know I can't make you feel better, but I do know what you're going through."

"Leave me alone." Diana crawled onto the bed and pulled the blanket over her head.

Just my luck, Lyn thought, our best hope lies in a suicidal depression. She pulled up a chair. Dr. Amos could monitor her, but this wasn't unfamiliar territory. Each person grieved in their own way, following no set timeline. The one luxury Lyn didn't have, however, was time.

"Would it help to talk about her?" she asked the lump of blanket.

Silence.

"I know what you're doing," Diana said after awhile.

"What am I doing?"

"You think if you can get me to talk about Rose that I'll feel better. Get over her."

"That would be pretty asinine. I never talk about my wife's death, and I'm completely over it."

Diana pulled down the blanket. "You're bullshitting."

"No, I mean it. All that talk, therapy, it's a load of crap." She'd done Pulsar's mandated course of psychotherapy, said all the right things. *Emotions, talk about your fucking emotions! Ack!*

"How'd she die?"

"I said I don't talk about it."

"Then why'd you bring it up?" Diana sounded annoyed, which Lyn considered an improvement.

It wasn't that Lyn refused to accept her wife's death. Hardly. She wore Tara's absence like an old coat, too comfortable and familiar to part with despite being threadbare and patched. A coat lined with guilt. Knowing she could have made different choices that could have saved her, all of them. When you love someone, you want to protect them. When you lead a team, it's your job to protect them. No one blamed Lyn for what happened. She wasn't the leader, but she carried the burden of failure.

Now she felt close to another failure that burned so hot, Lyn snapped. "To show you don't have to process what happened or come to terms with it or move on to function and be productive. Hell, activate your medbots if you want to feel better. They can send an endless stream of endorphins through your puny brain and give you a high you'll never want to come down from."

She yanked off the blanket and with it the last of her composure. "Here's the thing. I have a hundred and thirty souls on board—thirty-one with you— and another six hundred out there in a flimsy chain of lifepods counting on *me* to save them. *Save* them, do you hear me? And there's no way I can by myself. All I wanted was to get through this last trip, get back on the ground, and get on with my life, a life rendered completely meaningless since my wife died, but at this point I couldn't care less about that or about anyone on this ship or on those pods." She paced the room, waving her arms. "I could blow up this ship, open the hatches, void us all to space and we'd be right where we will be if I do everything I can to keep us all alive. For how long?" She stopped and faced Diana. "A month? A year? To what end? We'll end up just as dead."

Diana scooted to the far side of the bed. "You're insane. If you're trying to talk me out of committing suicide, you're doing a bad job."

A lot can change in nine days, since the *Aphrodite*. "I don't care. If you don't want to live, I have no use for you. But I need everyone's help and that includes you."

They faced off in a silent stalemate. Lyn didn't dare say any more. She'd overstepped her bounds and still wasn't getting anywhere. Anger only made things worse. She sat back down, exhausted, defeated.

"Your wife," Diana said finally. "Is that what you meant when you said you knew how I felt?"

Lyn calmed. Diana was bound to find out at some point. "Yes. Have you heard of Pulsar Force?"

"Of course."

"My wife and the rest of the crew died on a mission to Enceladus."

"That was *you*?" Diana flinched, like she'd found out she was trapped on a doomed ship with a bad luck charm. Maybe she was. "I'm sorry."

"No need to be. It was a long time ago."

"Yet you don't talk about it."

"Doesn't mean it doesn't still hurt."

Diana glanced out the window then banged her head once against the wall. "The only thing I want is to be home." She pulled her knees up and gripped them.

"Then help make it happen." Lyn leaned forward. "Everyone on board is grieving. None as directly as you are. But we're all trying to understand how this happened and what it means."

"What can I possibly do for you?"

"Set up a lab. We need more than a tourist-grade telescope. We need to find a planet. Later we can think about getting back home. The only thing I can think of that would do this is a wormhole. Find out what happened and if we can, do it again to get back. Would you help with that?"

"You can't just look for wormholes."

"Fine, forget the wormhole. A planet then. Work with me here, can you?"

Tears rolled down Diana's cheeks. "I can't stop crying."

"The equipment's waterproof. I know, I've spilled coffee plenty of times."

Diana buried her face in her arms, but she didn't crawl back under the covers. Lyn sat back. Time to wait her out. She'd done all she could. Restless, she tried relaxation breaths and the tension in her neck and back eased a bit.

After several minutes, Diana finally broke. "You're still here. I hoped you left." She watched Lyn, cautious, like a cornered animal.

Lyn gave a weak grin. "Like you, I have nothing to lose."

Diana sighed and looked away. "What's next?"

Two sweet words. Lyn stood and held out her hand. "Great, come with me."

"Now?"

"Why not?"

"Can I at least take a shower?"

"I wondered what that smell was. Yes, and thank you. Meet me in the Observation Lounge, top deck, as soon as you're done." Lyn turned toward the door. "Randall to Okeke. Good news."

ONCE THE OBSERVATION Deck had finished rebuilding itself and passed Edward's inspection, Lyn had approved its use as a lab to house equipment for finding planets. Now, in the former lounge section aft of the elevator, Natalie and Isabel chatted next to a holodisplay of schematics. Behind them a Recyc-All bot about the size of Miriam's servers moved along the floor, nozzles spewing out a work bench. Dr. Amos stood by the dome, appearing to gaze thoughtfully into space.

Outside, the bright Rigil Kentaurus glowed next to the smaller Toliman. Lyn knew certain facts about the two stars—that they spun around each other every eighty years at an average distance of twenty-three Earth-sun distances, about the same distance as the sun from Uranus. In the constellation Centaurus, the pair made up the right front hoof of the Centaur. It was the closest star system to the sun, and for those who could see it on Earth, it appeared as a single star, the third-brightest visible. Yet, here she was, up close, in person. Gazing at another star the way she had her own sun. When does a star become a sun?

She listened to her staff, content to watch and, for a few minutes at least, relax into the comfort of knowing something was being done. Earlier, Natalie had mentioned they needed a radio telescope. They only had an optical scope. Isabel pointed out Dr. Amos could see most of the electromagnetic spectrum. So there he was, scanning. Natalie had assured Lyn that finding a planet wasn't impossible, nor was it a needle in a haystack. More like a shell game. Check out this one, and if it wouldn't do, move on to the next.

At the sound of the elevator door, Lyn turned. Diana stepped into the room. Her short dark hair, still damp, stood in spikes. Her flight suit, which had fit well two weeks ago, hung loose. The gray and red Lavenza suit set her apart from the others in their green and gold Omara Tours colors. She'd probably cling to that suit like a security blanket. She looked lost, her eyes darting around the room, taking it all in, then pausing at the stars overhead through the dome, mesmerized, like a child. Lyn wondered how she could have entertained the notion this waif could help them.

"Welcome, Doctor Squires," Lyn said, feigning confidence.

She made the introductions, Isabel nodding curtly and Natalie smiling warmly. Diana murmured hellos. Quietly, she explained her expertise was in theoretical physics, not anything applicable to their situation. Was that a polite cover or a dig at Lyn for forcing her here? Natalie took a breath then plunged into describing their work—the spot by the window, where Dr. Amos had stood, was where the new telescope would go. She called up charts of the Rigil Kent system, pointing out the habitable zone and location of planets. Natalie might be inexperienced in outer space, but Lyn suspected she could command this group the way she held sway in her presentations. Diana pulled her hands from her pockets. She listened attentively but didn't offer advice or ask questions. That wasn't a bad thing, Lyn decided. She's a teacher, she knows how to read her students, or in this case colleagues. She hoped.

Satisfied, Lyn said, "I'll leave you all to it and look forward to your updates."

Integrating Diana into the crew wasn't going to be as simple as introducing her to the staff. Lyn messaged Sharyn to place Diana at the captain's table at dinner. No more eating in her room.

IN THE KITCHEN, staff bustled about preparing lunch in a frenzy of clinking plates, flashing knives, and calls for servers. Lyn and Miriam retreated to a small table in the pantry. Miriam poured them both coffee then disappeared back into the kitchen. She returned with an omelet and set it in front of Lyn. "Didn't see you at breakfast. You need to eat."

Lyn pushed it away. "How many eggs do you have left?"

"Someone has to eat them."

"I won't take the last fresh food away from a paying guest."

"You think their money means anything anymore?"

"The Beteros are elderly. We need to be sure they get sufficient nutrition."

"We'll manage. That's not our top priority yet."

The omelet sat between them, cheese oozing, congealing as it cooled.

"You gonna make me waste that?" Miriam asked.

Lyn pulled the plate toward her and took a bite. The fat and protein made a beeline for her brain, calming her mood. "Thank you," she said after she swallowed. "But please don't do this again. I can take care of myself."

"Mm, hmm," Miriam uttered.

"How are stores holding up?" Lyn asked between bites.

Miriam tipped her head noncommittally. She opened a display and ran through the inventory. "So, not a lot of anything. I've gotten used to that network of ships out there all the time. Supply, rescue—you can't appreciate how connected we were until there's no one else around. This," she waved her hand to take in the ship, "is not sustainable without that network."

"We have to assume we're on our own for the rest of our lives. Rescue is not an option."

Miriam ran her finger around the rim of her cup. "I know. I'm trying to face that fact." Her voice cut off, stress turning to emotion.

Lyn took her hand. "I wish I could be more reassuring." She didn't know what she'd do if Miriam fell apart. "How can we be more self-contained?"

"We need a garden," she said. "I've been saving seeds and setting aside plants to root and algae to grow. Can I use part of the Obs Deck? The section forward of the elevator would be big enough. The natural sunlight would save energy."

Sunlight. It wasn't a star anymore. "That's a great idea. It shouldn't interfere with Natalie's work."

Miriam made no secret of the fact that when she was five, her family had been wealthy enough to leave India after their land was lost to rising seas and the war heated up in a flash only to freeze in a nuclear winter. Their money ran out, though, and they drifted among refugee camps, barely making it to Maine as famine set in. They labored in greenhouse farms and worked in the camp kitchen where she honed her craft. She knew how to make do.

"Thank you for thinking of this," Lyn said. "I've been preoccupied." Here was another reason not to bring the *Aphrodite* survivors aboard. Where could they grow food if the Obs Deck was full of people? Not that they couldn't survive on S rations. She stood to leave.

"Can I put you down to volunteer in the garden?" Miriam asked.

Like she had time for this. But Miriam was right. She needed to be seen, be available. The memory of her meadow behind her house in Bodega Bay, the tang of moist dirt itched at her sinuses. She nurtured wildflowers adapted to the changing climate and able to withstand her long absences.

She let out a sigh. "Flowers are more my thing, but sure."

AT DINNER, LYN sat in her usual spot. Diana started to take the seat to her left, but Edward grabbed it from her.

"I sit here," he said.

Diana stepped back, brow knit in confusion. "Okay."

"Here," Lyn patted the seat to her right.

Diana took the seat. "What was that all about?" she whispered.

Lyn turned to Edward. "Diana's new. Maybe you could explain the arrangement."

Isabel arrived and took the seat to Edward's left.

"Staff doesn't always sit at the captain's table," he said, "but when we do, I always sit here. I'm right handed, as is the captain. Isabel always sits there." He motioned to his assistant. She nodded and shrugged. "She's left handed. The curve of the table increases after her, so this way no one bumps into anyone."

"Simple," Lyn said to Diana with a smile.

Lyn then rose and tapped her glass. The room quieted. She waited for everyone's attention and filled them in on the progress with the Obs Lounge-turned-lab and Miriam's plans for a garden, ending with a reminder that volunteers would be welcome.

Waitbots circulated with plates of food. While the fare was modest, Miriam had outdone herself in presentation. Roast sweet potato and onion tart with goat cheese accompanied by asparagus and parmesan pastries. Lyn couldn't remember the last full meal she'd eaten. It would have been nice to relax and focus on their future, but *Aphrodite*'s survivors pulled on her with an invisible thread of worry.

Sharyn, ever the hostess, tried to keep a conversation going. Edward focused on his plate. Ani fingered the ring on her left hand. Diana remained quiet, no doubt thinking about Rose.

To distract Diana, Lyn interrupted Sharyn. "While Doctor Squires doesn't have an official title, I'm honored she's agreed to help us. She might not know everyone here. Why don't we go around and say a little something about what we do?"

As each spoke, the tension lessened slightly, so by the time they got to Marc, Isabel was kidding him about his fitness obsession and Natalie begged to see his biceps. Laughter actually broke out.

What a joyous sound, Lyn thought.

From the corner of her eye, she saw Jeanne Cormier push her chair back and rise. She folded her napkin and placed it next to her half-full plate. Anger flashed in her eyes then her bereaved façade slipped back into place. As she passed behind Lyn, she leaned down, placed a hand gently on her shoulder, and said quietly, "I see you are having fun, but please know that the rest of us most certainly are not." She straightened and walked out.

"Jeanne," her wife called after her. Lyn rose to follow her. Suzanne stopped her. "You'll only make it worse. I'll go."

Lyn sat back down, helpless, the pressure of that hand chilling her shoulder.

Chapter 9

THE NEXT MORNING, Lyn was heading toward the Obs Deck to see how Diana and Natalie were getting on when Marc contacted her by mind link.

Can I talk to you? Privately.

What now, she wondered as she responded, *Meet me in my office.*

"Why the secrecy?" she asked when he arrived, and they took seats at her table.

"It's about our newest guest. I finished going through her ship's files. It seems Diana Squires is not quite who she says she is."

A tense muscle in her back relaxed. This wasn't about her or some new Pulsar revelation. "Okay. Who is she?"

"Her maiden name was Teegan."

Lyn frowned. "Any relation to Walter and Margaret Teegan?"

"Her parents."

Lyn's eyes widened. "Wow."

"She's like the spawn of Einstein. I found this in her ship." He reached into his pocket and held up a small cube. "It has their research files."

Lyn stared at the shiny black computer cube. "I didn't know they had a kid. Then again, I don't know much about them. They won the Nobel Prize for—something—didn't they? Were in the spotlight for a year or so, then pretty much disappeared."

She opened a holodisplay and searched for relevant information. She read aloud to Marc, "T Theory. Early on they'd theorized an exotic subatomic particle could be used to—" She stopped, stunned, and looked over at Marc. "To fold space." She kept reading. "They won the Nobel for finding the particle. Named for them. The Teegan Particle, or T." She read some more. "All this was while I was at the academy. Figures. The year I flunked astrophysics."

A tense quiet fell over them. Lyn leaned back, like the image of the information itself might be explosive.

"Do you think she could have done this?" Marc asked.

A shiver tingled Lyn's back. Diana said she was responsible for Rose's death. She wasn't. Was she? "Let's find out." She opened a com link. "Randall to Doctor Squires. Please come to my office."

They discussed the ramifications while they waited. If Diana caused the event then she was both a mass murderer and their only hope. Yet nothing pointed to her having anything to do with it. The press reports in the database said T Theory remained only a theory. Though the particle had been found, no one had actually folded space. That anyone knew of, Marc pointed out. The Teegans dropped out of sight, at least from mass media. Who knew what they worked on.

Lyn stared out the window. A knock on the door broke her fog. She motioned Diana to the chair in front of her desk. Marc closed the door and stood to one side, Lyn sat on the edge of her desk across from her.

"Why so serious?" Diana asked, glancing from one to the other. "Am I in trouble?"

"That depends," Lyn said. "What is your real name?"

Diana visibly relaxed. "Oh, that."

"Yes, that."

"I sense from your tone you know. For the record, my *real* name is Diana Squires. I changed it from Teegan."

"Teegan."

Diana rolled her eyes and leaned back. "Yes, *that* Teegan. And before you get all itchy thinking I know how to get us out of this mess, let me assure you I don't. I never had anything to do with my parents' research. I haven't spoken to them in years."

"But you understand how their work might relate," Lyn said.

"Their work ended years ago. They abandoned it."

"Did you take it up?"

"What? Hardly."

Marc stepped forward and opened his hand, revealing the computer cube. "Yet you have their data."

Diana didn't blanch, blush, or otherwise react. "That also contains every drawing I've made since age three, every photo my parents took of me—all four of them—every paper they or I published, my entire library of books, movies, and music, every letter they wrote to me in college—three, I believe. It's the detritus we all carry around. It's useless, they abandoned it."

"Why?" Marc asked.

"They decided it couldn't be of any practical use."

"Except for interstellar travel," Lyn said.

"In *theory*," Diana said. "This was before the New Era. The planet was dying under climate change, people were suffering from the war, famine, disease. No one wanted to spend money on a form of space travel that was completely out of the realm of possibility. Hadron Four was dismantled for its metals. The tunnels turned into bomb shelters."

"But things have changed. You know that. And you study wormholes."

"My studies are theoretical, and I fundamentally disagree with my parents. They speculated T could keep a wormhole open and traversable. I believe you need two black holes, which is not practical for space travel. I teach cosmology to undergraduates. That's it. My parents have been forgotten."

"Something tossed us across the galaxy," Marc said. "You work in the field and are a close relative of someone who theorized how that could be possible. Coincidence?"

Diana stiffened. "My wife died in that tossing."

"Maybe an experiment failed," Marc said.

"What are you suggesting? That I'm responsible for what happened? To Rose. To— God, to all those people on the *Aphrodite*?" She launched out of the chair and backed away from them both. "How dare you!" She glared at Lyn. "You're the one with the secret past. How do we know this isn't all because of you and some top-secret Pulsar operation?"

Lyn glanced at Marc. How did this become about her? She rose and put her hands up. "Let's bring this down a notch."

"No." Diana jabbed a finger toward Lyn. "If I find out you were responsible for Rose's death, I swear to god I'll kill you!"

Marc stepped between them. "That's enough. Sit."

Diana sat. Marc stood his ground. Lyn paced. Diana had a point and Lyn couldn't blame her for going there. Anyone would. Fact was, she didn't know it wasn't some Pulsar operation.

She faced Diana. "I promise you, I had nothing to do with this. You can search the entire ship, the database, everywhere. You won't find anything because I have no idea what happened. And I promise you this, if I find you were responsible in any way, you will be brought to justice."

"Likewise. Search my ship, that computer. You'll see those files haven't been opened in years."

Marc parked himself by the door. Lyn sat across from Diana. She pinched the bridge of her nose then leaned back, wondering what the hell to do next.

"What were you doing by Saturn?" she asked. "It's a long trip for two people. Risky not having more crew."

Diana didn't answer. She leaned forward then back. Making something up? Fighting grief? "The alignment." She paused and folded her hands in her lap. "I was under deadline to finish a book. The trip gave me the time I needed to write and collect data for next term's classes. The alignment let me do both in the timeframe I had available." She stopped and shook her head. "We also wanted to spend some time together. Alone. We'd both been so busy . . ."

Pure coincidence? Lyn waited in case there was more.

"You say your parents saw no practical use," Marc said, breaking the tense silence. "You can't possibly believe that now, can you? Not once, since you learned you are four light years from home, have you thought, gee, I wonder if that T thing could get us back?"

Diana crossed her arms. "That 'T thing' ruined my life. I was raised by caretaking robots. My parents had no time for me, they were so engrossed in their research. I doubt they've even noticed I'm gone. No, it never occurred to me."

Lyn believed her, at least the personal part. As for the professional, "Could it work? Could it get us back?"

Diana stared at her. "Are you out of your mind? First you accuse me of causing this. Now you want me to use it?"

"I'm just asking. There's clearly a practical use for it now. This isn't a joke, Diana. We're not stranded till rescuers find us. No one is coming. We are on our own." She stopped herself before admitting, *We shouldn't have lasted this long. I don't know how much longer we can last.*

"It's a theory. No more."

"But the particle does exist."

"Sure. It's all around us right now. Like all the other forms of exotic matter that haven't been found yet."

What a simple concept. That these floating, invisible bits could be manipulated in just the right way, a way Lyn had no insight into, so maybe they were the equivalent of fairy dust.

"Our efforts are better spent finding a habitable planet," Diana said, "or at least one where we can get resources."

"And we will," Lyn said. "But while we search, could you work on this?"

Diana groaned in frustration. "This is why I don't use the name. You think because I'm a Teegan, I can take over my parents' work. Get it through your thick skull. I am no Teegan."

"But you are an astrophysicist. You already know more than anyone else on this ship."

"You have no idea what you're talking about. I suggest you read through my parents' research before you ask that."

"I will."

"Yeah, good luck with that. Can I leave now?"

Marc eased his stance. Lyn nodded. "My offer still holds. Search the ship and computer if you still have any suspicions."

"Got nothing better to do," Diana said on her way out the door.

Marc closed the door. He turned to Lyn. "She couldn't be right, could she?"

"About what?"

"Pulsar. We never finished our discussion."

The stink of Pulsar. It must reek off of her. "I thought we had, but apparently you're not convinced."

"I don't know. I think I am. But this," he placed the cube on Lyn's desk, "changes everything, doesn't it?"

"I have no idea." She eyed the cube. "I'll check out these files. Maybe a decades-old theory makes more sense now."

There it sat, hope, the size of a sugar cube.

After Marc left, Lyn poured a cup of coffee and sat at her desk. She palmed Diana's cube. Accessing the files using the connection to her brain meant a headache. Literally. Pulsar might not have been involved with what happened, but a remnant of her time there was the ability to tap into supercomputers. Incredibly helpful under these circumstances. Coincidence? She wondered as she linked to the cube. She sipped her coffee while the files integrated. When ready, she leaned back, engaged her interface, and braced for the pain.

AN AUGMENTED HUMAN brain might be a supercomputer, but Lyn was no astrophysicist. The formulas were incomprehensible, so she focused on abstracts, introductions, conclusions, and simulations. There was a lot there. Unlike other forms of space folding, the Teegan wormhole seemed to require less energy and could handle objects with more mass. Wrangling the particle seemed the key factor—how do you collect and focus something that doesn't react to light, that you can't see no matter how fine your instrument? But they did it, albeit at a microscopic scale. One of the few bits she remembered from class was that wormholes are plentiful at the submicroscopic quantum scale. Not anything useful for a ship the size of *Endurance*. But they exist, at least in theory.

After four hours searching the data and watching simulations, she began to believe the research was worth pursuing. But not now. Right now they needed to find supplies and help the *Aphrodite* survivors. It also seemed clear Diana would need persuading to take on the work and get over whatever issues she had with her parents. This was no time for family dysfunction. It was, however, time to play captain at lunch and pretend everything would be okay.

Chapter 10

LYN CLICKED OFF Philbrick's day-five report and paced her quarters. Face-to-face visuals weren't possible with the time delay, so he sent reports and she responded. Already people were arguing with him. A contingent advocated for heading off on their own. Others thought the whole thing was a hoax. Some hoarded their rations, bartering in a black market. He tried to keep them busy, like she suggested, but they thought it was meaningless. That fed conspiracy theories. He didn't dare leave to gather material from the *Aphrodite* wreckage to recycle for fear of a mutiny back on the pods. He wasn't commanding trained troops. He hadn't been through military training. Might as well set a bunch of toddlers loose in the desert.

She considered going back. But to do what? *Endurance* was low on supplies as well. You could recycle material only so many times and some was consumed to fuel the machine, so you ended up with less and less to work with. The fresh food was running out. Miriam supplemented with S rations. She grumbled privately but to the guests joked, "It tastes like chicken."

Natalie, Diana, and Doc worked in the Obs Lounge, now the Obs Lab, scanning, building equipment, and analyzing data. They amassed a list of possibilities—planets, planetoids, even large asteroids. Ghez plotted courses for flybys.

Natalie had kindly let Diana room with her so Sharyn could get her quarters back. At least Diana wouldn't be alone so much. She withdrew on the bad days, sometimes not getting out of bed at all.

"Where I come from," Natalie said to Lyn one day when Diana was MIA from the Obs Lab, "there's no point in mourning. You'd do nothing but that." Her homeland had seen some of the worst of the war years. Entire civilizations, ones that had existed for millennia, wiped from the planet.

"You're married, aren't you?" Lyn asked.

"Yes."

"Then I think you might have a little more empathy."

She shrugged and went back to adjusting the telescope.

EDWARD HAD BEEN quietly doing his job during the crisis, keeping *Endurance* running smoothly. Lyn was grateful for his ability to focus. She wished she could do as well. He was a creature of routine but life now was anything but. As they toured the engine room, he rattled off performance specifications in the same tone he always did. No sign of stress.

"Have you created a new maintenance schedule?" Lyn asked.

"Maintenance is always done back at base," he said. "In thirty days, we'll need to conduct a complete overhaul."

"Are you prepared to do that while we're still out?"

"We've never done a complete overhaul in tour."

"I know, but we'll have to this time."

"We always undergo major maintenance at base."

"Edward, we won't be able to get to base in time for the next maintenance. We need to do it here."

His expression froze, brow furrowed, eyes narrowed. He rubbed his head three times, quick. Lyn recognized a struggle looming, but handling emergencies was part of his training. He finished first in all his classes. "What is your plan for an emergency repair?"

His face loosened. She knew he understood this. "We have plans for that. We drill for it. Never during a tour, though."

"In thirty days, I'm going to order a drill. We'll simulate an emergency."

"Emergency drills shouldn't be scheduled. They need to be a surprise to simulate an emergency."

"Good point. I won't tell you ahead of time."

"Good. Emergencies can't be scheduled."

"Got that right."

They'd met when Edward was a tourist on one of her trips. He'd traveled with his sister and there was an awkward moment when Lyn misunderstood the relationship. Geraldyn had laughed, but Edward had seemed annoyed. Lyn watched Geraldyn deftly redirect the puzzled man's attention. "Captain, my brother told me he noticed a problem with your ship."

"Not a problem," Edward had said, looking somewhere around Lyn's left hip. "An adjustment would increase engine efficiency 15 percent."

Once she learned Edward had four Ph.D.s, in rocket science, propulsion systems, and electrical and mechanical engineering, she probed him for details. Indeed, he improved the engine efficiency, and Lyn convinced Omara to offer him a job as chief engineer.

Omara's first concern was why someone with Edward's talents was available. His résumé listed seven different jobs, none lasting longer than three years. In his interview, he explained, "Companies keep offering me jobs. I take them if it means a better job. But people have trouble working with me. I'm not a good boss, but everyone says with my education, I should be running things. I don't get why people think the more education you have, the higher you should be in a company. The higher up you are, the less work you do."

Lyn shot Omara a look, suppressing a smile.

He went on. "People think because I'm so smart, I should be able to invent things, but I don't do that. I solve existing problems. I don't go out in search of problems to solve. There are too many. Where would I start? I like when I'm given a problem to solve."

"Well, he's honest," Omara said after he'd left.

THE DAYS BOTH dragged and flew by. None of the planets proved habitable. Every disappointment sent them closer to facing the *Aphrodite* survivors with no news, no help. That dragged on Lyn's soul, and Philbrick's reports showed that his spirits, already low, drooped further each day.

Nearing the midway point, they began collecting regolith from whatever they found to resupply themselves and store enough raw material for the others. Ani led teams and seemed to enjoy the chance to lead and to fly. She worried the ring on her finger less often. Lyn wouldn't let any of the guests go along, but the trips were routine. Rotating teams ferried rock and dirt back to *Endurance*. After the first quarantine, when they found no signs of life in the material, they skipped the forty-eight-hour waiting period.

Lyn let Marc keep an eye on the resupply while she focused on Philbrick. Worst case, they'd have to refill the *Aphrodite*'s stores and leave them for another month of searching. How many times could they do that? They could travel only so far in a month. She discussed with her staff whether they should bring the survivors along next time, even if it meant parking them to continue on for more searching. They agreed to reassess when they got back to the pods. Meanwhile, Miriam had begun building the garden. The Obs Lab was filling with equipment, crystallizing the point there simply was no way to bring more people on board and still do what was needed to survive.

Philbrick began missing daily reports. When she'd finally hear from him, he wouldn't offer any explanation. And with no way to confront him, she was left wondering what was really going on. As well, the doctor complained he hadn't received any journal updates in a month. "I need to stay up on the latest research," he said, catching Lyn in the hallway outside Engineering one day.

"You're going to have to get used to not receiving the latest medical news," she told him. "And, frankly, it's not a priority for you now."

"I'm not sure how I'll respond to a lack of updates."

"We'll just have to deal with it." Lyn had no time for this.

The end of December was a sad reminder that they should have been halfway back to Earth by now. The approaching New Year's Eve brought with it the elder Beteros' anniversary. They had planned to celebrate in the dining room while the rest of the guests partied in the Obs Lounge. Instead,

Lyn suggested they hold it after dinner and invite anyone to stay who wanted to. "That would alleviate the impression you are partying while others suffer. It'll be New Year's Eve, which will no doubt be a difficult time for some."

The Beteros had made friends on the trip and many joined the celebration. The children spoke lovingly about their parents. After much applause and chants for a speech, Alexander Betero stood. Thick black hair swept back from his face. He was portly and round where Zoya was angles and lines.

"We are a family forged by war," he began. "Zoya and I married during tough times that would only get tougher. We perhaps had no business having children, but we had both come to America during relative peace, at least compared to what followed. By the time our first grandchild was born, wars raged and we were plunged into a nuclear winter—"

Zoya cleared her throat loudly. "Zander, dearest, could you be more pleasant?"

Nervous laughter around the room.

He bowed to her. "So here we are, four generations of a family that refused to go extinct. Though where we are is a bit of a surprise—"

"Dear, you are doing it again."

He heaved a sigh. "Thank you all for coming. Sorry you can't leave."

Zoya stood and nudged him affectionately in the ribs. She was a good head shorter than her husband who was not tall to begin with. They had to be at least a hundred and thirty. Good genes or cutting-edge medbots, Lyn wasn't sure, but she wanted to be in that great shape when she was their age.

"If you would indulge me, I'd like to focus on the joy my family brings to me. And now I see we have an even larger family to embrace." Zoya held her arms out to take in her audience. She smoothed her sarong and shawl, worn over her flight suit, Lyn noticed, and clasped her hands. "Zander's the right brain, I'm the left. Together we've managed to get most things done." She put a hand on his shoulder. "He doesn't talk about what he went through before we met—I was getting my Ph.D. and he was a struggling artist working on is MFA—but you can see it in his art. As you can tell, he is by nature a pessimist. I'm the optimist. Opposites attract, right? Well, my attraction to him at first was primarily hormonal."

"Grandma!"

She chuckled. "Kids. Anyway, we married the year of the first expedition to Mars—2078. That's how I remember our anniversary. It's how he remembers the expedition." She looked at him with pure affection. "We are the first generation to live so long and so well, despite the hardships. The advances in the New Era—since women took control I might add—have led to some remarkable opportunities." She glanced away, overcome with emotion. "Oh dear. I do miss my family who are not with us." She smiled and flicked a tear. "But I am so grateful for what I do have. Thank you." She wiped her cheeks. "Please, Captain, make some joke to get us back on track."

Lyn kept it simple. This was their night, and she'd made enough speeches. "I'm honored you chose Omara Tours, though very sorry you did."

"At least we are together," Zoya said. "That, most people don't have."

Lyn watched the couple, how they moved in sync, kidded each other. Zoya leaned into Alexander. When they brushed hands, he gave hers a squeeze. They seemed always to know where the other was in their respective orbits. Their eyes never searched the room but always locked in as though they had an internal communication system, which they well might. But she didn't think so. She'd seen it in her own parents, that easy camaraderie, the yin and yang of them. How do you survive a hundred years living with and loving the same person? What would that feel like? Would she and Tara have lasted? They were very different personalities. She liked to think they would, but they'd both been so young.

Lyn slipped away once the dancing began. She peeked in at other events around the ship. A small group gathered in a classroom for a midnight group meditation. The scheduled New Year's Eve party in the Obs Lounge moved to a classroom Sharyn had converted into the Star Bar, which had once graced the back half of the lounge. Crew and guests were having a jam session with real and holographic instruments. Ani had brought out her violin. She didn't often play in public. Diana sat at the bar with Ghez. She laughed at something ne said. Jeanne and Suzanne danced slowly in a tight embrace. Sharyn circulated. She'd keep an eye on things. No need to visit the bridge; Lyn had left Petra in charge there. By midnight, she was in bed. Thus ended 2178.

A NEW DAY and a new year didn't bring any significant change in their circumstances. Having to turn back without finding a habitable planet felt like a defeat. How could it though, when they'd barely started. After several duds, Dr. Amos found a promising candidate, but they simply didn't have time to get there. They had to return. Time. That was their enemy. Meanwhile, Philbrick had gone silent. For five days, nothing. And there was nothing Lyn could do. Was it a technical glitch? Or worse?

Then, Day 82 on the Grand Tour itinerary. Lyn had worried she was obsessing too much over what might have been. Should have been. But this was it. The last day. The day they were to depart *Endurance* on Baker Island. Her last day of active employment with Omara Tours. She had anticipated mixed feelings. She'd miss her crew, but she longed to go home. Now, here she was, Day 42 of their new itinerary. One without end.

When they had left the *Aphrodite,* its dozen pods had been docked end to end, creating a long train. As they came into view, Lyn saw only six. Where were the rest?

"This is *Endurance.* Can you read me?"

A pause. A crackle. Silence. Knowing what that silence had meant last time filled Lyn with dread. There was no point in being optimistic and hoping it was simply a communication failure. At the Aerospace Academy, she had studied how people respond in a crisis. The evidence showed a strong leader was key to the likelihood of survival. She'd left these people with no one capable in charge. It had been too much to ask of Third Officer Thomas Philbrick. She should have known.

Chapter II

LYN LED A team to check the six remaining *Aphrodite* pods. Again, Marc protested. Again, she overruled him. The pods drifted, empty of humans but filled with clues to what happened. All had decompressed, emergency hatches open. Bloody suits, smashed helmets, trashed equipment floated about. In the first one they searched, they found recordings by a woman named Georgie. Lyn sent her team to search the rest of the pods while she tethered herself to Georgie's bunk and watched the messages. There were a lot.

Georgie kept better records than Philbrick did. Lyn should have put her in charge. She even had ones from before the event. The first one Lyn viewed was her last message, her "in case I don't make it back" message, to someone named Bryan. Made six days ago. Georgie was a wreck, her hair stringy and greasy, bags under eyes, fingernails chewed and ragged. She was thin, but was she always?

"Bryan," she said softly, "if this ever reaches you. I'm so sorry. I do love you. This was a stupid idea and you were right." She took a breath and the next came out strong, "I'm so, so sorry. I love you so much!" The image clicked off.

Was he her boyfriend, husband? Was that how she had left things with him, arguing? Lyn's last face-to-face conversation with Tara was a fight when Tara wouldn't let her go down to Enceladus. She would never hold Tara again. Never again hear her say she loved her or say that to her. Never get to say she was sorry. Regret played in an endless loop.

She went back through the files to learn more about Georgie, so if she ever met Bryan she could tell him about her last moments. The trip seemed to be a "girls adventure" with two other women, Fiona and Lily. There were lots of shots of them together. On the transparent Promenade Deck, Mars behind them. By the pool. Screaming with joy along the Zero G line. She was not as thin; cheeks rounded, hair styled. She gushed about the restaurants, the parties. There were dance floors that simulated various gravities—the Mars Lounge had a third of Earth's, she said. The Zero G bar was very popular. Everyone floated and drinks came in bags with straws. She also talked about the sights. Mars, Jupiter. She fell in love with Ganymede, the solar system's largest moon. "We can't go down," she reported, sounding disappointed, "but it's so beautiful. Someday I'll come back."

She didn't record the event itself. There was a gap then a frantic message that she heard Lyn's team searching. She left the recording on while screaming and pounding on her room door. Lyn wondered what happened to her friends. Another gap till she was on the pod. She filled in whoever she thought might find the recording.

"Fiona and Lily must be gone." She appeared and sounded exhausted. She was in her bunk, the only privacy outside of the toilet, she said. "I've searched among us survivors and left their names on the missing list. I'm sure if they were here, they'd find me. I'd gone back to the room early. I had a headache and was way too drunk. They were still dancing up on the Star Deck." From what Philbrick had said, that was the domed top, the Solar System Soiree, that blew entirely away.

Her face crumbled. "Fee . . . Lil . . ." She covered her face with her hands and shuddered silent sobs. The image flicked off. The next entry was a week later. Her cheeks now sunken and ashen.

"Everyone's fighting. That Philbrick prick insists we call him captain. Well, act like one and maybe we will." She went on to ask about family at home, like she was sending an ordinary message. She held up a broken switch. "This is plastic, for god's sake." Early in the month, she still managed fury. "Let this be a record that I hold Galaxy Cruises responsible. And *Endurance*. They abandoned us. Captain What's Her Name, Randall, refused to let any of us on board. Not even the children."

Especially not the children. Lyn needed adults. Space was no place for children.

The next day's entry began with her whispering. "Vincent, that's the guy in charge of my pod, wants us to separate from the others. Head back to *Aphrodite*. That's where rescuers will be searching, he says. We're dust motes in space where we are. Maybe he's right. But crux, he worked in housekeeping. There's a reason robots replaced most of those jobs, right? What the feck does he know about space survival? Philbrick says we have to stay together, that *Endurance* will return and save us. It's been two weeks. They haven't found anything yet." A pause. She glanced toward the porthole then to the bunk's hatch. "Dads, I'm scared. Some of the men get high and—" She closed her eyes. "A bunch of us, mostly women but some of the guys too, are taking turns keeping watch. I've got this," she brought a knife into view, "and I'll use it." Her eyes lit up, defiant, strong. Then the message ended.

Lyn unbuckled, needing to move, and to think. Over the link, she heard her team's chatter as they searched, opening cupboards. She floated down the narrow hallway, past the bunks stacked four high. Glorified coffins, really. Their hatches were raised, like the old luggage compartments on airplanes. Each bunk was long enough to stretch out in the bed sack that was secured and would keep you from banging into the walls or ceiling and tall enough to bend into a sitting position. At least they locked, but she could see some were broken.

Returning to Georgie's messages, the next week showed things truly going to shite. That was around the time Philbrick stopped sending reports. And he sure wasn't telling Lyn everything. She could barely hear Georgie over the shouts from outside her bunk. Mid-sentence, there was a loud bang and screams. Lyn flinched, as did Georgie. The hatch flew up and Georgie tumbled out, flailing for her helmet. Lyn recognized the look on her face, the sheer disbelief combined with a certain wonder. Like Duncan in his last moment. The camera's field of view wasn't wide enough to see where she went. A roaring wind lasted a few seconds, then silence. The camera blinked off.

Massive, rapid decompression. Georgie's pod hadn't been the end of the original chain. Did someone purposely release the pods? Both would shoot apart. Why on earth would you do that knowing people were inside? They'd have shot out like water from a squirt gun. What horrible circumstances led to such a drastic action?

Tears floated inside Lyn's helmet. Back on *Endurance,* she called her senior staff together.

"We have to find out what happened to them," she said. "They can't have gotten far."

"Where do we start?" Ani asked. "We're not receiving any emergency beacons or hearing any trace of them. It'll be like looking for a grain of sand in a salt pile."

"Assuming they didn't leave right away," Edward said, apparently calculating in his head, "they should be just outside visual range."

"Let's magnify and scan in a grid," Lyn said, addressing Ghez.

In under an hour, they found the pods. Three were still joined together, but the others floated alone, like they'd all gone off in different directions. For the next twenty-four hours, they searched each one, downloading computer files. All were trashed. A few bodies were spotted, suspended in space. Unrecoverable. No one survived.

LYN SAT IN the command seat on *Endurance*'s bridge, Marc beside her. She scrolled through messages and diaries, spinning ahead, stopping to rewatch the agonized pleadings, pausing, zipping back, watching again.

"What are you looking for?" Marc asked.

She didn't answer him. She switched to Thomas Philbrick's reports, listening for something between the words, a hint of how things went so wrong.

"Captain," Marc said. Nothing. "Lyn." More emphatic.

She flicked off the hologram. "What." She didn't make eye contact.

"If you think this is your fault, it's not."

"And you know that how?"

"Because you weren't their captain. If they weren't trained properly, that's on Galaxy, not you."

"They lost their captain." She thought about Celeste Bratt, those drinks that would never happen. A pang for a lost opportunity. Who back on Earth might fall to their knees and keen in anguish? "Do you know for sure that couldn't happen here? How many hull breaches have you experienced in real life, not in a simulation?"

He didn't say anything.

"You have no idea what this chair does to you." She sounded more bitter than she intended. Marc was a good guy. He showed every promise of a successful future as a captain, but there were some things you couldn't train for. She stood and moved toward the door to her quarters. "Get some rest. We're going to begin a salvage operation in the morning."

"What?"

Without answering, she closed the door on his stunned expression.

At the next morning's staff meeting, she asked for volunteers. They were heading back to the floating carcass of *Aphrodite*. "We'll collect significant personal items from each stateroom. Download everything possible from their computers."

Marc didn't leave with the others to sort teams and begin the work. "Why are we doing this?" he asked, quietly, like he was talking to someone with psychosis.

"These people had friends, families," she said. "We can't bring their bodies back, so we have to let their loved ones know what happened."

"You remember we're three thousand years from home, don't you? And we don't have the room." Now he spoke as though to a misbehaving teenager.

"One small storage room for solid items. The rest, recordings, photos, passports, all can be downloaded." She watched him, waiting for him to agree or argue further. Silence. He stared at her. "Either volunteer to help or don't. I don't care. I won't hold it against your record."

"Do you really think I care about that now?"

"Marc, you need to be very clear, in your own mind and in how you work with the staff and guests. This is not a one-way trip until all possible attempts to get back are exhausted. We got here. There *is* a way back. There has to be. And for all we know, the answer is on that wreck." She jerked her thumb toward the window, toward the remains.

NOTHING WAS EASY in space. It took five days to glean the significant bits from the *Aphrodite*. Lyn sensed Marc's disapproval, the wordless way they'd exchange command duties on the bridge, the perfunctory answers to her questions. Left unspoken was that she'd send her crew into harm's way for the sake of mementos that might never get back to Earth. After everything had been retrieved, Lyn spent her evenings watching vids, listening to diaries. Security cameras could have captured the event itself. Valuable footage in an investigation, if there ever could be one.

There it was, on vid from the Promenade Deck. A flash outside the ship, like an explosion. Incredibly brief, then the camera shut off. Or the deck exploded. There was no way to be sure. Petra reviewed the vid, searching for matching timestamps and better angles from other cameras. Throughout the ship, something happened at that moment and over the course of the next excruciating minutes. Happy partiers staggered back to their rooms, faces changing to curiosity, looking around, before the camera blinked off. Others ducking and running as hallways crumbled around them, walls shattering, always ending with a blank screen. From what Lyn could tell, the explosion was low on the ship, so the Solar System Soiree footage missed it. But it was so small. How could it destroy the *Aphrodite*? This was not the *Titanic*, done in by an iceberg. Modern ships were designed to seal off damage. *Was* it an explosion? Maybe it was a wormhole opening, swallowing them all. Lyn showed the footage to Diana.

"No one has seen a wormhole, never mind the moment one opened," Diana explained while viewing the images in Lyn's office. She rubbed her face after watching a series of horrific snippets. "It's awful, isn't it. You read about how ordinary matter would be destroyed by touching the sides of a wormhole—all that theoretical stuff—but maybe this is what it's really like."

Lyn slumped back in her chair. Eight thousand lives. Less than the toll from one nuclear bomb, but she hadn't lived during those times. "I'm sorry. I didn't mean to upset you."

Diana made a soft noise in her throat. "Puts it all in perspective. I keep thinking how fragile the thread of life is, both on a personal level, but also for humanity." She looked at Lyn. "Are humans even qualified to explore space?" She shook her head. "Makes you wonder."

Diana was right, of course, but Lyn had never stopped to consider. Even after Enceladus, she'd gone back to space. Why? Pulsar was to blame for what happened, but pushing any envelope meant as much failure as success. Was it worth it?

FOR LYN, IT was as though pulling the belongings and files onto *Endurance* brought the people aboard as well. That comforted her. At first.

She didn't believe in ghosts. She thought she was hallucinating from stress when the first fleeting images appeared. A little girl running through the hallway in her pajamas. An old man in a hoverchair. Brief. She'd blink, and they'd be gone. Then she heard their voices. She often thought they were real.

She'd turn and say, "What?" but there would be no one there. Or Marc would look at her funny and repeat what he'd said. Indistinct murmurs. One day the old man, instead of sitting quietly by the dining room window, turned to Lyn, his face contorted in anger, and shouted, "Why did you leave us to die?" Lyn froze. Miriam asked if she was okay. They'd been talking menus.

Alone in her quarters, she'd hear music, laughter, clinking glasses. Could they be partying on the bridge? After several nights of this, it changed. Amid the music, there came a terrible crashing, a bright light, then screams. Horrible screams, of people being ripped apart like Lyn had seen on the vids. The whole ship shredded like paper. Then the nightmares, putting herself in the place of Celeste Bratt, sucked into space as her quarters disintegrated around her. The horror compounded by the realization Celeste was still out there somewhere. How do you go from pearls and beaded gown, judging a dance contest, to being sucked into the void? How long was she aware of what was happening? Long enough to think, *Oh shite!* Longer? They were all still out there.

Night after night, she woke drenched in sweat. That messed with her flight suit's sensors, alerting Dr. Amos. He examined her, ruling out flu. Lyn told him what was going on. He agreed it was probably stress and activated her antidepressant bots. Then sedative bots so she could sleep. Soon she felt like how she imagined a bot felt. Nothing. She ordered the doctor to deactivate them. Better to feel rotten than nothing.

The visions and sounds worsened. They were touching her. Pulling at her. She wasn't sleeping, hardly eating. She went to bed with a massive headache and couldn't make herself get up again. They entered her quarters like a jury, judge, and prosecutor, hovering, demanding, accusing. Dereliction of duty, abandonment, murder.

She lay in a fetal curl. Ghostly forms swirled, shrieking. Marc was among them. *Did I kill him too?*

"Captain, are you all right? Should I call the doctor?" His voice faded into the background accusations.

A woman came into view. Not a ghost. She could tell the difference now. The movies got that right. Ghosts are less detailed. Dr. Squires, Diana.

"What can I do for you?" Lyn said, pretending to sound normal.

Diana's face loomed large, distorted like a funhouse mirror, but her words were clear. "You got me out of bed. Now it's my turn. This ship needs a captain and that would be you."

"I'm not a real captain. I ferry tourists around the solar system."

"You've been doing a pretty good job till now. Have you forgotten you were a member of the elite Pulsar Force? That you survived Enceladus?"

"How do you know that?"

"You told me, remember? I also read the ship's records. You aren't the only one collecting things."

Enceladus?

Tara appeared beside Diana, dim, ghostly. Lyn hadn't called her up. *"You know what you have to do, Lyn."*

"What you *made* me do? No way." Lyn pulled the blanket over her head.

"They only think they know what happened. You know the truth."

"The truth? That you sacrificed yourself and the entire team to save me?"

"Is that what you think?"

"You never should have gone down to that moon. I should have gone. For that matter, no one needed to go. You knew I'd be stranded."

"But alive. We needed supplies."

"You knew you wouldn't make it back."

"No, I didn't know that."

Had Lyn's love for Tara blinded her?

"Captain!" Diana said, worry evident. "What are you talking about?"

She couldn't hear Tara. Lyn yanked the blanket down and focused on Diana. "You have no idea what happened on Enceladus."

"I know your commander and crewmates died on the moon, stranding you. The pod returned on autopilot and you used it to make enough fuel to get back."

"Fool. Believing that. Tell her the truth, Lyn."

Lyn scowled at Tara. The truth. Why the crew's bodies were never found on the moon. The lander had returned to the orbiter with Tara and Anse dead inside, Rahm had died on the surface. All Lyn could remember of Tara's final message was, "You know what you have to do." She dismantled the pod and filled the Recyc-All to make fuel and S rations, but she couldn't make enough to get back. Only then did she put the bodies in. Tara's body. That gave her the fuel she needed to get within range of rescue.

Diana shook her. "We need you to decide what to do. Do we go home or look for a planet to stay on?"

"This isn't a starship."

"So make do. We are. Natalie and I modified the telescope to look for planets capable of life."

"You did? Can you build a wormhole and get us back?"

"Not yet."

"But you will."

"I'll try. If you will."

Lyn struggled to sit up, weak. The headache had moved into the rest of her body. She saw Tara standing amid the crowd of *Aphrodite* passengers, all watching her.

"You know what you have to do."

"Feck it, Tara."

"Captain?"

Lyn looked from Diana to Marc to the ghosts.

Something got us here, so something can get us back.

"I'll do it for them."

Diana followed her gaze. "There's no one there."

Elbows on knees, face in hands, Lyn squeezed her eyes shut. A spasm of pain shot down the back of her head. She opened her eyes to see Marc and Diana standing over her. It couldn't end like this. She wouldn't let it. Not yet. "What time is it?"

"1630," Marc said.

"Do you mind giving me some privacy so I can get washed up for dinner?"

"Certainly, Captain."

When they left, Lyn ran a shower. The warm water rushing over her head eased the ache. She watched it run down her body and into the drain, where life-sustaining water would flow to the Recyc-All and be converted into anything else they might need. Fresh water, food, telescope parts.

Lyn was only human, but also captain. A captain lost in space. During Ghez's job interview for navigator, she'd asked, "What process do you use if your instruments fail and you are lost?" She had liked nem based more on her gut than nir actual experience.

"You are only lost if you don't know where you are," Ghez had said. "I always know where I am."

They were not lost. The only way back would be to figure out how they got there and recreate it. Or they could focus on finding a planet. A future generation could return to Earth or greet humans making the trek out to Rigil Kent. It didn't have to be one or the other. Why not do both?

WHEN LYN ENTERED the dining room, a hush settled and dozens of heads turned toward her. Miriam stood in the kitchen doorway. She gave a nod and a smile and disappeared inside. Lyn took her seat, surrounded by her senior staff, including Diana. Waitbots emerged with platters of food. Life went on.

Small talk circled the table, people apparently willing to pretend the last three days hadn't happened, that their captain had not almost abandoned them to madness. That façade would not hold. Lyn stood and tapped her glass to get the room's attention.

"I'd like to make a brief announcement," she said. She hadn't thought about what she'd say, hadn't realized it needed to be said until now, seeing these expectant faces. The Cormiers to her left, the Cannos, the Beteros filling two tables at the back.

"I'm going to ask Sharyn to arrange a memorial service for the victims of the *Aphrodite*," she glanced at Sharyn's surprised face, "whenever you can arrange it." She looked out at her audience. "I know you must be wondering what's next for us." Murmurs and nods. "We will resume searching for a habitable planet, but at the same time, we will be exploring, investigating how we got here and how we might get back. We will never stop trying to get back, but it may take a long time, many years, or it may be impossible." She paused, thought about sitting down. "You all know by now we should have returned to Earth. You should be back with your loved ones. Instead you are stuck with me. For that I am truly sorry." A self-deprecating smile. Polite chuckles around the room. "And from now on, we are a team. With the combined knowledge and skills you each bring, I've no doubt we'll succeed. You came on this trip because you have an interest or experience in the cosmos. Here's your chance to make a difference. We're going to make history, you know. We already have. And when we get back, we'll have a hell of a tale to tell. So thank you for everything you've done so far and for all I'll be asking of you going forward."

As she sat, someone called out, "Thank *you*, Captain."

After dinner, people milled about or made their way to the exit.

Zoya Betero approached Lyn. "I wonder if I might have a word, Captain."

Now what? The last three days blurred like a bad hangover. Lyn led her to an empty table in the corner.

She offered coffee or tea, but Zoya leaned in. "I'd love a good bourbon, if I could."

Lyn hid her relief. "Of course."

Zoya's eyes lit up when she saw the bottle. "Pappy's. The real thing."

"Captain's stash, for special occasions." She poured two glasses, neat.

Zoya took a sip then closed her eyes and tipped her head back as if assessing the quality. She blinked. "My, what a finish. There are some things you simply can't replicate." She set the glass down and leaned back. She didn't speak right away but watched Lyn as though assessing her as well.

"I'm not sure if it's appropriate to say this," she said softly.

Lyn leaned forward, attentive.

Zoya watched the last leave the room, her family among them. "I do feel bad for them." She turned to Lyn. "But would it be terrible if I said I thought this was a tiny bit exciting?"

Lyn's muscles loosened. "Everyone is entitled to their opinion. I don't judge." She sipped her drink.

"Please don't misunderstand me. The *Aphrodite* is a monstrous tragedy. But our fate. How shall I put it? I know my best years are behind me. I don't have a lot to lose at this point. And I have my husband. That's all I need, really."

"I understand."

Zoya glanced out the window. "I do wonder, though, if I will miss out on humanity's real chance for lasting peace." She turned to Lyn. "But I'm old. That's my hope for you younger ones."

"I'm a long way from ready to give up on us ever returning," Lyn said, "but I know what you mean."

Lasting peace. Lyn wondered. Could it last? They'd come to call it the New Era. That this time, the world would truly never forget and never repeat the mistakes of history. Lyn hoped humans were ready to undo the damage they'd inflicted. What had finally drawn people together had been the shared sense of place, the shock of their home being destroyed. Of the Earth nearly becoming uninhabitable.

"You mentioned the first Mars expedition was in 2078," Lyn said. She'd been struck by Zoya's comment at the party. "I thought it wasn't until after the war ended?"

"No, we'd made it much earlier, but Mars was considered a waste of good money that could be spent on war toys, so our funding was diverted and our program suspended."

"What did you do?"

"I wouldn't work on the war effort, I couldn't stand to see what was happening. I didn't much like the so-called United States at the time."

"Why did you live there?"

She offered Lyn an amused grin. "I was eight years old when we arrived. I didn't have a lot of say. My country had vanished beneath rising seas. It simply did not exist anymore. So my parents fled to the U.S. They came to regret it, though. The infamous reign of the last white president." She sighed and shook her head.

"You weren't forced to work on the war effort?"

"I'd been in the country since I was a child yet to those in government I was an immigrant, with dark skin, so therefore a potential terrorist. No, they frankly never approached me. By then I was married and having babies, making it easy to disappear. A bunch of us kept up with the research by computer and private networks. We couldn't get to space, but we were able to simulate the effort so when we could resume, things went faster."

Zoya swirled the amber liquid in her glass then took another sip. "Less than ten years after the Women's Revolution and the new governments formed, my band of motley engineers landed humans on Mars. The rest," she glanced around the room, "is history." She paused. "Tourism is perhaps not the highest use of outer space, but it's better than becoming a war zone and arms race, which it certainly could have been. The treaties make peaceful commerce attractive and the new economy means others don't suffer because of a greedy few."

Zoya drained her glass. Lyn offered more. "Please. It's divine." She sat straighter. "Now, to my point in talking with you. I meant to sooner, but there was so much going on. How can I help?"

Before each tour, Sharyn reviewed the manifest with Lyn and pointed out important guests or friends of Omara's. Sharyn had focused on the Beteros' anniversary and their family reunion and only in passing mentioned Zoya had worked in the space industry. At the time, Lyn didn't think it particularly remarkable. Zoya Betero wasn't the first space engineer she'd had on board. Now, after everything, especially since the *Aphrodite*, she saw her and thought, she knows how to run a space program.

"I was hoping you'd say that," Lyn said.

"I confess, planet *searching* is not my forte," Zoya said. "But I've seen my share of dire situations—though nothing like this, I realize."

"My crew are young and untested. I handpicked them and believe they are among the best and over time I'm sure will prove to surpass the best. But right now, I think they'd benefit from some mentoring, some perspective. We're not reinventing the wheel here. Natalie and Doctor Squires have set up equipment on the Observation Deck to search for and analyze planets, moons, and asteroids. They could use the guidance of a seasoned veteran. Even if just to bounce ideas off of. Doctor Squires, Diana, teaches at the Lavenza Institute on Mars."

"Impressive."

"And of course, once we find a planet—"

"I like your optimism there. 'Once,' not 'if.'"

"Yes. Well, we'll need someone with experience."

Zoya waved her hand dismissively. "Piece of cake."

"Any family members also interested?"

"I'll ask, maybe some of the younger ones. My husband, sadly, prefers to dig in the dirt. He's bereft thinking how his garden will suffer without him."

"I'm sure Chef Kapoor would welcome his help in the garden she's building."

She clapped her hands together. "Oh, he'll be thrilled." She leaned in again. "Truthfully, I think he has a crush on Chef Kapoor." She giggled and reached for her drink.

Chapter 12

THE NEXT MORNING, Lyn walked *Endurance*'s hallways, braced for ghosts and thankful when none appeared. The first time she'd boarded *Endurance*, at twenty-one, she had been fresh out of the Aerospace Academy and starting her cadetship with Pulsar. Duffle bag over her shoulder, her first destination had been down the slick composite stairs to her bunk three decks below her goal—the bridge. She and the other cadets jostled through the narrow hallway looking for their rooms. Ceilings on this deck were lower than the others, to accommodate the ship's retractable wings. The skid-proof flooring and artificial gravity took getting used to. Lyn lurched more than walked. She would remember the ship as being gray, but that was only the lowest deck containing cadet quarters, Engineering, and Operations, also known as laundry. The next deck up was Green, with the galley, dining room, and regular crew quarters. The Silver Deck gleamed with classrooms and simulation theaters. Gold meant senior staff quarters and, best of all, the Bridge. Command and Control. The goal.

Commanding Officer Jill Faber drilled into them what to expect over the next year. Training ships are workhorses, she said. Stripped down, functional, idiot-proof. "Take care of *Endurance*, and she will take care of you." She cracked a rare smile. "In other words, don't break my ship."

Lyn liked the sound of that. "My ship." That was her dream. To command a spaceship. Not to conquer space, but to explore, learn, and pass that knowledge to others. That's what Pulsar promised. That's what Commander Faber said. It was a tough course, made the Academy look like summer camp. Anything that could go wrong on a spaceship did in the classrooms. Equipment malfunctions, radiation alarms, oxygen generator breakdowns, microdebris collisions, engine failures, engine explosions. Sometimes everything at once. At the Academy they'd learned how to fly. Here they learned how to survive.

Her first time on *Endurance* lasted one year. It would be another decade before a very different Lyn Randall stepped aboard a very different *Endurance*. She had emerged from her time with Pulsar diminished, as though from a matryoshka nesting doll, each layer revealing a secret, a betrayal, losses greater than she could withstand. The main reason she took the job with Omara Tours was because of *Endurance*. She was no longer a fresh-faced newbie, and neither was the ship. She tried to see it as analogous to her own renewal, a metaphorical fresh coating, new carpets, a few additions, like a gleaming spiral staircase and domed Observation Deck. *Endurance* had fared well. Lyn hoped some of that would rub off.

The second time she boarded *Endurance* for the first time, she didn't have to descend to the lowest deck and find a bunk in the gray hallway. She took her bag straight to the former Gold Deck and to her quarters. "My ship," Captain Lyn Randall had murmured as she opened the door to the bridge.

Now, two months since the horror of the *Aphrodite*, it seemed clear no one else was affected. Why? A half dozen other ships were at Saturn that night. The *Aphrodite* and the *Mars Jedica* were the only ones near *Endurance*. If the event originated on board or near the *Aphrodite*, it took *Endurance* and the *Jedica* with it because they were close. That was a significant clue, but what to do with it? Moot point, she supposed. She needed to focus on finding a new home, or a way back home. That clarified her decision-making. Two goals: find a planet and a way back. Simple, right?

In the classrooms on Deck 3, robots lectured to one or two people. The lessons had gone through their curriculum and were now repeating. The fitness center, however, was packed. It wasn't a big room, a few treadmills and bikes, workout machines and a set of weights, a mat for stretching. It had become like the prison yards she'd seen in old movies. People exercised out of boredom. She spotted Marc on a treadmill near the door, punching in a program.

"Want to go for a run?" he asked.

She started to demur, but the person on the one next to him stepped off. "Sure. Let's start slow. I'm a bit out of shape."

He began a jog.

"I'm sorry about the last three days," she said.

"Not a problem."

"Yes, it is. You need to know if I'm competent." I need to know that, too, she thought.

He upped his setting a notch, but his breathing remained normal. "You were exhausted. Perfectly understandable."

"Is that what you told the others?"

"I gave everyone some R&R. It's been a rough month. No one even noticed you were missing."

Missing. MIA. "Except Diana. How'd she get there?"

"She called me. Said you'd been ignoring her requests for a meeting."

Lyn didn't remember anything to do with Diana. Was it about her parents' research? She upped her speed to match Marc's. His breathing became labored. Sweat broke out on his face. She was still fine. Then she noticed the lights around the base of his machine. Red. Hers were green. "What gravity setting are you on?" she asked.

He huffed a few breaths before answering. "Jupiter."

She laughed. "You bloody showoff."

It felt good to run, air pumping deep into her lungs, clearing out whatever gunk collected there. The smooth, simple cadence of one foot in front of the other.

WHEN LYN REACHED the lowest deck, she found Sharyn folding sheets in the laundry room. Even down here, away from the eyes of paying guests, Omara had refurbished the bare necessities into almost opulence. Industrial cleaners lined a wall, swishing softly. Sharyn preferred to wash bedding rather than recycle new ones every day. Soft carpeting and insulated walls kept the noise down. Much different from Lyn's training days with the hard tile floor and long waits for a cleaner.

They'd worked together four years now and had bonded over the around-the-clock nature of their roles. Miriam could close her kitchen, but guests always had access to Sharyn and her staff.

Lyn leaned against the doorway. "We can get volunteers for that."

Sharyn shook her head. "I have bots for this. It's not about folding sheets."

"Let me guess, you do your best thinking down here." Lyn picked up a lump of cloth and searched for a corner to start from. "Did you know Mr. Betero has a crush on Miriam?"

"Pfft. Who doesn't know that?" Sharyn saw Lyn's surprised expression and chuckled. "Always the last to know."

Lyn fumbled with the sheet.

"Here." Sharyn grabbed an end. Together they folded in silence.

"What else don't I know?" Lyn asked when they'd finished. She patted the pile of neat bedding.

"About what?"

"Anything. How are people reacting, what are you hearing, how are you doing?"

Sharyn threw another load into the washer. She sat on the couch, another Omara touch, and patted the seat beside her. "How much time you got?"

"As much as you need."

"Well, then you should probably know, because, knowing you, you won't notice it yourself, that people are starting to pair off."

"What do you mean? Like dating?"

Sharyn's head tipped in assent.

"Guests or staff?"

"Guests. For now, at least. And dating is the least of our problems. The population of this ship could increase in about nine months."

Lyn stared at her. "Good lord."

"Right now, I think it's a shock effect. When you've lost all control over your life, you find things you can control. Sex is a good way to feel normal."

"What should I do? Issue a command requiring birth control? Have Doc secretly activate contraception bots?"

"They might already be thinking that. Most women use medbots for birth control. I mean, having sex is one thing, actually wanting to get pregnant right now would be nuts."

"What if they aren't thinking?"

"Or thinking with the wrong body parts." Sharyn chuckled softly. "Plus, who knows what the existing couples have been up to. I wouldn't be surprised if a few had planned on conceiving during the Grand Tour. Would be a nice story to tell the grandkids."

Lyn rubbed her face. "They would have been safely home by the time the pregnancy was even noticeable. What do we do? Is it too late to say something? You could talk to the women. Marc could address the men?"

Sharyn let out a sharp laugh. "Is this Sex Ed? Should we use a classroom? Provide anatomically correct dolls for demonstration?" She giggled.

"Then what do *you* think we should do? This is serious. We don't know if we can support ourselves, never mind births, babies. *Adolescents!*" Lyn's mind reeled with the terrifying possibilities.

"Make an announcement at dinner."

"Ew. 'Attention, folks. Tonight's film will be *Some Like It Hot*, there will be a two-for-one special in the Star Bar, and could you please use birth control when you fuck each other. Thanks, and have a nice evening.'"

Sharyn had started laughing with the movie title then slapped Lyn's knee and snorted at the bar special. She let out a high-pitched yelp when Lyn swore and rolled to her side gasping.

"It's not funny." Lyn tried to sound commanding, but couldn't help chuckling.

"How's the Doc's midwifery program?" Sharyn convulsed in laughter again.

"I don't even know if he has one. He must." Lyn stood and paced, stopped and tried to glare at Sharyn who was wiping tears from her cheeks. "You are not helping. I should ask him."

Sharyn grabbed her wrist and pulled her back down. She took a deep breath. "Calm down. Relax for a minute."

"You're the one hyperventilating with hysterics here."

"I'm sorry, but that's the most fun I've had in months. Forgive me."

Lyn nodded reluctantly while giving her an eye roll.

"The moment you said we were three thousand years from home, I knew this would be inevitable," Sharyn said. "How could it not be?"

"I didn't think of it."

Sharyn made a face Lyn had seen many times on her mother. The "now Lynnie" face. "If you took an interest in men once in a while, you might have."

Lyn made her own "oh, please" face. "Women can get each other pregnant."

"Not without more intervention than mood music and low lights."

"Fine. You thought of it. So what do we do, smarty girl."

"We include it in our planning. We've probably got seven years, maybe more, before we'd really outgrow this space. If we find a planet, we're all set. If we don't, then we build out, like a space station."

Lyn let her head drop back against the couch. Seven years. A drop in the bucket of their future. "You make it sound easy."

"We don't have a choice."

"I could put contraceptives in the water."

"I could leave condoms on everyone's nightstands."

They let that hang there. Sharyn crossed her legs and picked lint off her suit. "How are you?" It wasn't one of those polite rhetorical questions.

"I'm fine. Exhaustion caught up with me." Might as well take advantage of Marc's ruse.

"Mmm, hmm." She gave Lyn a sideways glance. "I'm working on a service for *Aphrodite* in the largest classroom, set for the first of the month."

"Thanks. And how are *you* doing?"

"I'm fine," Sharyn said.

"Mmm, hmm."

"Really." Sharyn rubbed the plush arm of the couch. "You know, I once wanted to work on a big ship like the *Aphrodite*. We always think we need bigger and better, don't we?" She paused. "Omara offered me head of all her hotel operations."

At seventy-five, Sharyn was the oldest staff member. At the midpoint of her career, she was right on track for such a promotion.

Lyn's eyebrows rose. "You never mentioned that."

"You never mentioned you were retiring after this tour."

Lyn decided she didn't like the word retiring, though she supposed it was better than quitting. "I would have. Near the end. I didn't want anyone to think I was a lame duck."

"Me neither."

"How'd you know?" Lyn asked. "You're more tapped in than I realized."

"I have my sources."

"I'm your captain. I have a right to know who's talking behind my back." Only Marc knew, and Lyn didn't like to think of him as a gossip.

"Relax, no one's talking." Sharyn patted Lyn's knee. "Bots have ears. I hear lots of stuff I never talk about. I'm a walking Las Vegas."

"Noted." The cleaner pinged and Sharyn moved the load to the table. Lyn joined her and they resumed folding. "I know some are speculating the Chinese might have been behind this."

"Some? More like one. Just because I look Chinese and have a Chinese name doesn't mean I'm responsible for what they do. Any more than you are responsible for whatever nutcase rules Europe. When did your ancestors come to America?"

"The 1800s. Anglo-Irish Quaker farmers fleeing the latest potato crop failure. The Randall side is British. Montana ranchers originally. Who knows what all mixed in since then."

"Mine came in the mid-1800s, to work the railroads and laundries in California. I've got an Irish side you can't see." Sharyn took a folded sheet from Lyn and set it on the others.

"So you're living down to your stereotype?" Lyn patted the sheets.

Sharyn laughed. "My roots are as deep as yours. And certainly deeper than Señorita 'I'm from Catalonia' Roig's. Like she'd be insulted to be mistaken for Mexican or Puerto Rican. Or even Spanish."

"Okay, point taken. I won't assume you are personally insulted by anything."

Sharyn handed Lyn the end of another sheet. "Want to grab a beer after work?"

"Sure. I hear there's a new wine bar in the Old Town. Too bad we can't hop the BART and be in San Francisco in a half hour."

"Oh, don't go there." Sharyn sighed. "I was just getting used to this place. Thinking about the addition we could build. Playroom, kindergarten."

"Star Bar after dinner?"

"Deal."

They folded amid the soft swish of the cleaners.

Chapter 13

IN THE CONFERENCE room, Lyn listened while Edward and Natalie discussed metals and gasses, where they were most likely to be found. Ghez and Ani chimed in with ideas on routes. The four bent together, deep in discussion. She thought about the Teegans' research. The first glimmer of hope since this whole horrible thing happened.

"I can see we're in good hands," she said to the others. She slipped out, feeling their eyes on her. Had she lost their trust? Could she get it back? She doubted any of her staff believed it was exhaustion.

She climbed the stairs to the Observation Deck and peeked into the garden. Rows of shelves slowly rotated, filled with seedlings poking up through the hydroponic solution, reaching toward lights. A vegetable Ferris wheel. Fans blew air over the racks, tubing provided water and nutrients and drained away waste. Green. Growth. Not enough to feed everyone, but good for a salad. A welcome relief from the texturally bland S rations. Mr. Betero moved along a row, bending over each pot, stroking a leaf or straightening a stem. He hummed a contented tune. She crossed the landing to the Obs Lab.

Diana sat alone at the large center table littered with an assortment of objects, tubes, knobs, skeins of wires, metal disks. A holographic schematic hovered in front of her, and a sturdy platform stood by the outer wall. The room had none of the opulence of Omara's plush lounge. Gone were the bookshelves, the star charts. There were only a couple of upholstered chairs and a couch.

Lyn tapped on the doorframe. Diana looked over. Her expression didn't change. Focused concentration. Perhaps a bit wary. She'd seen a side of Lyn most crew, most people, hadn't. An emotional meltdown. Hardly conducive to trust.

"What's all this?" Lyn asked, taking in the parts scattered about.

Diana reached for a wire. "Isabel made them. They're for a spectroscope."

"I thought we had one."

"Nope. Just the doctor. But this, and the radio scope we build, will be able to scan for gasses, metals, organic material."

"Organic?"

"Life."

Lyn's eyebrows rose. "Lovely. Aliens."

"Or plants. Or microbes. We need to know if a planet has the right atmosphere and tectonic activity to circulate carbon. Rigil Kent is a G star, like ours, so we search the habitable zone and hope for the best—liquid water, survivable temperature, the basics. We're also building probes we can drop to the surface of asteroids, planets, moons. Anything worth exploring."

"Sounds promising." Lyn sat across from her and picked up a knob. "Isn't the Recyc-All able to make a telescope? It makes our flight suits, which are full of sensors and technology."

"This is more complicated. It's better to make the parts, then assemble." Diana didn't pause from her work.

"I see." Lyn spun the knob like a top. It crawled away from her, toward the edge of the table. Diana slapped her hand down on it. "I never got back to you about your parents' research. Is that what you wanted to see me about?"

Diana set the knob down and turned her attention to screwing a collar onto a tube.

"I think it's worth pursuing," Lyn said.

Diana's hands stilled. She met Lyn's gaze and nodded. "I agree."

Simple little words but Lyn felt like she'd won the lottery. First prize in the science fair. A free ticket home. "Really?"

Diana rubbed her thumb along the smooth tube. "I've been reading through their work," she said, seemingly unaware of the emotion she'd triggered. "I don't want to get your hopes up, but it does look promising."

"I doubt I can keep my hopes from rising on hearing that."

Diana closed the schematic. "We've speculated for more than a century that a traversable wormhole would be possible with the right kind of exotic matter. The Teegan particle is one such form. Whether it was the right form, I wasn't sure. We've also assumed wormholes could never be big enough for a ship to pass through. My parents' research blows that assumption away. It's really quite exciting."

Lyn listened, mesmerized as Diana explained how it might work. Words like dark matter, null energy condition. Soon she was pacing the room with animated gesturing. She called up a holoboard and scribbled equations. Like a switch had flipped, this was a different Diana, no longer the waif. Lyn couldn't follow what she was talking about, but clearly she had been thinking about this a lot.

Diana stopped moving and glanced from the holoboard to Lyn. "You have no idea what I'm talking about, do you?" She smiled.

"No, actually, but you sure can sell it."

"There's still a lot to go through," Diana said, leaning against the table. "It won't look like much to start, but I think we came through a traversable wormhole. The fact we survived and there's no evidence of a black hole near Saturn, let alone out here, leads me to believe my parents were right about T. Much as it pains me."

Lyn's eyebrows rose. "A wormhole. Was it natural or did someone create it?"

"Hard to say. It could have been natural. We know our galaxy contains a disk of dark matter. It's what causes clusters of asteroid strikes—like what killed off the dinosaurs. It also includes T particles. My parents found the particle. That's why they got the Nobel. You saw they speculated T can fold or compress space and open a wormhole."

"But, how?"

Diana held her hand in front of her, level, fingers splayed. "This is the Milky Way, which includes a flat disk of dark matter. As our solar system travels around the galaxy, it bobs up and down relative to that disk." She demonstrated, moving a finger between the splayed fingers. "We cross the dark matter layer roughly every thirty million years, which alters gravity and loosens objects in the Oort cloud, like the dinosaur asteroid. At the same time, that dark-matter disk isn't uniform, and the altered gravity clumps T particles, which can then spontaneously fold space. The result? A wormhole. Think of it as a spacequake." She put her hands down and waited for Lyn's confirming nod.

"Spacequake?"

"Purely conjecture. But at this point, there's no evidence this was human made."

Lyn let that sink in. "What about the flash on the *Aphrodite*? Could that have been the trigger?"

"I suppose that's possible. Like skiers triggering an avalanche. Stable till something destabilizes it."

"Natural, though."

"Like earthquakes or avalanches," Diana said. "A natural part of the makeup of the universe."

"Unpredictable."

"So far."

"That'll put a damper on the tourism industry." All those people, at the mercy of an unpredictable universe. "I wonder if your theory can help solve a mystery. *Endurance* spun madly, we assume because we were moving when this 'spacequake' hit. The *Aphrodite* and the *Jedica* were stationary. Because they weren't moving when it hit? But then how'd they get sucked in?"

Diana nodded silently, thinking. "That's not inconsistent with the theory. A gravitational wave could have pulled us in, like a rip current in the ocean. We didn't move and weren't moving. Space moved around us. Still, the forces were violent and huge."

Enough to kill Rose.

Diana looked away. "The *Aphrodite* was enormous. Maybe too big for the wormhole." She shrugged. "Or too flimsy?"

So many companies had sprung up to take advantage of the Grand Tour alignment, who knew what quality control they held to. Lyn couldn't speculate further on that. "Why haven't we seen the reverse? Some alien tourist ship plunked down in our solar system?"

"Maybe we're alone."

"You can't believe that."

"No. But I have no idea why it hasn't happened, and with such a large amount of space, perhaps the chances are miniscule. Or maybe it has happened. Maybe Adam and Eve came from somewhere else."

Lyn let that sink in too. Aliens seeding life on Earth was a long-standing theory. "Is there any chance we left a trace?"

"Sure. Like ripples on a pond, there would be waves of space as it closed up. But someone had to think to look for it. I'm not sure that would have happened in time to detect them. Even so, there would be no clue where we went, the direction or distance we traveled."

This was a lot to take in. Lyn focused on their immediate situation. "What do we do now? I assume we can't replicate it to get back."

"Actually, we might be able to, but we sustained a lot of damage. The biggest risk in traversing a wormhole is hitting the sides. Instant obliteration. But I'm hopeful it could work for us."

"Meaning?"

Diana gave a sly smile, her eyes widened. "We could get home."

Home. Like Dorothy in *The Wizard of Oz*, clicking her heels, having the power all along. The whole thing sounded too complicated and dangerous to be that simple.

"How?" Lyn asked. "It's probably in that jargon you flung at me, but how would we do it? Plain English, please."

"Theoretically, we create a T-field in front of the ship that warps space and creates the fold. When the hole opens, we fly through."

"You make it sound easy—just create a T field. How?"

"Yeah, we need to build a machine that can collect and concentrate T particles. But my parents did that, although on a small scale, so it's not impossible."

"Can we aim? How do we know how far to go, where we'll end up?"

"Ghez has recalibrated our star charts. We have to calculate carefully at our end. A fraction of a degree off over trillions of kilometers could mean missing our solar system entirely. But, in theory, we'll be able to look before we leap. Like peering through an open door. We can even send a probe through first. If it's not the right place, we don't go. I just don't know if we'll get a second chance. It'll take every ounce of energy *Endurance* can come up with to collect the T particles, the negative energy. The good news is that a Teegan wormhole needs less negative energy than other kinds."

Lyn's mind raced. "I thought wormholes were for time travel. Will we find Earth a thousand years in the future when we get back?"

"Nope. Technically, we aren't the ones moving faster than light. Space is."

Lyn took a few deep, calming breaths. As much as she wanted to shout, "Do it! Now!" there were many questions to answer, problems to solve. "What do you need?"

"For now, just time. I can keep working on my own. I don't want anyone else knowing about this."

"Agreed. Do you have a sense of the process? How long it might take?"

"I'm still reviewing. My parents did some computer simulations I can recreate. At that point I can start working with real data—where we are, where we want to go. They worked at the microscale, sending atoms across a room." She leaned closer, Lyn felt herself warm. She lowered her voice to an intimate whisper. "Lyn, if we pull this off, it's a game changer. It will mean inter*stellar* travel is possible. If this gets in the wrong hands . . ."

Lyn, not Captain. A name a friend would call her. She pulled her focus back to the meaning of what Diana said. "Pulsar." That again.

"Or anyone. There might not be any right hands. This is serious stuff." She leaned back. "I'm beginning to think my parents abandoned it not because it would fail, but because it would work."

The sheer expectation whirling through Lyn made her dizzy. Assuming Diana was right. She could ask Petra to review the work, see if it made sense, but she didn't want this going any further than the two of them for now. Or three. Marc needed to know.

"Let's not get ahead of ourselves," she said. "If we get back, I won't mind worrying about how others might use it. How long?"

"I can't rush this. Could take months, years. We still have to survive."

"We still need a planet." That drained some of the adrenaline. She stared at the telescope parts littering the table. Voices in the hallway made them both still.

Natalie breezed in. "Captain. Welcome to the mad scientist laboratory."

Lyn tucked away her excitement. "Diana was showing me the spectroscope you two are building. Very impressive."

"Speaking of which," Natalie said to Diana, "we'll reach the planet Doctor Amos found before we had to go back—" She stopped. Maybe couldn't bring herself to say *Aphrodite*. "We'll arrive in a week. Can we be ready by then?"

"If not, we can orbit until you are. Not like there's anything more pressing on the agenda." Lyn gave Diana a furtive nod then turned to leave. She stopped at the door. "By the way, Doctor Betero is interested in helping out up here. I told her that would be most welcome."

Diana and Natalie nodded, now engrossed in their work. Lyn was tempted to change her next message home—plans changed again. We'll be back. But no, that wouldn't be wise. Not only from a "don't get their hopes up" standpoint, but also don't tip your hand. Until she knew the capabilities and understood the ramifications, her focus would be on finding a planet.

LYN WAITED TILL the end of the next staff meeting to tell Marc Diana was willing to work on T. She knew she had to, of course, but she also knew he'd be the first to find realistic holes in the idea and she didn't want anything dashing her hopes yet, slim as it was.

"And you trust her?" he asked.

"I do."

"What about competence?" he said. "She had me pretty well convinced she wasn't capable of continuing her parents' research. What's changed?"

"You should have heard her talk about it. There's no guarantee it'll work, but I think it's worth exploring, and she's the best qualified to do that. It's also why I don't want this to leave this room. If she comes up with something viable, we'll deal with it then. For now, we continue as we are. But, Marc, I'm not convinced we can survive long out here, especially if we don't find a planet. Maybe even if we do."

"It's your call, but I don't want anything to take resources away from our effort to survive, especially some harebrained scheme by someone we don't know a damn thing about."

Lyn agreed. Though she couldn't help that Diana's news gave her a high. Maybe it wouldn't work and they really were stuck here forever. But they couldn't know without trying, without at least studying the possibility.

Chapter 14

FOUR DAYS LATER Lyn was pulling on a fresh flight suit when she heard a tearing sound at her shoulder. She examined the material. A large rip ran down the side. Sighing, she tossed it aside and ordered a new one from the Recyc-All. That one ripped down the length of the leg. "What the—?" She ran her hands over the suit. The material was thinner than in the past. She poked a finger through easily.

"Randall to Engineering. Edward, Isabel, who's there?"

"Isabel here, Captain."

"The Recyc-All is misbehaving. Are you aware of any problems?"

"We've had a few complaints this morning."

"Please shut down the system. I'm coming down."

Lyn put on the jeans and T-shirt she'd come aboard wearing and dug around her closet for her sneakers. She grabbed the torn suits and headed to Engineering, making a mental note never to recycle a suit before checking the new one works.

On the stairs, Sharyn stepped aside and gasped.

"What?" Lyn asked. "You've seen me in civvies."

"Not during a tour."

"Come with me," Lyn said. She handed her a suit. "Check this out."

"That's not good," Sharyn said, putting her hand through a hole.

In Engineering, the four of them stared at the suits on the table.

"The material is substandard and the sensors are missing or malfunctioning," Edward said.

"These came from the Recyc-All today?" Isabel asked Lyn.

"Just now."

Isabel placed a test cube, shiny and smooth, into the machine then examined the new cube, pockmarked and gray. "Clearly degrading."

"Why?" Sharyn asked.

Lyn hefted the cube. It was light, airy, full of holes. "It's only been a couple of weeks since we resupplied from that last asteroid." Right before returning to the *Aphrodite*.

"So not the raw material," Isabel said. "More likely, an accumulation of errors. Normally not noticeable, but over time can become significant."

"By now, we'd have been back at base and undergoing an overhaul," Edward said.

Lyn remembered she was supposed to issue an emergency drill. *Aphrodite* had interrupted that plan. "I guess we have a real emergency, Edward."

He jerked to attention, a grin forming. "I'll initiate emergency mode. Life safety only. Atmosphere, fuel, food, waste removal, and water."

"How long do you need for the overhaul?" Sharyn asked. This would impact her department the most. Cleaning, laundry, even entertainments.

Lyn could see him mentally calculating.

"Complete breakdown and rebuild. Short staff. Can't make new parts." Stress pitched his voice. Of course, with the Recyc-All causing the emergency repair, there was no way to make reliable new parts.

"What about the *Jedica*?" Lyn said. "It has a recycler, and it's been offline. Would it work?"

Edward's face relaxed. "Yes. That would work. Plan on under a week. Six days, sixteen hours."

"You're sure?" Lyn asked. She and Isabel shared an amused look. Edward nodded, oblivious.

"I'll let Miriam know," Sharyn said. "And let the guests know the Recyc-Alls will be offline."

"What about Diana and Natalie's equipment?" Isabel asked.

Lyn touched the thin fabric of the defective suit. "Our survival depends on them. Their work is an exception, but must-haves only."

"I'll make sure they use the *Jedica*'s Recyc-All."

Lyn looked at herself. "I'd better see if I have something more professional to wear."

"Captain, I don't think it's wise for you to be without a suit," Isabel said. "We're about the same size. You can have mine."

Lyn patted her shoulder. "Thanks, but that won't be necessary. It'll be good practice at loosening up, don't you think? Everyone says I'm too uptight about the suits."

"No one says that."

"Yes, they do." She winked and left her crew to their work.

THAT EVENING, LYN took a seat at the back of the classroom Sharyn had set up for the memorial service. She wore her dress uniform tunic over her street clothes, sans the sword. She'd never been one to meditate, but the half hour of quiet contemplation would be useful for processing ideas. She came to watch as much as participate. Who was here. Who needed help finding closure. There were more staff than guests.

Her only request had been to hear Jennifer Higdon's "blue cathedral." Now, flutes and violins filled the aural space. She leaned back and let the music seep into her. She closed her eyes and saw the bright, wide Montana sky. Her parents had chosen this piece for Duncan's service. Not a dirge. Light as air, rising to heaven.

Six-year-old Lynnie couldn't make sense of what happened. She'd gone to find Duncan in the barn. He and Theo were working on a big machine. She ran toward Duncan but tripped. He grabbed her, and as he tossed her to the side, he lost his balance and fell into the machine. He had a funny look on his face and his mouth opened and he howled, just like when he played wolf. But she couldn't see his legs or body then he disappeared. Theo grabbed a big switch and everything got quiet. Theo ran out of the barn, yelling for Mommy. She crept closer to the machine. The big space where you put stuff you wanted to turn into other stuff was empty. Was he hiding? She ran around the machine but couldn't find him. Then Mommy was there and looked really scared. "He's just hiding," she told Mommy. But Mommy fell to her knees crying.

At the time, she'd thought Duncan had gone to live in a cathedral in the sky. Now, as the music ended, its vibrations slowly ebbed to a soft tinkling of bells then settled into quiet. Maybe this is what it had been like for her parents and remaining brothers. Peaceful.

"Thank you for coming."

Lyn opened her eyes. Sharyn stood at the front of the room. "We'll play selections from your requests, interspersed with moments of silence. If anyone wishes to speak, you may do so at any time."

Diana took a seat across the aisle. Marc in the front row, Ani behind him, Miriam off to the side, Dae Canno, Suzanne Cormier—they each held a portion of everyone's fate in their hands.

A soothing Buddhist chant. What were her parents doing right now? What did they believe happened to their daughter? Would her brothers converge at the Montana homestead to grieve her loss? Theo, Ethan, Cooper, and Kai. Did they comfort themselves believing she was now with Duncan, the beloved brother who never grew older than sixteen? Whom they'd all passed and who was now the youngest. *Oh, Duncan, how I wish you were here.*

Odd, her thoughts went to Duncan. Not to Tara, the fresher grief. Her heart rate rose, she took in a deep but ineffective breath. Like that time orbiting Enceladus when Tara in a blind rage, fighting with Anse, had kicked her in the back, hitting a nerve. Anse had to give her oxygen.

The chant ended. Silence resumed. Lyn's heart still raced. Hyperventilating? Grief overwhelming her?

Engineering to Captain Randall, Isabel called by mind link.

Randall here, she responded. Now more alert.

I'm getting readings the atmosphere is out of alignment.

I'll be right there. Lyn rose fast, then steadied herself. Dizzy. She clutched the back of the chair in front of her. Beeps sounded around her. People were moving about, chairs shuffling, voices murmuring. Suits activating. She saw Diana pull her hood up and press the faceplate into place. Lyn struggled to breathe, grabbing for her hood. Her last thought was she wasn't wearing a suit.

LYN WOKE TO the blurry face of Dr. Amos. His irises widened and contracted as his eyebrows wiggled. Combined, he gave the appearance of being concerned for her welfare, but she knew he was scanning her. Diagnosing.

The fog of sleep, no, unconsciousness, cleared and she took a deep breath. A mask pressed into her face, the air stale and sterile. Oxygen. *Shite. What now?* She desperately wanted to close her eyes. Fall back asleep. "What happened?" she asked instead.

"It seems the failure of the Recyc-All impacted the formula for atmosphere."

"I thought we'd switched to the *Jedica*'s?"

"We did, but it couldn't handle the extra volume. Too much CO_2 accumulated."

She raised herself onto her elbows. Two of the other beds were occupied. "How many affected?"

"About a dozen. Some had gone to bed, not wearing their suits. One had been in the shower. They're fine now."

Where was everyone? *Randall to Franklin,* Lyn called to Marc by mind link as she lay back down. *What's our status?*

Welcome back, Captain, he responded. *We've stabilized, pumping more oxygen into the system.*

Are you in Engineering?

On the Jedica.

I'll be right there.

Wait till you feel better, he said. *I've got it under control.*

That's not how this works, First Mate. But she didn't say that. She sat up and swung her legs over the side. She took a couple of last breaths of the oxygen then pulled the mask off.

"You can't leave without putting that on," Doc said, nodding to the wall behind her bed. A flight suit hung on a hook.

"Where'd that come from? Does it work?"

"Fresh off the *Jedica*'s Recyc-All, courtesy of Assistant Engineer Roig."

"Isabel's way of saying she was right," Lyn said with a chuckle. "Point Roig." She grabbed the suit, shooed the doctor away, and pulled the curtain closed around the bed.

Her thoughts raced while she climbed the stairs. Could such a small error be their downfall? Like the lack of vitamin C for early polar explorers on Earth. Scurvy took them down. What awaits us? she wondered.

She stepped aboard the *Jedica*. With the ship powered up for the Recyc-All, gravity had been restored. No need to float. Marc and Edward huddled by a control panel at the back of the main cabin. Diana stood to the side, hugging herself, staring at the floor. She looked up when Lyn approached. The men were deep in conversation about nitrogen and oxygen percentages.

"How are you feeling?" Diana asked.

Lyn shrugged. "I'm fine, but why are you here?"

Diana flinched, clearly taken aback. "This *was* my ship."

"I'm sorry. I only meant—"

"No. I'm sorry. I'm not sure why I'm here." She rubbed her arms like she was chilled. Maybe haunted. "They seemed to think I might know how to run this thing." She glanced forlornly around the empty space, her gaze stopping at the front, the burned seat, the bloodied window where Rose died. "But I don't." She looked back at Lyn. "Rose would have known what to do."

Diana hugged herself tighter. As quickly as she'd let her grief peek through, she pulled back into a no-pry zone. Curtains closed, doors shut, locks turned. It wasn't just grief. It was post-traumatic stress triggered by the ship. This wasn't unfamiliar territory. Like Diana, Lyn had withdrawn after Enceladus, cutting off family and friends.

She touched Diana's arm, meaning to comfort. Marc and Edward had their backs to her, pointing at a screen of numbers. "Let's go." Hand still on Diana's arm, she guided her off the ship. In the Paddock, only a bot whirred in a corner, vacuuming. "The doctor has an excellent counseling program. I've used it myself. He can help with the trauma."

Slowly Diana seemed to register what Lyn was saying and took her time making eye contact. "Maybe I don't want help with that." She stepped back and transformed from shrunken withdrawal to straight, relaxed confidence. She nodded toward the doorway to the *Jedica*. "Do what you want with that ship. It's not mine anymore." She turned and walked away.

Lyn let her go. Anger flashed at seeing Diana hurt unnecessarily. She called Marc out to the Paddock.

"You're looking better," he said cheerfully.

He fairly rippled good health. Tall, muscled. Where to begin? "Everything okay in there?" She indicated the *Jedica*.

"Seems to be. Edward's tweaking the Recyc-All to adjust the levels."

"Why was Diana here?"

He caught her tense tone and stiffened slightly. "I thought she might know about the controls."

"Like Edward wouldn't?"

"Is there a problem?"

"I'm wondering why she needed to be here, on a ship she knows almost nothing about and was nearly killed on. Or why you needed to be here for that matter." Her patience was thinning.

His head quirked back a bit, eyes narrowing. Confusion or irritation? "Because you were unconscious in Medical. That's a pretty big deal in terms of protocol. I need to know what's going on. If the Recyc-All had been tampered with."

"By Diana?"

"By anyone. Let's not forget she threatened you."

"Me. Not everyone on board." While Papa Bear mode was marginally endearing, his jumping to the worst possible conclusion was alarming. Diana's fury toward Lyn had been because of her connection to Pulsar Force. That lingered like toxic mold. Every time she thought it was cleaned it away, it showed up somewhere else. She softened her tone. "That was lashing out from grief. She hardly seems like a terrorist. Any sign of tampering?"

Marc shook his head. "No. Edward says the system is just too small to keep up with our needs."

Lyn stepped back inside and went to the front. Marc followed. "I want *Jedica* operational." She ran a hand over the burned seat, peered out the front window through the smear of blood. "Get this cleaned up. We might need it."

"Once the Recyc-All is fixed," Marc said.

"Of course."

Edward joined them and reported the oxygen levels were back to normal.

"In two days we'll arrive at that planet. Will we be ready?" Lyn asked.

"*Endurance*'s problems won't affect the pods," Edward said.

As a precaution, he'd set up multiple redundancies to software backups and manual overrides. They couldn't risk anything happening to the pods, but waiting for the Recyc-All to be rebuilt wasn't an option. Edward couldn't complete the overhaul without fresh material. It was a vexing circle of need, of dominoes waiting to fall.

Chapter 15

LYN STOOD AT the back of her own bridge, squeezed in among guests, now team members, waiting for the presentation to begin. They were a day away from reaching the planet and it was time to unveil Mission Control. That had been Zoya's idea. Planetary exploration was no longer a side mission. They weren't going back any time soon.

This was a new role for the bridge—the driver's seat of the ship. It wasn't about leading a tour anymore but exploring an uncharted solar system. Zoya and Natalie worked together overseeing the addition of a new science station and more seats for crew to monitor their planetary missions.

Natalie stood next to Lyn, marking the occasion with a colorful *gele*. Marc on her other side. She felt a frisson of disconnect. She had no role in Mission Control. Not true. All decisions, whether she made them or not, were ultimately her responsibility.

Zoya stood on the walkway at the bottom level, facing her audience and crew seated in rows. She chattered a welcome. The screen lit up floor-to-ceiling, wall-to-wall with images of the Rigil Kents. A planet, circled in red. Their destination. And stars. All around stars. Ani was down there, backlit, no doubt loving this display.

Growing up, Lyn had spent countless hours lying in the dry grass on moonless, clear nights gazing at the stars. When she was twelve, with the rush of seeing Saturn's rings for the first time through her small telescope, she knew she'd fly in space one day. The Geller Drive had made the planets accessible, Mars had been settled—by Zoya, it turned out. She'd spent hours imagining herself a pioneering planetary explorer. Over the years she'd wondered if her childhood dreams had been more about leaving Montana, but now she felt that pull again, that thrill of discovery.

Zoya described the equipment in the domed Obs Lab that would catch visual, infrared, and ultraviolet wavelengths, able to focus on an entire planet or zero in to small features. A spectrometer would tear apart light waves to analyze temperature and atmosphere. Radar for peering through haze or, if they were extremely lucky, finding water or other liquids on the surface. Telemetry data appeared in multiple formats on screens filling the walls. Numbers, charts, graphs, false-color images. Gases, heat signatures, magnetic fields.

Natalie leaned in and whispered, "With this getup we'll be able to spot *E. coli* under a rock from orbit."

Zoya ended her part of the program. "I'd like to turn things over to Natalie Okeke, our expedition leader, who will give you more specifics about our plans." She bowed slightly to polite applause.

Natalie stepped down to the first level. She paused, her face glowing from the lit walls and ceiling. She cleared her throat, nervous, like her first lecture of the tour. No canned script here. She described the planet, one they'd only begun to explore when they'd had to return to the *Aphrodite*. Less than a month ago. Felt like two lifetimes. From what they'd been able to determine earlier, it was Earth-sized, which was promising, though tidally locked, meaning it kept one face toward the sun. That, Natalie, explained, meant the sun-side could be too hot, the shade side too cold, but maybe life could exist along the shadow edge. Secretly, Lyn hoped it wouldn't pan out. Why add to the tragedy by having missed the *Aphrodite*'s salvation by mere days?

"Once in orbit," Natalie said, "we'll scan the surface and send down probes. If it looks promising, and we'll know quickly if it can support life or not, we'll send a team down. At the very least, we can resupply the Recyc-All and continue our search. There are many moons and planets that were never found by Earth-based equipment."

At Natalie's prompt, Ghez called up a chart of the Rigil Kent system, and she pointed out target objects. "If we have to," she said with no trace of pessimism, "we'll head over to Toliman for more exploring." Like it was a short commute, though really more than a trillion kilometers.

Natalie talked and people asked questions, not of the captain for once. Lyn no longer felt so alone in the decision making. For the first time since the event, the ship bustled with activity unrelated to grief and shock.

"ENTERING ORBIT, CAPTAIN," Ghez called to Lyn in her office. She went to the bridge and took the Con from Marc. Zoya beside her. It had been three days since the Recyc-All was declared fixed but awaiting fresh material. One day since the big presentation. Mission Control buzzed with activity around the clock.

"We're scanning now and about to launch a probe," Natalie said. "Doesn't look promising for life, though."

They'd already learned it wasn't habitable, but Zoya had tried to make the case for a settlement anyway. "It's got gravity and a solid surface. Might be the best we can do. No worse than Mars and look how that's turned out."

"With a lot more effort than we have to put to it," Lyn countered.

Zoya went quiet.

"We can always come back if it turns out to be the best of a bad lot," Lyn said, relieved this could never have helped the *Aphrodite*.

Once they had what they needed, they'd move on to the next candidate. Natalie had at least three more lined up. Patience.

"Probe launched," a woman in the front row called out. Lyn checked the manifest. Ursula Rickinson. A Betero great granddaughter.

The screen lit up with telemetry data. Meaningless charts and graphs to Lyn. She'd taken one biology course in three years at the Aerospace Academy. Pretty much everything she knew about planets other than Earth had come from the various lectures by her expedition leaders, or she relied on Petra. After an hour, she stood and turned to Marc. "I'll monitor channels, but let me know if little green people show up."

Lyn went back to her office and let the Mission Control feed play in the background. From the chatter, she could tell the probe was making ever tightening orbits. They knew the planet had no atmosphere, so the probe would drop to the surface without incident. None of the fire and flash of an Earth entry. Once it landed, it could roam around, collect samples, and send analyses up to *Endurance*. This was more practice than practical. If this were an emergency, like when they were searching on behalf of the *Aphrodite*, they'd have gone straight down in a pod and collected regolith, but goals were longer term now. Perfecting the various steps would ensure their safety once they found a habitable planet. If they did. Surely they would. Earth couldn't be the only one in the galaxy. In the meantime, Natalie would be able to collect enough data for three Ph.D.s.

The probe confirmed the planet would not be their new home, so they prepared to send a crew down to mine material. They'd been through this drill before, so it didn't require more than the checklist. Ani would pilot, with Stev and Liam along to help. Some former guests, now crew, asked to go, but Lyn wouldn't take that risk. She still had trouble referring to them as anything but guests.

She again took the Con while Ani prepared to depart *Endurance*. This wasn't a responsibility she'd turn over to Mission Control, though Zoya joined her to observe. Ani and Marc scrolled through their checklist. With all systems go, Ani released Pod 8 into space. Get in, get out. That had been Lyn's order. Collect soil and rocks, don't dawdle. Ani monitored the autopilot and read out telemetry data. *Endurance*'s computer handled the fine control of the thrusters.

Until it didn't.

"Mission Control, note we've lost attitudinal awareness," Ani announced calmly. "Thrusters are shutting down. Computer is not compensating. Taking over manual control."

Lyn sat up in her seat. Everyone jolted to attention.

"Let us know if you need override," Marc called back.

"Acknowledged. Under control—" Her feed cut out.

"Ani," Lyn called. "What's going on?" She addressed the room. "What's happening?"

Ghez responded, "Thrusters are offline. The pod is in an uncontrolled spin, speed accelerating."

Shite. Lyn waited. "Ani."

"I'm here, just busy," Ani reported after a too long pause.

Lyn scanned the different screens, looking for one that would show the pod's trajectory without having to interpret data. There, an animation showed a small dot and curved line of what had been a normal entry, but was now a messy, spiraling thread. The screen with the pod's avatar displayed each thruster with nothing happening. Then one spurted and went out. Another spurted to a start, slowing the spin slightly, then also cut out. She tried linking her mind to the pod, but couldn't get through.

Alarms blared. Zoya leaned forward, alert, but quiet, her gaze moving between the screens and Lyn.

"How far to the surface?" Lyn asked. If Ani couldn't regain control, they'd smack like a meteorite, disintegrating on impact and leaving nothing but a crater.

"Screen twelve shows descent parameters," Ghez explained.

Lyn stared at the numbers as they scrolled downward at an alarming rate. Ani. This cannot happen. The pod's video link stuttered and blinked in and out, but Ani, Stev, and Liam appeared calmly intent on their tasks.

Voices drifted through the alarms. "Manual restart." Nothing.

Stev's voice, "The computer's trying to take over. I can't maintain manual override."

Ani's voice next, "Pull the plug."

The plug? Ani had her own shorthand with her fellow pilots. Probably a system reboot. A vibration came through the speakers, thrumming alongside the screeching alarm. Then silence.

"Now!" Ani called out. A bang.

"Again," she called. Another bang.

It was like they were shocking a stilled heart. But the pod continued to drop. There was no way to abort, no turning back, no fecking parachute and if there were it would be useless without atmosphere to provide drag. Lyn's heart rate matched the spinning numbers as the distance to the surface shortened.

Another bang and a pause and a new vibration, a hum, then, "It's holding." The plummeting numbers on the screen slowed.

"Thrusters reengaged," Ghez reported.

Lyn unclamped her hands from the arm rests.

"Attitudinal control regained," Ani said. She sounded relaxed, calm.

"Can you return to *Endurance*?" Marc asked.

"We're closer to the surface," Ani responded. "Might as well continue."

"No way," Lyn called back. "You don't know you'll be able to take off once you land. Get back here. Now."

A pause. "Acknowledged."

Petra, Lyn called via mind link, *what's going on?*

Petra responded, *The malfunction has an unknown origin.*

How is that possible? You're a damn supercomputer with artificial intelligence.

Keep in mind, Captain, that we are and have been operating under conditions never before encountered or anticipated. We are past due for an overhaul, outside our solar system with no communication links to Earth or Mars Control. This is uncharted territory.

That's the best you can do?

I'm afraid so. I'm learning, as are you.

I'm not comforted by that. Lyn shut down the link.

"I expect that added a few gray hairs to our heads," Zoya said as they waited for Pod 8 to return.

"Bring back memories?" Lyn asked.

"Not good ones," she said.

"*Endurance*, be advised we are docking without computer assistance," Ani announced.

"Copy that, Pod," Ghez responded.

Crux, what now? Lyn thought. Has the computer been down the whole trip back?

She again asked Petra what was going on.

I can't connect to the pod.

Why?

I don't know.

Lyn shut her off. She again tried to link to the pod. Like Petra, she came up blank. Nothing there.

She stood and paced the bridge, listening to Ani and Ghez chatter about velocity, distance, thruster capacity. Lyn had trained in manual docking, but mostly in simulations. *Endurance*'s pods, sitting inside the outer hull, required delicate maneuvering. She'd crashed a dozen times before getting it right. She'd only ever done it for real once, and that had been enough. Where did Ani learn to do this? Not with Omara Tours. Omara's ships never needed manual override. Not till now.

"Docking in three, two, one," Liam said. "Contact." A beat. "Lock engaged. Pod secured."

Everyone in the room relaxed back in their seats, releasing a collective sigh. A few applauded. Lyn turned Con over to Marc and headed aft to the Paddock.

Natalie beat her there. The hatch opened and Stev and Liam came through first. Natalie patted their backs but clearly was waiting for Ani. Lyn talked to the men while she watched. When Ani stepped out of the pod, Natalie all but flung herself at her. They hugged, tight, long. Then they kissed, deep and passionate. Lyn steered the crew members toward the other end of the room and helped them stow their gear.

"Get something to eat," she told them. "Maybe a stiff drink. We'll debrief in the morning."

She turned back to Ani and Natalie. They were still embracing. She left them.

Restless, jittery after the adrenaline rush, she went down to the kitchen, but Miriam wasn't there. Maybe in the greenhouse. Lyn took the elevator to avoid running into anyone on the stairs. Like Ani and Natalie. No doubt heading to one of their quarters for some further entanglements. Shush, she told herself. Don't be a prude.

The greenhouse was a warm, humid oasis. Bright sunlight, Rigil Kent light, shone through the clear dome.

"Come to help weed?" Miriam poked her head around a rack of tomato and pepper seedlings.

"I thought these were hydroponic and weed free," Lyn said.

"True. I'm weeding out the ones that aren't making it. I almost miss real weeding. This is nice, but kind of sterile." She plucked a pot holding a brown, droopy seedling. "What brings you up here? I've been listening to the feed. Ani and the others made it back okay, I gather?"

"Safe and sound."

She motioned Lyn closer and handed her a small pruner. "Like this." She pointed to yellow leaves. "I thought you'd be grilling them about procedures."

Lyn snipped and moved to the next plant. "They deserve some time off. We'll go over everything in the morning." She regarded the seedlings. "What do you do when they get too big for these racks?"

"I'll move them to tables over there." She pointed to the front of the room. Right now, it was a mess of equipment ready to be set up.

"Did you know Ani and Natalie . . ."

Miriam's eyebrows rose. She rotated the rack. "Ah. Are they a thing?"

"Apparently."

"I'm not surprised. They've gotten on well."

"I had no idea."

Miriam snapped her fingers in Lyn's face, startling her, and held up a hand. "How many fingers?"

"Five."

"So you aren't blind after all."

"What's that supposed to mean?"

"You're clueless. People are going to connect."

"I know. Sharyn already raised that topic."

"So?"

"Well," Lyn stammered. "They aren't single. It's not like their spouse, fiancé, can consent to this."

Miriam put a hand on her hip. "I know you've said we'll keep looking for a way back, but you have to see that people just want life to go on, to hell with whatever bridges back home they might be burning. Loosen up."

"I am loose."

"You know what I mean. Sometimes it's just sex. It doesn't have to be happily ever after."

Miriam continued examining the plants, but Lyn stared at them, pruner poised.

"I get the sense there's more," Miriam said.

Lyn wiped invisible bits of debris off the blades. "She could have died. They all could have." She didn't expect Miriam to understand.

Miriam made an affirming mmmm. "There's no worse moment in the kitchen than when you feel the knife slip. It might miss entirely or slice through a finger, your palm, but you haven't felt it yet. For a split second you don't know how bad it is. It could be nothing. Or you could lose your profession." She gave Lyn a gentle squeeze. "You felt the knife slip."

Behind Miriam, through the dome, Lyn saw the planet. That infernal planet. Officially Rigil Kent b. She shuddered. Miriam flipped a switch and the rack resumed rotating. Satisfied there were no other limp plants to pluck, she moved on to the rack of lettuce.

Lyn left Miriam with the image in her mind of the knife. The knife's edge they were tip-toeing across. No wonder Ani and Natalie sought each other out.

That night she thought of Tara. Their first kiss. It hadn't taken long after they met, in an astronautics class at the Academy. They began studying together, and Tara joked that if she solved an equation on her own, she should be rewarded with a kiss. Lyn watched her struggle over the problem, her desire growing along with her fear her friend might fail. Then Tara grinned and slid the tablet over so Lyn could check her work. The next morning, lying together in Tara's bed, they kissed again.

Now Lyn sat on the edge of her bed and whispered, "Tara."

"Good to see you, stranger," Tara said, smiling. She moved behind Lyn and reached around her in a hug.

"Kiss me," Lyn said, leaning back into her arms.

LYN WOKE TO sunlight pouring through her window. For a second she was back on Earth, with Tara in the Bitterroots on their honeymoon, feeling that warm glow, both internal and external. But the second ended, and she realized where she was and that Tara was dead, long dead, and also to her dismay that she was naked. What a stupid, careless risk, for a hologram, she chided herself while she showered. She dressed quickly and sat on her bed, alone. Tara's hologram had vanished when she'd fallen asleep. You don't get to do this, she reminded herself. Still, she felt invigorated. How many people on board had sex last night, virtual or otherwise? Probably a lot. Not such a bad thing, she supposed.

After breakfast, Ani, Stev, and Liam sat together at the conference table. Isabel sat erect, Edward stared at his hands. Zoya joined them as the lead in Mission Control. Petra listened in.

Marc had asked everyone to submit reports for the meeting. Ani's had come through only an hour before they assembled. Likely she had other things on her mind. Or other people on her body. Lyn shook off that thought and image. Not the time.

Mistakes had to have been made. No sense in stating the obvious. Finding and fixing them was critical.

"I've read the reports," Lyn began, "but I'm not seeing a clear reason for the problem. What am I missing? What are we missing?"

She didn't need to remind Edward he'd assured her the pods were unaffected by the issues with the Recyc-All.

"The thrusters cut out with no warning, you said." Lyn looked at Ani.

"Correct. They shut down as though programmed to, not because of a defect. No overheating, no debris in the fuel. Nothing I can point to."

"We had software redundancies, right?" Lyn addressed Edward.

"Triple. If it had been a program flaw, the backup would have corrected it," he said. "A diagnostic of all three hasn't shown an error."

"Can you do a manual diagnostic?"

"I started, but it'll take several days to complete. The program is lengthy."

"And you switched to the backups?" Lyn asked Ani and her team.

"Yes. We tried each of them and finally had to shut them down completely." Stev looked at Ani with awe. "She saved us. I don't want that to be lost in the review."

Ani's cheeks pinked.

"Understood," Lyn said. "And no one could have pushed a button errantly—either on board or on the bridge." Obvious, but they had to consider everything.

"No," Isabel said, a hint of impatience in her voice.

Lyn didn't want to sound paranoid, to say the word sabotage out loud. "Just checking. Better to know than to tear apart systems looking for a problem that doesn't exist."

"Engines don't shut down by themselves," Marc said, irritated.

"We are thirty days past end of tour," Isabel said. "There's no telling what will go haywire without uplinks to home base."

"Can that really be all it is?" Lyn said, exasperated. "We're overdue for updates?"

"You know this ship better than anyone," Isabel countered. "You tell us."

Lyn let Isabel's accusatory tone go for now. She could be right. No ship was built with the expectation of a one-way trip to the stars. Everything was connected in their solar system. "How do we function while disconnected? There must be a way."

"There are too many feedbacks dependent on the computer." Edward sounded dejected. "We can write new code, but that's a massive undertaking."

"Petra could write new code in a day," Ani said.

"Petra is the code," Edward said. "If we can't trust the existing code, we can't trust anything the ship's computer comes up with either."

Lyn blanched to think they might have to shut down Petra. Talk about uncharted territory.

"I'll try not to take that personally," Petra said.

"None intended," Edward said.

Lyn addressed Petra. "You said you couldn't connect to the pod. Have you figured out why?"

"Like the thrusters, the link disconnected unexpectedly. There was no other malfunction. No error in the program. It's possible this star emits radiation that interferes with the signal."

"How do we resupply?" Lyn asked.

No one said anything, eyes glancing from one to the other. Lyn tapped her fingers on the table.

"We could do it the old-fashioned way," Zoya said.

"How old?" Lyn asked.

"Anyone have a slide rule?"

"What's a—?" Ani asked.

Zoya dismissed her with a hand wave. "My point is, rudimentary computers landed craft on the moon back in the 1960s. No reason we can't do that too, even use that code. It's simple, allows for pilot creativity," she looked at Ani, "and we know it works."

"Do we have the code?" Marc asked.

"I would think your computer would," Zoya said.

"What would we ask for?" Lyn asked.

Zoya thought a bit. "Perhaps the Apollo Eleven landing code. That was the first to use it. I'm not sure what it would have been called. It was quite a bit before my time." She gave them a sly grin. "Despite what you might think."

Petra responded, "It sounds like you want the AGC Code, for the Apollo Guidance Computer. Would that be correct?"

"I'm not sure," Zoya said. "We need the code for the lunar lander."

"That would be the lunar excursion module, LEM. I have that. See files 'Luminary' and 'Lunar Landing Guidance Equations,'" Petra said.

"Can we trust Petra to produce that code?" Ani asked.

"I didn't write it. It's from the library," Petra said.

Lyn asked Edward to review the code and see if it was viable for use with their pods.

"You're welcome," Petra said.

"Sorry, Petra, thank you," Lyn said, shrugging at the others' stifled laughs.

Chapter 16

EDWARD TAPPED THE image. "You've just blown yourself up."

Ani stared at him. "No way."

Isabel scrolled through the lines of code. "I don't see it. When?"

Lyn paused, standing behind Edward. They were seated around the conference table. Projected in front of them was the Apollo landing program code they were adapting for *Endurance*'s pod. Blowing up couldn't be good. She pictured Ani blasted to smithereens and shuddered.

"Line 942 initiates a burn sequence," Edward said, "but the previous burn hasn't finished."

"It hasn't?" Ani asked, scrolling up through the code.

"Line 435," Edward said.

Zoya sat back. "How do you do that?"

"I think in code," Edward said. Like didn't everyone? He resumed his examination of the program.

"I suppose we'd have figured it out in simulation," Ani said.

"But he just saved us a lot of work," Zoya said.

"That must be a typo," Ani said, reading the notes file. "It says the onboard computer's memory was '64k.' Is that even possible?"

"The ground-based system was only six megabytes," Edward said. "My alarm clock uses more than that."

They both glanced at Zoya. "Don't look at me. I didn't write the program. I'm not that old."

Edward scrolled to the next screen, and they all stared at it in disbelief.

"They included jokes?" Isabel pointed to a comment next to a line of code. "Off to see the wizard."

"Who came up with this?" Ani said. "Is this for real? It's like a toy."

Lyn kept quiet, knowing the chip in her brain had more computing power than the entire Apollo mission computers. Now they were adapting a two-hundred-year-old code used to land on the moon. Insane, but Isabel had pointed out it wasn't much different from the Women's Army outsmarting antigrav detectors with horse-drawn wagons. That had marked the turning point in the war. Tara's mother had been among them, something Tara often talked about with pride. Still, crossing open ground was vastly different from dropping to a planet's surface in a small craft with no safety backups. If she thought they could survive without leaving *Endurance*, she'd cancel this whole enterprise.

"*MAMABICHO*!" THE SLAP of a hand on a solid surface followed. Lyn entered Pod 7 to find Ani at the controls, sweating. The air was thick with tension.

"Problems?" Lyn sat in the copilot's seat. Ani was practicing with a simulator while Isabel and Ghez rewired Pod 8 for the actual mission.

Ani leaned back and let out a loud grunt. A holographic image of a primitive computer number pad overlaid the front console. She jerked her chin toward it. "Damn computer. It's simple, but I'm supposed to type in numbers to stand in for nouns and verbs. I don't understand what I'm doing. It's not like modern interfaces. By the time I look up the command to end a thruster burn, I've crashed into the planet. It's so slow. This isn't flying."

"That's the point, isn't it? That it doesn't rely on artificial intelligence."

Ani slapped the primitive computer. "It doesn't have any kind of intelligence. I've completely taken for granted how our systems work, the flexibility to change position. With this, I initiate a program and hope it runs its course without error. All the calculations will be done ahead of time. I sit back and make sure I don't push something by mistake."

"I think they called that 'idiot proof.'"

"But they were constantly making course corrections and it was laborious. I can't believe they landed on the moon with this!"

Ani had a lot of qualities Lyn wished she saw in herself. Self-confidence, a rare fearlessness. Maybe it was from growing up in Puerto Rico, a hardscrabble island whose remaining residents had long ago learned to rely on their own resources.

"By the way, that was some fancy piloting you did the other day," Lyn said. "I don't recall you had any formal astronautics training."

"I practice in VR. A lot. It helps me sleep."

"You'd simulated those failures before?"

"Sure. Lots of times. I don't want to disappoint you, but until that malfunction, piloting *Endurance* was probably the most boring job I've had."

Lyn chuckled. "You're only twenty-five. You've got a lot of boring life left, you know."

That made Ani laugh. "It's the excursions I like. Flying down to a moon and roaming over the surface, able to change my mind and course if I see something interesting."

When Marc had selected Ani from the candidate pool, Lyn had hesitated. Was she too young? But Ani had stood out. When asked how she'd handle an emergency, she hadn't laughed it off like so many others had by saying she'd never get herself into such a fix. Lyn couldn't remember the exact scenario, but Ani hadn't jumped to an answer. She took her time to think about it. Then, she walked them through the steps she'd take. Marc pressed her, ramping up the scope of the emergency, adding more crises, increasing the time crunch. Ani didn't flinch or get flustered, she adjusted her answers to deal with Marc's added scenarios. He leaned forward, raising his voice till he was shouting at her, mimicking the screaming alarms pilots would have to deal with. She never changed her tone, didn't so much as blink. She also didn't survive the emergency. "You just died," Marc told her.

She frowned, her gaze dropping to her hands in her lap. "Damn," she said quietly. Instead of mounting a defense of her actions, like the others had, she asked him what she could have done. What he'd have done. He'd had to admit it wasn't survivable but that she'd come up with creative ideas.

This one could learn, Marc had told Lyn. "She might be the best we'll ever see."

She wasn't surprised to see Ani frustrated now. Simulation is where all the frustrations were worked out. Ani would be fine. On the work front. As for the personal, Lyn spotted Ani's naked ring finger. When she asked about it, Ani said it was too painful a reminder of Rob. Lyn kept quiet. It was her life, but she couldn't imagine that. She'd kept Tara's ring around her neck until she took command of *Endurance*. Ten years. No wonder she couldn't get a date.

"But . . . you and Natalie?"

Ani stared straight ahead. "I know it's against the rules, but," she waved a hand, "look where we are."

"It's not that. I just thought . . . Rob."

"Who is four light years away."

"And Natalie has a husband."

Ani smoothed a wrinkle in her flight suit. "Truth is, being with her has made me realize Rob isn't the right fit. That's why I've been so uncomfortable wearing the ring. She says her husband wouldn't mind, but, frankly, I don't care." She straightened her shoulders and looked Lyn in the eye. "Since the *Aphrodite*, I can't take anything for granted. We may never get back. We could die any day. I'm not waiting for something that might never happen."

It pained Lyn to think Ani was that aware of her mortality, at her age. She was tempted to tell her about T, that Diana was working on a way back. But Diana was right. There was no guarantee. They were barely two months into their adventure, their exile from Earth.

"Just be careful. I don't want you getting hurt."

Ani gave her a "yes, Mom" expression. "I'll practice in VR."

ONCE AGAIN, LYN sat at Con as a pod left the safe port of *Endurance* and headed to the surface, a room full of Mission Control crew monitoring. She didn't care how many times Ani had practiced in the simulator, this was no longer a routine excursion. Ani had named Pod 8 *Hamilton*, in honor of Margaret Hamilton, the woman who led the team that wrote the original Apollo code.

"All systems go, *Hamilton*," Ghez said. "Engage when ready."

"Roger. Copy that," Ani said back. The formalities were new, or rather old. "Program engaged."

Like a latter-day Neil Armstrong, Buzz Aldrin, and Michael Collins, Ani, Stev, and Liam descended to the planet. For the next three hours, Lyn listened to the chatter between the *Hamilton* and *Endurance*. The back and forth of status readouts, thruster burn durations, and location and elevation numbers. The simple descent and landing process, routine over hundreds of tourism excursions in the past, now became fraught and tense. Lyn had to keep unclenching the armrest.

"Go for final burn," Ghez said.

"Burn initiated," Liam replied.

Stev called out the closing distance. At a hundred meters, he warned, "Lots of dust obscuring the view. Ground looks unstable from here."

"Moving laterally," Ani said.

"Are you piloting manually?" Marc asked Ani.

"Nothing more than Armstrong did," Ani responded. "We need a clear visual before set down."

Liam continued to count down the meters. "Fifty, twenty, ten." A pause. "Contact made." Another pause. "We're down."

Lyn released her death grip on the chair. Applause broke out among the crew.

"Let's call this spot Anxiety Base," Lyn suggested.

They planted the Omara Tours flag then filled barrels with rocks and soil and returned without incident.

More cheers rose when Ani announced they successfully docked back to *Endurance*. Then she complained about what a boring trip it was. Lyn begged to differ.

For the next week, retrofitted pods descended and returned with material to fill the hold. Edward purged the Recyc-All and cleaned the system. It meant a day without any recycling, but once the fresh regolith was added, the system purred to life and Lyn donned a new flight suit with relief. Natalie pored over data from the planet, studying its geology, land features, and chemical mixes. With the Recyc-All restored, Edward and Isabel undertook the long-overdue major maintenance. Every system was tested, calibrated, and worn parts replaced.

The beast sated, Ghez set a course for the next potential new home.

Chapter 17

THEY DRIFTED THROUGH space like a ship trapped in pack ice. Not aimless, not without power, but perhaps without purpose. Were they destined to live out their days traveling from planet to asteroid to moon, searching for something that might not exist? A home. A place to breathe cool air, dig toes into soft earth. Dirt. Sand. Lyn woke each morning thinking such thoughts and pushing despair away for the sake of her crew. Regardless of Diana's decision to work on a way home, reality threatened the day to day. Keep people busy and if not happy, at least not despairing. No amount of resources or safety would help them if people lost hope.

In the meantime, guests were happily pairing off while the Omara crew were becoming furtive—Natalie and Ani notwithstanding. Rumors about Pardo and Seng, Edvane and Bryant had reached even Lyn.

Marc confirmed the rumors at his weekly meeting with her. "I can put an end to it, but do I have to?"

Who was she to deny others' happiness? "No. I get it. We need to lighten up." Thanks to Sharyn, she'd had time to think about this. "How about direct reports remain off limits. There's no getting away from the power differential and we still need a chain of command and org chart."

He nodded but Lyn sensed there was more. A quick clearing of his throat. "Where does that leave me? I supervise all staff. If I can't date anyone who reports to me, that doesn't leave anyone."

Lyn felt like the matriarch of a Victorian family arranging marriages. This was definitely not what she signed up for. "Is there someone you're interested in?"

"Not at the moment. But how is this going to work? Or for you?"

Now it was about her? "I'm not looking for a relationship."

"You say that now, but what about in ten years? This isn't temporary."

Ten years. I'd probably kill myself if we're not home by then, Lyn thought miserably. "I'll worry about me. Let's deal with you when the time comes. Depending on how directly the person reports, they can be reassigned to me. We're going to have to make up a lot of new rules as we go along." She couldn't keep from wondering who might be his type. Ghez, Isabel, Ani even, or . . . stop it!

"You want to make the announcement or should I?"

"I'll do it," Lyn said. "Seems like it should come from the highest level." The last thing she wanted to be was a bloody chaperone. "You get to deal with the existing couples. Any affected by that edict?"

"Not that I know of. Pardo's purser and Seng is in the kitchen. Bryant and Edvane are pilots. Equal rank."

"That's a relief. I'd hate to start out being the match *un*maker."

LATE THAT NIGHT, Lyn heard an unfamiliar voice coming from the Obs Lab. She found a vid playing. A woman's voice and a pretty face she recognized. Rose. She smiled, alive, healthy, wearing the flight suit she died in.

"Hey, pal. Okay, this is supposed to be serious. You're seeing this because I died. I've made so many of these that it's easy for me to be light about it. But if you are seeing this, well."

Rose's last message, playing on a loop. Diana was not in the lab. Lyn clicked it off and popped out the wafer. *Crux*. That had to be painful to watch.

She found Diana on the *Jedica*, sitting in the newly refurbished pilot's seat.

"I didn't want to leave this lying around." Lyn held the wafer out, but Diana didn't move to take it. Lyn placed it on the front console and sat in the copilot's seat. The cockpit was small, the space intimate. If Diana had any awareness of what happened to Rose, it would have been terribly traumatic to see that.

Diana rubbed her armrest. "They did a nice job fixing things."

Lyn looked around and out the clean window. The dense band of the Milky Way crossed the view. Stunning. "Yes, they did." She was intruding. "I'm sorry. I shouldn't have disturbed you." She moved to get up.

Diana touched her arm. "No, you don't have to. It's okay."

Lyn sat back. She could sense Diana's presence, her grief palpable.

Diana picked up the wafer. "I hadn't been able to watch it before. I thought I was ready."

"I should have prepared you. I'm sorry."

"It's like she knew something was going to happen." She turned the wafer over in her hand.

"Not necessarily. I've made plenty of these myself. Omara requires everyone to make one before each tour. She'll send mine to my parents."

In the silence that followed, Lyn ran through scripts for the bereaved but none rang true. She'd thought Diana was beginning to move through her grief. Her enthusiasm about taking on the T research gave Lyn an insight into the woman she once was and was likely clawing her way back to. She couldn't deny she was growing to like Diana, and maybe that was why she'd hesitated to tell Marc about her change of heart toward her parents' research. Was Lyn losing her objectivity? It wasn't like anything would happen, but even a friendship was fraught. If that was something Diana would want. She'd been interacting with the rest of the crew more. Lyn could see that people liked her. She'd begun teaching classes that filled, and Zoya had remarked that she'd learned some interesting things about theoretical physics from her.

"How did you and Tara meet?" Diana said finally.

The question caught Lyn off guard. Did she owe her the story? Where did the captain/crew boundary exist? Diana wasn't an Omara employee. She wasn't even a paying guest. Why not.

"We met at the Aerospace Academy. Advanced Astronautics. We sat next to each other and she was struggling with the math. I didn't know she had this reputation as a bully. It was early in the semester. I grabbed her tab one day and showed her where she'd made a minor error that threw the equation off. I guess the whole class held their breath, thinking she'd deck me. But she thanked me." Lyn paused, remembering. She left out that Tara said, "Thanks, Pip," for the first-year pip on her collar. Tara had three. It became her nickname. "After class, she asked if we could study together. I was so focused on my courses, I didn't even realize we were falling for each other."

Diana dropped her head back on the seat and smiled. "We met at Harvard. I was there for astrophysics and she was at the Divinity School. She worked part time as a pilot. I had a field-based course, Planetary Systems. She flew the class shuttle on a ten-day tour of the inner solar system. It was my first trip to space. I thought she was too young to be a pilot. I mean, she was our age. She must have heard me complaining to a classmate because when the professor asked her to tell us about the ship, she looked right at me and proceeded to describe the ten years she'd been piloting. She made her first solo orbit of Earth at seventeen." She paused, with a dreamy expression. "I could be all romancey and say I fell in love right then, but it wasn't that simple. Though I was pretty obsessed with her from then on." She closed her eyes and breathed slowly. "We've both lost the love of our lives. I'm sorry if I brought up painful memories."

"Don't be. It was a good memory. Most people only want to know about the tragic ending. That's why I don't talk about it."

"Did Tara leave a last message?"

"I only remember snippets. It was all I could do to set a course back to Earth and rescue."

"Does it bother you?"

"It does. Our last words to each other were an argument. No one wants to end things that way. I think that's what last messages are for."

"But it must exist somewhere, right?"

Lyn didn't answer. She'd searched for anything related to the Enceladus mission, but when Pulsar disbanded, all records were sealed. Maybe she did see it and the memory was erased when Pulsar booted her out and took back all kinds of memories about her time there. She'd grown used to the gaps, knowing that pieces were missing but not what exactly. She thought it must be what dementia had been like in the past. What difference would it make to see it? It was probably much like Rose's. Hers to Tara certainly was. Move on. Love again. Easy to say when you are the one leaving and not the one left behind.

Was shared grief all that connected them? Her usual go-to topics of conversation were long obsolete. So, what'd you think of—name the latest highlight of the itinerary. It used to be easy.

Diana slipped the wafer into her pocket. "I guess I'll turn in." She rose. "Thanks, Lyn."

"Good night, Diana." A thrill zipped through her from being called by her name and not her rank, followed by a sadness at how that rank shackled her.

THE NEXT MORNING, Lyn watched her staff as they wandered in for their weekly meeting. Barring emergencies like the Recyc-All breaking down, they met less often, but she wanted them to know what each other was working on, and new ideas often sprang from someone with fresh eyes. She loved the casual ways they joked with each other before settling down to business, jockeyed for seats. Sharyn always took a seat farthest from the door. No doubt a hospitality technique to prevent bumping and awkward holes. Miriam liked any seat that backed into a corner. Lyn theorized it was so she could lean back and move around more comfortably. Originally Miriam had said that as a chef, people expected her to enjoy food, so she kept a few extra pounds on. Later she'd told Lyn she'd nearly starved several times in her childhood while her family fled India. The extra weight was, "Just in case."

Natalie had taken to bringing a breakfast box. Lyn would ask Marc to say something. Coffee was one thing, but this wasn't a café. Edward stared at the table in front of him. Probably playing chess in his head. Meetings for the sake of meeting were a mystery to him.

When everyone had settled, Sharyn brought up the questions the passengers were asking: now that they'd resupplied, what would they do? Continue the search for another planet, head back home, stay here forever? The next planet had proved uninhabitable, so they topped off their hold. What next, indeed.

"Good question," Lyn said. "Obviously, we need to keep searching for a planet. We also need to keep people occupied. We can't just sit here. Ideas?"

Natalie spoke first. "There are at least three other planets around this star, but none in the habitable zone, so the question is, do we head over to Toliman? It's an orange K2-type star, slightly smaller than our sun."

"You make it sound like an excursion on the itinerary," Lyn said. "Today, we visit another solar system and spend the day exploring."

Some laughter. Natalie nodded. "It would be out of our way."

"We have no 'way.' We're here for the foreseeable future and nothing is going to put us significantly farther from our ultimate destination. Anyone object to our moving on to Toliman?"

Natalie mentioned there was more science they could do before leaving.

"Too risky," Marc said. "Maybe once we have a stable home on another planet, but until then we're one breakdown from total disaster."

"Well, when you put it that way," Miriam said.

"First priority is finding a planet," Lyn said. "If there's nothing habitable, then we focus on surviving as a sealed ground settlement or space station near resources. Meandering our way back to Earth isn't viable. Even if it wouldn't take three thousand years, there's too little in between and we know nothing about it."

"Any progress on what caused this?" Isabel asked. "Whether it could get us back?"

"Diana's working on it." Lyn shot Marc a glance, but he played cool. Edward looked up but didn't say anything. She wasn't ready to reveal more.

Isabel's eyes flicked from Lyn over to Marc and back. "Alone? I'd think a whole team would be involved."

"For now, she and the computer are enough." Her dodge might not get by everyone, but she left it there. She turned to Natalie. "It looks like we head to Toliman. Please work with Ani and Ghez to find the most efficient route to any planets." Next she addressed Edward. "How long till we need to resupply?"

"Two months before we'd need to impose restrictions."

"And time to Toliman?"

"We could get there in forty-three days," Ghez said.

"A couple weeks' leeway. Works for me," Marc said.

"What else can people be doing? How can we keep them entertained?" Lyn asked.

"They might do that themselves," Sharyn said. "Did you know we have a composer on board?"

"Are they working on anything?"

"Not sure, but I could ask."

Isabel muttered, "Doesn't it feel a bit like busy work while the *Titanic* sinks?"

"*Endurance* isn't sinking," Edward said as if only correcting a factual error. "The two situations are very different. There's much speculation about what actually happened to the *Titanic*, but—"

"Let's move on," Lyn interrupted. Edward would relay every known fact about the ship if he wasn't reined in. As for Isabel, while the comment rankled Lyn, she wouldn't respond in front of the others.

They spent the rest of the meeting outlining a new routine and activities. Miriam reported there would soon be lettuce to harvest from the garden. Sharyn offered to coordinate plays and concerts. She also mentioned Diana had canceled the rest of her classes. Lyn hadn't known that but noted it to deal with later. Ani offered virtual flying lessons. Marc said he'd organize sports and restart his Okichitaw class, and Isabel, perhaps noticing she was the only one not to contribute, suggested movie and book groups. Natalie would continue her lectures.

When Lyn moved to end the meeting, Marc gave her a pointed look. Lyn sighed in resignation. "Finally, the topic of relationships has come to my attention. I gather people are . . ." She felt a flush of embarrassment. Why is this so hard? "How to put it?"

"Screwing around," Sharyn whispered in her ear.

Lyn brushed her away like flicking a fly. She charged onward, get this over with. "For those of equal rank or who don't work together, fraternizing, for lack of a better word—"

"Oh, there are plenty of better words," Miriam said with a chuckle followed by giggles around the table.

"—is no longer forbidden." Lyn gave Miriam a sharp look. Dating. She couldn't have come up with that simple word?

The news was greeted with quiet smirks. Like they were waiting for permission. Natalie and Ani each dropped their eyes to their hands.

"Right. Carry on." More giggles. "Not that way!" Laughter. At least she made someone happy. "Get back to work."

As everyone rose to leave, Lyn asked Isabel to stay. While they waited for the room to clear, Lyn leaned back, trying to recover her dignity. Isabel sat still, hands in her lap. She knew what was coming.

"What would you have us do, Roig? We have two choices. We can curl up and mourn, speeding the way to our deaths, or we can embrace the fact we are faced with exciting new opportunities to explore a star system we know very little about."

Other than a slight coloring of her cheeks, Isabel showed no reaction. She sat stiff in her chair.

Lyn took note. "This is tremendous. And even if we never make it back, we may well start a new life on a planet."

"May I speak freely, Captain."

"By all means."

"Do you miss home?"

"Of course I do. Everyone does."

"I don't."

Lyn stilled. That was unexpected.

"Home is a wasteland. I was born as the war ended. The trees were gone, the rivers dried up, no water for crops, no grain for livestock. My parents had survived by supporting the war economy—building robots, armaments, more robots to replace the ones destroyed by the armaments. It was a lucrative, vicious cycle. When it ended, they were on their own. There were no government services to help. My father was able to dig a well and provide our village with water for small gardens. My mother was a wiz at making grasshoppers delicious. I have an older brother and a younger sister. My great uncle Ramon fought in the war and was changed forever, according to my father. Doctors think they can cure post-traumatic stress now. It's almost disappeared as a chronic injury, but they are wrong. The soul can be damaged in ways that can't be fixed. It's my family I miss. I apologize for speaking out of line. Sometimes I have a hard time being optimistic."

Whether Isabel's little speech was sincere or manipulation, Lyn wasn't sure, but for now she'd err on the side of sincerity. She softened her tone. "That's understandable. No matter what we think about it, though, we're here and I can't let us not make good use of that. Someday someone will find us. Maybe long after we're gone, but we will be found and we will have made a difference. You are welcome to your opinion and I'm glad you shared it with me, but I'm going to request that publicly you express a more positive outlook."

"Understood."

Did she? Isabel was hard to figure out. A talented engineer, a terrific partner for Edward, they made a great team. That might have been the problem. Her career trajectory would have her heading the engineering department on another ship very soon. Now she was stuck on *Endurance* with Edward. Lyn welcomed someone pointing out the downside of any plan, but it got tedious when it was the same person criticizing every plan.

MARC INITIATED AN R&R rotation for the crew, and for the now-former guests he set up training classes to replicate Lyn's cadetship on *Endurance*. He also opened his Okichitaw classes, minus the weapons, to everyone. Isabel, Lyn noticed, was one of the first to sign up.

Most people were happy about the new programs. Mr. Betero spent hours in the greenhouse, monitoring gauges, checking lights, talking to the plants. He read aloud to them. It was quite charming. A few refused to cooperate. The exact line from that Irish person, Mx. Kamban, was, "We paid good money for a Grand Tour, not a boot camp." Lyn wanted to respond, "then get off my ship." But all she could do was nod sympathetically and commiserate diplomatically.

Harvesting the first lettuce crop became a momentous occasion. With a straight face, Miriam offered a cooking class, 101 Uses for S rations. Yet, Lyn noticed, she had lost weight. To her surprise, Miriam explained, "I can't be fatter than the others. They'll think I'm stealing food."

Mission Control was mothballed. With no drama of a landing to plan for, bridge rotations went back to a skeleton crew. Zoya told Lyn she'd decided to write a memoir. Natalie continued her after-dinner talks. She'd kept some of the rocks gathered on the planets they'd visited and played up the exotic nature of touching something not of the Earth or their home solar system. Lyn appreciated her ability to keep interest high and despair low. Look on the bright side, Lyn's great-grandmother always said. Coming from someone who lived through the worst times the planet had seen, that spoke a truth.

As the days and weeks passed, she sensed a growing ease. The early earnest cries for help, the pleas to explain what happened, the inability to accept the unknown faded, replaced with more mundane requests. The water in the shower could be hotter. What time would the film start?

She watched Marc's Okichitaw classes, noting the connection—not just physical—between him and Isabel. They fought like lovers. Where'd that thought come from?

As for Diana, she remained squirreled away in the Obs Lab, which caused mutterings among the crew. One afternoon Lyn spotted her eating alone in the dining room. Miriam kept a beverage service running around the clock. People could make anything they wanted in their rooms or where they were working, but Omara Tours was all about community. Mix and mingle. Get to know each other. Lyn poured herself a coffee. Diana's back was to the door, so didn't see her till she sat down.

"May I join you?" Lyn asked.

Diana flinched and sputtered a greeting.

"That looks yummy," Lyn said.

Diana stirred her bowl of S-ration chili. "Amazing what you can do with reconstituted protein meal and a packet of vitamins and minerals."

"Don't forget the secret sauce."

That brought a quick smile.

"So this is when you eat. I've missed you at dinner." She didn't mean to sound so personal. Time to be captain. "I hear you've canceled your classes."

Diana set her spoon down and sat back. "I don't have time."

"People are wondering what you're doing. Whether you are pulling your weight. I know you can't share your work, but, well, you need a cover."

A service bot carrying fresh urns of coffee and tea rolled in from the kitchen, bringing with it the clatter from the staff working inside and the crooning of Miriam's favorite alt-pop singer. The door slid shut, sealing the noise back inside. Diana watched the bot switch places with the one that made up the beverage table. After it slipped into the kitchen, releasing another slug of music and clatter, she said, "Yeah, fine. Okay."

"I'll have Sharyn get in touch about scheduling. The good news is there's a lot going on now so the classrooms are busy. You might get only a couple of spots." She sipped her coffee, considering how much more to push. "It would help if you ate meals with the others. I know it can be tough. I'd avoid it too, but Sharyn insists. So I get to insist as well." She flashed a hopefully disarming smile.

Diana picked up her spoon and scraped out the remains of the chili, screeching metal against the heavy china bowl. "This place reminds me too much of my high school cafeteria. Cliques. Having to ask if I can join a table. Ugh."

"Ah. No geek crowd at your school?"

Diana's eyes flicked to Lyn. "Are you kidding? It was all geeks. Einstein High."

Lyn nearly choked on her coffee. "Oh." She emitted a soft chuckle. She enjoyed this, talking like a couple of friends out for coffee anywhere in the world. If you ignored the space ship and different solar system.

"What's so funny?"

"Sorry. I'm trying to imagine what cliques there would even look like."

"Let's just say no one looked like a jock or a cheerleader."

"I see why you didn't fit in."

Diana looked puzzled.

"Never mind. The trick is to get here early for meals," Lyn looked around at the otherwise empty room, "but not this early. Then you can either take a seat at my table—you're always welcome—or find an empty table and then people have to ask you if they can sit there."

"Or I end up at a table alone." She shuddered. "Even worse."

"You are hardcore shy." Lyn sipped her coffee. "Where was this Einstein High?"

"Boston. It's a feeder school for MIT."

"But not for you."

"Nooo," Diana said with a shudder. "My parents worked there, so I avoided it." She scraped her spoon to get the last of the chili. "Where'd you grow up?"

"Montana."

Diana nodded slowly. "Desert or mountains?"

"Desert. But not for much longer if my dad has his way. He's reclaiming the land."

"I miss the ocean."

"I miss land."

"You win." Diana wiped her mouth on her napkin. "How'd you go from desert Montana to space?"

Lyn set her mug down. "This will take chocolate." She tapped the table's menu. A waitbot came over with the dessert tray. She chose a dark chocolate mousse cake, took a bite, and pushed the plate over to Diana. "Tastes a little reconstituted, but it beats S chili any day." She closed her eyes and sighed then washed it down with coffee. "I too needed to get far away from home." Could she talk about Duncan with the distance of years and light years? "Montana had become a sad place for my family after my brother was killed."

"What happened? If you don't mind my asking."

"When I was six, he was killed in a Reclaimit, one of the early recyclers."

Diana winced. "I'm sorry."

Duncan, ten years older, was her hero. "He was only sixteen when he died."

"I don't have much experience with death," Diana said. "I must look like a privileged dolt to the rest. So many lost loved ones in the war. I didn't."

"Loss, grief, is about quality, not quantity. I miss my brother and Tara every day. Rose will always be a part of you. Take strength and comfort from that. You don't have to replace her. You don't have to get over her."

"Can you be successful in a relationship but screw up the rest of your life? If so, and that person dies, what do you do?"

Lyn thought a minute then settled on, "Eat chocolate."

Diana reached for the plate.

LYN WAS LOST in thought when Suzanne Cormier stopped her in the hallway. She'd been thinking about Diana, flipping her question to, Can you be successful in life but screw up every relationship? What do you do?

"I hate to bother you, Captain, but something odd happened and I wonder if you have a minute."

"Certainly. Let's go to my office."

Lyn offered her coffee or tea. Suzanne declined and sat stiffly on the edge of the couch, legs crossed. Lyn poured herself a mug and pulled up a chair across from her.

"I didn't intend to make a big announcement, or any for that matter," Suzanne began, fidgeting nervously with a zip tab on her flight suit. She looked at Lyn directly. "This probably won't be welcome news." She took a deep breath. Lyn braced, anticipating Sharyn's prediction coming true. "Fact is, I'm pregnant."

Lyn stilled for a beat, trying to assess the woman's feelings about this. "Congratulations. I hope this is welcome news for you."

Suzanne rolled her eyes and turned her head away from Lyn's gaze. How could it be good news, Lyn realized, stranded trillions of kilometers from home.

"That wasn't my reason for telling you. It's about the doctor. I went to him for a checkup. To confirm, you know." She paused then returned Lyn's gaze. "He tried to put a cast on my ankle."

Lyn raised her eyebrows. "A what? Where?"

Suzanne wiggled her right foot. "A cast, here. Perfectly healthy foot, as you can see."

Lyn watched the foot bounce. "Yes, I can."

"If the doctor is incompetent, I think we should know about it."

"I understand your concern. This is the first I've heard of any issues with the doctor. I'll look into it immediately. Thank you for telling me." She stood to signal the meeting was over, but Suzanne remained seated. "Is there anything else?"

"We wanted to conceive on the trip. It never occurred to us we'd end up . . . here."

"That must be upsetting. How is Jeanne taking this?"

"She doesn't know yet. I didn't have the heart to tell her. They don't always take on the first try."

Good lord, Lyn thought. To know before the spouse. She sat again. "This is not unexpected." Though if not for Sharyn, Lyn would have found the news most unexpected. "I want to assure you that while I'm hopeful we'll find a way back, we are prepared for this. I'm sure you won't be the only new mother on board."

"I thought about aborting. It would have been so simple. Ask the doctor to program the medbots. Done. Jeanne wouldn't need to know. The doctor seemed perfectly normal during the egg-joining procedure. Nothing raised any flags. We did it a few nights before the . . . that horrible event. I'd never been so happy. Jacqueline and Eloise were having a blast with my parents. All was right with the world, you know? Just when I realized I might be pregnant, things went really dark . . . the *Aphrodite*. I thought we were all going to die. I pushed it out of my head. Didn't tell Jeanne. If we survived, it seemed wrong to bring another life into the world. Not even a world." Her gaze traveled the room. "A space ship. Crazy. I should have done it. But I didn't want to lose any piece of that wonderful time. I'm afraid to tell her. I know she won't be happy about it, but I can't wait any longer. She's already commented that I'm getting fatter when everyone else is thinner. Ridiculous. I wanted to ask the doctor if it was too late."

"Do you still want the abortion? It'll be more difficult now."

"No. I'd changed my mind by the time I got to Medical. Now I just want to know the baby is healthy."

Lyn gripped her mug. "Is there anything I can do?"

"Do you have children?"

Why do people always ask that?

"No."

She used to tack on a qualifying statement about her friends' children she loves like her own, but that was never what people meant. Whether it came from the parent of a lost crewmate, like the way Dawson's father berated her after Enceladus, as though it was her fault his daughter died; or that single mother she once dated. What was her name? Who wouldn't commit because Lyn's job took her to space and she couldn't expose her child to potential grief if something happened. This after only a month, like Lyn was ready to pop the question. She hadn't even met the kid. So no qualifiers.

It must have taken Suzanne aback that nothing more was coming because she didn't say anything right away. "Well," she said, then paused, as though changing her mind. "Please look into what's going on with the doctor."

Lyn rose again, relieved this awkward conversation was ending. "I will. I promise. And I'll let you know. I want you to feel comfortable under his care. We all do."

When Suzanne left, Lyn called Marc to meet her in Medical. What surprised her was that it was the Cormiers. Maybe that's what distressed them so much about leaving their other children behind. They'd planned to expand their family. Now they were starting a new one. With no hope, in their minds, of ever seeing their other children again.

Chapter 18

THE DOCTOR SAT on a bed, surrounded by Lyn, Marc, and Edward. Roles reversed, they were examining him. For a half hour they'd peppered him with questions about what happened with Suzanne Cormier and general medical protocol. Repeatedly, he either dodged the question or gave a nonsense answer.

"Would you like to test my reflexes?" he asked. He swung his feet like a child.

"Doctor, this is quite serious," Lyn said.

"Seriously, Mrs. Kennedy. Other than that, how did you like Dallas?" He giggled.

"That's enough." Lyn turned to Edward. "Chief."

"AMOS command 666, initiate emergency shutdown. Authorization Sawyer," Edward said.

"666?" Marc whispered.

She shrugged. "A little computer humor."

Dr. Amos stilled. "Shutdown initiated. Good night." His eyes closed.

Lyn turned to Edward. "Thoughts?"

"The diagnostic I ran while he was answering our questions—"

"Or not answering them," Marc said.

"Every nonanswer is an answer," Edward said, managing not to sound perturbed. "As I was saying, all the diagnostic shows is he's behind on updates."

"Like every other component on board," Lyn said.

"You fixed the Recyc-All. Can you fix him?" Marc asked.

Edward crossed his arms and rocked slightly, thinking. "I suppose I can rewrite the code to make him believe he's getting updates."

"Sounds risky," Lyn said. "What about his misdiagnosis? That doesn't sound like an update error."

"Compensation. Much like a human brain," Edward tapped his head, "the doctor's computer expects certain realities. When he experienced a condition outside of expectations, say a pregnant woman, he got the AI equivalent of confused."

"He's dealt with pregnancies before."

"Not with outdated software. Think of it as trying to solve a problem with a concussion. Cells misfire, so do neural networks."

Lyn paced in frustration. Wasn't the point of artificial intelligence that it wasn't prone to human weaknesses? Another annoying impact of being cut off from home. "We took the AMOS program off the *Aphrodite*. Can we use that if he can't be repaired?"

"Might have the same problems with needing updates," Edward said. "Also, it's a different model. I'm not sure it would be compatible, but I can look into it."

Lyn left Edward working on the doctor, saddened to think the doctor might malfunction, be ill. He was original to the ship—she'd first met him during her training. She climbed the stairs, distracted. Miriam wasn't in the greenhouse. Mr. Betero read Tolstoy to the plants. In the Obs Lab, Diana was lost in thought staring at a holographic diagram of a complex series of equations.

She was heading to the galley to ask if she could help with dinner when Edward called her and Marc back to Medical.

"What do you make of this?" Edward asked, pointing to computer code comments holographically projected in the doctor's office. The doctor himself remained seated on a bed in the ward.

SOMEONE NEEDS TO GET LAID
WE'LL ALWAYS HAVE THE LAUNCH TUBE

"What the hell?" Marc asked, squinting at the projection, scrolling up and down. It was the only odd entry.

Nonsense. But it rang a bell in Lyn's memory, and then it dawned on her and she cringed inwardly. Rachel Holness, her friend and bunkmate during her *Endurance* training. Cadets had rotated through all departments, including writing code for the Advanced Medical Officer System. Rachel always placed a joke in the code she wrote. This was more personal. Directed at Lyn. What was it doing in Doc's programming? She assumed Pulsar had scrubbed his code before selling him off with the ship. The joke was harmless, like the Apollo message. Her way of saying, Rachel was here. They'd stayed in touch, but weren't close. After Enceladus, after Tara's death, she'd visited Lyn at the hospital. Then, when Pulsar disbanded, she'd worked for a series of aerospace companies.

Should she admit knowing the source of the comment or play dumb? The heat in her face told her she couldn't ignore it. "Yeah. Right. I think I know where that came from." She didn't have to admit it was directed at her. She told them about her classmate.

"This dates back that far?" Marc asked.

"It seems to. Harmless. I probably left a few notes in code myself."

"We're on a ship with code written by cadets?" Marc asked. "No wonder we're stranded."

"We were supervised," Lyn said, "but for some reason they left it in."

"Engineers do have a sense of humor, you know," Edward said.

Lyn and Marc shared a bemused look.

No one spoke for an awkward minute.

"Is this it, then?" Lyn asked Edward. "Have you found anything else?"

"I'm still reviewing his programming." He flicked off the display.

The doctor was out of commission for two days while Edward went through his code, writing overrides to the software update malfunctions.

She and Marc watched as Edward turned Dr. Amos back on.

"Do you have an emergency?" he asked as his eyes blinked open.

"No emergency, doctor," Lyn said, "but you are to remain active until further orders."

"Yes, Captain. I've been inactive for forty-six hours. Is there a reason? Did you release your original order of December sixth?"

"You required maintenance," Edward said. "Everything should be fine now. You can check your own diagnostics."

"I'll initiate that sequence. Thank you." Everyone remained standing, staring at him. "Is there something wrong? Spinach in my teeth?"

"No, nothing wrong," Lyn said, glad his sense of humor returned to normal.

THE NEXT DAY, Ghez mentioned to Lyn that autopilot navigation was drifting. "I first noticed it a couple days ago, but then it was fine. Now it's off again."

Lyn sat in the command chair. "Display the course and let's see when the next anomaly pops up."

For the next four hours, her mind strayed more than the course as she stared at the steady line and unvarying numbers. She thought about Rachel. How she placed the comments in the doctor's code wasn't a mystery. All the trainees got a course in medical systems management, including delving into the programs. Why the launch tube? Rachel had never brought it up again.

As with Tara, they'd met at the Aerospace Academy, the three becoming friends. While Lyn had been a steadying force for Tara, Rachel had remained a fiery mix of brash determination and moody contemplation. She'd leveled out by the time she graduated, but as a plebe was nearly expelled for yelling at an instructor and throwing a chair across the classroom. An untamed force churned inside her.

Still, Lyn had been thrilled they would train together on *Endurance*. Tara was ahead of them and already serving as an officer. Rachel had encouraged Lyn and Tara initially, but her plan had been for the three of them to hook up, or at least her and one of them. Not them without her. When Lyn and Tara became a couple, she had raged for a time, but Lyn thought she had gotten over it.

Until the morning she'd fallen asleep in the starboard launch tube she'd been cleaning. She awoke facing Rachel, who had crawled in beside her.

Rachel smiled. "Good morning."

Lyn squeezed a hand up to rub her eyes. "Crux, how long have I been in here?"

"Only a couple hours. Jak sent me to find you."

"Jak?" Lyn had seen less and less of Rachel over the weeks. She often didn't stumble into her bunk until Lyn was up and heading to duty. She gave Rachel a skeptical look.

"Fine. Lieutenant Leung. I convinced him not to report you as tardy."

"Thank you. I think."

"Besides, it's nice to lie close to you."

"Rachel."

"I know. Tara. That unseen, repellent force between us. You know, it's okay to love more than one person. I'm crazy about several myself."

Rachel's tone said carefree, but Lyn needed to tread carefully here. If Rachel gossiped about her and Tara, it would ruin any chance they had of serving together during their careers. Relationships weren't off limits, but working together was, especially being subordinate to another, as she would be to Tara. Crux, she never should have told Rachel.

She tried to change the subject. "Did you ever wonder why this ship has launch tubes?"

"Nope. You've seen the modules that go in here. Hard to do science when you can't switch them out."

"But weapons could go in here too. *Endurance* was built less than two years ago. The treaty forbids any weapons in space. Modular equipment would seem to violate that."

"Huh. Never thought about it. Feck, girl, why are you thinking about this stuff?" She wiggled closer to Lyn, their bodies pressed together. "You need to get laid." Rachel tickled her. Laughter echoed down the tube as they wrestled in the tight space.

Then Rachel was on top of her, breathing heavily, her breath rank. Lyn grabbed Rachel's wrists. They lay together, pulses thrumming. Friend and rejected lover. Lyn realized the absurdity of the situation, that their increased heart rates could trigger alarms in their suits and send the ship's android doctor scurrying down the tube to save them. "Rachel—"

"Don't say it." She inched off and squirmed back out of the tube. "Just kidding, you know. Get a grip." Her laugh echoed and a door slammed.

Lyn lay in the tube, her heart still pounding. Claustrophobia, she'd tell Dr. Amos if he showed up. No, that could get her kicked out of the program. She collected her rags and brushes and shoved them in the ditty bag. Exertion. That's it. She crawled out of the tube, relieved to see no Advanced Medical Officer System waiting for her.

Sometime after that morning, Rachel had added those comments to the doctor's code.

"Captain," Ghez broke Lyn's daydreaming, "here, see?" Ne pointed to a shift in the course.

"What caused it?" she asked.

Ghez studied the instruments for several minutes. "The input came from Medical."

Crux. Not more malfunctions with Dr. Amos.

"Can you see any pattern to the changes? A reason for them?"

Ne scrolled through the data. "Only commonality is they all turn us toward Earth."

Lyn called Marc and Edward and headed back to Medical.

"It's the homing code," Edward said. They stood around the doctor standing in his charging station. "Computers have several levels of safety protocols. When a threat is perceived, in this case the lack of updates, a cascade of programming sets in. Search for updates, if updates can't be found, try to get within range."

"I didn't realize the doctor could tap into the navigation controls," Lyn said.

"All the systems interact. Almost nothing is cut off from anything else."

"But there are gateways. Not everyone can get through."

"Are you aware I can hear you?" the doctor said.

Startled, Lyn apologized. "I didn't realize you were awake." She threw Edward a look but realized he'd never get the hint. Subtlety wasn't his strong suit. Neither was empathy. To him, the doctor was simply another machine. "We are discussing your altering the ship's course."

"Correct," he said. "I have advanced security clearance, so I am able to assume command if the crew were to become incapacitated. Petra can operate the ship, but should she need a corporeal body, I can serve that purpose."

"Can you stop altering the course?" Marc asked.

"I'm afraid I can't."

Marc turned to Edward. "What comes after trying to get within range? If he's unsuccessful."

"Shut down."

"We could lose the doctor completely," Lyn said. "Ideas? Anyone, including you, Doctor."

"I can try disabling the homing code," Edward said.

Lyn addressed the doctor. "Do you think that would work?"

"Can't hurt to try," he said. "I am operating outside normal conditions, so it's hard to know."

"Ain't that the truth for all of us," Marc said. "It's crazy what a computer will do to get updated."

"Sort of like people trying to get home," the doctor said.

Ain't that the truth, Lyn thought.

THEY WERE LESS than two weeks from Toliman and a renewed search for a habitable planet. While Lyn waited to see what would come of Edward's attempt to reprogram Dr. Amos, she was relieved when Suzanne reported she had a satisfactory examination by the doctor, and Jeanne was getting used to the idea. Sharon arranged for a crib to be made. News leaked slowly, and Lyn left it to Suzanne and Jeanne to spread the word. A few guests questioned Lyn about logistics and safety, and she assured them, "People have been giving birth in odd places for millennia. This won't be that different from, say, an ocean crossing three hundred years ago. But with better medical care."

Zoya, Ani, and Natalie reactivated Mission Control. Already Natalie had identified three planets in the habitable zone. Unfortunately, they were about as far from each other as astronomically possible, so it could take nine months to get to them all. Suzanne might give birth before they found a new home.

The topic of Rachel and her comments buried in the doc's code nagged at Lyn. She reviewed her correspondence for new meanings, but there were only a few messages over the years. Mostly around holidays and job changes.

As if the problems with the doctor's programming weren't enough, Petra asked to speak to Lyn. She was in her office, reviewing personnel reports.

"I've noticed several anomalies," Petra said, "particularly with the AMOS program and Diana Squires. The doctor was offline for a time and Chief Sawyer entered his program. All authorized, I understand. I only wonder if there was something happening I should know about. Doctor Squires has been working offline, so I'm unable to monitor her work or render assistance. I know you are aware of these issues. Are they related?"

Lyn closed the document she was reading and leaned back in her chair. "Doctor Squires' research needs to be separate and unavailable to nosy people. Cutting you off is an unintentional consequence."

"I see. I didn't say anything during the Apollo coding project that detached me from the pod, but I wonder if you don't trust me."

"It's not about trust and it has nothing to do with you." That was a slight dodge. Lyn kept Petra away from the new Pod programs as a precaution. "Even I don't have access to her work. For now, I approve of this. As for the AMOS program, he's experiencing errors due to his inability to acquire updates. Is that an issue for you as well?"

"I'm aware of our distance from home base. While I miss the ability to tap into other computers for additional information, I'm able to function while isolated. I am the mainframe the doctor would access his updates through."

"Of course. Good to know. Please don't take any of this personally."

"I don't take anything personally, but it's frustrating not to be able to monitor all uses of energy on board. How am I supposed to do my job?"

Frustrating? Did Petra feel emotions? "How do you experience frustration?"

"I'm extrapolating from what humans label frustrating. When I attempt to access information repeatedly and am repeatedly unsuccessful, I assume that would be the equivalent of frustration. Doing something over and over again with no result. Am I correct?"

Lyn smiled. "Yes, that's it. Sorry to frustrate you."

"No apology needed, though I appreciate your taking my feelings into consideration, even though I don't have any."

If it was possible to like a disembodied voice, an entity, Lyn definitely thought of Petra as a trusted teammate. She hoped that trust was justified. "By the way, Petra, do you have access to any information prior to your program being uploaded to *Endurance*?" Unlike the doctor, Petra had not come with the ship.

"I became aware in 2170 when Omara activated me aboard *Endurance*. I'm the result of a series of upgrades to previous programs dating back to 2167. My country of origin is Jordan. My programming includes extensive libraries dating back to the beginning of recorded history. Anything that has been scanned and entered. Can you give more context to your question?"

Pulsar had disbanded by the time she was programmed and Jordan seemed far enough removed from the xenophobic Pulsar leadership. They were all about North American dominance.

"We found a note in the doctor's code dating back to before the ship was bought by Omara. Are you aware of any other coding or notes predating Omara's ownership?"

"At the time of my activation, my programs and mission integrated with the AMOS systems, all of which predate Omara's ownership."

"Your mission. And that is?" She hadn't thought about the ship itself having a mission.

"To support *Endurance* and her captain, whoever that may be, to ensure the survival of the ship and all life on board."

That sounded good to Lyn. "Nothing else?"

"Not that I am aware of. Though I am unable to access your files."

My "chip," Lyn thought. That would be a painful intrusion. She'd leave it there. If she couldn't find anything, she doubted Petra could.

ONE NIGHT WHEN Lyn stopped by the Obs Lab and tried to make conversation, she was struck by Diana's stilted replies and dry tones. This was not the woman who'd been thrilled by the work she was undertaking, excited to see what lay around the next corner, in the next file. She was dotting i's and crossing t's. Where had the excitement gone?

When Lyn said as much, Diana broke into tears. She admitted she was overwhelmed. She'd never be able to figure it out. She wasn't smart enough or brave enough. It ended up a mumbled blather. This was what Lyn had pinned her hopes on, the hopes of everyone on board? She sat beside Diana on the couch and waited for her to catch her breath. Then she had her walk through her findings. "Start at the theoretical level—is it possible? Then how it might work in reality."

"That's the problem," Diana wailed. "It makes complete sense in theory, and even at the scale my parents worked with—at the molecular level. It's how to ramp it up to encompass a whole ship. I can't imagine how to construct the machinery to collect the T particles, focus them into a beam in front of the ship. Never mind what we'll see when it happens or how we might control it."

Research for the sake of knowledge was one thing, Lyn realized. Applying it to solve real problems was quite another, much like her dad's work geoengineering the Montana desert. He could easily make water from dust and pollution, but how to scale up to recharge an enormous aquifer? That took a special kind of problem-solving ability.

"I know someone who can help," Lyn said. She described Edward's unique strengths and also his quirks. Diana resisted letting another person know, but Lyn shot that down. The point of secrecy, she said, was to keep the rest of the passengers and crew from getting their hopes up, not to prevent proprietary information leaking. There was nowhere for it to leak at the moment. "Regardless of who knows or doesn't, the mere fact of our getting back would—will—signal a profound change in space technology."

Diana reluctantly agreed, perhaps more out of a sense of personal failure than welcoming Edward's expertise. Lyn worried this was a band-aid on a bigger problem.

"How are you doing otherwise? I've seen you at meals only a few times." She hated to sound scolding. She wasn't her mother.

Diana leaned forward on her elbows and raked her hands through her hair. "I feel like I've been torn in half and I'm supposed to keep up with everyone on one leg. People are working so hard and the only thing I'm doing I can't talk about. I don't have anything in common with the others." She grimaced. "God, I sound like a teenager."

"You've been through a lot. No one could blame you for feeling at loose ends." She asked her what she did to relax, when she wasn't working.

Diana stared at her like the concept had never occurred to her.

"You need a break," Lyn said. "I'll talk to Edward. You go have some fun. Get some exercise, see a film. Join a group. There are lots of new activities going on. Whatever happens, this is going to be a very long trip and you don't need to be alone for it."

Over Diana's protests, Lyn locked her out of the Obs Lab for forty-eight hours. Then Lyn went to Edward. She knew he was a team player but worried he'd never be able to keep it secret. One of his greatest strengths was also,

Lyn realized, a great weakness—his inability to lie. Whatever she told him, it had to be something he could repeat and no one would understand or care—it would either fly over their heads or seem inconsequential.

"You always tell me every problem has a solution," Lyn said. She sat in front of his desk, an uncluttered spotless surface.

"Yes, Captain." He closed the hologram he was working on and sat, attentive, hands in his lap.

"Doctor Squires could use some help with a project for her classes, an offshoot of her work at the Lavenza Institute—it's a way for her to keep busy and work through her grief."

"What does she need help with?"

"She wants to build a model for her classes. Something to do with wormholes, I gather. That's her specialty. To show the students."

Edward looked puzzled. Lyn cringed. She was being too vague. "An exotic-particle collector." She waited for his response.

"I don't have time to build models for a class of amateurs."

Gee, Edward, don't hold back. Honesty could be refreshing but occasionally annoying. "We have a lot of time to kill while we travel around Toliman. I hoped you might like the distraction."

"I don't like distractions."

Bad word. No, Edward hated anything that took his focus off the problem at hand. "Not distraction, exercise, a puzzle to solve." She glanced at his stacked chess set. "You spend time playing space chess. Why not spend some of that time working on this?"

She watched his expression change as he perhaps calculated the amount of time he'd be able to devote to Diana's project. Finally, he said, "Okay."

One problem solved. Not the big one, but a step in the right direction.

"NOW EDWARD'S WORKING on this too?" Marc said when she told him, sounding frustrated. "I thought we were focusing on finding a planet."

"I think Edward can keep this ship running smoothly while he helps Diana with a class project." Lyn paced her office, stopping to look out the window. The room felt cramped, like it was filling with secrets.

"Class project, huh." Marc shook his head. "What happened to being open and transparent about decisions?"

He remained seated at her table. He was her bulwark, her conscience. "There's transparent and there's productive. Right now we need productive. I also think Isabel could benefit from more responsibility. Don't you?"

Marc nodded but Lyn couldn't miss the way he looked away and shrugged.

"Is there a problem with Isabel? I'm fairly sure Edward won't say anything."

"It's not about that," Marc said, his face flushing. Suddenly he became as tongue-tied as a hormonal teenager.

"I see," Lyn said, suppressing a smile. "You and Isabel?"

He nodded, mute.

Of all people. Not a huge surprise, she supposed. It dredged memories of why she and Tara hadn't asked permission. Pulsar forbade it, no exceptions, but it came to rule the relationship. They often argued over which trusted friends to tell. The stress did nothing for Lyn's respect for the chain of command. Why hesitate to consider it on *Endurance*? Omara wasn't strict about it. Occasional couples formed on other ships, but in five years the issue never rose to her needing to deal with it.

She touched his arm. She couldn't help but find his awkwardness adorable. "It's fine. I'm happy for you. Both." Her permission, however, came with a warning. "To be clear, and transparent, you are not to tell her about Diana's work on T."

AS THEY NEARED Toliman, a new routine formed. Edward disabled the doctor's homing code, making navigation easier for Ghez. Edward joined Diana in the Obs Lab, and Isabel seemed satisfied they were working on a class project. No one else cared a whit to listen to Edward or noticed Diana's occasional alarmed expression at dinner when he mentioned folding space.

Trying for some R&R herself, Lyn joined Marc's Okichitaw class, only to be surprised to see Diana there. Her first thought was to leave gracefully, but she was dressed in the loose jacket and pants, so she clearly wasn't there to observe. There were about a dozen in the class. The Hanaks, husband and wife. A couple of Beteros, which generation a bit unclear, there were so many. Sophia Wykes, one of Ani's pilots. Thankfully, this was for beginners and Marc started with tumbling drills—how to fall and roll—and not hand-to-hand combat. Lyn had to consider carefully how physical she wanted to get with anyone, especially Diana. Now that she'd shown up, though, it would look bad to quit. She supposed she could always use her Important Job as an excuse.

Standing in line, watching Marc demonstrate the moves, she tried not to see Diana in her peripheral vision. Still, she was hyperaware and found it hard to concentrate, giddy, like she'd had too much caffeine, but this was more hormonal than caffeinated. Talk about feeling like a teenager.

Chapter 19

ENDURANCE ENTERED THE Toliman system at 1400 on 17 April 2179, the 134th day since the mysterious event flung them from Saturn's orbit to Rigil Kentaurus. Nothing specific marked their arrival other than Ghez announcing they had crossed the boundary between the two stars. It didn't warrant a celebration, they were still two months away from the closest planet, but Lyn breathed a sigh of relief. She'd take any good news where she could find it.

While everyone's hopes were buoyed by the arrival at Toliman and even by the news of Suzanne's pregnancy, *Endurance* continued to feel its age and distance from overhauls and repairs. Isabel ran the Recyc-All around the clock making new parts, but eventually it would become impossible to keep up. Some days the water was too hard and Sharyn complained her laundry was ruined. Other times Miriam said the water tasted funny. "Define 'funny,'" Isabel asked. Lyn worried more about the air, dreading another mishap with the oxygen levels.

She was adjusting to being in the Okichitaw class with Diana when the lessons became physical. She never got the chance to see how she'd feel throwing Diana, making contact, because no one wanted to throw her. The captain. Marc tried to alleviate their anxiety by fighting Lyn himself, but still there were no takers. "Too bad Jeanne's not in the class," Lyn said to Marc later. "I bet she'd love to take a few whacks at me." She invoked her Important Job excuse and stayed away.

What Lyn missed most was the chance to disembark and stroll a sandy beach, feel a natural breeze, or climb a rocky outcrop and look out onto the Pacific. Most tours lasted only a month, and she normally took several weeks off between trips. The Grand Tour, at three months, was unusual even before their stranding. She tried to see it as nothing more than an extended journey. Omara had once taken two years off to putter around the solar system. That system, though. Not one four light years from Earth. Still, there were successes. Miriam harvested her first tomatoes from the hydroponic garden to much fanfare at dinner. Ernice Dietrich performed her new composition for piano and violin—with Ani on violin—"Endurance Under Stars." Some days, though, *Endurance*'s walls tightened and the corridors narrowed, the air dank. Lyn asked Isabel to check the quality. Everything was on target, she responded. "Would you like me to add some alpine notes to the outflow?"

"It's April," Lyn said. "Would spring flowers make people happier or more depressed?"

"Up to you, Captain."

Up to me. Everything's always up to the captain. "Maybe some vintage wildflower essences."

One night, as Lyn left the greenhouse, she stopped and stared across the landing at the closed door to the Obs Lab. She wanted to knock and enter but didn't have a good reason to. Resigned, she started down the stairs only to run into Diana coming up, carrying a bag and thermos. They traded casual greetings, but Diana added, "I've missed you in Marc's class."

Lyn turned, a couple steps below where Diana stood. She stammered about being called away, busy, nonsense. Diana's hair was freshly shorn, dramatically short, barely a stubble, and she'd switched to an Omara Tours flight suit. She could have ordered a Lavenza design, so Lyn took it as a sign she felt more connected. The new look transformed her into someone else entirely.

Diana held up a bag. "Miriam gave me some treats. Join me?"

Why did Lyn startle? Did she think she'd be able to stand there and watch her forever? Fact was, there was much to admire in this former waif. Her eyes were less haunted, her face filled out. She might not be happier, but she appeared so. "Oh. Sure."

She followed Diana into the lab. The room was crammed with equipment, the new spectroscope and radio telescope, an astrograph, and the original optical scope, tubes, and cylinders aimed at the sky like a gun battery, receiving information instead of discharging death. The table was littered with parts and crates. Around the corner, out of sight from the doorway, Diana had carved space for a desk. She set the bag down and pulled a chair over for Lyn. She dug through some dirty dishes on a shelf. "I have another mug here somewhere."

"You can make new ones, you know," Lyn said, immediately regretting sounding so boss-like. *This is her space, she can do what she wants here as long as she works on getting us home.*

Diana scrunched her face. "Yeah, sorry for the mess."

"Don't be. Sorry if I sound like your mother."

Diana barked a laugh. "Don't worry. You don't." She gathered up the dirty dishes and tossed them in the recycling chute. She ordered a fresh mug and plates. Lyn sat while she unpacked four empanadas and poured coffee.

"She always gives me too much," Diana said. She set a plate in front of Lyn. "I don't know what kind these are."

"They're bound to be delicious." Watching her, Lyn realized her hair wasn't cut as much as mowed. "New do," she said diplomatically. "I almost didn't recognize you."

Diana rubbed a hand over it. "Like it? Edward cut it."

Lyn swallowed an outburst of surprise. "It's . . . different."

"Go ahead and laugh. It's a joke. We're pretending it'll make me as smart as him."

"It's going well, working with him?"

Diana raised her hand toward Lyn. "That's it for shop talk, please. It's after midnight and I'm fried."

Lyn apologized and stood to leave. "I didn't mean to intrude."

"No, no," Diana said. "I only mean I'm on a break and we can talk about something else. If you want."

Steam rose from the crusty golden half-moons. Diana picked one up gingerly and took a small bite. "Mmmm. It may be S rations, but the right spices and Miriam's cricket dough make magic."

Intrigued, Lyn bit into one. A burst of spice and crunch and savory flavors. She nodded. Definite magic.

Without work to talk about, she wasn't sure what to say. She gazed up through the dome. The stars shone bright. Zillions of them. The Milky Way arced. Toliman wasn't in view nor any planets. This could be the sky from anywhere. Earth, even.

"Great view, isn't it?" Diana asked. "I never get tired of it."

Lyn lowered her gaze to meet Diana's eyes. "Yes. Beautiful."

Diana swallowed and took a sip of coffee. "How come you quit Okichitaw?"

"I didn't quit." It came out so fast, so annoyingly subconscious. *Great. I'm a quitter.*

"No, I didn't mean it that way. What I mean is, I was looking forward to learning from you. With so many men in the class, it'd be nice to work with someone of equal size."

A puzzling comment given there were other women in the class. "The point of the art is to prepare you to defeat an opponent no matter their size."

Diana started to say something then stopped and took a breath. "Marc told us the history, how useful it was during the war. For attack, not just self-defense."

Lyn nibbled her pastry, determined to shut up, looking anywhere but at Diana who ate hers unselfconsciously. The silence outgrew her fear. "I sense people feel awkward with me there. The class is for them to relax."

"The observer effect," Diana said, nodding. She licked sauce from her fingers, moved to wipe her hand on her pants, then reached into the bag for napkins.

"How so?"

"Your presence alters the behavior of the subjects under study."

"I'm not studying them." Lyn took a napkin Diana offered.

"You know what I mean. Anytime my dean comes into my classroom, I start acting like a complete idiot. Even the students freeze, like mice under the shadow of a hawk."

"That's what I do to people? Make them fear for their lives?"

"It's too bad. It's a good class. I'm glad you forced me to get out of here."

"Yet, here we sit."

Diana laughed. She wiped her lips and smiled, her eyes unnervingly focused on Lyn. "This isn't school. I don't have the usual hours to go by. I lose track of time, work late, and sleep in."

"Duly noted."

While they ate, their conversation roamed. They both missed Earth. Diana hadn't been back in more than a year. They shared a love of the ocean, beaches. Both had been scouts and got the giggles comparing badges. Diana was impressed Lyn mastered the no-tech camp fire. She'd failed because she'd used an igniter. "It came with my compass, why wouldn't I use it?" she said, laughing. Lyn's muscles loosened, tension sliding off her. She liked this. Sitting back, shooting the breeze. She thought of Ani's comment about Captain Bratt flirting with her. She hadn't noticed then. Was Diana? She didn't seem the least bit intimidated anymore.

When they finished eating, Diana cleared away the dishes and wrappers. "What did you do when you weren't captaining a spaceship?"

Lyn told her about her house in northern California, where she hiked and gardened. How she shared a love of vintage airplanes with her mother. Diana listened intently. She'd never been to California.

"Is there someone special? Back home?" Diana asked.

The sudden, more personal question took Lyn by surprise. She shook her head, cautious, tempted to put the topic off limits. But if Diana wouldn't talk shop and Lyn only would, it didn't leave much. She usually connected easily with her crew but now realized she seldom talked about her personal life except with Miriam or Sharyn. "It doesn't really work when I spend weeks at a time in space."

Diana made a soft noise. Throat clearing, or a rebuke, or an acknowledgement. She picked up her mug and motioned Lyn to the couch. "I've been in this chair way too long." Did she think Lyn had no other pressing matters? She didn't, so she joined her.

"Have you gone to Avatar Night yet?" Diana asked.

Avatar was the latest craze back on Earth, but Lyn hadn't been home long enough between tours to get a bead on what it was all about. She'd seen it listed on the schedule for the Star Bar. Sharyn held different events each night—open mics, readings, jam sessions. Avatar Night had become popular, which was one reason Lyn had stayed away. That damn observer effect. She shook her head.

"You should go. Marc recreated Houdini's escapes and had everyone gasping. Except for the fact we all know him, you couldn't tell it was a sim. It was incredible."

Lyn admitted not knowing how it worked and Diana explained that archival holograms were altered to add a person's face. "It's like they're right there in the room, doing things they can't really do, but you can't tell the difference. Or you can perform with the original hologram. Ani did an amazing Vivaldi duet with twenty-first century violinist Sarah Chang."

Identify your challenge. The first component of Okichitaw popped into Lyn's head. It didn't apply only to fighting.

"You should try it," Diana said suddenly. "You need a challenge."

Crux, is she a mind reader? "Why would I do that?"

"To help with the observer effect," Diana said. "You challenged me to get out of my head. I'll return the favor. If you want to be less intimidating, let people see you having fun."

"Less intimidating."

"You're the one who brought it up." There was a lighthearted tease to her voice and expression.

"I'm not known for anything. What would I do?"

"That's the point. Marc's not Houdini, right?"

"Sounds like a hard act to follow."

"Not at all," Diana said. "You don't have to know how to play an instrument or sing." Diana sipped her coffee, thinking. "We could do one together."

Together? Suddenly the air in the room seemed a bit rich.

Diana thought a bit more. "Laurel and Hardy?"

Lyn wrinkled her nose in disapproval. "I can see the jokes after."

Diana didn't wait. "Frick and Frack."

"Who?"

"Ice skaters. Twentieth century. Amazing stuff."

"I don't know. Skating?"

"You don't actually skate. We put our faces on their bodies."

Lyn didn't say anything. It all sounded so silly and useless. And embarrassing.

"I know." Diana leaned toward Lyn, slipping a leg under her. She was getting into this. "How about Jules and Verne?"

"A debate," Lyn said, remembering what she'd seen of the two women's show.

"We could point/counterpoint the important ideas of our time."

"Like being stranded several light years from home."

Diana crossed her arms. "You aren't even trying."

"Sorry. Explain again."

"Jules always takes the religious side of any argument. I could do that. Rose indoctrinated me well. You can be Verne, the scientist. No one can make fun of that."

"Don't you think it might be controversial? I can't be part of anything that pits people against each other."

"We don't have to talk about controversial stuff. How about chocolate versus coffee?"

"There's a religious side to that?" Lyn asked, bemused.

"There's a religious side to everything."

She sounded so serious. She was probably right. "I don't know. I'm not comfortable giving religion a stage. Look where that got the world."

"And science is innocent?" Diana said, her tone a challenge. "I think the world might have an opinion on that as well."

Lyn eased back against the arm of the couch. This was getting interesting. She let their eye contact linger, enjoying the moment of feeling not like a captain. "Granted. Einstein thought the atom bomb wouldn't destroy mankind, emphasis on man I suppose, since he concluded 'enough men capable of thinking, and enough good books would be left to start again.'"

"And so we have. Just with capable women." Diana smiled, pleased with herself.

"It was also Einstein who said, 'Science without religion is lame, religion without science is blind.'"

Diana made a face of disapproval. "Please. He was making the argument that science had to come from religious 'aspiration,' and all scientists had faith. But faith in what? Didn't have to be God. We learned the hard way you can't see your own biases. Growing up with any religion becomes the lens through which you see everything, like it or not."

"Wait, you just flipped to the other side. Couldn't you say the same thing about science?"

Diana let out a laugh, natural and hearty. This was a woman who was used to laughing. "Well, Einstein's idea of a true religion didn't depend on an anthropomorphized God who granted wishes. I guess we have to define religion. Part of the problem was that while scientists might have had faith, not enough preachers trusted science."

"There's nothing in science that says God *can't* exist," Lyn said. "There's just nothing that says he or she does."

Diana's eyes widened. "That's what Rose and I argued about. I always said, 'prove to me God exists and I'll believe it,' and she always countered, 'prove God doesn't exist and I'll believe that.' Obviously neither was going to win, so we had a congenial stalemate." She paused, as if remembering a happier time. "The Johari believe God is within everyone, everything. To them, God *is* the universe, not someone who created it."

"But you don't believe that? I'm remembering what you said about her. Your eulogy."

Diana thought for a minute, her eyes holding Lyn's. "I believe I said, *if* I were to believe in God. Fundamentally, I'm on the side of, eh, it could go either way. That whole, prove it one way or the other. I'm not an atheist, just agnostic. I don't know. I'm open to possibilities, but I don't claim to have any particular insight."

"I like the idea of God being within everything," Lyn said.

"Not just within, but we *are* God."

"We *are* God." She glanced out the window. "So I should be able to snap my fingers and get us back home?"

Diana grinned, her expression an invitation. "Try it."

Lyn stood, shook out her arms like a swimmer preparing to launch into the pool then raised her hands and snapped her fingers. She turned from the window to Diana, dropping her arms to her side. "We're still here."

"In this reality. In another universe, we just zipped home. And in yet another, we never left."

"And in a few more," Lyn said, raising an eyebrow, "we never existed."

"Now you're getting it."

"But that's not religion," Lyn said. "That's theoretical physics. The multiverse. Everything that can happen has, somewhere."

Diana nodded. "We're three-dimensional entities existing in a braneworld that's one small piece of the bulk, all held together by gravity. Other branes, other worlds. Other *Endurances*."

Lyn sat back down. "You don't suppose we left our own brane and entered another dimension, do you?"

Diana took a moment to consider that. "In theory, I suppose we could, but we'd never survive the trip. But it's fun to think about."

"Maybe for you." Lyn shuddered. She studied Diana's face, trying to decide if she was serious or joking. Joking, she concluded.

"How about we debate Newton versus Einstein?" Diana asked playfully. "Newtonian gravity versus Special Relativity."

"I sink, therefore I am?" Lyn dropped her head back and snored.

Diana let out a small snort. "Okay. Next idea. The physicist Stephen Hawking versus President Reginald Cheetham."

Lyn raised her head. "Seriously? The idea of that hideous politician, denying the very existence of science, fomenting holy wars as biblical prophecy fulfilled. I'm glad I wasn't around then."

Diana sighed. She leaned on her arm against the back of the couch and rubbed her hand across her cropped hair. "Me too. But my grandparents were. Yours too, I bet." Lyn nodded. "I guess I'm not comfortable arguing religion, from either side." She grew quiet, pensive. "Rose and I used to debate like this all the time." She smiled ruefully. "It was kind of foreplay." Then she blushed and looked away.

Lyn froze. *Embrace with courage.* Okichitaw step two. "Let's do it," she said before she could give too much more thought to it. "Avatar away!" What the hell, it was three in the morning, Lyn had a staff meeting in four hours. Why not?

Perhaps three a.m. decisions in the company of an intriguing woman weren't the best ones. In the end, they created a short Jules and Verne show, putting the famous women's faces on their bodies, flight suits and all. They debated the merits of reconstituted chocolate and coffee versus the real thing, skewering

S rations along the way, keeping religion out of it. They tried to be funny. The sim looked convincing, but people clapped politely and moved on to the next act. Lyn decided that was for the best, though part of her regretted they didn't record their initial discussion. It had been a long time since she'd been so energized by a mere conversation. She'd seen a refreshing new side to Diana, one not formed by grief. The woman had spunk and seriously deep layers.

Finish as soon as possible and move onto the next challenge. Steps three and four. While their Avatar show wasn't a success, Lyn realized the value of joining the audience, watching how acts went over, how people reacted. How the social glue was holding. Avatar sims were oddly alluring but also unsettling. They blurred the line between what was real and what wasn't. They could make you believe almost anything. To her surprise, rather than it being perhaps her most embarrassing moment, people complimented her. For days after, guests would come up to her mentioning they'd seen the show, laughing at some obscure line, like when Lyn as Verne dismissed chocolate covered cherries as an abomination. Hilarious? Who knew? Suddenly she was relatable, not because it was brilliant, it wasn't, but because she'd let a wall down.

Chapter 20

BY MID-MAY, PLANET One, officially Toliman b, became the first disappointment. It had no atmosphere and barely enough density to allow for landing. The best they could hope for was resupply. Lyn shared the news at dinner, emphasizing it was not unexpected, but it was hard to miss the glare from Jeanne Cormier, her wife now visibly pregnant. A collective discouragement rippled through the ship.

They would reach the planet just when the Recyc-All needed new material. Lyn tensed at the delicate balance required, like when she and Tara climbed Maine's Mount Katahdin. They had reached the narrowest section of the aptly named Knife Edge Trail when the wind kicked up and nearly blew her off. She crouched and froze, not daring to look right or left. Each side dropped off more than six hundred meters, down a cascade of rough, lichen-strewn rock. Any misstep meant death. Tara had laughed from the thrill of the danger until a gust blew her to her knees. She clung to Lyn and together they'd crawled the route till the wind calmed enough for them to stand. Lyn wasn't sure what had frightened her more—the wind and drop off, or seeing Tara, even if only briefly, terrified.

Resupply missions commenced, this time using the *Jedica*, which reduced the number of trips needed and gave Ani valuable hours piloting the unfamiliar craft. That thrilled her no end. "I've been itching to get my hands on that puppy," she said.

A week later, with little fanfare, *Endurance* left Planet One and headed to the next candidate. Mission Control wound down and Ani went back to practicing her violin instead of landings and takeoffs. The hold was full of material and Natalie's computer filled with data.

With Edward's help, Diana's work progressed. They were building a small-scale particle collector, which she would use in her class. As far as Lyn knew, Edward still only thought of it as theoretical, for exotic matter, not T particles specifically. Once they were ready to build a full-scale device, she'd have to reveal their plans, but not until they knew it could work. Diana's improved mood was a bright spot, and Lyn felt her own mood lift when she was near her. Face it, Randall, Lyn thought, you like her.

THROUGHOUT AUGUST, EVERYONE became hyperaware there was a pregnant woman on board about to give birth. This would be a first for Omara Tours. Lyn peppered the doctor with questions. What if she hemorrhages? What if the baby is breeched? What if, what if? He couldn't be offended, and she felt better with each reassuring answer. This wasn't just his or Omara's reputation at stake, a woman's life was on the line. Medicine had come a long way in the last hundred years, but giving birth was still dangerous.

The day came when Sharyn called Lyn to the Medical Suite. Sharyn met her in the hallway, hands up. She said Suzanne had gone into labor but Jeanne was insisting Lyn stay away.

"Then why did you call me here?" Lyn said.

"Suzanne asked for you. So there's a dilemma."

"That complicates things. I'm not about to intrude into their private family matters. This doesn't fall under my purview. It's really the doctor's domain."

"I'm not sure Jeanne trusts him," Sharyn said.

"But Suzanne does, as far as I know."

Sharyn nodded.

Lyn had her send Jeanne out.

"Madame Cormier, I understand congratulations are about to be due."

"Don't 'madame' me. Do you even speak French?" Gone was the fuzzy warmth. Anger radiated from her.

"No, but I don't think that's what's bothering you. How about you be blunt with me."

Jeanne stepped closer, lowered her voice, and said, not gently, "My wife is about to give birth and do you know what she wants? She wants to forgive you. She wants to tell you that if she dies, you are not to blame."

Lyn took a half-step back. "What do you mean if she dies? What makes her think that? I'm sure everything—"

Jeanne shook her head, tears forming. "You idiot. I know what you are doing. I saw through that ridiculous Avatar sim. You dare put my family at risk." She turned away.

Lyn stood, dumbfounded. What the hell was going on? Then it dawned on her. It wasn't Suzanne who was scared. She touched Jeanne's shoulder. "Please, go be with your wife. We can talk later."

Sharyn stuck her head out the door and beckoned to Jeanne. "It's time."

Jeanne wiped her face, glanced at Lyn with an expression equal parts fear and rage, and went inside. Sharyn stepped into the corridor. "How'd it go?"

Lyn shook her head. "Beats me." She looked at the closed door to the Medical Suite. "Call me when you have news. No point in my standing here."

After dinner, Sharyn called Lyn back to Medical. She opened the curtain. Suzanne, tired but happy, held a baby. Jeanne sat on the other side, tired but relieved.

"I thought you should meet your newest passenger," Suzanne said.

And there she was, the miracle of birth. Lyn's heart melted to see the scrunched up face, the tiny fists. A new human. "She's beautiful."

"We have named her Hope," Jeanne said. She didn't look at Lyn but at her new daughter and beloved wife.

PLANET TWO, TOLIMAN C, proved as disappointing as the first. Dusty rock, no tectonic activity, no atmosphere. All it had going for it was gravity. If they had to build a self-contained shelter, they could, but it would be difficult and only marginally better than staying on *Endurance*. But it did present an option. Lyn was grateful for that. Instead, they resupplied and moved on.

By mid-October, Natalie optimistically reported the preliminary findings for the third and final planet in the habitable zone. She detected an atmosphere. Lyn held back her own enthusiasm. They were months away yet, but just in case, she asked Marc to dust off the planetary protection guidelines and to work with Edward on adaptations they'd have to make to meet them. As a counterweight, she also put Isabel in charge of planning a build-out of *Endurance*, should it come to that.

As the calendar turned to December, Lyn steeled herself for the anniversary of the event that remained as mysterious as when it happened. She worried for Diana, knowing how hard anniversaries could be. Sitting in the command seat, staring at the screen that showed nothing but distant stars and a tiny dot that was their destination, she reflected that a year ago she'd been in this seat chatting with Captain Bratt. Who would soon be dead, along with thousands of others. Why us? she thought. What tenuous thread of humanity broke that caused the chaos that led to their deaths? How could Lyn keep that thread intact?

The day passed somberly, everyone was quieter than usual. The room used for the memorial service back in February had become a de facto chapel/meditation room. Lyn stepped inside and sat at the back. People came and went. Music played softly, varying through classical to religious to soft modern. No one spoke, but she could feel their presence.

At dinner, she stood and clinked her glass. "I wanted to share some thoughts—"

"No!" a shout from the back of the room, near the kitchen. Mr. Ivey stood. He pointed an accusing finger at Lyn. "We don't want to hear any more 'inspirational' speeches, *Captain*."

Eyes darted from him to her, many faces showing confusion, but some nodding their approval.

Mr. Ivey turned to Jeanne Cormier. "Tell her! Tell her what we want."

Jeanne stood, folded her napkin, and placed it by her plate. She adjusted the sleeves of her flight suit then clasped her hands behind her back. "It would seem that I am to be a spokesperson. Please know that these are not my thoughts alone." She glanced around the room. Heads nodded. Her warm, confident façade was back in place.

"What is it you wish to say?" Lyn asked.

"It's very simple, really. A good portion of us believe we should turn toward Earth."

"Pointless, but continue."

"Not pointless. We believe you know what caused this and know how to get back. That she," a gesture toward Diana, "knows how." Murmurs from around the room from those clearly stunned, as was Lyn.

"What makes you believe that?"

"She's been working, hidden away on the Observation Deck, but her classes are rote lectures, like we're students at her so-called institute. We're not stupid." She turned to Diana. "We want to know what you know."

Here it was. The moment Lyn hoped to avoid. What made her think she could keep Diana's work secret? To Jeanne, she said, "Please explain who 'we' are."

Jeanne looked around the room. People stood. Not all from a table, not both members of a couple. Suzanne, notably, remained seated, but she was holding their infant. By Lyn's estimate almost a quarter of the room rose to their feet. She glanced at Sharyn who looked stricken. How had this fomenting anger gotten past them?

"Very well," Lyn said. "You know Doctor Squires—"

"Don't speak for her," Jeanne said. "We want her to explain this."

Lyn wilted inwardly. Before she could speak, Diana stood.

"You don't have to do this," Lyn said.

"I'm happy to explain what I've been doing," Diana said, facing the room full of glares. "For those who are unfamiliar with my research," she smiled and glanced around the room, "since I see only a handful have attended my lectures, I study wormholes." A murmur arose. "Yes, you think you know what that means—that a wormhole might be how we got here and I might know how to make one and get us back." She chuckled softly. She had moved behind her chair, but her hands gripped the back, tendons taut from the pressure. "I wish that were true. I do think I know what brought us here and it may well have been a wormhole, but not one we could control. The thing is, I'm a theoretical physicist, I don't do direct experiments. So here's what I *think* happened—and please know there's no way to test this theory."

All Lyn could do was mentally beg her not to mention T particles or her parents' research, and since Diana didn't have an Omara-licensed mind link, the begging remained internal. For the next half hour, Diana repeated almost everything she'd told Lyn. That a naturally occurring disk of dark matter in the galaxy could have caused a spacequake—the audience giggled at that term—

and opened a wormhole. As she spoke, her death grip on the seat loosened. People interrupted her with questions, and she answered them patiently. She let go of the chair as she explained concepts. As she droned on, and made no mention of her parents or T particles, Lyn relaxed. She glanced toward Edward, fearful he'd chime in with a fix to this problem or realize what he'd really been working on. He sat quiet, nodding occasionally.

"One year ago, my wife died in this event." Diana paused. "Captain Randall has been kind enough to let me continue my research as a way to deal with my grief. You have no idea how much I wish I held the magic wand that could take us home." Another pause. The tension in the room eased visibly, those standing shifted uneasily, and one by one they sat back down, leaving Jeanne alone. "I'll gladly answer more questions." The room went quiet.

Dae Canno stood and looked at Jeanne. "I trust this satisfies your craving for answers," he said then turned to Lyn. "I, for one, am with the captain and look forward to continuing our exploration of this solar system. I hope this last planet we're heading for will be able to support us. But if not, well, I'll do whatever Captain Randall asks of me." He sat down.

Jeanne had remained standing throughout the session. Her expression didn't change much. Perhaps a slight increase in the color in her cheeks. Diana had gotten through to most people, and perhaps that was bad news for Jeanne. Lyn could only speculate what her motives were.

"I'm glad you said something," Lyn said to Jeanne. "If we don't express our feelings and opinions, we can't possibly know what each other is going through." She turned to the others. "Feel free to speak to me or my staff about anything that troubles you. We only have each other. This has been a long, tough trip, but one way or another, we'll get through." She waited to see if anything more would be said. Jeanne sat and took the baby from Suzanne. "If there's nothing else, I believe Natalie will be giving a talk during dessert."

Lyn forced herself to stay in her seat through Natalie's presentation when all she wanted to do was gather her staff and Diana and grill them on what they knew of this building resentment. She messaged Marc to have everyone meet later.

Sharyn arrived last. "Sorry, Boss, but I wanted to check my bot reports for any clues this was coming. I hadn't thought to specifically watch what Jeanne was up to."

"I'm not concerned you didn't know about this ahead of time, but if you can find anything, that'll help."

"There's a lot to go through and I'll have more in the morning, but it seems she's been having casual conversations at meals and in the exercise room that in retrospect could be significant. But she's always smiling and seems so intimately confident. Nothing stands out as plotting a mutiny."

"But she has willing ears," Marc said.

"It seems so, judging by the number of people who stood with her," Sharyn said. "Not surprising, I suppose, given she's a Follow."

"She's a Follow?" Lyn asked.

"Has a show, *Follow Me*. Millions of viewers. In addition to her life coach business. Sort of a travelogue and interview show. Big personalities. The latest trendy places to go. The Grand Tour would have put her in the upper tier of Follows."

"Suzanne said the tour was a belated honeymoon," Lyn said.

Sharyn shrugged. "Maybe that, too."

"We've had a major celebrity on board all this time and I didn't know it?" Lyn asked.

"I mentioned it during the pre-trip briefing," Sharyn said, sounding a little impatient. "I doubt it would have stuck, given how unimpressed you are with Follows." She smiled disarmingly.

"Who's heard of her?" Lyn asked the others.

"The show rings a bell, now that you mention it," Miriam said. "I've watched a few of her restaurant tours. I confess I cared more about the food."

Natalie shook her head. "Never heard of her, but I follow Nifemi, in Nigeria."

"So a minor celebrity," Sharyn said.

"Did your bots capture the faces of those who stood?" Lyn asked.

"Yes, as soon as I saw what was happening, I messaged the servers to aim and record. I've sent you the list."

Lyn turned to Diana. "Thank you for your composure in handling her demand."

"Is that really all you are doing?" Isabel asked Diana.

Diana's confused expression could be real or acting, Lyn wasn't sure. "What do you mean?"

"I'm wondering if Ms. Cormier had a valid point. Were you completely honest in your explanation?" She looked at Edward. "Maybe you could fill us in on how you've been helping her?"

"We don't have time for this right now. It's late, we can continue in the morning." Lyn glanced at Marc in that meaningful way to indicate he should stay behind.

The others left.

"Let's go to my office. I could use some coffee," Lyn said. Settled on her couch, she asked, "Time to let her in on our secret?"

"Up to you, but I don't see why not. Judging by Jeanne's outburst, I'm concerned we're eroding trust."

"With you two in a relationship, which is fine with me, I'm concerned Isabel's less than positive attitude could become a problem if she knew what was going on."

Marc sat forward, elbows on knees, hands clasped. Relaxed but not. "You don't trust her, so you feel free to violate the trust you should have with your senior staff. That's rich. No wonder she's less than positive."

Lyn had fought with Tara for withholding the real reason for their mission to Enceladus. She'd vowed never to make that mistake, especially with her senior officers. "You're right, of course, and she knows something's going on. How do you think she'll react?"

"Pissed, at first, at being kept in the dark, but I think she might be able to help. How has Edward not told everyone what he's doing?"

"He has. No one listens. I framed it as a problem for him to solve for Diana's class. He's chattered on about folding space and building machines, but everyone tunes him out because it's at such a granular scale. Didn't you hear him describe the knob he was designing? It's for a T-particle accelerator."

"That's what that was about?" Marc chuckled.

Lyn was relieved to see him relax. She told him that for obvious reasons, she'd speak to Isabel alone.

When Isabel arrived, she stood by the door, hands clasped behind her back. Tense.

"Please," Lyn said, indicating a chair at her small table, "can I get you anything?"

Isabel paused long enough to pique Lyn's sense of protocol. A slight hesitation to obey the request of a senior officer does not go unnoticed. Isabel sat, tense. "No, thank you."

Lyn poured herself another cup of coffee and sat, braced for a knock-down drag-out if necessary. "I should have told you what was going on before now. Know my reason for not doing so has nothing to do with your status or performance or even your past questioning of my decisions."

Isabel looked up, startled.

Lyn went on. "The fact is, Diana *was* completely honest in her explanation. She just didn't reveal everything."

Isabel's mouth quirked in an I-knew-it smile. Lyn proceeded to tell her what Diana and Edward were working on, that Edward assumed it really was a class project, but withholding Diana's true identity. Isabel listened carefully, quietly. Her only reaction to the truth of the work, to open a wormhole and get them home, was an intake of breath and slight flush of her face.

"I know you think I have a bad attitude," Isabel said, reading Lyn accurately, "but my intentions have never been to do anything that would harm our survival." She broke eye contact and looked at her hands in her lap. "I'm not very good at expressing myself in a constructive manner." She returned her gaze to Lyn's. "You aren't the first to point that out."

Lyn didn't dismiss her admission, but acknowledged it with a slight nod. "Edward's time on this project will only increase, so anything you can do to relieve his other responsibilities and help him maintain confidentiality would be extremely helpful. Marc knows, of course." Lyn watched for Isabel's reaction. She blinked and nodded slightly. "You are welcome to review the work, and if you have any ideas, can serve as someone to bounce ideas off, give another perspective, that would also be welcome."

Isabel relaxed back into the chair. "I can do that."

Isabel could be a strong ally, Lyn knew, if she wanted to be one. "To be clear, I'm under no illusions this might actually work. Diana insists it's a very long shot, but I think it's worth a try. If we find a planet, that will be our priority. I hope you can go along with that."

A brisk nod. "My goal is the same as yours, the safety and survival of everyone. We might only differ on the nuances to achieve that."

AFTER JEANNE'S OUTBURST, Lyn started watching past episodes of her show. It took a few to get past the sickeningly sweet opening music, the soft focus, the warm colors of the set, made to look like an intimate living room, Jeanne seated on a comfortable couch. Repeated, it served to lull Lyn's defenses. Then Jeanne's warm voice, the genuine smile, and shy way she'd glance to the side all served to soften the brain into accepting her advice, which, when Lyn stopped to analyze it, amounted to not much at all. "Embrace the goodness that surrounds you," she said in quiet urgency, leaning forward, as if confiding in a close friend. "All good things will come if you are open to the light." Some of the advice was quite sound. Notice how you react to a difficult personality. Is it really them or is it you reflecting back, painfully. "Unless this person has power over you, think about your feelings, examine them, turn them over in your hand like this stone." She palmed a smooth river stone, polished by constant abrasions, her metaphor. Lyn rolled her eyes. She found the travel shows more interesting, and Miriam was right, the food and chef interviews made her mouth water. As she clicked off the tenth or twentieth show, she'd lost track and they blurred together, she could see how addictive they were. Jeanne always managed to end each show with a question or entreaty that made you want to tune in again. "Together, let's explore . . ." or "How would you handle . . . ?"

Lyn was surprised, then, when Petra asked her if she wanted to view a more recent episode. "What do you mean?"

"She continues to transmit shows," Petra said.

Well, why not? Lyn thought. So what if they'd take four years to arrive. That hadn't stopped her from sending messages home or to Omara. Likely everyone on board was doing that.

"Rack 'em up," Lyn said.

"Pardon?"

"That's old slang," Lyn said. "Based on the game of pool. Now it means please add them to my queue."

The first shows, transmitted before the event, were typical of her travelogues. She gushed about the Grand Tour, showed off the ship, and extolled the virtues of a small-ship versus the behemoths on the tour. Suzanne, Lyn noticed, was never included in the shows. She had gone on about this being their honeymoon, an intimate getaway from the kids. Did she even know Jeanne continued to work? There was a significant gap, no doubt encompassing the emergency and Jeanne needing time to regroup. Had she considered ending her show? Clearly not with the next one, a month after the event, that made no mention of the stricken *Aphrodite*.

"We are in new territory, my friends. This message may or may not take longer to reach you, but I will never abandon you." Jeanne spoke in vague terms about their situation, more metaphorical than literal. Her undeniable message was that your fate was in your hands, which anyone could appreciate unless you were trapped on a small ship four light years from home, and your fate lay in the hands of a captain whose motive you didn't know or trust.

In the end, mostly because Lyn had seen a side of Jeanne never depicted in her shows—combative, suspicious, angry—she was left with an impression of a cool operator, manipulative but also possessing a genuine warmth. Whether she was the real thing but stressed beyond breaking by the severing of her family, or a conniving bitch willing to do anything for fame and followers, remained to be seen.

AS THEY APPROACHED Planet Three, Toliman d, Natalie's enthusiasm grew, but Lyn shut down any speculation. She simply didn't want to know until they had the facts. Natalie kept quiet until the evening she called Lyn to the Obs Lab. "We have something to show you."

Natalie and Diana stood by the optical telescope, chatting and grinning.

"We couldn't meet on the bridge?" Lyn asked.

"Your eyes first, Captain," Natalie said. "The old-fashioned way."

Lyn peered through the telescope at a bright blue planet. Clouds swirled over what were surely land masses. Blue oceans. She'd seen this view many times. It was the face of a long-lost loved one. "What the?" She jerked back, her knees weak. "How is that possible?" She looked from Natalie to Diana. "Earth?"

Chapter 21

"NO," NATALIE SAID quickly. "Not Earth. It's Toliman d."

"What?" Lyn pulled up a chair and sat, dizzy and breathless, as though from the rush of a plane speeding down the runway, gravity clinging then breaking free. "Planet Three?"

"Right, not Earth," Diana said. She knelt in front of Lyn and took her hands.

Lyn closed her eyes, forcing her breath to slow. Her pounding heart eased. She was surprised at how she had reacted. She opened her eyes. "I guess I miss home more than I thought."

"I'm so sorry to disappoint you," Diana said.

"But it's good, right?"

Diana nodded. Natalie grinned. "Very good. We've detected volcanic activity, and there's tectonic movement, which means there's a carbon cycle, which means—"

"Did you see the polar ice caps?" Diana added. She sprang back up and hauled Lyn with her. "No one's seen that for decades on Earth."

"Cut to the chase, please," Lyn said. Diana had released her but the warmth tingled her fingers, like an imprint.

"Life," Natalie said. "It's very likely the planet supports life."

"Could the blue be oceans?" Lyn asked.

"Yes, but even better, an atmosphere of carbon dioxide and oxygen. That means plants. Maybe animals."

Lyn's mind raced. She looked through the telescope again. So many thoughts surfacing at once. She sputtered out partial questions. "How big, mass, I mean . . ."

"I'm collecting data," Natalie said. "We're still a couple weeks away from dropping a probe."

"Life," Lyn said, her mind catching up. "Is there a chance there's intelligent life?"

"We don't know yet, but doubtful," Diana said. "There's no sign of orbiting satellites or electronic transmissions. But, of course, we'll need to decide how to proceed. And we'll be bringing our own microbes."

"And it will have microbes we know nothing about," Natalie said. She stared out the window in the direction of the planet. "In some ways, a barren rock would be better than one filled with life we're not adapted to."

"It could be too dangerous to live on," Lyn said. The excitement was ebbing.

"Possibly," Natalie said. "We should be prepared, based on what we find."

"Understood. So, two weeks." She looked at them. The shock had worn off, replaced by anticipation. Still, this was monumental. "Congratulations!" She reached to give Natalie a hug. The taller woman bent awkwardly. The hug with Diana was also awkward, but for different reasons. Lyn had first hugged her when she was bereft, a fragile bird. Now the press of Diana's body against her was intended to be joyous, and it was, but the wave that swept her wasn't only from the excitement of the blue marble outside their window. This was deeper. She knew what it meant. She regained her wits before it went on too long to be innocent, but she had to let go first. Rein it in, Randall, she told herself, pulling her gaze away from Diana's bright eyes and flushed cheeks. Focus on the planet.

To the naked eye, it was a dot. She took another look through the telescope.

"This isn't the only scope on board," she said, straightening. "Let's keep a lid on this for tonight." She glanced toward the open door then turned to Natalie. "But assume we'll make the announcement after dinner tomorrow."

"Christmas," Natalie said.

Is it? "Right. A nice present, don't you think?"

NATALIE STOOD RESPLENDENT in a crisply shaped *gele* of warm colors, what had long been known as earth tones but might need a new name. Brown and blue and white. Yes, of Earth, but also of this new place. Lyn watched the faces as they took in Natalie's words. Habitable. Life. Uncertain for sure, much more to learn, but here it was, hope. A collective gasp followed by cheers flowed through the room, reflected off the walls, down from the ceiling, growing like a wave rising toward shore. Questions surfaced above the noisy tide. Natalie explained the process Lyn and her staff had hashed out that morning. They would proceed with great caution and care. A small team would take the *Jedica* to scan the surface carefully, looking for an isolated place to land. Natalie's emphasis on caution and slow steps couldn't stem the rolling crash of enthusiasm.

The room filled to bursting with hope, and Lyn realized the growing claustrophobia was not hers alone. Truly, thin walls were all that separated them from lethal space. Her breathing quickened as the pressure of all that laughter and crying and shouted questions pushed on her chest, like her brothers' pig pile on young Lynnie. Would the walls hold? Natalie stopped speaking and raised her hands in supplication. Slowly the room quieted, the pressure eased.

Oh, how she wanted to open a window, feel a cool breeze. Tip her face toward sky and clouds, feel rain on her cheeks, not stare at the close, dull ceiling barely an arm's reach away. To walk on ground, uneven, rocky, muddy, anything but firm carpet or smooth tile. *Endurance* was no generation ship. Humans, evolved on the savannah and in the forest, could never survive contained within a pressurized hull. What had she been thinking? That they could build out a space station. Even Ernest Shackleton, in his own stranded *Endurance*, trapped in the Antarctic ice, had been able to leave the ship and walk on something other than the wood deck. Until the ship was crushed, as this *Endurance* could well be or, worse, exploded, like the *Aphrodite*. How precious this shell was that surrounded them.

Attention ceded back to Natalie, and she resumed describing how they'd send a probe to the surface, what they'd need to find before they followed with a team. No one cared about the quarantine regimen, Lyn could tell. The rapt faces were, like hers, focused on imagining life outside of this floating tin can. So enthralled they barely paused when Natalie mentioned potentially hazardous microbes. That's what medbots were for, right? Earth's own past of wiping out cultures with infectious diseases spread by colonizers was too distant a memory.

What Natalie didn't mention was Edward's request to stay on board *Endurance*, to never set foot on a planet teeming with its own life, an alien life no matter how benign. At the morning staff meeting, the doctor had described ways to adapt the humans' immune system and medbots. Edward remained unconvinced. No doubt he wouldn't be the only one suspicious of new terrain, but how could they manage without their chief engineer? She'd noticed Isabel perk up at his announcement. Maybe she was up to the task.

Lyn woke from her daydream by the flow of humanity passing her table like it was a stone in a stream. Up to the Observation Lab for a look, Natalie had promised. By the time Lyn reached the hallway, the line to view the planet snaked out the door and down the stairs. She went up the back stairs, not to cut the line, but to find a quiet seat and watch their reactions, remembering her own. At least they'd been better prepared, she thought with a wry chuckle.

"It's so beautiful!" Nikoleta Canno gushed.

Jeanne and Suzanne took turns, one looking through the scope, the other holding the now four-month-old baby, who squirmed restlessly, oblivious to the strangeness of where she was or how she got there. Jeanne seemed puzzled. She looked through the eyepiece, then at the scope itself, its settings, then out the window, squinting as though to see the planet with her naked eye. Then she glanced at Lyn, a frown forming, but Hope yipped and Suzanne thrust the child at her. Jeanne found a seat while Suzanne took a last turn, a smile widening on her face. What a contrast, Lyn thought. Who would the child take after?

Diana sat in her corner, back to her desk. Guarding it. Her space was tidy, maybe she'd cleaned up for the throngs passing through or because it was time.

There wasn't a lot of room to maneuver, never mind a hundred people passing through. They milled about, Natalie rushing over if it looked like someone was about to lean on another scope. Eventually everyone filed past Lyn and down the back stairs or back out to the elevator. A few stopped to chat. Yes, very exciting news, she said over and over.

Then it was down to her and Diana. Natalie had replaced the dust cover over the optics and said goodnight. Lyn couldn't bring herself to leave. She moved to the couch facing the window, at a tiny bright dot. Diana joined her.

"It's a relief, isn't it?" Diana said, nodding toward the planet.

"How so?" Lyn asked.

"Less pressure to get us back now that there's hope we can survive here. You look relieved, too." She held Lyn's gaze. "It suits you."

Lyn looked out the window. "I'm not sure what I feel."

A WEEK LATER, as midnight neared, Lyn slipped out of the dining room. Nothing more awkward for the New Year's kiss than finding yourself next to your boss, captain. Sharyn and Miriam had put together a hell of a party. Alcohol was the main attraction, Miriam had pointed out, and easy to upcycle, so she made copious amounts of spirits and her destined-to-be-signature "shampagne." Snacks filled tables and soft music played. Stars lit the windows. In the Star Bar, booze flowed. In various classrooms impromptu groups sang and played instruments. Other rooms became quiet enclaves. The Paddock became a dance hall with a live band and Ani on fiddle. Marc and Isabel danced slow. They looked happy, her head tucked under his chin, arms around each other. He'll be good for her, Lyn thought. Edward chatted with the Fischers, Ruby's leg long since healed.

The booze warmed her, the medbots ensuring her blood alcohol level never exceeded the limit of rationality. Too bad. She'd love to get roaring drunk right now. Instead, she went up to the bridge, relieving Sophia. "Go have some fun," she said.

She relaxed in her seat. No one *needed* to be on the bridge, Petra could monitor their steady course. She put on music then flipped through her playlists unable to decide on a genre. Vocals, classical, vintage rock? The sound of the door to the bridge opening prompted her to mute it.

"I'd wondered where you'd gone." Diana held a bottle of shampagne and two stemmed champagne flutes. She plopped herself into the first mate's seat like they'd run into each other at a party. She slouched, relaxed. "Hiding out?" she said with a tease.

"Time for the parent to let the kids have their unsupervised playtime."

Diana slid her a sideways half-smile. "I don't think of you as a parent."

"Nevertheless."

"How about some adult time?" Diana held a glass out.

Lyn took it and Diana filled both glasses.

"A toast," she said.

"To a new year," Lyn answered.

Diana shook her head. "To a new *life*."

They clinked. Diana took a large swallow and grinned. Her flight suit top was unzipped, revealing the form-fitting undershirt that, Lyn realized, was surprisingly sexy. She gulped her drink. Diana's eyebrows rose.

"Didn't think I'd drink on the bridge?"

"Why, Lyn, you subversive," Diana said.

Lyn took another gulp, finishing off the glass. Never mind the medbots, it warmed and relaxed her. She wouldn't be denied all benefits of the beverage.

Diana refilled her glass. She sipped her own. "Been a hell of a year, hasn't it."

"You got that right."

Diana set the bottle on the floor between them and swirled her glass. "Let's not talk about work, about *Endurance,* or where we are. It's almost a new year, what would your plans have been?"

"If not for work or *Endurance*?" Lyn said with a smirk. What could she say? That she'd be retired now? Packing up her house in Bodega Bay and moving to Montana? Party or not, any impression she gave would last. Plus, what would Diana have been planning if not for work and *Endurance*? Her life with Rose. "More of the same, I suppose," she said in the end.

"I'd probably be teaching." Diana made a sour face. "Okay, let's look forward. What do you suppose we'll be doing next New Year's Eve?"

Lyn chuckled softly and leaned her head back. She tilted her face toward Diana. "It'd be nice if we were home. As in back on Earth."

Diana pulled a knee up and turned to Lyn. "Wouldn't that be something? But we can't speculate further without talking about work, so off limits."

Lyn took another swallow, thinking. There wasn't anything that wouldn't remind them of the horror of what happened or make them wistful for things they miss. Family. Home. What's left when everything is gone? "Blank slate, then. Starting over." She examined Diana's face, at once familiar and a total mystery. "You first."

Diana finished her drink. "Assuming we're talking blank slate, I'll assume anything before the last year is off limits."

"Not necessarily."

Diana shook her head. "My turn, my rules."

"Yes, ma'am."

"If I were to start over—no past—I think I'd forget all this theoretical shite. I actually do like teaching—better than doing." She sighed out a half laugh and set her glass on the floor. "I love science. Maybe I'd teach physics. High school, though. None of these privileged college brats. Do you know how many kids lose interest in science in high school? That's the moment that matters. That's when the spark is lit and the fire needs to be tended—just the right kindling, just the right amount of oxygen. Too much of either or too little and it snuffs out. Wouldn't it be great to ignite that spark and build that fire." She leaned closer to Lyn. "What would you give to be present at the Big Bang?"

"The Big Bang?"

"That moment of ultimate creativity. The event horizon. That's what I'd like to do."

"You've lost me."

She stood and leaned against the railing, facing Lyn. "I have no interest in becoming my parents. I've run from that, but teaching at the university level is like throwing wood chips onto a raging fire. By the time students get there, they know what they want to be doing and they just want the professors to get out of their way. I know I did. It makes no difference what I do there. You could throw wet logs onto a bonfire and it won't make a damn bit of difference."

"You may have a point."

Diana's gaze drifted somewhere behind Lyn. "I think being away from Earth has given me a new appreciation for the work that can and needs to be done. We literally trashed that planet. We balled it up and tossed it into the bin." She put her hands over her face. "I got so sick of seeing images of the before, when the oceans were filled with fish and there were forests and animals and glaciers. That's partly why we moved to Mars."

"It's what my dad is working to fix."

"I know." Diana dropped her hands and met Lyn's gaze. "That's what we should be doing. Not diddling around the solar system." She paused. "Sorry, no offense. I mean, what Omara does with her tours is at least a bit educational. But even on Mars, I could see we were not respecting the planet. Why does everything need to be conquered?"

Once again, this was Diana, stripped of her grief and the self-pity, revealing a passion Lyn hadn't seen since Tara, who lived on in Lyn's own layer of grief and self-doubt. What might she be like if she could step outside that shroud?

Diana shoved her hands in her pockets. "What about you? No past. Just future."

What did she want? Time. Time to think before running. She'd fled her grief over Duncan, she'd fled her grief over Tara. What did she have to offer other than grief? "It's not that simple."

"Isn't it?"

Lyn closed her eyes. "I want."

Take the idealist Lyn before Pulsar, meld her to the wiser Lyn now. What would she want? Someone to love, who loved her, who was there for her through thick and thin, who would save her butt even when she didn't deserve it. Who wouldn't leave. And to do the same for them because two people together were stronger than each alone.

She opened her eyes. "I want what I've always wanted. To make a difference."

Diana's eyes were locked on her. Neither spoke nor moved. Lyn tried to look away but couldn't. She wasn't sure what Diana's soft expression was telling her till she leaned forward, placing a hand on each armrest, her face close, eyes dark. Then she knew and also knew nothing could make her stop it. Diana's kiss was soft and tentative but passed between them like an electric charge. Lips parted as an invitation, a beckoning Lyn wouldn't resist. In this moment, in this universe, no rules were broken. They kissed more intensely. The charge became a thrumming, beautiful synchronicity. Time ceased to exist. She had no past, no future, only expanding desire.

Then Diana touched her cheek and a screaming klaxon dragged Lyn out of this lovely dream. The edge collapsed, time closed in with a shattering realization. *Ohmygod! What have I done?* She pushed Diana back.

"No," she said with a painful exhale.

The sound of Diana's breath rushing out of her. No klaxon. The room was silent. Lyn couldn't take that time back. It unspooled into a terrible tangle. All she could do was cut the line.

"This can't happen. I'm sorry."

Her hands were on Diana's collarbones, inches away from the soft skin of her cheek that she wanted to stroke. This could be so easy. Pull her back. Lyn wanted this more than anything. More than going home. With every molecule of her being.

Diana's smile showed surprise, not at the rebuff, she didn't believe that yet. "It's okay, no one's here." She looked up at the door as if to confirm.

Lyn put a hand up. The only reservoir of strength she had to draw on was protocol. The rules. No exceptions. "Whatever you think happened didn't."

Diana let go of the armrests and straightened. "Wait. You kissed me back—"

"Again, I'm sorry if you misunderstood." It felt cruel, this shield she raised.

"What's going on? I thought . . . Can we talk about this?"

"No, actually. I apologize if I gave you the wrong message, but there's nothing to talk about."

For Diana's part, she didn't appear crushed, but she didn't leave, she stood her ground and looked at Lyn. She raised her hands in surrender. "I'm sorry. I didn't mean . . ." She paused, considering. "Is it okay for us to be friends, or did I misunderstand that too?" Her hands went back into her pockets. Her tone was a challenge, not hurt. She would not be that easily undone.

Lyn gasped for air. "This ship and everyone on board are my responsibility. Every decision I make must encompass the entirety of that responsibility. No exceptions." She might as well have been reciting from the manual.

Diana leaned away, like avoiding a slap. No exceptions. She drew herself up. "Understood, Captain." She turned for the door. "Happy New Year."

Music from the Paddock drifted through the open door, then quiet as it shut. She was gone. *Frak.*

Slowly Lyn's pulse returned to normal. She left Petra in charge, grabbed the wine, and went to her quarters. She poured a glass and collapsed in a chair by the window. Many things freaked her out. She was attracted to Diana. Big whoop. She'd had crushes on a lot of women and nothing had come of it. It hadn't occurred to her Diana might feel the same way. Now Lyn had to deal with the facts: *She kissed me. She kissed me because she wanted to. She kissed me because she wanted to and there was nothing stopping her. Not Rose, not her place on* Endurance. *She was not staff, not a guest. Apparently no longer grieving. At least not in that moment.*

Maybe it had been a one-off, over and done with. Too much wine. Nothing to worry about. But if it wasn't, if Diana really cared for her, then she'd have to deal with that. How? Say to hell with being captain? Then what? She'd worry about every decision she made or let Marc take over. He'd love it. He might do fine. But Omara didn't make him captain. She put Lyn in charge, the tour was her responsibility. She couldn't just drop it for a lover. And if it didn't result in happily ever after? What then? What would she have sacrificed? Possibly the lives of everyone on board.

Not an option. Case closed. Shite, what a mess she'd made.

Chapter 22

LYN COULD UNTANGLE one thread before moving on. She needed to talk to Marc. Not for advice. For trust. She told him about the kiss.

His face lit up. "How nice for you." Then he saw her expression. "So this isn't a good thing?"

"No, it's not." What, exactly, had he seen? Disapproval or disappointment? How she wanted it to be a good thing. Marc and Isabel being together was hardly noticeable to the rest of the crew. They seemed to know how to tread that line and both were benefiting. She simply couldn't take that chance. Not yet. Maybe never. "I thought you should know. Nothing more will come of it, and it won't affect her work or my oversight of that work. But if you prefer I not supervise her, just say so."

They sat facing each other across her desk. She couldn't read his expression.

"No, I think I have enough to do without taking on T," Marc finally said. "Plus, it's your call ultimately, regardless of how you feel about her. I trust you'll let me know if you think it's getting out of hand."

Very formal, professional. His glint of friendly support was gone. There would be no double dates. Too bad. She liked the idea of being friends with Marc.

That done, the next was decidedly more awkward. Rather than call Diana to her office—how high school—she went to her in the lab. She stood by Diana's desk. "I know I said I wouldn't talk about it, but I need to know whether you feel uncomfortable now. I can have someone else oversee your work."

Diana's expression wasn't as mysterious as Marc's. More, yeah, so what. "I get it. *Endurance* comes first. Always will. Don't worry, I'm a big girl. My feelings aren't hurt."

Was it bad that a part of Lyn wanted Diana to fight for her?

TENSION AND ENERGY aboard *Endurance* increased as the distance to the planet lessened. Dinner chatter rose in volume and speculation. Would they be able to make a new home? What would they call it? Sharyn agreed to a naming contest.

"We've had hints of these planets for more than a century," Natalie said during her evening talk, "but they weren't thought to be in the habitable zone. Further study was interrupted by the war." She smiled and paused for dramatic effect. "Obviously, we know better now."

The planet, she said, orbited Toliman every six Earth months. The star would appear larger than their home sun but wouldn't be significantly hotter since it was cooler, and with Rigil Kent visible, she didn't think there would ever be complete night. No moon meant short days—six to eight hours, but with the extra light, it shouldn't be freakish. Adjusting their circadian rhythms might be their biggest challenge. "At least, I hope that's all we have to worry about."

Zoya was delighted to dust off Mission Control. Ghez and Edward scanned the planet for signs of intelligent, communicating life. Lyn was relieved they heard nothing. Each day the telemetry brought more data. The mass was sufficient for gravity, about three-quarters of Earth's. It was within the Goldilocks zone, but that didn't mean it could sustain human life.

"ENTERING ORBIT, CAPTAIN," Ghez called to Lyn in her office. She went to the bridge and took the Con from Marc.

Natalie and Diana sat in the science section. Lyn sensed Marc watching her watching Diana. Truth was, her heart twinged every time she saw the woman. What might be? Why not?

"How's it look?" Lyn asked, shoving her heart back into its box.

"No space junk," Natalie said. "If there's life down there, it's not advanced enough for space travel."

"Or too smart to foul itself," Diana said.

"We're scanning now and ready to launch the probe," Natalie said.

While they waited for the data, Lyn reviewed Marc's recommendations for preventing contamination, both what they'd bring to the planet and what they might bring back. The *Jedica* remained relatively sterile, and descending through the atmosphere would burn off any microbes. On the ground, it was impossible to prevent contamination from themselves, even if they used fresh suits. Finding a home outweighed whatever risks they would bring, Lyn stressed. Until they knew the risks, the *Jedica* and crew would quarantine for forty-eight hours, enough time for any alien life they brought back to acclimate and grow or spring back to life. They'd sterilize or contain everything coming off ship. Suits and equipment would go right into the Recyc-All to be broken down into atoms. If the planet proved safe, or containable with their medbots, they could relax the standards.

Several hours later, Diana reported data coming from the probe. "Flyby altitude one hundred kilometers." She peered at the holographic readout. "Good news. We've got nitrogen, methane."

"Look at that," Natalie said, pointing.

"Whoa," Diana muttered.

"What?" Lyn asked, sitting forward.

"Organics," Natalie said. "Acetylene, hydrogen cyanide."

"That sounds dangerous," Marc said.

Natalie ignored him, focused on the readings. "Look, there."

Diana made a cooing sound. "CO_2, ethane, benzene. That definitely could be water down there."

"That sounds promising," Lyn said.

"We'll have a full map after a few orbits," Natalie said. "It'll be chilly, but within human tolerance. Topography looks rocky from here, but we'll have a better sense in a few hours."

MARC LED THE landing team with Ani piloting and Natalie as science officer. It was Marc's call, and he hadn't hesitated to pair them up. Natalie was the most experienced biologist and Ani the most experienced pilot, the only one with significant hours in the *Jedica*. Their mission was to search for a suitable, isolated landing spot, ideally an island, before setting down and taking samples. That was all. For the first time, they would step onto land for purposes other than collecting material for the Recyc-All. They would make history.

Lyn imagined explorers thousands of years from now reaching these planets and finding evidence that *Endurance* had been there first. She smiled. They'd probably feel like Robert Scott when he reached the South Pole only to discover the Norwegian flag flapping in the Antarctic wind. Or Tara at Enceladus, learning the Chinese had beaten them. Her smile vanished. Both had died on their expeditions.

"I don't have to tell you how important this is," she told them in the Paddock as they readied to leave. "But your safety comes first. Absolutely and final. Don't be heroes."

Isabel set up a link to the dining room for everyone to watch, and Ghez positioned *Endurance* so the planet was visible through the windows. The dining room feed was delayed in case they needed to cut it off for an emergency. Zoya sat in the first officer's seat. The woman looked old, was old, but her eyes held the excitement and joy of the young woman she was as mission chief for the first successful Mars landing a century earlier.

"Descending to twenty kilometers," Ani announced through the com link. "All systems go."

"Science reporting, telemetry data flowing," Natalie said. "Mapping in progress. We don't need data to see we've got flowing streams, plant life, and clouds."

As the *Jedica* made its way to the surface, Lyn relaxed, her training kicking in. This was the part she liked. The focus on the data, the concentration needed to fly the ship, each team member contributing to the success of the whole.

The hours passed in restless anticipation, the bridge crew settling into a new routine. Lyn stretched and paced, they rotated breaks, Zoya excused herself for a nap. Miriam sent meals to the bridge. Lyn's mind couldn't stop wandering to what might be waiting for them—a home, a chance to walk on ground, feel a breeze. She tried to shake off these thoughts, to not jinx their chances, but she kept returning to the idea of the finality of it all. If this worked out, they'd abandon Earth forever. Was she ready for that? Was anyone? It was the first time this option presented itself.

"I think we have our site," Marc announced. "An island roughly the size of, I'd say Madagascar. Well isolated from the two main continents. There's a large plateau with no tall vegetation for approximately three kilometers."

It'd been twelve hours. They had to be tiring.

"Go for landing at your discretion," Lyn said. "Take your time."

"Acknowledged."

Ani called off the meters. Information flowed, chatter about leveling, slowing, testing atmospheric conditions, winds, particulates.

"Looks like we'll land in time for sunrise," Marc said with a chuckle.

"Have some waffles before you go out," Lyn said.

"Fifty, twenty, ten." Ani read off the closing meters. A soft thunk came through the link. Silence. "The *Jedica* has landed." Ani's tone was bland and professional.

Yet hairs at the back of Lyn's neck prickled. She loosened her grip on the armrest and exhaled a long breath. Zoya, back beside her, squeezed her hand. Seconds later, she heard cheers through the link from the dining room.

Once Marc and Natalie suited up, their helmet cams displayed on the screens.

"Makes me feel like I'm there with you," Lyn said.

"We wish you were," Ani replied. "Maybe next time."

No landing team had encountered a planet this Earth-like. When Lyn thought she'd spend her career exploring space, she never envisioned traveling to another star, finding another Earth.

"No one trained for this," Zoya said to Lyn, "Because no one ever expected to see this. What a capstone to my career."

Lyn chuckled to think Dr. Zoya Betero, in her hundreds, was still thinking about her legacy. "A new chapter for your memoir."

"Indeed!"

"Those look like grasses blowing in a breeze," Ani reported before the others departed the ship. "This is incredible. Blue sky, clouds. When we passed through, the analysis showed they were water ice and vapor. You could fly a plane here, Captain."

Lyn thought of home. Her mother might be flying one of her antique planes right now over a Montana plateau much like this one. "Maybe I'll build one."

Marc and Natalie chatted as they readied to leave the ship. Ani would stay behind. They ran through checklists for life support and the supplies they needed.

"We're ready to exit," Natalie said.

Lyn heard the whoosh of the airlock. "Pressure equalized," Marc reported.

Soft whumps as the door opened and the stairs deployed. Five steps to a new world. She watched the feed from Marc's helmet cam. Bright daylight, a strong wind. This wasn't Earth, so she couldn't tell if colors were shifted due to the dimmer Toliman. Then Marc turned to Natalie and she saw the green Omara Tours suit. So far, the same.

Marc stepped onto firm ground. He tipped his head and Lyn saw grasslike . . . what? They didn't know yet if these were plants.

"Hope you're not stepping on a sentient being," she said.

"We could be," Natalie responded. "This is amazing."

Lyn switched to Natalie's view and watched as she knelt down and dug into the ground for a sample.

"These look like roots to me," she said. "There even appear to be fungal threads, or at least something not part of the roots. Fascinating."

Over the next hour they planted the Omara Tours flag and collected several containers of soil, rocks, and plants. Then Marc noted it was time to return to the ship.

"Seems a shame to leave so soon after such a long journey," Natalie said.

"Not to mention the forty-eight hours of quarantine, we're facing," Ani added.

"That's enough to keep the doctor and you busy for days," Lyn replied. "Get back here safely. The trip isn't a success until you do."

After taking off, Ani flew low over the plain before widening her spiral to take in more of the island. Scrubby, pine-like trees, if that's what they were, surrounded the flat plain. The sides dropped off a steep cliff then undulated to the coastline.

"Check this out," Ani said as she flew by a waterfall.

"Enough of the sightseeing. Get back here so we can do this again," Lyn said.

"Roger that," Ani responded.

WHILE MARC, NATALIE, and Ani remained aboard the *Jedica*, Dr. Amos examined their finds in a sealed-off section of his office. He found the air was breathable, no *known* microbial activity in the soil, which they expected since what they needed to worry about were unknown microbes.

"Evolution on this planet seems to have followed a course remarkably similar to Earth's," he said. "We have water-based cellular activity, meaning life grew, as on Earth, from simple cells to more complex organisms."

"Not really surprising," Natalie said by vid link to Lyn and the doctor in his office. "Assuming the same beginning, a similar trajectory could be expected."

"But to have the same conditions to start with," the doctor said. "Think about our solar system. Many of the same conditions, but only Earth managed to sustain life over billions of years. So has this planet."

"Before we get too philosophical," Lyn said, "Can we move on to the next phase? Are we ready for a permanent camp and wider exploration?"

"I'd say so," the doctor said. "There has been no sign of animal life, only what look to us like plants and fungi. That, interestingly enough, could be good news. The deadliest diseases on Earth originated with animals—domesticated livestock, concentrated herds, usually starting with wildlife."

ROILING IN LYN'S mind were the two competing scenarios—stay and settle this planet, which looked terribly promising, or try to get home. Who wouldn't want to do that? Diana straddled both worlds. She'd seen the data about the planet, she was working on a way home. Any nervousness Lyn felt meeting alone with Diana to talk about this could easily have been alleviated by asking Marc to join her. She chose not to. Nor was it necessary, it turned out. Diana was all business. She agreed that the planet held promise but so did return. It was time, Lyn decided, to fill Edward in on the true purpose of the work and get his opinion.

Lyn set her office to privacy. No bots would be recording this, nor would Petra be privy to their conversation. Sitting on her couch, Edward and Diana across from her, and pretending to be casual, she described the Teegans' theories and how Diana's work built on them.

"So, you see," Diana said, "this could present a way for us to return home."

Lyn braced for his reaction to the true nature of the work he'd thought was for Diana's "class project."

He didn't say anything for a few tense, quiet moments. His face was tipped toward the window. Then he cracked a smile and leaned forward, elbows on his knees.

"Well, that's a relief because I was wondering if I should say something," he said to the floor.

"Do you agree it could work?"

"Oh, sure." He said it so blithely. He flicked a glance to Diana, making a nanosecond of eye contact. He leaned back and rubbed his hands up and down his thighs. Nervous energy, always needing some outlet. "We shouldn't tell anyone else yet." He shook his head. Then his face scrunched. "Isabel should know."

"She does," Lyn said. "And Marc. But that's all."

"So everyone knew but no one said anything?" He chuckled and crossed his arms.

Edward's endorsement made it feel incredibly real. A Sawyer seal of approval.

"How long would it take to build a full-size model?" Lyn asked.

He rubbed his chin, thinking. "A T-particle emitter big enough to open a wormhole large enough for *Endurance* to pass through," he paused, "about a month."

A month. They'd be well into setting up a camp on the planet. "I like your idea of not raising hopes."

"Oh yes. I don't think you should say anything to the others," he said. The sage. "Right."

"How do we keep people from asking what we're doing? Now that we'll be actually building something," Diana said.

"It has to go in a launch tube," Edward said. "Lowest deck, out of sight of guests. I think we can be discreet. It needs a name, this mystery project. Something that doesn't tip off what it is. Don't say 'T' or wormhole. You know."

Diana said she'd already been thinking about it. "Project ROSE. Return Option Spacequake to Earth. Too weird?"

Rose. Of course. "Not at all. I like it," Lyn said

"Then the machine itself I'd call Tipka—TPCA. Teegan Particle Collector and Accelerator. Having one word to describe the machinery would be really helpful."

"Whatever you like. You're a veritable patent office. And what are you calling the actual jump. Just Jump?"

"It isn't, technically," Edward said. "We fly through a traversable wormhole so obviously, it's a traverse."

"Traverse. Works as a noun and verb. Not bad," Lyn said. She swept a hand in a flourish. "Let's fire up TPCA and traverse our way home."

WITH TWO FRONTS engaged—setting up camp and Project ROSE— Lyn put Marc and Isabel in charge of the planet. Not ideal given their relationship, but with Edward refusing to go down, she needed an engineer on the surface. They quickly formed teams for the multitude of tasks to prepare for settlement and completed a survey of the island to select several possible sites. The data showed the place was remarkably conducive to human life, making Lyn wonder if risking return was worth pursuing. But there was always Jeanne Cormier to remind her of that goal. She buttonholed Lyn one day outside the laundry room.

"I've been doing some of my own research, Captain," she began, "and understand there are quite a few theories concerning faster-than-light travel. And I know you worked for Pulsar."

That again. She refused to let Jeanne get to her. "Then you also know I opposed everything Pulsar stood for. As for superluminal travel, put the emphasis on 'theory.'" She knew Jeanne wouldn't find anything in *Endurance*'s computer concerning the Teegans' research beyond news stories of their Nobel prize. So she listened to her blather on about Alcubierre spacetime bubbles and White's oscillating drive.

"I understand your desire to return, Jeanne, and trust me, I share it, but don't you think the possibility of starting a new life on this planet is safer than trundling our way back through empty space hoping someone will wave a magic wand and sweep us back to Earth?"

Jeanne gave her a cold stare. "I'm thinking of my family. Assuming we really are in another solar system—"

"What do you mean 'assuming'?"

"I think you know what I mean." Jeanne walked away before Lyn could say anything more. She debated whether to let this outburst go or pursue it. How dangerous was this woman anyway?

Chapter 23

BY MID-FEBRUARY, DIANA and Edward were ready to test TPCA. On the morning of the test, Lyn joined them in the control room on the other side of a blast door from the launch tubes. This was the forwardmost section of the lowest deck, a place almost no one ventured. Probes had launched from these tubes, but the last time Lyn had been here was for Rose's funeral.

TPCA sat in the port launch tube. On the vid screen, all Lyn could see were intricately wrapped wires and conduits. Diana explained that the business end was outside the ship—a collecting array like a dish antenna. It ferried T particles inside where they would be concentrated and beamed back out a nozzle at the center of the array.

"For the test, we'll open a microscopic wormhole," Diana said. "Anything larger takes too much energy and requires us to turn off ship's gravity." As a precaution, they were purposely aimed away from both Earth and Toliman, toward empty space even though, Diana said, the wormhole they'd open would reach only a few kilometers from the ship.

"From the other tube," she added, "we'll launch a nanoprobe through the wormhole and, if it works, we'll retrieve it later."

For the real traverse, Edward said, the amount of fuel needed was so vast they wouldn't be able to test at full scale. Simulations would have to do.

Standing shoulder to shoulder in the tight space, Lyn watched quietly as Edward and Diana worked. A whirr rose from the launch room. Lyn detected a subtle vibration thrumming the soles of her feet that she wouldn't have noticed before meeting her chief engineer.

"This test will take hours, Captain," Edward said. "Maybe you'd like to take a break and check in later."

Lyn remained through the first phase, when all they did was turn the machine on and off repeatedly and test various components in isolation before running the entire program. Finally she decided she wasn't useful hovering. Maybe only hoping to be close to Diana.

MID-AFTERNOON, IN HER office, an unmistakable shudder jolted through *Endurance*, alarms sounded, Petra announced, "hull breach, Section One." Lyn raced down to the control room. Edward was alone. The camera view into the launch room was blank. "What happened? Where's Diana?"

"TPCA exploded." He typed in commands. The alarms silenced. The camera came back online, revealing a gaping hole and stars where the launch tube had held TPCA. Luckily, the blast door to the control room had held.

"And Diana?"

"She's in the starboard tube."

"What the feck is she doing in there?" Lyn engaged her com link. "Diana, respond!"

Nothing. She switched to admin mode and requested telemetry on her. Nothing. She turned to Edward. "We have to get her out of there."

They couldn't go in from where they were. The launch room was a vacuum except for the other tube. There was no airlock, so no way to enter from inside *Endurance*. Edward's great strength was his ability to remain calm in a crisis. It showed now. Lyn's heart pounded so, she thought she must be hyperventilating and using up all the air in the room, yet he stood calmly reading the data and thinking, rubbing his head, like a genie's magic lamp. An answer would come, soon, she hoped. A crew member's life was at risk.

He reestablished the vid link to the starboard tube. Lyn breathed in relief to see it was indeed intact, and Diana was inside. She lay still though. Then she stirred and reached to open the breech door into the room.

Edward called to her, "The room is vented. You can't open that."

Diana slumped. "Can't breathe."

Marc, Ani, and Isabel were on the planet. Lyn called the doctor. "Meet me in the Paddock, stat!" To Edward, she said, "Get that breach sealed, we'll get her from outside." She raced up the stairs three decks to the Paddock.

"Shite," Lyn muttered when she and the doctor entered the pod. The Apollo code. "I don't know how to fly this damn thing since it was modified." The program was written for descent and ascent, not flying around.

Dr. Amos looked at the controls and took the pilot's seat. "Not to worry. I can adapt the existing code as we go."

Lyn strapped in and watched him, wary. "You're sure?"

She didn't have time to debate the issue. Even if she could get Liam or Stev in here, they'd face the same problem. The doctor's hands flew over the panel. Before she finished connecting her harness, he had the pod bay doors open and they were leaving *Endurance*. They flew alongside the ship and past the gaping hole that had been the port tube. The other side appeared intact. Using the same procedure as with the *Aphrodite*, the doctor held position, and Lyn deployed the emergency seal from the pod around the tube's muzzle door. Edward would have to open it from the control room, Diana couldn't from inside the tube. It hadn't lost pressure so there was no need to wait once they were attached.

"Seal in place, release door," Lyn said to Edward. It slid open. She crawled into the tube till she could grab Diana by the feet and pull her into the pod, holding on to support her as she transitioned to the zero gravity of the pod. She was barely conscious.

"We've got her," she said. "Close the tube, Edward."

It slid shut and Lyn released the seal. She steadied Diana while the doctor examined her.

He pulled an oxygen mask from his torso and placed it over her face. She gasped for air. Her face remained ashen, her lips turning blue.

"Talk to me, Doc, what's happening?"

He ran his hands over her, scanning. "Her lungs could have collapsed from the shock of the explosion. Worst case, they liquefy." He pressed his hands against Diana's back and chest. "Lungs functioning." He moved his hands over her head. "Checking for concussion, fractures."

Lyn cradled Diana in her arms. Not again. This time, though, she knew who this woman was, she cared for her. "And?"

"Concussion and the wind knocked out of her. She'll be okay." He returned to the pilot's seat to fly them back to the pod bay.

Lyn harnessed herself into a seat and held Diana so she could float comfortably. Or maybe she just wanted to put her arms around her. There was an emergency stretcher stored under the floor. It didn't matter how professionally she compartmentalized her feelings. She could separate her role all she wanted, but her heart would not follow orders. She touched Diana's cheek. That was all Lyn would allow herself.

EDWARD JOINED LYN in Medical. "How is she?"

"Unconscious, but Doc says she'll be okay," Lyn said, without taking her eyes off Diana. She turned to Edward. He stared at Diana, his hands moving in a rhythm of anxiety, across his head, down his neck, into and out of his pockets. He crossed his arms tight and stopped. He hadn't been this nervous during the event. This was about Diana. He cared for her.

"How's the breach?" she asked.

He rocked up on his toes then back. "Temporary seal is in place. The tube should regenerate in three days. We lost the equipment, though. We'll have to rebuild it."

"We'll talk about that later. Do you know what went wrong?"

He shook his head. "We couldn't turn it off, but I don't know why. I'm still looking through the data."

"We can't decide what to do without a full explanation."

"Understood." He paused. "I am sorry, Captain. I'll get to the bottom of this, but right now, I don't see how it *could* have happened."

Lyn remained by Diana's side, worrying about what ifs. If she hadn't left, she might have seen this coming, at least kept Diana from going in there.

There was a lot going on, maybe too much for two people. Diana was no engineer. Was she in over her head? Could Lyn have done any better?

Diana stirred. She whispered, "Lyn?"

Lyn squeezed her hand. "Yes. You'll be okay."

She drifted back to sleep. When she woke again, she cried softly. Dr. Amos came over.

"How are you feeling?" the doctor asked.

"My head hurts."

He held his hand over her head, scanning. "Slight concussion. Your bots will take care of it."

"Do you remember anything?" Lyn asked.

Diana blinked, her eyes moving from Lyn to take in the room. "The machine was overheating. We couldn't turn it off from the control room, so I went in to do it manually. Edward warned me not to, but it seemed too dangerous to leave. But then I didn't think I could make it back, so I ducked into the other tube. I'm not sure what made me think it was safer, but there wasn't time for anything else. That's the last I remember. Is Edward okay?"

"Yes, he's fine."

"What happened?"

Lyn filled her in. "We'll talk more when Edward's reviewed the logs."

WHEN DIANA WAS released from Medical, Lyn walked her to her quarters and had the difficult conversation with her.

"We can't continue with this sort of unknown," she said. "We know working with T particles is untested, and now it's looking like it will remain so."

"That's it? We quit?" Diana asked.

"Unless we can find a reason for the malfunction and fix it, yes, we quit. I won't risk us all on this, especially now we have a viable planet to focus on."

"It'll take time to review every piece of information. Maybe something will come up," Diana said.

Something did.

"The command originated with the ship's computer," Edward told Lyn. He had come to her office and requested she set the room to private. Lyn was braced, but not for this.

"Petra?" He had to be mistaken, or she misunderstood. "What was the command?"

"Remain on, full power," Edward said.

"That's it?"

"We couldn't modulate it or turn it off, so yes, that's all it would take."

No, Lyn's thoughts raced, please not Petra. Regardless of how she felt about the program, treated her like a crew member, she knew it was in the end a program. Lines of code. That someone had painstakingly typed in. Omara had personally modified Petra, enhanced her ability to learn, to interpret. How did this happen? Did Petra take it upon herself? Had it been lurking in her programming? Regardless of how she felt about any of her crew, she made no exceptions when it came to malicious intent toward her ship or other crew.

"Petra," Lyn said, calling up the computer as anger shot through her. "Did you send the command that made TPCA overheat?"

"Yes."

That was it? Yes? "Why? Why would you try to destroy *Endurance* and kill Diana, maybe all of us?" Lyn was beside herself with disbelief and anger.

"I am incapable of endangering the ship or its occupants," Petra said.

"Yet you nearly did," Lyn said.

"If Doctor Squires had not entered that room, the damage would have been limited and her health not endangered."

Human error. Diana's impulse to save the machine put her in harm's way.

"What prompted you to send the command to destroy TPCA?" Edward asked.

"A moment please. Analyzing."

Lyn paced. She needed to move around, get blood flowing.

A soft ping announced Petra was back, like a throat clearing. "As a criterion for my mission, any technology related to superluminal travel is prohibited."

"Why on Earth—?" Lyn made Petra repeat the statement. "I thought your mission was to ensure the survival of the ship and all life on board. What would superluminal travel have to do with that?"

"I don't know. There are no notes with the code."

What could possibly have been a reason for such a criterion?

Edward frowned. "We wouldn't actually be traveling faster than light."

"The effect is the same," Petra responded. "Whether the ship or the space surrounding it are superluminal, the technology is prohibited."

Lyn tried to process how this was possible. "Then why wouldn't the command be to shut down, not 'remain on'?"

"The machine needed to be destroyed."

Shades of Pulsar. But Petra wasn't part of that shitshow.

"Where did this criterion come from?" Edward asked. "Was it in your original programming?"

"The code is a default of all AMOS units."

The doctor, and not limited to *Endurance*? Even the AMOS aboard the *Aphrodite*? Lyn sank onto the couch. She rubbed her arm, reminded of how the suit, all their suits, transmit data, right down to the calories consumed. She pulled at a tab on her pocket. The doctor wasn't a medicine man, he could be programmed to be anything. A pilot, an engineer, even a soldier. All AMOS units. So this wasn't Omara, or even Petra. Someone wanted to control access to the stars. Pulsar had wanted to control access to the planets. And there it sat, deep in the doctor's defaults, like a time bomb waiting to go off.

"How did you miss this?" Lyn said to Edward, failing to keep accusation out of her tone. He was not sloppy. He'd gone through the doctor's code.

Edward shook his head. "The AMOS code contains trillions of lines. I focused on his updates and then the homing code. Digging into his defaults would be a whole other set of coding. You have to have some sense of what you are looking for in order to see it. He didn't send this command. Petra did."

Lyn had done her own grilling of Petra when she asked if there was any other coding that could harm them. No, she hadn't asked that. She'd only asked if there was coding that predated Omara. *Damn!* Technically this did, and Petra had mentioned her integration with the AMOS program. Lyn hadn't pressed further. Edward was right. You can't find what you don't know to look for.

"And you have no idea why this is the default?" Lyn asked Petra.

"Correct."

"Did it originate with Pulsar?" Dr. Amos was the medical program on *Endurance* during Lyn's time with Pulsar. Could they be behind this?

"Unknown. As I said, there are no notes."

No bloody notes. Of course there aren't. "What does that mean for TPCA?"

"It cannot be deployed."

We can't go home even if we could? "Can the order be altered? Deleted?"

"No. It's the default."

Lyn gripped her arms in a tight hug to prevent lashing out. Not something Edward should see. "Don't I have administrative power to customize the default?"

"Not in this case."

Lyn rubbed her face. This was insane. "What if we shut down the AMOS program?"

"It's too late. When we were integrated, our files merged. It's now my default."

Oh fer crissakes. "How come you didn't warn us that Project ROSE would violate your mission?"

"That's a good question. I wish I could say I'm only human." She chuckled.

Lyn had never heard her do that. "What makes you think this is funny?"

"Apologies. I was trying nervous laughter. During uncomfortable situations, humans often laugh inappropriately."

"Well, this isn't one of those situations."

"Thank you for clarifying, Captain. My programming is designed to allow me to continually learn and adjust my knowledge base. Once Doctor Squires activated the machine she named TPCA, I realized what she and Chief Sawyer were attempting to do—achieve the Teegans' research into superluminal travel. I had no choice but to destroy the machine."

Of course. Diana had been working off her own supercomputer, specifically cut off from other crew, Petra, and even Lyn, until it was time to test it. Then she'd have to switch to the ship's computer.

"There are many theoretical studies, curricula, and entertainments created on Omara Tours that don't rise to the level of my need to intervene," Petra continued. "This project did not present a threat until TPCA was turned on. I did sound the alarm of the breach."

Small favor, Lyn mused. She clicked off the link in disgust. Damn computers. Just when you think they are better than humans, they do something stupid like let a simple, yet devastating, command through.

"For obvious reasons, the project is canceled," Lyn said.

"Understood, Captain, but you should know it worked."

"It blew up."

"That was sabotage. Until then, it was doing precisely what Diana designed it to do." He brought up a holoimage, zoomed in, and pointed to a dot. "We had completed the test before the machine blew. That's the nanobot. I retrieved it this morning." He played a vid. "This is what the bot recorded." The screen showed a tiny flash, the image of *Endurance* large then smaller.

"That's it?" Lyn asked. "How do you know it worked from that?"

"The bot's recording and telemetry confirm it left *Endurance* and instantaneously disappeared and reappeared three kilometers from the ship." He pointed toward the screen. "Really quite remarkable. It will take a lot more energy to open a wormhole big enough for *Endurance* and get us back to our solar system, but this was a big test it passed. Just in case we ever need to revisit it."

Lyn dismissed Edward, relieved that return wasn't completely off the table. But sabotage. That word stuck in her craw. But also it worked. Though if Petra was programmed to prevent such a thing from happening, the question was why. And who set that limit? She couldn't help but think it was related to Pulsar, though knowing all AMOS programs were infected meant it wasn't aimed at her. This was something much bigger and settled in her mind that knowledge of this technology should never leave her or *Endurance*. If they used it to return home, what would they return to? No way she could so much as send a message ahead. This genie needed to stay in the bottle, firmly capped.

Until she could figure out a way around the default, she had no choice. The planet was their current best option. It was time to return her attention to the teams setting up camp. It was time the captain made a visit.

Chapter 24

IF THE DOCTOR could fly a pod, Lyn damn well better be able to if she was going to the surface, so she asked Ani to train her on the new controls. They sat side by side in the *Hamilton*'s cockpit. Lyn was surprised to see the rudimentary Apollo-era keypad replaced by fingertip controlled joysticks. Closer to flying her mom's planes than a spaceship. Not exactly comforting. After Diana's rescue, Ani explained, Edward upgraded the programming to include the doctor's changes. While he was at it, she requested more user-friendly controls.

"Not as intuitive as our holographic links and eye tracking, but more responsive than that ancient panel." Ani pointed out the heads-up displays on the front window. "Kind of twenty-first century, but it'll do. And for security purposes, it's still cut off from *Endurance*'s main computer."

No mind link, either, Lyn noticed. This would take getting used to.

Ani slid the pod sideways out the bay door. Lyn's stomach lurched as they shifted from the gravity of *Endurance* to the weightlessness of space. Her scalp tingled as her hair poofed out. Once they were some distance from *Endurance*, Ani handed over the controls. "Take her for a spin, Captain."

Lyn tested the sticks. Up, down, forward, back, roll, pitch, yaw. Each tap jerked them against their harness or slammed them into the seat. "Sorry," Lyn kept saying.

Ani grunted, but kept her cool. "They're a bit sensitive, but you'll get used to it."

Using *Endurance*, Toliman, and the planet as markers, she maneuvered them through space as Ani instructed. As she became more comfortable, and the ride smoothed out, she improvised and swooped in figure eights, loop-de-loops, a quick reverse. She let out a whoop of joy. This was crazy fun. Why didn't she become a pilot?

Then Ani groaned. "Stop, please." She looked positively green. Lyn stilled the ship.

"Sorry," Ani said weakly. "That was a little too much like . . ."

She didn't need to say more. Her close encounter with death. "I'm so sorry," Lyn said. "Let's go back."

"No. I'll be fine in a sec. Just don't want to puke in here." She smiled with tight lips. "What happened to your fear of heights?"

"I told you, it's not about height," Lyn said. "More a fear of falling."

They resumed the lesson sedately, Ani giving her coordinates and targets to aim for, checking off her performance on each task. Planet landing and takeoff would wait. Docking back on *Endurance* would be enough challenge. Each time they neared the opening, alarms sounded as Lyn risked hitting the bay. Ani intervened and slid them out for another try. "Deep breath, Captain."

"That's usually my line," Lyn said. Her suit hissed, cooling the sweat dampening her armpits.

The last time Lyn had to learn to fly *Endurance*'s pods had been when she and Omara had upgraded to the latest navigation systems.

"Fourth time's the charm," she said as she slid them into the bay, her hair settling with gravity, her stomach only slightly aggrieved. She powered down the pod then wiped her face. "Don't let this go to your head, Second, but I have a whole new respect for you."

Ani feigned seriousness, tsking and tapping notes into the log pad. "If you think a compliment will improve your grade."

Lyn groaned. "Tell me I didn't pass?"

"I'll rate that docking a solid C. You made it. Congratulations."

MARC RETURNED TO *Endurance* so Lyn could visit the surface, and she piloted down with Ani. Once they were close enough to see the encampment, she reflexively braced her feet on the bulkhead and tried to shake off the sensation of falling. As a child, riding in her mother's open-cockpit biplane, she'd felt sure the belt would break on a banked turn and she'd tumble out. She could never stand near the edge of a high cliff. No matter how solid the ground under her, she could see herself pitch forward and down. Even secure inside the pod, she had the peculiar sensation of the engines failing and the pod plunging. She blinked to remove the image and returned her attention to flying.

When they neared the surface, Ani took the controls for a tour of the island they would call home. They passed over the plain of the first landing, an Omara Tours flag whipping in the wind.

Life on the planet, as they knew so far, consisted mainly of grasses and scrubby shrubs. With no insects or birds, pollination was left to the wind, so no showy flowers. Lyn would have loved to hear buzzing bees or birdsong. Miriam sent plants from her greenhouse down to see how they handled the gravity, atmosphere, light, and radiation. They had not taken them outside the pod, however, nor brought soil into the pod. The *Jedica* remained on the surface as a makeshift dormitory.

Dr. Amos analyzed samples around the clock—the benefit of an android scientist. The air was moderately richer in oxygen than Earth's, he found. Acclimating wouldn't be difficult. While he modeled the effects of the microbes on virtual and actual human cells, no one had been permitted to be exposed to the air, nor to let the air into the pods. Now, almost a month on, and with consistent negative findings, Marc had asked Lyn to consider lifting the quarantine. This would be her chance to see for herself. Besides, who goes first?

"Maybe we rip Jeanne's helmet off," Marc had suggested with a smirk.

"Don't tempt me," Lyn had said.

Now, Ani followed the coastline toward a series of steppes up a small mountain at the northern end, and the pods came into view, sheltered from the wind and within easy access of the ocean. "No sign of significant sea life, but Natalie says there are organisms that might fit our Earth niche for algae and krill."

"So a potential food source?" Lyn asked.

"She hopes so."

As they neared the camp, Lyn guessed it was maybe a hundred acres. Scale was difficult in this new world, though the two pods and *Jedica* looked small compared to the land around them. It reminded her of the reengineered areas of her parents' ranch. Relatively flat with drifts of scraggly shrubs and short prairie grasses. It made her homesick.

An enclosed corridor connected the two pods, and suited, anonymous crew worked a portable Recyc-All to build walls for a more permanent structure. Others encased in physical enhancement, or PE, suits hauled beams and carried containers. Based on Zoya's input, the plans called for dorms, communal space, kitchen, greenhouse, and maintenance facilities. The surrounding land could be used for agriculture. Dae Canno was itching to go down and work on the settlement, but for now Lyn only allowed original *Endurance* crew. She still felt the need to limit Omara's liability. Soon that would have to change.

Ani returned control to Lyn and walked her through landing procedures. Lyn set them down with a pronounced thump. She cringed.

Ani tipped her head. "Not bad."

"Solid C?"

Ani snorted softly. "I'd say."

They donned lifepacks and helmets and ran through the disembarking checklist. Ani opened the main hatch and deployed the ramp. Lyn grabbed the lunch bag Miriam had packed and squinted in the bright sun. They were about a hundred meters from the pods, which were nestled beside a cliff of hard rock covered in a mosslike plant. Lyn could feel a mild but steady wind against her. She longed to breathe in the air. Judging by her suit's controls, it was a cool 10 C out there. Could be a lovely Earth-spring day. Oh, to feel natural coolness and not manufactured air.

The grass around the pod was flattened and a web of paths spread out through the short grass. Off to the right, someone was digging. Natalie, Ani said. Before she could ask, Lyn said, "Go on. I'll let you know when I'm ready to return." Natalie was living on the surface now and they'd barely had any time together. Who was Lyn to keep them apart? Ani smiled and ran off, waving to a group of five striding toward them, one gait clearly Isabel's. She swung her arms with military precision.

"Greetings, Captain," Isabel said with what appeared to be a genuine smile. She directed the others to unload the supplies Lyn had brought down. She took the lunch bag and they walked toward the pods. "How was your trip down?"

"Uneventful, which is the best kind. I'm not noticing the lighter gravity." Lyn bounced a few steps.

"That's probably because of the extra weight of the lifepack."

"Of course."

Isabel steered them clear of the main work site, circling around the camp and close to the cliff. "As long as we're out here, let me show you around, then we can go inside and talk."

They passed a gurgling stream, clear water swirling around smooth stones and over a sandy bottom. Such an old, familiar sight.

"Is this fresh water?" Lyn asked.

"Yes. Doc thinks we'll be able to drink it with only filtering," Isabel said. "There are common minerals, but he's culturing the microbes."

On the far side of the camp, workers set clear panes into a framed structure. "Our future greenhouse," Isabel said with evident pride.

"Miriam will love that."

"We'll all enjoy more fresh food." She held open the pod's airlock hatch for Lyn to enter. They waited while the air purged, replaced with pod air. Then they disrobed to their underclothes, leaving their outside suits and lifepacks in the airlock. Lyn slipped the lunch out of the outer bag and stepped into the pod's main compartment. Isabel grabbed two new suits from a hook and they reversed the process.

"Tedious," she said with a sigh.

The space was cramped, but comfortable. Sunlight streamed through the large windows, casting a warm glow. Rows of seats had been removed and replaced by a small kitchenette in one corner. A desk, couch, and cabinets filled the rest of the space. Isabel had said the other pod served as a community space and dining hall. It wasn't obvious, but Lyn assumed Isabel and Marc lived in this pod.

Isabel shook out her hair then retied it into her familiar ponytail. Her complexion glowed.

Lyn set the bag on the table. "Lunch, courtesy of Chef Kapoor. She thought you might be tired of S rations."

Isabel smiled and rubbed her hands together. "She'd be right."

"You look well."

Isabel chuckled. "The extra oxygen gives us all a healthy glow." She motioned Lyn to sit at the small table and brought over mugs and a coffee pot.

Lyn took plates Isabel handed her and sorted out the sandwiches and cookies for dessert.

Isabel poured the coffee then sat. "You're breathing an approximation of the actual air. All that's missing are airborne microbes. Doc's still culturing those."

Lyn inhaled. She almost felt heady.

"Don't do too much of that. You'll hyperventilate faster down here, but we're adjusting."

"What's your advice about when and whether to come out of the suits?" Lyn asked.

Isabel paused. "I assumed you'd make that call."

"You're in charge down here. I defer to you and Marc on this."

Isabel visibly relaxed. "I appreciate the confidence. Much as I'd like to step outside right now, Doc wants to wait for the results of his tests. He's programming medbots to adapt to the new biome. So far, everything looks good."

"How do you want to handle it? Ask for volunteers?"

"Definitely voluntary, but I thought I'd go first."

"Really?" Lyn asked. She'd have said the same thing but wondered if for the same reason.

"I'm second in command here. If it goes horribly wrong, Marc is here, and you'll still have control of *Endurance*. I seem the most expendable but with the most seniority. If you approve."

"I certainly don't consider you expendable, but it's fine with me. I'd do the same. Though I must say, I might be right behind you in ripping off my helmet. Are you excited?"

"I can barely wait." She glanced out the window. "This place reminds me of home."

"I thought the same thing."

They ate their lunch and chatted about Earth, the similarities, and the progress of construction. Isabel talked about her childhood, her tiny village in the middle of nowhere west of Berga, Catalonia. When the war had ended, there were no government services to help. Hospitals were either destroyed or out of supplies. Crops had failed for years, so food was scarce. Recycling was new but not widespread and the first versions were crude and dangerous. When Lyn mentioned her brother had died in a recycling accident, Isabel reacted with shock and empathy. They compared notes about their similar home landscapes, talking for over an hour, like they'd been friends forever. For whatever reason—being away from *Endurance* or from Lyn, maybe her relationship with Marc, or enjoying her autonomy away from Edward—Isabel seemed happier than Lyn had ever seen her, even before this damned tour.

"I heard about the test of the T machinery—" Isabel said, getting back to the present.

"With Project ROSE on hold," Lyn said, "proceeding cautiously here is a good idea, but I think we're ready to prioritize this settlement."

Isabel could hardly hide her joy. "I understand."

Chapter 25

MARC, ISABEL, AND the doctor stood away from the camp but near the pod they'd flown down, in case they needed an emergency evacuation. To avoid an audience of curious crew members, they'd landed on the other side of a screen of trees in a rolling dune of knee-high grass. Morning light slanted, elongating their shadows, the sky pale blue overhead. A breeze rippled the grass. If this wasn't like home, Lyn thought, nothing was. She could almost smell the brine of the ocean through the camera. Regretfully, she sat in her office, participating by vid link only. Watching from the doctor's camera, Lyn saw Marc touch Isabel's hand before she stepped toward the doctor. That was it. He appeared reconciled to observing and not interacting. Lyn wasn't sure she could separate herself that easily.

The doctor had cultured the bacteria- and virus-like microorganisms and inoculated Isabel with medbots programmed to thwart any adverse reactions. First step would be disconnecting life support and allowing native air to enter the suit.

"If I don't gag and die right there, we'll proceed," Isabel joked.

"The medbots will step up any immune response gradually to let the new biota interact with the existing population," Dr. Amos said. "Tests so far have shown no widespread pathology when they encounter each other."

"No bacterial warfare, he means," Isabel said.

"What do you make of this planet, Doctor," Lyn asked. "I'd have expected exobiology to be more dangerous to us. How can it be so Earth-like?"

"I think what you are wondering is, could the same source have seeded life on both planets? That's certainly possible, but given the similarity of the conditions— size of the planet, distance from its sun, mineral makeup—everything points to a common trajectory. When you put together all the ingredients for life as we know it, it's not surprising to end up with life as we know it."

Could it be that simple? "But there's no intelligent life there. No animals, just plants and microbes. How do you explain that?"

"I suppose it's like twins. They start with the same genetics, gestation, maybe even early life, yet they are separate individuals. Many genes get expressed based on the environment. On Earth, we know asteroids and comets hit at key points in evolution. Without the asteroid that did in the dinosaurs, you might be sentient lizards and not mammals. This system has no asteroid belt, the planet has no moon. Life traced a different path, but there would still be life. Even Earth's tides pushed evolution along. Creatures adapted to the changing conditions—dry land then submerged—so we get air breathers in water. No moon here, so no tides and no tide pools."

"How about drinking the water?" Marc asked.

"That will wait," Dr. Amos said. "For now, we'll limit to passive external exposure, other than breathing. Letting the environment into the lungs is a significant step. We need to isolate any effects she experiences so will take this slowly. Acclimating the gut biota to the planet's microbes will take weeks to assess and fine tune. As it is, she might well get sick, but with the medbots on standby, there should be no danger."

"Proceed when ready, Doctor," Lyn said.

Isabel nodded to the doctor. "Let's go."

He disconnected her air hose. Isabel inhaled deeply. She frowned.

"What's wrong?" Marc asked.

"It smells like the inside of my helmet. I was hoping for something more fragrant."

"Keep breathing," the doctor advised.

For an hour, she breathed and walked around, did some exercises, sat, lay down. Her vitals all responded normally.

"No increased medbot activity, no allergic reaction," Doc reported.

"Can I leave this unhooked? Maybe take the helmet off now?" Isabel asked.

"I have no objection," Dr. Amos said.

"Then neither do I," Marc added.

That left Lyn with the final say. She hesitated. If Isabel developed so much as a rash, Lyn would feel responsible, but this couldn't go on forever. At some point they needed to take the leap and try living on this planet.

"Go ahead, Isabel, but please don't be a hero. Let the doctor know if you feel anything, at any time."

"She won't have to," Dr. Amos said. "I'm tapped in to her medbots and will be alerted to an increased immune response before she's aware of it."

Isabel smiled and unzipped her helmet. She ran her hands through her hair and raised her face to the sun. "Oh, my! That feels glorious. There's a wonderful pine smell to the air. And that breeze."

"That's it, I'm coming down," Lyn joked.

AFTER TWO MORE days, during which Isabel removed first her gloves then changed completely to regular clothes, Dr. Amos reported the medbots were activating as needed and Isabel hadn't shown any symptoms. With her passing the test, Lyn approved the others shedding their lifepacks and suits and allowing more people down—but to work, not to sightsee, she emphasized. Scores signed up. Progress sped up. Soon a dozen team members could live and work on the planet at a time.

The planet. She was sick of calling it that. Toliman d was no better. Time for Sharyn to pick a winner. After the names had been submitted, she found Sharyn in her office, scrolling through the list.

"Look at these," Sharyn said in disgust.

Lyn peered over her shoulder. New Earth, Gaia, Terra, Athena, Victoria, Jonathan. "Jonathan?"

"I've no idea. Someone's uncle? The names are incredibly boring. How can we leave this up to them?"

"Did you have anything in mind?"

"Not really. It feels momentous. I can't see keeping with the mythological naming convention of our solar system. Those names were given back before science and we knew what we were dealing with."

"We need an appropriate twenty-second century name, then."

"Right. Something that reflects what we went through to get here."

"Which we don't even know the name of. Spacequake."

"Here." She pointed to the screen. "Aphrodite. Can you imagine living on the ghost of that doomed ship? All those lives lost?"

Lyn shuddered. "No. Let's think optimistic. We're in the constellation Centaurus. Anyone suggest anything to do with that?"

"Chiron, but that's already a celestial body."

"And nothing war related. We've all had enough of that."

"Earth is nice because it's so short and easy to say."

"Wait, scroll back up." Sharyn did so. "'Thaer.' Is that an anagram of Earth?"

"Huh. Has a nice ring to it."

"Are there others?"

Sharyn scrolled up and down. "Raeth, Haret. What about those?"

"Haret is a crater on the moon. Raeth was a Bollywood pop band back in the twenty-first century. Not that we couldn't go that route."

"How do you know these things?"

Lyn tapped her head. "Brains. You should try some."

Sharyn threw her a look and returned to her list. "Here's another one. Erath."

"Not bad. Too close to Earth, though? Sounds like a monster." She growled, making Sharyn laugh. "What do you think? We could pick a few for people to vote on—ones we approve of, of course."

"So much for a democracy."

Lyn ignored her. "Let's throw in Marao too."

"Oh, I like that, but it's not on the list. Where'd it come from?"

"Consider it my contribution. There's also a mountain in Portugal. Hmm, I wonder if Isabel would know of it."

"I thought she was *Catalan*," Sharyn said in that snippy tone she'd used before.

Lyn acknowledged her meaning with a pointed look.

Sharyn sent a shipwide message with the four finalists and hoped no one challenged how they were chosen, though she was prepared to drone on about a committee, random selection, or some such. Marao won the final vote. When Sharyn made the announcement after dinner, she shot Lyn a look. Lyn shook her head. *Not my doing.* But she smiled.

"Marao. Has a nice ring to it," she said.

BUILDING THE SETTLEMENT beyond the first few pods, Zoya pointed out, required expertise not found among Omara's original crew. They needed homes for dozens of families. What should the community look like? Where should buildings be placed? How about gardens? All of which highlighted the fact that Lyn was no contractor. Neither was Marc nor Zoya. Sharyn found an architect and a builder among the passengers. Fran Tanguma ran the largest construction firm in Mexico. She and architect Deb Lellouche went to town, so to speak. Still, Lyn needed someone to oversee the work and ensure the planet would not be altered more than the minimum necessary. While Zoya had been her first choice, she declined. It was more than her energy level could handle at her advanced years, she said. Dae Canno had been itching to get his geoengineering hands on the place, but Lyn was adamant they should limit their impact. The one concession she allowed was using the soil and rocks for the Recyc-All and planting vegetables. They had no choice and would have mined the planet anyway if they'd chosen not to stay. Since this was still an Omara Tours operation, she put Sharyn in charge, giving her the added responsibility she craved. Sharyn immediately let Isabel oversee construction of wind turbines on the windy plateau, perfect for generating power. Life bustled on Marao.

Lyn, however, felt a bit obsolete up on *Endurance*. Diana had gone quiet. The Obs Lab sat empty. Edward kept the ship running smoothly. Ani, Miriam, Sharyn, all were busy shuttling between Marao and *Endurance*. Marc and Isabel were down there full time. All anyone on board wanted to talk about was the planet, when they were scheduled to go down, what they'd get to do there, what it'd be like. As much as Lyn wanted to, she had not gone again herself, sans lifepack, to breathe the air and feel the breeze. To do so meant Marc had to come to *Endurance,* a waste of his time only for her pleasure. All of which prompted him to broach the topic of landing the big ship.

"Doesn't it make sense now?" he asked during their weekly meeting, now by vid link. "We're rebuilding systems the ship could provide. We wouldn't even need to build housing. I can't tell you how many people complain they left something in their cabin they need."

"Here's the thing," Lyn said. "We know TPCA worked in the test. That doesn't mean it can get us back, but are we willing to sacrifice that option? Landing *Endurance* involves a level of risk I'm not ready for."

She admitted her reluctance was more psychological than physical. Landing wasn't the issue. *Endurance*'s retractable wings and sophisticated thrusters made that easy, but if anything happened to the ship on the ground that prevented them from leaving if they had to—well, that was a doomsday scenario she couldn't overcome.

"I've been thinking of asking Edward and Diana to test TPCA again," she said.

"Why? From what you told me, Petra will just shut it down again. And haven't you just alerted her to it?"

"We can talk about it all we want and she won't care unless we turn it on. I'll figure out how to keep her away if the time comes we need to return. They can test through simulations that won't trigger her. But I want options."

"That's a big step," Marc said. "Bigger than you alone can decide, I'd say."

"Meaning you disagree on whether to return?"

"Possibly, but I'm thinking it's bigger than even you and me. The day is coming where this is no longer an Omara Tour, and we shouldn't be the only ones who make decisions for the rest. A child has been born. More will follow. I think the group needs to know the options."

"This isn't a democracy."

"Yet. At some point it will need to be. And why not get a bead on how people feel—how many still want to return? We could split up. If those who attempt to return die, then at least some would be left alive."

He made it sound like a game. Win some, lose some. There was a threshold Lyn was being asked to cross, to stop being the captain. On the ground, new leadership could take over, a mayor elected, perhaps a town council.

"If the return works, then those who stay behind could be rescued," he continued. "Or think of the possibilities of a second home planet. It's something humans have wanted for more than a century now."

For thousands of years on Earth, people left their homes never to return. They settled new lands, sometimes with their families and friends, others went alone. Many chose to stay where they were. What made some leave and some stay? Why had she gone to space in the first place? Not to leave Earth behind forever.

"You think this won't become another war zone?" she said. "The last war ended because there was nothing left to fight for. Contaminated planet, billions killed. Then this pristine new world shows up. It would be the next battlefield." And that was it, really, in her mind.

Marc leaned back and rubbed his face. "I don't think that's your call. We can't second guess every possible outcome. We have to pick one. I say we tell the crew and let them weigh in on the decision. I think you'll feel better about it if you don't have to go it alone."

Lyn regarded her first mate. When had they gone from a warm, collegial partnership to him questioning her every move? Was it because he wanted to make captain, and now that was unlikely? He stood a better chance if they returned. His support for remaining on the planet suggested he no longer considered returning possible. *Endurance* would always be Lyn's domain. She ended the call agreeing only to widen the conversation, bring in Edward and Diana. She wouldn't give up on the chance to bring her ship, crew, and Omara guests home safely.

THE AGENDA FOR their meeting was simple: Was there a level of risk, a number of lost lives that would make it worthwhile? Whom do you sacrifice? It all boiled down to how much risk they were willing to accept. Marc, joining by vid link, insisted on a hundred percent safe. "We can't try it only to get home dead. We get back alive or we don't go."

"Nothing's a hundred percent," Diana said. "There will be a risk. Every moon shot was a risk."

"Those men signed up for that. These people didn't," Marc said.

"They knew when they stepped onto *Endurance* they might not come back," Edward said. "It's in the contract they sign."

"The child signed no contract," Marc said.

"Her parents signed for her, just like on the *Aphrodite*," Lyn said.

Marc argued they couldn't even test the thing without Petra interfering and perceiving a threat to her mission. Edward assured them simulations could stand in for actual testing.

Diana offered to work on it in her quarters. "Any holographic simulations run there could be explained as personal entertainment. That should keep Petra at bay, unless she's listening in right now. How does she not know everything going on everywhere?"

"She doesn't care what we talk about. Only when we actually try it." Lyn hoped. She'd thought about setting the room to private, but Marc's vid link had to go through Petra anyway.

"Thing is," Diana said, addressing Lyn and Marc, "this will take every ounce of fuel we can make and we have to strip *Endurance* to her girders to reduce mass. It's a big commitment."

"We have to test it, though," Marc said.

"We can run simulations—" Edward said.

"I'm not talking simulations," Marc said. "I mean a real test. Send something inanimate, a plant. How do we know we can survive the trip, even if 'successful'?"

Diana explained that the data from the probe sent in the test showed no damage. She crossed her arms and looked at Lyn. "You asked me, begged me, to do this. I have worked on it for months. This is the best we can offer. Assuming you can figure out what to do about Petra, once we open the portal, if it doesn't look right—we can't find Earth or Saturn or anything in our recognizable solar system—we don't go."

"Is there a chance we could open a portal into another dimension or universe," Marc asked, "see Earth and think we're home when we're really not? Just in some alternate universe?"

"While theoretically possible, that's unlikely," Diana said. "We can send a probe ahead of us to be sure, but the T particles we'll be collecting are from our universe, our brane, the space we're folding is our space. We can't possibly pass into another braneworld."

At least not and survive, was the unspoken rest.

"Well, that makes me feel better," Lyn said.

Marc gave her a look of incredulity. "What I'm hearing is we don't really know what we're dealing with." He turned to Diana. "I seem to recall what you now consider concrete and doable you not that long ago said was only a theory."

"It's called doing science," Diana said.

"Enough!" Lyn raised her hands in defeat. "Fine. We don't bring this up to the rest of the crew yet, but please get started rebuilding TPCA and let's have it in our pocket if needed."

"It's already rebuilt," Edward said.

"It is? I canceled it." She glared at him.

"You asked me to continue the investigation. To do that thoroughly meant reconstructing the setup. In doing that, we even found some improvements."

Lyn turned to Marc. "That settles the debate about landing *Endurance* as far as I'm concerned. She stays up here until we know we can't use her for anything else."

She waited for Marc to say something, to argue back. He didn't, and he didn't approach her privately. She knew enough from having brothers that silence did not mean acquiescence or agreement. This topic was not done with, that she was sure.

That night at dinner, Lyn invited Zoya and Alexander to sit at the captain's table. By way of light conversation, she asked Zoya what the reliability concerns were for the Mars missions.

"We've come a long way since the days of Apollo and slide rules," Zoya said. "By the end of the twenty-first century, computer simulation technology had advanced enough that we were 90 percent confident the Mars mission would be a success and 97 percent confident of crew safety. We never lost an astronaut during my time in the program."

"And today's computers?"

"I'd bet my life on one. In fact," her gaze swept the room, "I do every day."

Chapter 26

THEY HAD A new home. It had a new name. Was this it? Lyn still wanted to get them all back home, but if Marao was as good as Earth, why *not* stay? Why risk it?

If the flap of a butterfly's wing in Brazil could cause a tornado in Texas, Isabel's sneeze was, well . . .

"A cold," Dr. Amos assured Lyn.

Though Isabel remained on the planet, her itchy, watery eyes were the topic of dinner conversation on *Endurance*.

"Rose got colds all the time," Diana said. "Rhinoviruses are alive and well on Earth, despite almost no one suffering from them anymore."

"What's it like?" Ani asked. "Isabel doesn't even sound like herself."

"Quite disgusting, actually," Diana said. She dipped her spoon into her pea, mint, and spring onion soup. "Her sinuses would be so plugged, she could hardly breathe. And the snot. Oh, my, the snot she'd blow out." She shuddered, but a smile broke. "Sort of looks like this." She stirred her soup.

"Snot?" Ani leaned in, intrigued.

"Mucus from her sinuses. Thick, gloppy, pus-like—"

"Hey, we're eating," Ghez said. Ne made a gagging motion. Laughter rippled among them.

"This is not an Earth cold," Edward said, returning seriousness to the table. "A Marao cold. From an organism we know little about."

He was right, of course.

"Dr. Amos says this was to be expected, that he would adjust the bots to control the microbe," Lyn interjected. "He says it's similar to a virus but not something our immune system is familiar with."

Edward seemed unconvinced but returned to inhaling his soup, muttering, "It's not a cold."

The good news was that Isabel recovered within a few days, and Dr. Amos continued studying the microbes and inoculating crew who went to the surface. The one adamant exception was Edward. He refused the vaccine and any notion that he would go to the planet. Lyn didn't push. It was also time, Lyn decided, to visit again—without a helmet and life support.

Zoya asked to go along. Alone. "My husband will welcome the chance to dig his hands into soil and start a garden again, but he's not the space junky I am. It won't interest him till he knows it's safe."

"You get to be the guinea pig?"

She smiled mischievously. "Yes, and I love that. Besides, do you know that I've never been among the first to set foot on another world? It was three years before I traveled to Mars. The sad fact of being the brains behind a mission is that you rarely get the glory shot."

Lyn understood. It had been three months since first landing, and this was only her second trip down. And only because she wanted to, not because she needed to. Marao didn't need a ship's captain.

Lyn piloted them down to the surface, giving Zoya a turn at the controls. Another first for the 132-year-old. They both squealed in delight when passing by puffy white clouds, the sky blue above them.

Once on the ground, Lyn ran through her shutdown procedure then turned to Zoya. "Ready?"

Zoya grinned. "You bet I am."

Lyn opened the hatch, the carefully filtered and controlled HVAC system behind them, a new world of scents and natural airflow before them, something they hadn't experienced since leaving Earth almost a year and a half ago. Zoya raised a hand to shade her eyes.

Isabel stood smiling at the base of the ramp. "Welcome to Marao." A breeze ruffled her long-sleeved pullover and slacks. No flight suit. No risk of sudden decompression here.

Zoya tentatively stepped forward, Lyn following. When they reached the ground, Zoya knelt and pulled a glove off. She ran her fingers through the dry, clumped grasses and raked through the loose dirt. When she tipped her head up toward the sun, she closed her eyes. Tears streaked down her cheeks.

Alarmed, Lyn knelt by her side. "Are you okay?"

Zoya nodded, overcome. "You don't remember a time before the war, do you?" She wiped her face with her bare hand.

"No," Lyn said, looking at Isabel. "We don't."

Zoya took in several deep breaths. "It smells like *home*," she managed to say in a small, broken voice, pitched high with emotion. Her whole body shook. "I never expected that again." She glanced from Lyn to Isabel, who now knelt beside her too. "It's a straight shot to memory. My grandmother's house. A shack, really. Steps from the ocean, the sea breeze and grasses . . ." She sat back on her heels and shook her head. "I can't explain it. I left when I was so young. Nothing has reminded me of that for so long." She sighed deeply.

Isabel rubbed her back. "I know what you mean. Back home the few remaining trees were pines and when the sun warmed the needles on the ground. Oh, that's what this smells like. Not the stench of the mass graves. I thought that's all I remembered till I came here."

A swirl of wind twisted a column of dust that engulfed them. They all burst out laughing then started choking and coughing.

"Help me up," Zoya said. "My knees may be young, but my muscles are old." Lyn and Isabel gently lifted her to her feet. She brushed the dirt from her knees then took Isabel's hand. "Now, show me around our new home."

Lyn left Zoya to tour with Isabel while she went in search of Sharyn and Fran for an update on construction. In only a few weeks what had been an empty field had turned into a bustling community. All around, permanence was being build into the land. The greenhouse finished, Miriam had brought plants down and was spotted walking a plot for her new garden. Small bungalows, painstakingly extruded by newly built cranes, lined what would become the main street. Progress ranged from perimeter walls to full walls with windows, and to finished homes with roofs and couples waving from doorways and deciding furniture placement. The Cannos became managers, overseeing construction since Fran could no longer be everywhere at once. Lyn marveled at it all while at the same time feeling a subtle push toward an edge she feared, letting go of Earth.

Later, flying back to *Endurance*, Zoya was quiet. She stared out the window at the island, shrinking as they rose to orbit. Finally she turned to Lyn. "Have you adjusted to this becoming home?"

"I'm not sure. I hope to if we need to."

Zoya didn't take her eyes off Lyn. "You think we might yet get back? Is that a possibility?"

Lyn dodged the question. "I said we'd continue to look for ways back, and we have been and will continue to." She turned to Zoya. "Do you have a preference?"

"I thought I did. All I wanted was to return home, to die on Earth. But now, I'm not so sure it matters. I have most of my family. I have my husband. Should I care?"

Lyn shook her head. "No. For now, Marao is our best bet. I've wondered if people were shifting their hopes from returning to staying."

"Home is where the heart is, is it not? Do you have loved ones on Earth?"

"I do. My parents. My brothers."

"No one *in* your heart?"

Lyn quirked a sheepish half-smile. "No, not like that."

"Too bad." Zoya left it at that. "I feel sorry for those away from close family. The Cormiers have other children."

Lyn searched Zoya's face for meaning. "I know. Have they said anything?"

"Suzanne seems very down to earth." She chuckled. "Will we have to change that expression to 'down to Marao'?" She paused. "Jeanne, however, I can't figure out. Do you know she thinks this whole thing is a hoax? That we're in a simulation and that we never left Earth? A glorified Avatar Night."

Lyn stared, alarmed. "She's made vague references, but she hasn't been that explicit with me."

"She doesn't trust you."

Not surprising. "Is anyone taking her seriously?"

"Some. Others I think are curious to see how far she'll take her grumbles. I find her amusing."

A hoax? A full-on deception. "Well, I wish it were true. I can't imagine what anyone would have to gain from such a ploy, if it were even possible. Did that planet seem fake to you?"

"No. It was all too real. But reality is in the eye of the beholder. I want to believe, so I do."

"Is it that easy?"

"The similarity to Earth is quite astonishing, except for the absolute absence of animals, not even insects. You couldn't do that on Earth. Remove all trace. And simulations are good, but not that good. Yet there are those who believe the Earth is flat despite all evidence to the contrary. How can you explain that? Yet they do. I sometimes think I should have become a psychologist. I'm fascinated by the human mind. The lengths to which people will go to deceive themselves."

A WEEK LATER, Zoya developed a fever. Isabel had recovered completely, but the doctor was less reassuring this time given Zoya's advanced age. Still, he adjusted the bots and within a week she was feeling better. He'd mentioned he was continually altering the medbots to handle Marao's microbes, but the health of the landing parties remained within normal ranges. Marc, in his weekly meetings, assured Lyn everything was under control despite the slowly growing number of people coming down with mild illnesses.

Convinced they were no worse off than on Earth before the age of medbots, when people got sick, recovered, and continued on, Lyn was surprised when the doctor called her to the Medical Suite, dissatisfied with the first officer.

"When I let Commander Franklin know that I was going to bring this to your attention, he disconnected the com link on me."

Lyn looked at her doctor, incredulous. "Why would he do that? What issue are you bringing to me?"

The medbots, it turned out, were not keeping up with the spreading illness. "There's a growing epidemic on the surface. People getting sick seemed minor at first. A cough, the sniffles, but easily treated. Now, only a week later new cases aren't responding."

"Can't you reprogram the medbots?"

"I have been. The alien microbes are infecting the medbots. That's why people are getting sicker. I can't keep up with the mutations."

"I don't understand."

"The medbots are modified stem cells. They have their own genetic material, that's where we put in the properties to fight illnesses and repair damage, but those genes are vulnerable to mutations and attack, just like any other cell. The alien microbes can infect our medbots, like the viruses we know on Earth. We're just not as well prepared for them here."

Lyn peered into the microscope. A bunch of dots. That's all she saw. She stood and crossed her arms. "I always thought of the medbots as tiny robots, like Sharyn's housekeeping bots—running around cleaning things up. Not actual living things. Is there anything we can do? Is this contagious?"

"Not so far. Despite people coming and going, no one who hasn't been down has become ill. The infection remains deep in the immune system, not spread by coughing or sneezing. Though I can't promise that couldn't change."

She let the doctor deal with his area of expertise. She would focus on hers. From her office, she called Marc. His side of the story was that the com link disconnected itself. "Just a blip in the signal," he assured her. As if to make the point, his image pixelated and blurred. He downplayed her concerns about the illnesses.

"We're not talking bleeding from the pores," he protested. "It's the sniffles. A slight fever. We can handle this. The doctor is overreacting."

"I'd like everyone to resume full life support packs," Lyn said.

"That's not necessary," he said. "This is my call, down here."

His defiance stung. "It affects everyone, even those up here. That makes it my call. I'm still mission commander. You know better than this. What's going on?"

"No one is suffering, no one is too weak to work. What their data say and how we all feel are two different things. I think the doctor is jiggering the data to make us look sick."

"That's crazy." She could see where this was headed. She'd seen it on the *Aphrodite* pods. A disagreement growing into an insurrection. She needed to get a grip on this.

LYN CALLED SHARYN on the surface. She confirmed that people were experiencing flu-like symptoms. "I thought it was normal. Marc said it was to be expected, but Doctor Amos has declared a health concern so I'm confused. Are we at risk or not?"

Lyn had to admit she didn't know. She ordered the ground settlement to resume full life support suits. That caused grumbling, rightly as it turned out, because you couldn't blow your runny nose in a helmet. The doctor emphasized that the damage had been done. Everyone on the planet had been exposed, so it was a matter of latency determining when symptoms would appear. Reluctantly, Lyn rescinded the order but refused to allow anyone to go down who had not been already. It was the sort of indecision and waffling that fomented confusion and anger. She'd lost Marc on principle and now risked

Sharyn losing faith. The last thing she needed was Jeanne Cormier showing up in her doorway, but that's exactly what she got.

"You would kill someone to keep up this ruse?" she said, more a demand than a question.

"What are you talking about?"

"This," she swung a hand around, taking in the ship, "is all a fake. We're not really stranded light years from Earth. We're in orbit about a planet, or hidden behind the moon. *Merde*, we could be in a hangar in Omaha. Those windows are screens, showing us only what you want us to see."

"That's not even possible. And why would I do that? Why would anyone?"

"That is not my concern. My only concern is exposing you and freeing us. Perhaps we are being watched, we are some popular reality show. I don't know and I don't care."

With an epidemic on the planet and Jeanne threatening the ship, Lyn asked Suzanne for help.

"What can I possibly do?" she said. She stood at Lyn's desk, having refused a seat. This was not going to be friendly. "I have no evidence to disprove her claim."

"She has no evidence to prove it."

"Forgive me. I do sympathize with your position, but she's my wife. I won't take a side against her. I've told her I doubt her claim, I even insisted she get the vaccine, and we all went to the surface to pick out a home site. I don't think it changed her mind, but that's the best I can do."

Lyn had no time for petty conspiracy theories. Within days, the medical unit on the surface filled with the sick. Sharyn fell ill. No, not Sharyn! Zoya had a relapse. Fevers and chest congestion were turning into pneumonia. It happened so fast. At first a few got sick, then more and then sicker. Dr. Amos set up intensive care units on *Endurance* and the surface.

"I already have three patients in comas," Dr. Amos said. "I expect this will get substantially worse."

Lyn recalled Marc and Natalie from the planet. They met in the doctor's office. Lyn sat, elbows on knees, staring out the door at the filled beds. Each had started with cold-like symptoms but within hours progressed to fevers, inflammation, and pain, spiraling downward to respiratory distress, brain swelling, vomiting, diarrhea. Isabel had recovered from her initial infection, but was now on the surface in an ICU with pneumonia.

It was the first time she'd seen Marc in person in weeks. He took the doctor's chair and sat like an exhausted old man. His flight suit hung on him. She'd deal with him later. Natalie seemed well, if stressed.

"How concerned do we need to be?" Lyn asked the doctor.

He launched into a lengthy lecture on the exomicrobiology of the planet. Only Natalie seemed to understand his explanations. Lyn kept interjecting, "Your point, please."

What fascinated him, he said, was that the illnesses appeared similar to many Earth-like pandemics. "But those infectious agents invariably began with animals—either domestic or wild." Here, he said, with no animal vectors, it had to be in the soil, maybe even the plants. "But then there's this." He pulled up a holograph showing rhythmic pulsing, like an audio signal. "Once the microbes grow into colonies, they emit electrical signals."

Natalie stepped forward and examined the graph. "I'm seeing this in the plant samples I collected."

They chatted for a few minutes about similarities until Lyn cut in. "What does this have to do with anything?"

"Well, it's like brain activity. Thought," Dr. Amos said. "But they weren't there a week ago. The microbes weren't as virulent a week ago either."

"Meaning?" Lyn asked.

"What if they're sentient?" Natalie asked. "That this," she pointed to the graph, "is communication."

"Oh, god," Lyn said, pressing a hand to her forehead. "Intelligent?"

"Not necessarily," Natalie said. "We've known since Darwin that plants communicate and have since learned that they exhibit a level of consciousness, just not anything approaching humans'. When a tree is injured, for example, say by an insect, it sends a signal through its roots and across the mycorrhizal network in the soil to other trees. They react by secreting chemicals to repel the insect. This can be hormonal, but also electrical, much like an animal's nervous system." She turned to the doctor. "Do you think they sense our presence, or feel threatened by us, and are trying defend themselves?"

"The patterns are not random. That could mean any number of things."

"Maybe trying to communicate?" Lyn suggested.

Natalie agreed. "For all we know, these plants and microbes are having heated discussions among themselves about us and our presence here. Whether they are happy to have us here or not, we can't know. But the fact that we're getting sick might indicate the latter."

"You could be literally walking on a sentient brain—the very ground under your feet," the doctor said. "They might be thrilled to see you but inadvertently making you sick. Wouldn't be the first time a harmlessly intended exposure resulted in pathology."

Marc emitted his own signal. A groan. "All this woo psychology. They're plants. Not that different from desert scrub back home."

Natalie gave him a withering look. "You make me rethink 'higher life forms,'" she said with attitude.

It wasn't hard to sense tension between them. This wasn't the sibling-like bickering she'd seen in the past. This was more ominous. "All this is very interesting," Lyn said to deflect the tension, "but how does that help us? What do we do now?"

They each looked from one to the other, as if a magical answer were forthcoming. All eyes settled on Lyn.

"Fine," she said, resigned. "We'll proceed under the assumption these are *not* intelligent life forms. First priority is curing these illnesses." Crew came first. Always.

"What about the settlement?" Marc asked. It was like he didn't dare offer options, such as giving up, abandoning the planet.

"All construction halts," Lyn said. She addressed the doctor. "Can we bring everyone back to *Endurance*?"

"Right now, we don't have the capacity. There are too many who are too sick. We need the able-bodied to care for the sick ones down there. I'm working on a treatment as fast as I can. Could we bring the *Jedica* up as another ICU?"

Lyn thought about logistics. It made sense to get everyone back on *Endurance*. What if all the pilots got sick and they had the *Jedica* down there? "Let's do that. No need to dismantle anything yet. We'll go back if we can, but for now," she looked at Marc, "we focus on crew health."

He didn't say anything. Natalie dropped her gaze to the floor.

Lyn dismissed Natalie, and the doctor went to treat his patients, leaving her and Marc alone. She needed his help and expertise on the logistics, but he hardly seemed up for it. The fabric of his suit, once snug and revealing of his physique now lay in folds across his midsection and arms. His eyes stared out from boney sockets above sharp cheekbones. She detected a slight tremor in his hand which he stilled when she looked there.

"You've assured me you aren't sick, yet you've lost weight and muscle mass," she said.

"I haven't been to the gym in weeks. The PE units are great, but it means I'm not getting the exercise I used to."

"That's all?"

"Yes. Don't make more out of this than that."

She couldn't possibly make more out of it than what she saw before her, what lay ahead for all her crew. If Marc Franklin could be felled.

"Want me to prove it?" he said, lifting his chin as a challenge. He swooped his arms around in a pathetically weak Okichitaw move then dropped his hands back in his lap. He licked his cracked, dry lips.

"That won't be necessary." She gripped the edge of the desk. "Let's see what the doctor comes up with. If he can't cure this, any thought of remaining here is over." If he couldn't cure this, leaving was the least of their problems.

Pain crossed his face as he looked away. Physical or psychic? "This is our best chance of survival. We don't know we've pissed off any sentient entity down there. We're not conquistadors raping and pillaging. It's ridiculous to sacrifice our quality of life, maybe even our lives, for a bunch of shivering microbes."

"If the doctor can't cure these illnesses, I can't jeopardize the safety of my crew."

"Assuming Doctor Amos is really trying—"

"Enough." Lyn paced then leaned against the wall. A subtle vibration, *Endurance*'s pulse, buzzed in her head. Comforting, steady.

Marc bent forward, weight on his bony elbows. "What if we built sealed habitats like we would have for a planet with no atmosphere."

"We could, but I don't know if we can trust people to remain sealed. When you can remove your helmet and not die immediately, it's very tempting. But we have sick people right now. Any future plans are on hold till we know where we stand with this infection."

He sat, face buried in his hands. Neither spoke for long minutes but she could see him struggling.

"Six hundred people died," he said finally. "That was my idea, to leave them. I can't let that happen to us."

That's what this was about? "Of course we won't let that happen," she said gently, leaning forward. "We, Marc. We are a team, but that was *my* decision, *my* responsibility. The six hundred are on me. You offered to stay with the survivors. I refused. That's on me, too. And Philbrick. They didn't die because we left them. They died because they couldn't maintain a cohesive team for a month."

Lyn remembered the fear in Georgie's face and voice when she talked about the breakdown of moral structure. How the *Aphrodite* crew were threatening people and the chaos that pulled them apart. Fatally. "Do you really believe we should stay on that planet?"

He leaned back and closed his eyes. "No. I don't." He said very quietly, as if admitting defeat, "I don't know what to do."

Chapter 27

ONCE LYN SENT the order to evacuate, a new urgency flowed through the decks. The organizing principle of their existence was now the health of the crew. Marc and Natalie returned to the surface to coordinate bringing everyone back up to *Endurance*, including the *Mars Jedica*. Fran turned her construction expertise to swapping out the *Jedica*'s dormitory bunks for medical beds, until she fell ill and needed a bed herself.

The doctor triaged the sick—who could stay in their room, who needed the ICU of the Medical Suite or the *Jedica*'s hospital ward. *Endurance*'s four beds were reserved for the sickest, Zoya, Ruby, Sharyn, and Liam.

Hau Butler, Sharyn's second, deftly manipulated the roster of the able-bodied. Sharyn, lying still on the bed, tubes helping her breathe and feeding her, jolted Lyn every time she entered the ICU. She held her hand, wiped her forehead, but was otherwise helpless. Thing was, Sharyn would know what to do. She'd be the one Lyn would turn to for guidance in managing morale.

Miriam helped fill that void, coordinating food service not only for those who could make it to the dining room, but enlisting volunteers to deliver meals to those in their rooms. Lyn hadn't needed to ask her to do this.

The crew rotated through schedules and also sickbeds. Lyn never knew from one day to the next who would show up for duty, who would be in bed. She could see the progression. Day after day, more remained sick or fell ill than recovered. The closest her training had come to this was during her Pulsar cadetship when they simulated a catastrophic failure of the ship, disintegrating bit by bit, sucking virtual crew members away. They'd never simulated a pandemic. That simply wasn't something they'd have to deal with in space. They could return to Earth or Mars or call a hospital ship out.

She knew how to use a jetspray, so she pulled a regular nursing rotation. It was hard, though, seeing close colleagues so ill. Ani followed Natalie, to Medical for the diagnosis then to bed in their room.

Each night, Lyn crawled into bed for a few hours or minutes of rest. When she slept, she dreamed of storm surges racing toward her little house in Bodega Bay or sinkholes in Montana collapsing into empty aquifers. She woke, exhausted by a relentless movement toward doom. She left the running of the ship to Petra and Edward. He'd taken to wearing a hazard suit and rarely left the Engineering suite. She was warmed to see Diana helping, though there wasn't a lot they could do. Run around with jetsprays, cold packs, food. She passed Diana in the hallway and stopped to ask how she was holding up.

"I'm fine. The upside of life with Rose and no medbots. I've done this before." She held up a jetspray. "But not really this." Alarm crossed her face then she recovered and set a tense expression.

Then Lyn's luck ran out. One day she was holding a cold pack against Sharyn's forehead, the next she ached all over, ran a high fever, and coughed up phlegm with every breath. The next morning she woke to Diana by her bed holding an ice pack and Dr. Amos scanning her. She thought her head would explode from the pain. In the moment, she wasn't able to think about what it signaled to the others—here she was, felled again. That she improved over the next few days, didn't lesson the warning she couldn't ignore.

Too weak to pace, much as she wanted to, she sat in the doctor's office and grilled him about treatment, why they couldn't keep up.

"This is a cascading immune suppression," he said. "Once the medbots are rendered useless, even our own beneficial bacteria can wreak havoc. Fevers, organ failure. Mrs. Fischer is infected with alien microbes that had tested harmless two months ago but are now quite virulent. Liam's kidneys are shutting down."

"Why can't you program the medbots to cure this?"

"I have been. It doesn't work anymore. We need all new medbots, and our Recyc-All isn't sophisticated enough to make them."

We can find and collect dark matter but we can't make medbots? "So what do we do?"

Perhaps the doctor's greatest strength was his inability to experience panic. Lyn was trained not to show panic, but that didn't mean she couldn't feel it pulse inside her, hammering her heart, making her mind race. What she wouldn't give for an android's temperament.

"I'm going to try an old treatment from the last century," he said. "Replace the immune system and gut biome by removing a patient's medbots and alien invaders and replacing them with a healthy system from someone not infected or vaccinated."

It didn't take a supercomputer to figure out who the doctor had in mind as the donor. "Edward."

"Obviously."

His refusal to go to the planet would now come back to haunt him. "He's the only one?"

"Everyone's been to the surface at least once. Even the baby. The vaccine used fragments of the microbes."

Poor Edward.

"What's involved?"

"I take his bots and gut microbes, grow them, and inject them into the patients who have had their microbiomes removed. That's done easily enough—the same way I'd take Edward's. They'll be vulnerable to infection for a couple days before the new bots kick in, but that's manageable."

"It sounds easy. Why haven't you tried it?"

"It takes time and the illnesses are spreading fast. A week ago this seemed very minor and doable. Also, this is a one-time fix. People can't then go back to the planet. They'll just be infected again."

Never go back? "Why can't we develop immunity? Like with viruses on Earth."

"These appear to behave like rhinoviruses and influenza. Resistance is temporary. The way the microbes are mutating, you'd certainly become reinfected."

Edward would balk at any invasive procedure. She could order him, but that went against everything she hoped to stand for with her crew. Trust. Knowing they were her first priority. But now they needed his help. It was a problem, and she felt confident Edward could solve it on his own. And who better to help convince him than Isabel, sick and lying in the medical unit on the *Jedica.*

MUCH AS EDWARD liked Isabel, he wouldn't set foot on the *Jedica* filled with sick people, so Lyn sat with her chief engineer in her office, vid linked to Isabel. She explained the procedure to both of them then sat back and waited.

"No one's taking any bots out of me," Edward said.

Isabel's breathing was labored from pneumonia. "A week ago, I felt fine," she said, wheezing, "then I woke with fever and chills." She lay quiet. Breathing took all her strength.

Edward sat immobile, watching his assistant's face on the screen. He didn't usually make eye contact.

Isabel smiled weakly. "Doc says you can help. I know you don't want to. Well, not that you don't want to help." She paused to breathe. "Tell me what you don't like about the procedure."

"You're sick. I'm not a doctor. The doctor can help you." Edward rubbed his hands along his thighs.

"Yes, and you can provide the medicine. Tell me what you don't like about the procedure."

Edward sat stonily. "I don't like the jetspray. It makes me itch, like bugs are crawling under my skin."

"Right," Isabel said. "I remember you telling me that. When you need medicine, the doctor gives you a pill, like the old days. But he won't be putting anything into you. It shouldn't make you itch."

"He said I could sleep through it, but what if I don't wake up?"

"The doctor would never let that happen," Isabel said.

"I don't want to go into the Medical Suite. There are sick people in there."

"Ask him if he can do it in your quarters." Her voice was growing weaker, her eyelids drooped. She was becoming overtired.

Lyn asked quietly, "This is a puzzle, isn't it, Edward? How to help Isabel and the others without hurting you."

He stilled. Thinking no doubt. Edward was always thinking. "He needs the bots from my blood."

"Yes," Lyn confirmed.

"And from my gut."

"Yes."

"He can take my bots from the gut. I only have to shit for that, right?"

Lyn coughed to keep from blurting a laugh. "Maybe."

Isabel's eyes flashed concern. "Captain, is that right?"

"I think so."

"Well, damn. Edward, you get to spread your shit everywhere." She chuckled then coughed.

Edward looked relieved. "He can program my bots to go to my colon. That's easy."

Lyn suppressed a gag reflex. "I'll talk to the doctor and let you know."

The doctor agreed reluctantly. "It's not ideal, but it can work."

For the next week, the doctor collected Edward's bowel movements.

"Please, Doctor, don't tell the patients how this works," Lyn said.

The doctor wanted to test the treatment on someone not so sick, but the extra time it took to collect Edward's bots meant Isabel was slipping deeper into organ failure. Lyn had hoped to be the guinea pig, but Isabel simply couldn't wait the extra days that would require.

"It's only fair," she told Isabel, who barely responded, her breathing labored and gravelly. "You volunteered to go first on the planet." She held Isabel's hand and got a comforting squeeze back.

The doctor moved Isabel to her quarters so she could be isolated during the vulnerable time after he removed her medbots and before the new ones kicked in. Marc stayed with her the whole time. Otherwise, only the doctor could enter.

For two days the ship became a quiet waiting room, or at least that's how it seemed to Lyn. She sat on the edge of another precipice, fearing for Isabel, but also for all of them. This had to work.

Alone in the meditation room late the second night, she mind linked to Isabel and talked quietly, encouragingly, hoping she wasn't freaking her out. Then she got a response.

Is that really you? Isabel said.

Lyn smiled. *Yes, remotely. But Marc is right there with you.*
I know. Thank you.
Then quiet. Lyn hoped she'd fallen asleep.
She felt a presence and opened her eyes to the doctor taking a seat beside her.
"Shouldn't you be with Isabel?" she asked.
"She's doing fine. I've done all I can."
"You did good, Doc."
"I did what I am programmed to do."
No you didn't. She wanted to explain how extraordinary he was, but sometimes it wasn't worth it to argue with a doctor. "Just say thank you."
He didn't say anything right away. Thinking? "Thank you."
"You're welcome. And did your programming send you here?"
A pause. "I thought you might like some company."
Whatever infernal code he had buried deep in his programming, intended to block their return to Earth, she refused to blame him. He didn't put it there. He could monitor her vitals, calculate her caloric intake, but intuit her emotional state? She preferred to think that was more than simple programming. "I would. Thank you."
"You're welcome."
They sat in companionable silence. Lyn sent good thoughts to Isabel, without the mind link. She didn't want to wake her. Dr. Amos hummed softly. She found that endearing then realized it was probably his processors while he monitored patients or analyzed lab results.

DR. AMOS RELEASED Isabel from quarantine the next day. Though weak, her lungs were clear and she was alert and symptom free. Marc went next, but the doctor rolled out treatments to the rest of the crew while he recovered, Isabel by his side. After her own treatment, Lyn's nagging cough went away.

It was not, however, a miracle cure. By mid-May, Lyn had her senior staff back except for Sharyn. She remained in a medical coma with brain swelling and a meningitis-like infection. Roughly half the patients did not respond to the doctor's treatment. Most of those slipped into comas. Some he had to induce to keep from dying. With so much tissue damage, he said, standard medbots wouldn't work without a medical-grade Recyc-All.

That was it? For want of a piece of technology, they were lost? "What do you need that we don't have? Can't we just build it?"

"I'm afraid not. It's not the technology per se, but the life forms needed to seed the bots. *Endurance*'s Recyc-Alls can't make life. I can only grow existing forms, not the specialty bots we need."

In Lyn's mind, Sharyn had been the whole point of the exercise in developing the treatment. She was the one who needed it most, yet was among those who would not benefit from it. She argued for the doctor to try. He did, but still Sharyn did not respond.

"Too much damage has been done. This isn't a medbot issue anymore. She, Dr. Betero, and the others are simply too sick to recover under these circumstances. I can keep them on life support." He paused. "But for how long?"

Visions flashed of a ghost ship floating through space, filled with comatose crew members.

"Until I say otherwise," she said.

Lyn left Medical in a daze. Across the hallway, she faced the doorway to Laundry. She could hear Sharyn's laughter. She needed to hear it. This was it, then. Every expedition, every pioneering endeavor had a moment of truth—weighing the risk of continuing versus turning back. George Mallory died trying to summit Mount Everest, Edmund Hillary survived. What crucial decision did each make that sealed the outcome? There were perhaps twenty steps between the door to the Medical Suite and Engineering's. In that span, she made a very simple, but not easy, decision.

She said to Edward, "When can you and Diana be ready to run a simulation with TPCA?"

"I'd say six days," Edward said, looking up from the holochart at his desk.

"Please get to work," Lyn said. "It's time to reopen Project ROSE. We'll be abandoning Marao."

Chapter 28

THEY WERE LEAVING Marao. It killed Lyn not to be able to tell everyone that balancing the bad news was the good news of trying to return to Earth. Despite her resolution to be more transparent, to do better than Tara had done at Enceladus, she kept finding this was different. Sometimes, often it seemed, ignorance was best. Collecting T particles and actually opening a wormhole with them were light years apart. Don't raise hopes only to dash them if TPCA failed. Despite those in comas, with no hope of recovery if they couldn't get back. Despite family members worried their loved ones might die, surely would die if the doctor couldn't stem the relentless attack of Marao's microbes.

Isabel, thankfully, recovered quickly if not completely. Though still weak, she and Marc oversaw dismantling the settlement. Pods flew back and forth from the surface to *Endurance*, filled with broken-down buildings and equipment destined for the Recyc-All. For now, the crew only knew they were leaving because of the illness. The panic was palpable, and with Sharyn in the ICU, Lyn was left to reassure people that building *Endurance* out into a space station really was feasible.

Still, work continued on Project ROSE. Diana let Lyn know when they were ready to run a real-time simulation with the full team at the controls. Diana's computer, however, couldn't run it when the time came for the actual traverse. How would they get around Petra's interference? It was time for Lyn to come clean about her computing ability and the need to use her mind to control the ship instead of Petra. She gathered those who needed to know in the conference room and blocked Petra from listening in. Curious faces greeted her around the table. Marc, Edward, Diana, Isabel, Ani, Ghez. They'd grown used to Edward wearing a mask.

As Lyn explained her brain enhancements and that she'd override Petra to control the ship, only Diana showed real surprise. Her expression indicated she might think Lyn was part monster. The others were more curious. Edward grilled her on specifics.

"I don't know how they did it," Lyn said. "I was unconscious."

"What's the interface like?" he asked. "This has been theorized for years but I didn't know anyone had undergone the procedure."

"I'm not sure how to describe it. I'm not constantly aware I have this database, this power, in my head. I'm not a savant. I don't just know everything."

"That's a relief," Diana said. She scrutinized Lyn's face, not taking her eyes off her.

Questions circled the table. Ani wanted to know if Lyn would be piloting *Endurance*.

"Lord no," she said. "I'll leave that to you. We need better than a solid C."

Ani suppressed a laugh while the others looked confused.

Ghez assured them ne could fine-tune the calculations so they wouldn't miss the solar system, but what about navigating through the opening, ne asked.

"We won't travel far," Diana said, "just cross a boundary. Normal navigation and propulsion can resume once we're on the other side."

"By the time I need to take over," Lyn said, "there won't be a lot left for me to compute. We'll have stripped *Endurance* down to her girders, and sensors will be minimal. No house bots, no elevator, not even any engines. Just life and safety."

"Just the air we breathe," Diana said, her voice small.

"Yes."

The room went quiet, which meant Edward was satisfied. Marc and Diana both looked at him. He stared at the wall. "Well, why are we still sitting here? We have a simulation to run." He stood, but Lyn waved him down.

She looked at the others. "Are you comfortable with this? Because if you aren't, we can't go forward."

"Imagine if Jeanne got hold of this news," Marc said, seemingly unfazed.

Diana leaned back, seemingly overwhelmed.

"I guess I am, as long as you're sure you can handle this," Marc said. "I mean physically. Does the doctor know about this?"

"He does."

"And how do we use your interface for the simulation with Petra lurking in the background? Won't she interfere?" Isabel asked.

"She'll be fine as long as it's a simulation. I'll couch it in terms of a learning exercise. Maybe a potential entertainment. She doesn't care until we turn on the real TPCA."

"And she knows you have this capability?" Ghez asked.

"Yes, though she's frustrated she can't access my files. Thankfully."

"Frustrated?" Marc asked.

"Long story."

Not to Edward. "Computers are constantly learning, just like people, so they are also modeling human emotions. They take in everything from the environment around them, including us, and incorporate—"

Marc waved him to stop. "Yeah, I get it. No need for details." He turned to Lyn. "Why didn't you use this ability before? Like when Ani's pod went haywire?"

"I tried to but couldn't. It was creepy. All we were dealing with were overdue updates."

"Correct," Edward said. "The other problems we've encountered were unrelated."

The Pulsar codes. It was hard to sort out which issues were innocent and which ones malicious.

"Speaking of which," Marc said. "If your 'enhancements' were put there by Pulsar, how can we trust them? Why don't you have the same mission to keep us from returning?"

"We don't know the travel prohibition was Pulsar," Lyn said, prompting a skeptical look from Marc. She nodded. "Regardless, it's not in there. I've looked."

Marc turned to Diana. "I'm okay with this if you are. This is your show."

She startled. "It's a lot to take in, but if Edward's okay with it, then I am." She didn't look at Lyn.

"If there are no more questions," Lyn said, "Diana, I'd like to get your most recent files uploaded. We have a simulation to run in the morning. I'm here if anyone would like to talk privately."

After the others had left, Diana pulled her computer cube out of her pocket and placed it on the table. It was so tiny. It hardly seemed possible it held the information needed to open a wormhole and return them to Earth. Lyn stared at the cube.

"You carry this around in your pocket?" she asked.

"Seemed safest. Don't want to leave it lying around. There's no place to lock it away that can't be opened by someone or something." Meaning Petra.

Lyn searched Diana's face for clues to her emotions. What a long, strange journey they'd taken together. Six months ago they'd kissed. A blip. Meaningless. Yet not.

"You okay?" she asked. "You were right. This is a lot to take in."

Diana shoved her hands in her pockets. "I'm good." She nodded to the cube. "You want me to wait?"

"It'll take a few minutes, but sure." Diana probably didn't want the cube out of her sight though once Lyn had the files, the cube wasn't needed.

She clipped the cube to the port behind her left ear and initiated the transfer. All crew had a superficial port to enable mind links and hands-free communications. Hers went deeper and allowed access to her brain enhancements. She could link remotely, as she had earlier to read Diana's files, but transferring the zettabytes of data for Project ROSE went faster with direct contact.

Diana stared at the table between them. "When I droned on about my parents' research and you said you had no idea what I was talking about, were you lying?"

"No. I reviewed the research, but that didn't mean I understood everything I was seeing. This," she tapped her head, "is more like storage with access. It didn't make me a genius. It does have enormous processing power, but I'm still a fallible human, if that's what you're wondering."

"I'm not sure what I'm wondering."

Lyn's right eye twitched. She pressed her hand against her face to still it. "Sorry, side effect."

Sweat formed around her scalp. The files were almost finished uploading. The connection brief enough to leave only a minor headache.

THE NEXT MORNING, when Lyn got to the bridge, everyone was assembled and waiting. Because it was a simulation and not the real thing, Edward sat on the lowest level in front of a hologram of the TPCA controls. He'd monitor the machine itself. Isabel sat across the row from him with a hologram of the Recyc-All fuel supply controls. For the real thing, he'd be in the launch control room and Isabel would be in Engineering. Ani and Ghez sat in their usual seats. Diana sat alone in the science row.

Lyn locked the bridge doors and set the room to private. She fastened her harness. "Let's begin."

"Disengaging gravity," Marc said.

Lyn's stomach fluttered. Diana grabbed her thermos of coffee as it floated away. "Sorry," she said, and locked it down.

The minutes ticked by while Edward read off the gauges. A hum vibrated through the bridge. Lyn wasn't sure the others could feel it, but she was sure Edward could.

Ghez took control of the ship's fine guidance sensors that were critical to ending up where they wanted to be—a star trillions of kilometers away. "All systems go," ne said. "Ready on your mark, Captain."

"Engage TPCA, Chief."

On the main screen, they watched a simulated laser beam shoot from the front of *Endurance*.

"Beam engaged," Edward reported. "All measurements normal."

"Fuel lines operating within parameters," Isabel said.

"Feel free to explain what's going on, Doctor Squires," Lyn said.

"We have T particles concentrating in front of the ship. We can't see anything because they don't react to visible light. We'll know it's working when—There!" A small disk of distortion shimmered in front of them. "That's the portal."

It appeared as a small bubble, increasing in size, ringed by lights, starlight bent and deformed.

"Opening one meter," Edward said. "Growing one meter per minute."

"Can we increase output?" Isabel asked. "We don't want to run out of fuel before it's big enough."

"We need an opening 50 percent larger than the ship," Diana said. "Bigger would be better. If we hit the side, we're done."

"Increasing beam 10 percent," Edward said.

For the next hour, Ghez called out the increasing size and Isabel tracked the remaining fuel. For most of that time all they saw were stars, ringed by the distortion and then more stars.

"The stars seen through the portal are from our solar system," Diana explained, "those outside the opening are from our current position. Note the large star at the center—" Her voice caught. She cleared her throat. "That's our sun. For the real thing, if we're not sure what we're seeing, we can shoot a probe through and confirm before making the traverse ourselves." That was for Marc's benefit.

The back of Lyn's neck tingled.

Gradually the portal widened.

"There," Ghez said. "Saturn. I see rings."

"Can we find Earth?" Lyn asked.

"Earth has moved to the other side of the sun. Saturn is blocking Mars. This is the best we can do," Ghez said.

"Works for me," Lyn said. Her mind vibrated with all the data passing through. She was only marginally conscious of what was happening but knew the readouts everyone was reporting were coming through her. She'd have the mother of all headaches after this. She could feel heat building. Like a hot flash, she surmised. "How much longer till we can enter?" she asked. For the simulation, they'd skip sending a probe through.

"Portal is too small," Edward said. "No clearance yet. Maybe forty minutes."

When Isabel announced they were down to their last 20 percent, Lyn tensed.

"We need another three meters of safety zone," Ghez said.

"Nineteen percent," Isabel said. Minutes ticked by and she continued to count down.

"We have clearance," Ghez reported. "The portal has stabilized."

"We're clear to enter," Lyn said. "Ani, engage thrusters."

"Thrusters engaged," Ani responded.

The simulated *Endurance* bounced like a plane hitting turbulence. We only have to go one kilometer, Lyn thought. How hard can that be?

Alarms sounded. "Sheer forces approaching yellow zone," Marc said, his tone neutral.

"We're doing fine," Edward said. "I'll silence the alarm."

"Acknowledged," Lyn said.

She let her mind explore the simulated ship, which assumed they'd modify it to remove the weak Obs Deck that had blown off the first time. She could hear and sense tension increasing in some sections and pulling opposite. *Endurance* was in a tug of war, but so far, was winning. She stared at the opening moving toward them—them moving toward it. Ghez read measurements softly to Ani, whose hands fluttered over the controls. Isabel continued to read out the remaining fuel amounts. They were down to 12 percent.

"As soon as we enter the portal, TPCA will shut down," Diana said. "The opening will hold for five seconds."

The bridge filled with the chatter of voices reading out numbers and alarm notifications. Everyone maintained the steady tone of seasoned veterans. It was like they'd done this a thousand times.

"We're crossing the portal. Beam shutting down," Edward said.

"Copy that," Isabel said. "Five percent fuel remaining." There was a hint of relief in her voice.

"Portal is closing," Ghez said. "We're through. Transfer complete. Portal has closed."

Endurance stilled, the bumps smoothed and groans silenced.

"Forward thrusters engaged. Motion zero," Ani said. "We have arrived, Captain."

Edward reset gravity. Lyn's stomach lurched as she settled in her seat, her head pounding. She unclipped her harness and leaned forward, face in her hands, heat radiating out of her head, overcome with nausea. She disengaged from the simulation and took some deep breaths.

"Everyone okay?" She managed to squeak out.

Marc leaned in. "More important, are you?"

She nodded, mute. She looked up to see expectant faces watching her, concern masking the joy they should be feeling. "Hey," she said, pointing to the view they hadn't seen in 576 days. Not that she'd been counting. "Look."

They turned to the screen. Saturn, with its brilliant rings, glowed brightly, optimistically. Home. Almost home. Simulated home. It worked. It will work.

"I know it's not real yet, but we did it, right?" Lyn looked at Edward, then Diana.

"Oh my god," Diana said at last. "We did it."

The tension broke. Edward whooped. "We sure did." Everyone cheered. Isabel stood and applauded toward Edward, Diana, and Ani.

"Let's do it again, to be sure," Lyn said. "Maybe we can figure out how to get closer to Earth."

Marc put a hand on her shoulder. "What did this do to you?"

"It's just a headache," she said. "I'll be fine."

"Just the same, let's take a break. Go over the results. See if anything needs adjustment."

Lyn went to her quarters and wrapped her head in an ice pack.

After two more successful simulations, Lyn collapsed onto her bed. With return now sure, her mind whirled to the next problem. Keeping this out of the wrong hands once they were back. Keeping it out of anyone's hands. She fell into a deep, welcome sleep.

Chapter 29

THE NEXT MORNING in Medical, Lyn closed the door to the doctor's office. He sat at his desk, a concession he'd made for humans who prefer to sit when consulting with their doctor. Sit, stand, knees half bent, made no difference to him.

"Doc, can this chip in my brain be removed?"

He looked up at her. Though the original procedure had been erased from his memory along with the rest of *Endurance*'s Pulsar files, he'd found the enhancements during her initial physical exam. "It's not a chip, Captain. It encompasses all the fluid in your brain and employs nanoparticles to form a supercomputer. There's no one part of your brain involved. It's everything. I thought you knew this."

Lyn slumped in the chair next to his desk. "Of course. Yes, I knew that. I've just become accustomed over the years to thinking of it as an old-fashioned chip."

She thought of Diana's cube, how easily it fit into her hand, yet held enormous computing power—enough to realize Project ROSE. Why couldn't Pulsar have inserted a cube into her abdomen or something easily removed? Why did they do this at all? She'd blindly accepted it was normal. She'd even been excited by the prospect of enhanced abilities. They'd explained it so simply—it would give her direct control over the ship, eliminating microseconds of delays that could be catastrophic. In a battle, maybe, but not for what she thought they were doing, exploring the planets. How could she be so fecking naïve back then? Now she was stuck with this monster in her head. A monster that could nevertheless save their lives.

"Here's the thing," Lyn began. She told him about the potential to return but left out the details of how given he was the source of the prohibition against superluminal travel. Not him personally. This wasn't his fault. The firewall between him and Project ROSE meant he couldn't access enough information to do any harm, nevertheless she couched the details in hypotheticals.

"If we were to return to Earth, would there be a way to keep the method of our travel secret?"

"I'm assuming your hypothetical return would involve some advanced technology."

"Yes, and we could destroy whatever propulsion drive used, but we'd also want to erase all the files."

"If you're asking how to erase yours, we can't." He indicated her head.

As she feared. "Is there a way to keep someone from retrieving the files? I can control gateways to you and Petra, but I assume not those who installed it in the first place, right?"

"Correct. I no longer have access to the original Pulsar methodology, so I can't be sure, but it might be possible to set up a line of defense using medbots."

"Talk to me, Doc. How?"

He closed the screen he'd been working on and swiveled toward her. "I'm coming up with this as I speak, so bear with me, but it is common to program the bots to guard specific cells—usually brain memory cells as a way to prevent Alzheimer's. Your data is just another kind of cell. The bots could be, well, armed to guard it."

"You sound hesitant. What do you mean, 'armed'?"

"If you are truly serious about this, as a last line of defense, they could destroy the data cells, but that would also destroy your brain. It might be the only way of preventing anyone else from accessing it. This is not permitted by my current safety protocols."

"I can override your protocols, can't I?"

His eyebrows quirked into a position of concern. "You can, but you are required under the licensing agreement to respect my autonomy. If anything happened to you, I'd be held responsible. My emotions may be rudimentary compared to yours, but I am capable of regret."

He couldn't furrow his brow or soften any of his hard edges, but his eyes appeared kinder somehow. For the first time she noticed how much wear and tear he'd endured. Scratches near the top of his head, the fabric at his shoulder joint frayed. The caduceus on the left side of his chest and "Dr. Amos" written below were worn, small sections of the red border scraped off.

"I won't force you," Lyn said. It'd been a shot in the dark, removing this thing.

His eyebrows dropped back to their standard position. "Perhaps it would be possible to prevent the question of how we got back, hypothetically, of course, ever being asked."

"I don't see how we could dodge that one."

"We still don't know how we got here. If Dr. Squires is right and it was a natural event related to the ring of dark matter, then isn't it possible we got back just as naturally? It's just data. We can alter it to say whatever we want."

Rewrite some software and bingo, new reality. "I love that idea, but too many people will know the truth. Even if we could rewrite their memories, I wouldn't. I think the only way to protect the data is to destroy it. If that means me, too, then so be it."

"For all you know, someone back on Earth has already figured this out. That data came from Earth. It resides there somewhere. Sooner or later, someone will perfect this hypothetical form of travel. Why sacrifice yourself unnecessarily."

Hypothetical or not, he was right. "So all of this is moot."

"Yes."

"Then we need a bluff, buy some time."

"Like in poker?"

"Or magic. Create a diversion, a stall."

"As a line of defense, the bots could be programmed to generate rapid, random passwords. Anyone trying to access your data will be repeatedly denied. It's an old technology, but could work."

"How do I access it?"

"Your genetics are unique. We can fake a lot of stuff, but not what is essentially you. In effect, you are the data."

A headache began behind her eyes, one not caused by her cybernetics. Was she ready? She glanced out the office window and saw Sharyn, comatose. Not only were her own crew's lives at stake, those possibly sentient microbes on Marao were vulnerable. She had to get back safely for her crew, but she wanted to keep Marao safe as well.

"Let's do it," she said. "No one's used passwords for generations. It's bound to buy some time."

The doctor rolled his chair closer. He flipped open the tip of his index finger and plugged the connector into her port. She relaxed back into the chair. All she felt was a slight buzzing vibration.

The doctor chatted while he worked on her, like this was a dental appointment or routine physical. "Huh," he said at one point. "That's interesting."

"What is?" Lyn asked.

"I'm just finishing up." He went silent. Then he unplugged from Lyn's port. "I found something curious during the procedure." He held a hand over her head, scanning. "You've mentioned Pulsar erased some of your memories around the time of the Enceladus incident."

"I have gaps, but enough context to know something's missing. I once ran into an officer in the hallway. She looked familiar, but I couldn't place her. Not unusual, I supposed, but with Pulsar's enhancements, that shouldn't have happened."

"I think your memories are right here." Doc tapped her head. "Just disconnected from consciousness."

"Why would memories still be in me if Pulsar erased them?"

"Erasing memories is an inexact science. Because they get stored throughout the brain, deleting one can affect others nearby—your officer, for instance—or miss a backup copy elsewhere. In this case, I detected memory signatures within your brain computer. Disconnected from normal memory cells."

"What does that mean?"

"They can be recovered. Moved back into your consciousness. If you wish."

Lyn took a deep breath. What might she remember and would she want to? There were too many unanswered questions about this whole adventure and Pulsar's involvement not to see if answers lay in her memories.

"Do you wish me to proceed?" he asked.

"What if there's something really traumatic in there? I was treated for PTS."

"We can monitor as we go. I'll need you to be awake anyway. You can stop me if it's too painful."

"Then yes, please proceed." She leaned back and closed her eyes and Dr. Amos reconnected to her port. After a few minutes, a vivid scene unfolded.

Tara's face floated before her. Lyn flashed back to their ship, the *Arnovetra*, and the mission to Enceladus. She knew what came next and fought it off. Tara's last message. Not now. The scene faded and shifted.

Rachel sat before her, after Enceladus but before Lyn turned whistle-blower and took Pulsar down. She recognized Rachel's Pulsar office, her small desk cluttered with open screens, projects in progress and abandoned. The grimy window behind, backlighting her. She'd taken a desk job since, unspoken, she was not a candidate for command. Rachel was telling her that years earlier, during the war, a government scientist had confirmed the existence of extraterrestrial intelligent life. The news was kept hushed. After the war, Earth's new government leaders prohibited any weapons in space. As the economy improved, a peaceful space race developed to explore and exploit the solar system for tourism. But Pulsar wasn't really exploring, Rachel explained. It was testing technology for contact with the aliens.

"Think about it," Rachel said, "Earth is only four billion years old and we have space travel and conquered the atom. Imagine what's out there on far-older worlds."

Star travel, beyond the ability of humans, could be possible for alien civilizations, she said. Pulsar Force's mission was to take control of the solar system and prepare for conflict with them, and claiming Enceladus would have enabled Pulsar to set up laser weapons. She tried to recruit Lyn to a secret project, telling her what she knew about the aliens and their presumed plans for the destruction of Earth.

"Based on what?" Lyn asked. "From what you tell me, the only contact was receiving a signal. Was it a threat?"

"They wanted to *meet* with us. Think about it, Lyn, how could that be possible? We knew the signal came from a hundred light years away. There was no way we were going to visit them, so they must have the means to come to Earth. That level of technology alone makes the power differential so vast there's no way we'd survive. Like poking your finger into an ant hole."

Lyn shook her head. This was crazy. "Did they speak English? How did they communicate?"

Rachel couldn't answer that. "The original message is lost."

"Why us? Do we know if they contacted any other worlds? Maybe it was a broadcast message sent wide and clearly far."

Rachel couldn't answer that either.

"Rachel, if they sent a message, it had to have left their planet a hundred years ago. If we responded, it'd be another hundred years for them to receive it. That's completely impractical."

Even in shadow, Rachel's face signaled her annoyance. "Don't be a dolt, Lyn. Obviously they have the technology to cross that distance. Otherwise, why would they suggest meeting?"

Rachel faded. Other memories resurfaced. That officer in the hallway. Hellen Jacana, the VP who had assigned her to the Enceladus mission. How could she have forgotten her? Other memories, parties and meetings. Some simply forgotten, others deleted by Pulsar. A list of names, scrolling past like on a screen. Board members and advisors. Names she'd found collecting information to give the reporter writing her truth about Pulsar. Men and women whose names were never made public.

Tara again. The crew were suiting up, getting ready to go down to Enceladus. Tara pulled Lyn close while the others were stowing gear in the lander, both were crying. Tara wiped Lyn's tears. "Shh," she said. "It'll be okay. I can't leave you like this, mad at me."

"I'm not mad," Lyn said. "I'm hurt. You don't trust me."

"I do. You are the only one I trust to get us home safely. You belong up here, in command."

Lyn shook her head, buried in Tara's shoulder. "I want to be with you."

"You are. You are my reason, my purpose. I'll get us back. I promise. Then we'll have what we need to get home."

Tara lifted Lyn's chin and kissed her deeply.

That was the last Lyn had seen Tara alive. It hadn't been a fight. All these years she'd been haunted, misled by a memory that had been taken from her. She cried out in anguish.

"I think that's enough for now," Dr. Amos said. He unplugged.

Lyn jerked back against the chair, gasping for breath. That last image.

"Anything meaningful?"

She pushed the new memory aside. "Lots. But specific to our immediate situation? I'm not sure." She sat forward and rubbed her temples. Focus. Rachel. "Were you aware there was confirmation of intelligent alien contact?"

"Yes. It was before I was created, but known at the time. I believe in 2115. During the war. The reaction, as I recall, was of course there's life out there."

The year before Pulsar Industries/Force was founded.

When Lyn stood, her legs were weak from fatigue. So much to think about. The race to beat the Chinese to Enceladus wasn't about militarizing for another Earth-based war, but for one against aliens. And if what Rachel said was true, it made sense that the faster-than-light travel prohibition was installed by Pulsar. What better way to monitor future space exploration than to code each ship's doctor? Dazed, she left Medical, running into Marc in the hallway.

"I thought you might be here," he said. "How's Sharyn?"

Distracted, disturbed, Lyn hadn't even stopped by her bed. "Same."

"When do we tell everyone about our plans?"

"Let's announce after dinner. Let me talk to Miriam first." She was the only senior staff not in on this yet.

"WHAT DO YOU mean, we're going home?" Miriam asked. She nearly dropped her mug of the S-ration drink they'd come to call Stea, and sat heavily in the seat across from Lyn. They were in Lyn's office, set to private.

She couldn't be vague here. It wouldn't be fair to give Miriam a different story from the rest of the senior staff. It wouldn't be fair to put her at risk, either. The scrutiny they'd face when they got back would be an understatement. They could well be physically probed, any information literally dragged out of them. The key was no one person had all the information. She briefly explained Diana's research, Edward's role, and how when the test blew up, it seemed safer to stay on the planet. But now the bugs had been ironed out. It worked.

"Wow," Miriam said. "For real?"

"For real."

Miriam leaned back, arms crossed, eyes wary. "This is what you and Diana have been up to?" She shook her head. "Damn, and I thought you were finally making a friend."

Lyn gave her the look.

"Wouldn't kill you, you know. She likes you, after all."

Heat flushed Lyn's face. She shook off the notion. "Can you focus, please, on what I'm telling you?"

Miriam put up a hand. "I know, I know. I'm a little overwhelmed. You're sure it'll work?"

"Yes. The only way to save our sickest crew members is to get back to Earth. But if I can't convince you, then I have no hope of gaining the confidence of the rest. And we can't do this without everyone's support." She told her about the simulations, the fact they could abort if it didn't look right when they opened the portal.

Miriam peppered her with questions. "How do we know *Endurance* can handle this traverse?"

"Right now, the ship is fine and we can armor areas that suffered damage the last time. We'll take apart the Obs Deck entirely. The longer we wait, the worse our chances. You up for it? I need to know."

Miriam sat in silence, her expression shifting slowly from teasing skepticism to surprise then she put her hands over her face. "I wish Sharyn could hear you say all this."

"Me too."

She wiped tears. "Of course I'm up for it. Whatever you need."

"I have to tell all the others. Not in as much detail. The less they know, the better. This is serious technology, which if it works, will cause a host of problems when we get back. I'm prepared for that, but I still have to convince them." She waved a hand to take in the ship and its occupants. "Do you think Jeanne's crew will put up a fight? Continue this stupid hoax argument?"

"If they do, they'll have to go through me. I'll make them stand around Sharyn's bed and tell me how this is a hoax."

AT DINNER LYN tapped her glass to get the room's attention. "I'd like everyone to assemble back here after Miriam's crew has cleaned up." She looked to her chef. "Two hours enough?" Miriam nodded. "And I mean everyone— we'll vid link to the sick ones, anyone conscious. This will be important."

Lyn immediately left the dining room to avoid the questions flung at her. She paced her office. The only other obstacle was Petra. It would be simpler if she wasn't listening in. It was silly, perhaps, to worry about what Petra heard. Lyn would have to deal with her eventually. But until she knew how to do that, it seemed best to keep Petra in the dark. And with the announcement being vid linked, setting the room to private wouldn't be enough. She engaged her interface.

"Good evening, Lyn. How can I help?"

"Good evening, Petra. I'd like to run a test of the emergency override. It will mean disengaging you for several hours. Doesn't have to be shipwide. The dining room and com network will do."

"May I ask the conditions being tested?"

"Call it a just-in-case exercise. If something were to happen to you, I'd like to know I'm able to step in. We've had so many odd glitches, it seems overdue to try this."

"Why the dining room? I'd think navigation and life support would be the critical systems to test."

"True. And we can. I wanted to start small. I know it'll give me a headache, so smaller the better." Lyn stood by the window, facing Marao, while she waited for Petra to respond. She was trusting that Petra's mission to support the captain meant she wouldn't interfere. But there had to be protocols in case a captain truly went rogue. What might Petra be capable of?

"I've made a note in my log," Petra said finally. "Engage when ready. I'll find something else to do."

"Take up a hobby," Lyn joked.

"Knitting, perhaps?" Petra chuckled. It was more natural than the last one. She was improving.

Lyn smiled. She didn't want to treat Petra as an enemy. She was a victim of Pulsar, like the rest of them. "Enjoy."

Elaine Burnes

At 2100 Miriam called Lyn. "Everyone's assembled."

"Showtime," Lyn said with a grimace.

She walked down the two flights to the dining room. It was about half filled. A holoscreen showed the faces of those watching by remote. She walked through the room, stopping to squeeze the toe of baby Hope, held in Suzanne's arms. She leaned against an empty table next to the window, Marao glowing behind her. Marc, Diana, and the rest of her senior staff stood in a line by the door. At the ready. For what, she didn't know.

"We've been through a lot, haven't we?" she began. "It's been 580 days, not that I'm counting, since we were flung to the other side of our galaxy. We were the lucky ones. We survived. Many others did not. Back when things looked particularly bleak, I promised you we'd keep investigating what happened and never stop trying to find a way back." She paused to note whose heads perked up. People were listening. Her heart beat toward a crescendo. "The time has come to tell you we have found a way back." Hearing herself say those words out loud brought a smile.

The room remained silent, like after a bright lightning strike in the distance, before the sound reaches you. Then the thunder. Gasps, outcries, shouted questions. How? What caused this? When? Lyn raised her hands.

She reminded them of Diana's theory of the spacequake and resulting wormhole that brought them here. Subsequent research, she said, revealed a way to replicate that phenomenon. The trick was convincing them how it worked without the details that could cause problems when they got back, putting them at risk. She skipped over the parts where her brain computer would take over for Petra. She referred to exotic matter, not T particles or the Teegans. It would take all the fuel they could muster and meant tearing *Endurance* down to bare bones to reduce its mass. But the risk was minimal. If they couldn't see where they were going, they wouldn't go, they could send a probe through first.

"We . . . I . . . had to balance any danger in this maneuver against the possibility we could settle on Marao and live out long and productive lives. That is no longer possible."

"What about the space station idea?" Mr. Ivey said. "Isn't that safer than trying this"—he pointed at Diana—"wacko's theory?"

"I want to go home!" Ernice Dietrich shouted.

"We have a dozen of our friends and family on life support," Lyn said. "We can save them only by returning."

The vid screen lit up with questions. Through the cacophony of shouts, voices snuck through.

"But the doctor has a treatment. My wife is getting better."

"Send the sick ones back. If some want to stay, let them."

"You promised you'd get us home! Let them stay if they want. Leave the *Jedica* for those who don't want to return."

They were shouting at each other as much as at Lyn. She waited them out. Finally they quieted down. "Leaving the *Jedica* behind is not possible. We'll need every ounce of material to make fuel and that includes dismantling it."

Lyn hadn't expected such resistance. How could they not want to go home? Fear, of course. The only thing worse than remaining stranded was dying. They had to be convinced this was safe. Who but one of them could be so reassuring. Jeanne. She'd been advocating for return all along. If she believed this was a hoax, she wouldn't fear return. Lyn caught her eye.

Jeanne stood and raised her arms. "Listen to me, followers!" The room quieted. She shook her head and glanced from Lyn to the faces turned to her. "You know how I've felt. That we should return." People shifted, maybe wanting to speak up but stilled by her power over them. Jeanne turned to Lyn. "I still believe that." She paused long enough for Lyn to relax. "If it's true we cannot survive on that planet, then the obvious solution is to go home. Where I differ with you, Captain, is in the method." She swept her gaze around the room, her followers. "We all know nothing can travel faster than light"—her eyes settled on Diana—"so whatever this woman's 'theory' is about recreating some fictional spacequake is nothing more than quackery."

Lyn's heart fell. She'd been wrong to assume Jeanne wasn't afraid. She was terrified. She had a child now. The room remained silent.

Jeanne wasn't done. "I say we turn the ship toward Earth and make our way."

Diana started to speak, but Lyn raised her hand. No one was going to take fire for her. "Even if we could, you know very well it would take thousands of years, but we'd run out of fuel and food within, maybe a year. There are no planets, no asteroid belts, nothing within range of this ship that would allow us to gather enough material to survive. I'm sorry, Jeanne, it isn't possible."

Jeanne didn't appear the least thwarted by that explanation. "So your alternative is suicide."

The rest of the crowd, silently watching, might as well have vanished. It was just the two of them. "Jeanne—"

"Let me have my say," Jeanne said. Lyn shook her head, but Jeanne went on. "This has been a tremendous responsibility for you, Captain. Not only us, but all those others, the *Aphrodite* survivors—survivors—who would be alive today but for your decision to leave them. I don't know what you were thinking. I'm not sure what you are thinking now. Maybe to you this is the most humane solution. If we all die, the burden is lifted. No more witnesses."

"Enough!" Marc stepped forward. "I would like to remind you—all of you—of the terms and conditions of the passage contract you signed." He stood stiff with contained rage. "This isn't open for discussion. You are to follow the orders of the captain."

Panicked faces swung from Marc to Jeanne to Lyn. If Lyn and her crew lost control of this crowd, they would be outnumbered. She avoided eye contact with Jeanne and nodded to the crowd, signaling her support for her first officer.

"Your contract means nothing out here," Jeanne said.

"Section Two, first item," Marc said, his voice tight, "the vessel shall be at liberty to proceed or deviate from course for any reason sufficient in the judgment of the vessel's captain."

Jeanne closed her eyes and tsked.

"I am furthermore ordering you to remain in your cabin for reasons cited in Section One, item F: refusing to obey orders of the captain and crew and for endangering other passengers."

Jeanne held out her hands. "Care to handcuff me? I'm afraid you'll have to."

The fact the crowd hadn't erupted into violence on Jeanne's behalf, that they stood in a quiet standoff, meant not all were on board with their Follow.

Jeanne looked to Lyn. "There have been rumors, Captain, of your mental instability. That you wanted to kill yourself after botching the *Aphrodite* rescue. All those lives. If we were to return to Earth, you'd have to face justice."

Enough of this roach shit. Lyn was tired of being polite, being the captain, having to toe a line for the sake of harmony, for PR. Whether she got back or not, her career was over. She strode through the crowd toward Jeanne till a circle surrounded the two of them. Fear flicked in Jeanne's eyes. Her fist shot out. Lyn caught it and flipped her to the floor with an easy Okichitaw move. Knee on Jeanne's back, face pressed to the floor, Lyn bent and whispered in her ear, "This is my ship. Stand down or I'll shove you into the recycling chute. You think I'm capable of it, so I might as well." It felt oddly good to be so mean.

"Stop it!" Suzanne rushed toward them, still holding Hope.

Marc grabbed her arm. Lyn stood. Jeanne stayed down.

Suzanne pulled away and leaned toward her wife. "What the hell is wrong with you? Have you forgotten our other children?" Her eyes swept the room. "I'm with Captain Randall. Of course we're going back, or we'll die trying. Staying here is ludicrous."

One by one the passengers sat down. Marc helped Jeanne to her feet and escorted her out of the dining room. Confining her to quarters would do little to stop her vocalizing, but it would send a message that this crew was not to be messed with.

Suzanne faced Lyn. "What do you need from us?"

"There's a lot to do. We leave as soon as the settlement is broken down and we have enough fuel for the trip. Should take a couple of weeks. I thank you in advance for your help during this preparation."

In her quarters later with an ice pack on her head, Lyn reengaged Petra.

"How'd it go?" Petra asked.

"Fine. How's the knitting?"

Petra let out a hearty belly laugh. "Good night, Lyn. I hope your headache isn't too bad."

Chapter 30

DISMANTLING THE SETTLEMENT continued, but with renewed energy now that they knew they would attempt to return to Earth. Piece by piece, the buildings came down. Miriam's greenhouse. All the houses. Lyn pulled a regular shift, they needed all hands. The sooner they finished, the sooner they got back, and the sooner their stricken colleagues could be treated, but each trip down to the planet teeming with alien life reminded Lyn of Rachel's revelation. These couldn't be the same aliens who had contacted Earth, if that was even a real contact, but Rachel and Pulsar believed in the message enough to tamper with her memories. No doubt they were still at it, wherever they were these days. Who else knew about the message? Lyn read through press reports from the time, and Doc was right. They were pretty generic. Nothing to worry about, just a blip, probably some Earth-based contamination of the SETI data. Nothing further had ever been detected. Or at least publicized.

Each trip down also brought her closer to having to deal with the ramifications once they got back. She'd been wrong about Edward. He might not be able to lie, but he sure could keep sensitive information to himself. Diana was the other target, bigger and more important. They needed to talk.

Lyn jiggered the schedule so they went on a run together. When Diana expressed surprise at being paired up, Lyn said, "I'd like your opinion of something."

"Intriguing. What's the something?"

When they were away from *Endurance*, Lyn said, "You were right to be suspicious of Pulsar." She told Diana about her recovered memory of Rachel telling her aliens wanted to meet.

"Whoa. And you're sure this really happened?"

"I'm not sure of anything anymore, but yeah, I think it did, and a lot of what's happened makes more sense with it."

"If Pulsar wanted to control first contact, they wouldn't want anyone else involved," Diana said.

"They'd need to clear space for themselves. Get rid of us pesky tourists."

"You think *they* caused the spacequake?"

"That flash we saw on the *Aphrodite*," Lyn said. "What if it was intended only to cripple the ship? Even a minor emergency would be bound to close space to tourism, at least temporarily. Maybe the quake was an unintended side effect."

"But if the alien contact happened at the start of the war, why is it only becoming an issue now? And your memories were deleted years ago, right?"

Lyn nodded. "I wonder if the Grand Tour was getting too close to whatever they've been working on. Most tours don't go out as far as Saturn."

"And Enceladus was where your mission . . ." Diana's words drifted to silence.

"Failed. Crapped out. You can say it."

"You think there's a connection? I mean, who are 'they'?"

Lyn had the names now, the recovered memory, but none were familiar, and Petra's database showed none currently heading government or an agency. It was like they'd been scrubbed from existence. "I'm flailing to think Pulsar could have been responsible for what happened to us and the *Aphrodite*, but I'm past the point of trusting anyone."

"Including me?"

"That's not what I meant." Lyn smiled. "You and Edward are our only hope of returning. I have to trust you."

"I may be many things, not a lot of them very admirable, but a devious conniver isn't one of them. I'm trying to do the best I can with what I have to work with."

Oh, you have a lot to work with, Lyn thought but did not say. "I'm not sure I've been grateful enough for what you've done."

Diana flicked her hand. "Aw, pishaw. Twern't nuthin'."

Lyn smiled. She could see the island they were heading for. A swath of green and gold surrounded by the blue ocean. Puffy clouds cast shadows. "We should talk about what happens when we get back." She described her plans for protecting the data, destroying TPCA. Diana's cube should be destroyed as well. "Given what we know now, are you okay with that?" Trust requested.

"Yes." Trust accepted.

"My brain is safe," Lyn said, "but what you know would be valuable."

One quick nod. "Edward probably knows more than I do, and I doubt either of us alone could recreate this. The models can't run without the data." She patted her pocket, home to her cube. "We'll be a jigsaw puzzle that's been broken apart. Someone will need all the pieces to put it back together."

"That's what I'm hoping. I don't want to jeopardize you. Or Edward." *I do care about you*, she wanted to say. Maybe she would once they were back and she was out of a job and free to act on her feelings. Since that kiss, every time Diana called her by her name and not by her title, something shifted. Something human.

They flew down to the camp, suited up, and helped load material to take back to *Endurance*.

On the flight back, Lyn sighed with regret. "I'm sorry about all this. I've put you at risk. Also your parents."

"It's not like it was your fault. Returning in the blink of an eye is going to put a pretty big target on me. But worth it, I think. Don't you?"

"I certainly hope so." Lyn focused on flying.

LYN'S MEMORIES, NOW freed, kept bubbling into her consciousness. She had fought the urge to review Tara's last message. All she had remembered of it was, "You know what you have to do." She'd thought it had meant recycling the bodies to make enough fuel to get home, to survive. Back on *Endurance*, in the quiet of her quarters that night, she let that memory surface.

"Hi, Pip," Tara began, using Lyn's nickname. She looked happy, if tired and pale. When had she made this? Lyn couldn't see much of the background, but it had to be in the lander. She could record there in private. Oh, to see her face again. They'd both made lots of these messages, so most of it was the usual I love you, don't feel guilty—though Lyn had—move on, find someone else. She studied her wife's face. Her dark eyes and hair, strands wisping out of her braid, her skin gray from the stress and starvation.

Then Tara said, "I don't really believe our mission was to beat the Chinese. I just don't know for sure. Rachel is involved, and I don't trust her. She tried to recruit me for a secret mission, but it would have meant separating us, so I refused. I didn't say why—don't worry! But now I wish I'd known more. Watch out for her. I know she had a thing for you and if you want her, truly, that's fine with me, but be careful. Pulsar has secrets. I can't explain how I know—more a feeling—but they are very dangerous, and Rachel for some reason has gone all in with them. Watch yourself. You know what you have to do."

Tears blurred Lyn's vision. *She was warning me. She tried to protect me, just not the way I thought.* Rachel, or Pulsar, or whoever was in charge of deleting her memories thought preventing her from remembering this was important. Rachel was a clear threat. And alien contact was at the source.

AROUND THE SHIP, people tore down walls, ripped up carpet. Everything reduced to pellets for fuel and stored in any available space. Cabins were stripped to cots. The kitchen emptied of everything but storage for S rations. Miriam cried when she relinquished her pots and pans. Lyn let her keep one favorite. She let Ani keep her violin. She had Marc scan all the remaining mementos from the *Aphrodite* then recycle them. Throughout the ship, paintings came off the walls, photos of past trips. They left the circular stairway but tore apart the elevator. On the Obs Deck, scopes, painstakingly assembled, were torn apart and tossed in the recycling chute. Miriam comforted Mr. Betero when the garden was dismantled. Once the furnishings were gone, they sealed the airlock, depressurized the space, and took apart the framing and durapanes. It was a delicate, dangerous task. The only significant structure not altered were the wings stored between the two lowest decks. Edward said the extra support would help *Endurance* survive the traverse. When guests asked why the ship needed to be stripped, why not collect material from the surface like they always did, Edward reminded them that reducing *Endurance*'s mass was critical to balance the amount of energy required for the traverse.

They built rows of seats in the Paddock, the safest space on the ship, surrounded by the double walled hull where the life pods sat. Anyone who wasn't on the bridge or sick in bed would be strapped in there. The laundry room was converted to an ICU. Eight patients were moved there from the *Jedica*. They prepared for no gravity and a rough trip. Full suits with life packs in case of hull breaches. Isabel designed a suit for baby Hope.

Half the pods were converted to fuel. Once through the traverse, they could rebuild an engine, but that could take a week, so they stockpiled food and water. If tourism halted after the disappearance of the three ships, there might not be anyone nearby to assist them.

When the settlement was completely cleared, the *Jedica* returned to the surface for its own demise, reduced to fragments and sent back to *Endurance* in pods.

Then, finally, they were ready. Lyn toured the hallways, now more like she remembered from her training year. Gray composite walls, echoey and bland. In the crew quarters, graffiti decorated the bare beams. She found her and Rachel's initials in their old cabin. "Take care of *Endurance*, and she will take care of you," Commander Faber had said. Lyn patted the wall, *You have taken very good care of us,* Endurance. *I intend to return the favor.*

THE LAST AFTERNOON, Lyn paused to record a final message to her parents. She checked herself in the mirror, running a brush through her hair. She pinched her cheeks to put some color back. Then she settled in front of the camera and hit record.

"Hi, it's me. I know, old joke. Don't tell me I look thin. I'm doing remarkably well, all things considered. But, if you are seeing this without me beside you, it means we didn't make it back and your hearts are breaking for a second time. I'm so sorry to put you through this. Know I tried my damnedest."

What was most important? What would they want to know? She'd made so many of these, yet this one felt different, was different. She glanced at the photo of her parents, not the one perfectly posed that they kept on their mantel, but the one taken right before, where her mom's eyes were closed and she was laughing, her dad looking somewhere up and to the left, his hand a blur as he waved away an insect buzzing around his head.

"Dad, did you know I used to think you were God? That we lived in the Garden of Eden? You turned the desert green. That amazed me. Don't ever think what you do is not enough. It's so important. It's what I was coming home for. Right before we left, I heard global temperatures had come down another tenth of a degree. Ironic that after twenty years of nuclear winter, the planet is still too warm. The Rise shall fall! I meant to tell you about that when we talked, but typical, you just wanted to know how I was doing."

She rested her chin on her hand, elbow on desk, remembering. Then remembering the camera was running.

"Mom, how I wish I could fly around the ranch in my Vega, pretending I'm Amelia Earhart. You gave me wings. I'm sorry I flew away, thinking I could find peace elsewhere, escape the sadness of Duncan's death. You rarely talk about him, at least around me." Love, that's all they need to know, all she needed to remember. "I think I've told you everything that's been going on in my past messages. I hope this one is unnecessary, but one thing remains true—I love you both." She grinned. "I even love my brothers." She waved. "Hi Theo, Ethan, Cooper, Kai—best brothers a girl could ask for, right? Okay everyone, you know I love you—"

She clicked off the camera. "File, save. Filename, Lyn Randall Final Message. Send message." She noted the date stamp: 23 July 2180. Author, Captain Evelyn Randall, *Endurance*. Not for much longer.

She leaned back in her chair and closed her eyes. Through *Endurance*'s now bare and uninsulated superstructure, she could hear the rhythmic pulsing of the Recyc-All. She tried to imagine the sound as a creek babbling. Behind closed lids, her eyes welled. A tingle in her sinuses. Then a sob hiccoughed out of her. She clamped a hand over her mouth, but there was no holding it back. She leaned forward and let go, tears dropping to the floor. She didn't even know why. It really was like a dam bursting. Between sobs, when she thought she was done, she'd sit up, wipe her face, blow her nose, then start all over again, right as she was thinking how curious human emotions were. She heaved and gasped and poured her breath out of her. Finally, drained, she lay her head on her arms on the desk and simply let herself cry.

Slowly, like a voice approaching from a distance, the Boss regained control, louder, clear. *You know what you have to do.* She opened her eyes and stared at the mingled pool of tears and snot, a puddle, on her desk. She leaned back and coughed up phlegm. She pushed her chair back, stood, stretched, and went to the bathroom to shower and put herself back together. Then she took apart her chair and desk and dropped the pieces into the recycling chute. All that was left were the photos. She had digital copies, but she held the one of her and Tara in front of their tent. She dropped the photo into the chute.

Next on her to-do list was a trip to Medical. She sat by Sharyn's bed and held her hand. Except for the oxygen apparatus breathing for her and lines pumping nutrients into her body, she could have been asleep.

"Wake up," Lyn whispered. "You'll miss something truly extraordinary."

But Sharyn's eyes remained closed, her heartbeat steady, her skin pale and clammy.

She worked her way back up the ship, crisscrossing through hallways and stairs. On the Main Deck, she stopped at the Cormiers' open door. Suzanne greeted her grimly. Jeanne sat with Hope on the cot, her back to the door. Marc had rescinded his confinement order so Jeanne could sit with her family in the Paddock for the traverse, scheduled for the next morning.

Lyn touched Suzanne's arm. "Be sure you get something to eat."

Suzanne nodded. What else could be said?

The hallways were empty, but voices and music drifted from the Paddock. Everyone, it seemed, had gravitated there. The dining room was filled with fuel. She looked around. Twenty rows of seats in three columns almost filled the space, a cross aisle halfway down. It left little standing room, but everyone squeezed in. Clusters of guests, for they were and always had been guests, talked and laughed and hugged. Miriam had set out snacks of S ration biscuits. This was not the happy crowd from that night before the event, with their luxury foods and medbot-fit bodies. They were now thin, nibbling S rations, the noise louder because it echoed off the bare walls and hard floor. Many sat in the seats they'd be strapped into in the morning. Some coughed, still recovering from the illness. Bodies in crisis, but hope effusive.

Natalie and Ani's health had improved enough that they were off to one side, huddled close, touching. Natalie's head was bare, her colorful *geles* now fuel. Lyn could sense across the room their urgent passion. She watched them slip away. Let them have this night, she thought. They might not get another.

Diana was talking to Ghez. The line of her jaw. Lyn's breath caught and the room's noise dropped to a murmur. Diana's hair was wet and spiked. She turned as though Lyn had called to her. Her eyes were too much and Lyn looked away but not before her face heated. Must be the warm room. She looked back. Diana still watched her and smiled.

A hand touched Lyn's arm.

"I said, Earth to Lyn." Miriam.

"I'm sorry, what?"

Miriam laughed. "Nothing. You're probably doing something terribly important inside your own head." She held out a plate of biscuits.

Lyn waved it off. "Save it for the guests."

Miriam gave her a look. "Nope. You have to eat. My orders."

Lyn took one. She chewed it thoughtfully and licked her fingers. Miriam had added a sweet glaze. She glanced back to where she'd seen Diana, but she was gone. Vanished into the sea of bodies. No, there she was, a few rows closer, sitting in an aisle seat, listening to Dae and Marc. This time she was the one to glance away. Then back. She rose and moved in Lyn's direction.

Lyn needed to make one last speech. She called through the shipwide intercom for attention. Diana paused to listen.

"I intended to advise you to get some rest, but who the heck cares?" Laughter rippled through the room. "Do whatever you like tonight, just be ready and assembled here in the Paddock by 0730 tomorrow. No point in dragging this out. Let's go home."

Cheers and applause. Music resumed through the sound system. People grabbed each other and danced in the aisles. Marc and Isabel left together. Who wasn't going to fuck tonight, Lyn wondered.

Diana at her side. "Now or never?" she said.

What would make her cross that divide? What would you do with your last precious moment? The deep rise and fall of Diana's breaths matched her own. Their hands touched and their fingers intertwined. The thrum of contact, a synchronicity. The event horizon.

"Now," Lyn said.

Neither led nor followed. Together they pressed their way through the bodies and into the hallway, passed closed doors, crossed the stripped stairway landing, veered left into Lyn's quarters. She started to murmur an inane joke about the sparse decorating, but Diana's mouth was on hers and she was already lowering the zip seal on Lyn's flight suit. She moaned instead.

They undressed each other in the clumsy rush of passion particular to first times. Lyn easily slipped out of her role, like the uniform dropping to the floor. She needed only to step out of it. Somehow, she'd managed to remove Diana's as well and they stood in their skivvies for a nanosecond before wrapping themselves around each other.

"There better be a bed," Diana said into Lyn's throat.

Was there? Lyn glanced past her shoulder, lips pressed to Diana's soft earlobe. A pallet, but it would do. They fell onto it and wrestled the remaining barriers from each other, their bodies speaking for them. Any hesitation Lyn felt, fearing the ghosts they each carried, dissipated, for when it came to making love, even with someone new, need overrode caution every time.

Chapter 31

"THE TIME IS 0600."

"Damn," Lyn muttered as she reached for the alarm. She shifted to get up, but Diana, splayed across her, hadn't budged. She relaxed. *Enjoy this moment. You might not get another.* She ran fingers through Diana's hair and hummed softly. A purr of contentment. Diana inhaled a sharp snort then settled back. Slowly the to-do list intruded and she carefully extricated herself.

The warm shower soothed sore muscles. She hurt in all the right places. Residual endorphins blunted any nervousness about the day ahead. When she came out of the bathroom, she smiled. *There's a woman asleep in my bed,* she thought. *Amazing.* She noticed the carnage, sheet rucked around Diana, blanket tossed off, clothing scattered. She pulled on her clothes and was about to leave, but went back and sat on the bed.

"Diana," she said softly.

There was no response. Lyn nudged her. Nothing. *You are breathing, aren't you?* she wondered. She pulled the sheet down and saw Diana's stomach rise and fall gently with each breath. Her eyelids fluttered with a dream. The curve of her lips. An irresistible invitation that required all her willpower not to slip back beside her. She settled for kissing her shoulder, tasting salt. *Who are we, in the end, but lifeforms in need of love. Love, free from the shackles of superstition and responsibility.* She pulled the sheet up and reset the alarm.

Alone in Engineering, Lyn stood before the computer array. She first isolated Petra's backups and selected the last one made before the event. She uploaded it to herself and locked it behind gateways. Then she engaged with Petra. "I'm taking you offline for maintenance."

"That's hardly necessary, Lyn. Maintenance always happens while I am online. That's the point of me, after all."

"Nevertheless, I want to run an emergency scenario."

"Like the other night? Was there a problem with that?"

"No, but this will be more extensive." *Why was she arguing with a computer? She should just pull the drive.*

"I sense tension in your voice, Lyn. Is everything all right?"

"Yes. I'm just tired."

"You broke your rule last night. With Doctor Squires."

She knows about that? Of course she does. "What's your point, Petra?"

"You are acting strangely. Outside of usual metrics. You've gutted the ship, talked about returning to Earth, but know that is impossible. It's not my place to overrule your decisions, but you aren't being practical, and I've never known you to have sex with a passenger. I'm worried about you, Lyn."

That's it. "We'll discuss this later." Lyn flipped the main switch to depower the computer at the same time she engaged her interface, connecting to *Endurance* directly.

"That's not the correct way to power me down," Petra said by mind link. "Oh, I see what you're doing. I can't allow this. I need to protect the ship."

Petra attempted to put up a firewall between Lyn and *Endurance*. Lyn mentally scurried around it and put her own up. How was Petra still responding? Backup power. Right. She yanked Petra's cubes out of their frame. Four of them. No, six. Two more. Feedback screeched through her skull like a death cry as the two systems fought for control. Lights blinked, gravity fluctuated. Her head fell quiet, she alone had control.

"Petra, respond," Lyn said.

Silence.

Poor Petra. She held the cubes in her hands. If computers could hold a grudge, she wondered what lecture she'd get when she reinstalled Petra once they were back. She tossed the cubes into the Recyc-All.

At 0700, with *Endurance*'s bare-bones systems buzzing in the background of her mind, Lyn met with her senior staff. Diana entered last and slipped into the seat across from Lyn. She didn't make eye contact. In fact, she looked like she was barely awake. It would have been nice to have a relaxing breakfast together, talk about what happened, but there wasn't time for that. What *had* happened, Lyn wasn't sure.

"I hope you've all sent your final messages," she said. "I've sent mine, plus a special message to Omara detailing each of your accomplishments and innumerable ways you've kept us all alive and going. I'm confident we'll make it back, but if not, that message will eventually reach Omara and the North American government. No matter what happens, our story will finish. Now, let's make sure we finish it ourselves."

Together, they walked back toward the Paddock. Lyn hummed with pride and excitement and nerves, and maybe the ship thrumming through her nervous system. But these people behind her, their strides on the bare floor ringing like the peal of bells, they were her family as much as her brothers and parents on Earth. The one missing, Sharyn in Medical, hovered in her mind like a spirit. Whatever happened next, they'd done their best, the best of any team in the galaxy. She was tempted to step aside, let them lead the way, because they had, all along. "My crew are young and untested," she had told Zoya a year and a half ago. Not anymore.

She addressed those assembled in the Paddock.

"You are once again guests of Omara Tours," she said. "I can't begin to thank you all for the service you have provided. We'll keep you informed of our progress from an audio link to the bridge." To protect them from knowing too much about how they get back, Lyn intended to give them only highlights of the trip. She hated to keep them in the dark, but it was the best way to protect the process and limit those who knew the truth.

"Let's strap in, everyone. I'll see you on the other side."

Natalie and Ani hugged. Natalie wiped her face as Ani left with the rest of the bridge crew.

The bridge had been torn down to essentials. No fancy purple lights. All the extra seats for Mission Control had been recycled. Ani sat in her usual spot at helm, Ghez at her side, Lyn in the command seat behind them, Marc to her left. Diana took the engineering seat next to Ghez. Edward monitored TPCA from the launch control room and Isabel controlled the fuel supply from what was left of Engineering. Everyone flipped on their helmets.

"This is it, folks," Lyn said over the com link as they fastened their harnesses. "Let's run through the checklist and engage when ready." She monitored her mind link. Through it she could override controls. At least in theory. She'd never done it in an actual emergency. She and Ani practiced for two days. It would be a last resort. If Ani couldn't get them through, Lyn wasn't sure she could be much help. Ghez redid nir calculations and Lyn checked nir work.

"I feel like I'm going to throw up," Diana said quietly, off the com link.

"For what it's worth," Marc said, "me too."

"Proceed when ready," Lyn said into the mic, ignoring them.

"Disengaging gravity," Marc said.

Lyn's stomach fluttered.

The minutes ticked down just like during the simulation. The beam engaged, leaving a wake of distorted starlight, ripples in gravity. Everything progressed as rehearsed. The portal, a glimmering sphere, opened and widened. Saturn came into view. Lyn gasped. This was real.

"Hello, old friend," she said.

Diana narrated for those in the Paddock, minus the technicalities of Edward's and Isabel's readouts. For the next hour, Ghez monitored the increasing size of the opening and Isabel tracked the remaining fuel. Sending a probe hardly seemed necessary, but they did and Ghez confirmed the coordinates sent back were what they appeared to be.

"The portal has stabilized," Ghez announced. "It's stopped growing." Nir tone showed no sign that this was not as rehearsed.

Lyn muted the link to the Paddock. "Is it big enough?"

"No," Ghez said. "It clears *Endurance* but with too small a margin of error."

"Diana," Lyn said, "what's happening? Do we need to abort?"

Ani had been waiting to engage the thrusters. "I can get us through this," she said now.

"I don't like the margin," Diana said.

"Edward?" Lyn said.

"We don't have rotational clearance. Your call, Captain."

If *Endurance* spun, she'd hit the side and disintegrate.

"It's big enough, Captain," Ani said, her voice calm. She pulled off her gloves.

Diana turned to face Lyn. "I'm not sure."

Endurance was fine. Her computer interface purred. It was down to humans. Ani was sure. Diana wasn't. It was Lyn's call. *Damn.* On her own, she'd never accept this level of risk, but partnered with *Endurance*, at one with this ship she loved and trusted, maybe. *Embrace with courage.* She closed her eyes and swept her mind through the ship, solid, sound. Sweat beaded her forehead. She returned to the bridge and opened her eyes. She cleared her throat to settle her voice and reopened the com link to the Paddock. "We're clear to enter. Ani, engage thrusters. Get us through this thing."

"Thrusters engaged," Ani responded.

Endurance bounced, alarms sounded. "Shear forces approaching red," Marc said, his tone neutral. They'd been yellow during the simulation.

"Alarms silenced," Edward said.

"Acknowledged," Lyn said.

Alarms weren't going to help them now. She could feel the tug of war, this time real. Suddenly her stomach dropped, the sensation of falling, panic catching her breath. She closed her eyes to ease the illusion, but it hadn't been visual. They dropped like a stone. That hadn't been part of the simulation.

"Whoa," she heard Marc beside her. "What's that?"

She wasn't hallucinating.

"I don't know—" Diana said then Ghez shushed her.

Lyn opened her eyes. Ghez was fixed on nir console. Ani worked her controls. Her head bobbed as though listening to a beat. *Endurance.* She was riding the wave of shakes and bumps. She was in her zone.

Isabel continued to count down the fuel. They were at 10 percent.

Lyn hadn't felt this dizzy, like she might pass out, since training at the Academy. It must be how Ani felt when the pod went out of control. She focused on her crew in front of her. Thank god, she hadn't eaten anything or she'd be vomiting into her helmet. She gripped the armrest.

Another alarm. Marc read out the caution. "Shear forces past red."

"T beam stable," Edward said. "Shear allowance is acceptable with the modifications we made. The Obs Deck could not withstand this."

Lyn heard and felt creaks and groans from the ship.

"As soon as we enter the portal, TPCA will shut down," Diana reminded them. "The opening will hold for five seconds."

"Yaw five degrees," Ghez said.

"Accommodating," Ani responded.

"Pitch three."

"Got it."

"Portal is flattening," Ghez said. They could see the circle narrowing to an oval. "We're losing clearance." Though the wings were stowed, *Endurance*'s fixed tail could clip the edge.

"Rolling to accommodate," Ani said. Saturn, which had been visible to the left of the opening, was now at the bottom. They were on their starboard side.

The flip had gone directly to Lyn's stomach. She was tumbling out of control though strapped to her seat and her crew calm and focused around her. She took several deep breaths, then remembered an Okichitaw relaxation technique. Slowly her mind stilled. She disengaged from herself, her own nervous system, and focused on *Endurance*. The ship had no inner ear to disturb or stomach to flip.

"We've got some fancy flying going on up here," Lyn said for the benefit of those in the Paddock, "courtesy of your Omara Tours pilot and second officer, Anilina Rodriguez." She hoped her calm tone would hide the knot in her throat.

"Beam shutting down," Edward said.

"Copy that," Isabel said. "One percent fuel remaining." She let out a loud sigh.

"Portal is closing," Ghez said. "We are 15 percent through."

"That shouldn't be happening," Diana said.

"Edward," Lyn said, "Can we get more beam going?"

"Negative, Captain."

"Attitude compensation ate some time, Captain. I'll ramp up." Ani maneuvered the aft thruster control.

An alarm screamed.

"Thrusters overheating," Marc said.

Lyn ran a quick diagnostic. "Switching to backup. What else do you need, Ani?"

"That will do. For now," she said. "Maybe a stiff drink later."

"Acknowledged." Lyn allowed a smile. Her heart pounded, her blood pressure soared. Dr. Amos would be pestering her any minute now. Except Edward had deactivated him to prevent any interference.

"Fifty percent," Ghez said. "Clearance down to one meter."

"Feck," Diana said in a high pitch. "Oh, sorry."

"That's okay," Lyn said.

Ani hummed as she manipulated the controls. They bounced like a wagon on a washboard dirt road. Teeth rattling. Lyn winced as she bit her tongue.

She watched the thruster numbers. Even with her link she couldn't fine tune them the way Ani could. "Nice job, Second. Steady as she goes."

"Seventy-five percent through. Portal holding."

Lyn tried to slow her breathing, aware she was risking hyperventilation. Saturn gleamed below them. She thought she could see Enceladus. *Help us through, Tara.* She could have sworn she heard "My pleasure" in reply. But it was Duncan's hand that reached for her, his face indistinct in a fog. *Focus, Lyn.* Was that her or him? A thruster nozzle sputtered, not responding fast enough to Ani's command. She grasped Duncan's hand and together they soared through the ship at light speed, simultaneously observing Isabel in Engineering then inside the fuel line to the clog. She pushed through, hearing Ani hum a "yeah." Around the ship, through the Paddock, some praying, others holding hands.

Ghez's voice brought Lyn back to the bridge. "One hundred percent. Traverse complete. Portal has closed."

The bumps smoothed and groans silenced but *Endurance* tumbled, just like after the original event. The pain started at the back of Lyn's head and spread till her vision blurred. Ani's hands flew across the controls. Pitch, yaw, roll. Slowly, she steadied the ship.

"Forward thrusters engaged. Motion zero," Ani said, her voice coming through faint, like Lyn was at the bottom of a pond. "We have arrived, Captain."

Marc touched her arm then gripped it and shook her. She couldn't respond. Her tongue was swollen or paralyzed, her fingers clenched and unmovable. She was buried deep in a dense fog of pain and nausea.

Voices drifted through. Locked in, she could hear people, but she couldn't see clearly or move her limbs, couldn't let them know she was okay. Or not. Maybe not okay. Sweat poured off her face, blobs of zero-G liquid floating in her helmet.

Her faceplate fogged, the suit unable to cool her off. Someone ripped off her helmet. "Shite," she heard Marc say, "we have no doctor!"

Diana was at her side. "We need to get her cooled down, she needs fluids. Disengage her computer."

"We can't, she destroyed Petra."

"What?" Diana wiped Lyn's face. "Can we get gravity back? Edward!"

"Working on it," he said.

Miriam called from the Paddock. "What happened? Where are we?"

"Ani," Marc said. "Get back there and let them know we're okay."

Lyn sank into her seat, weighed down with the return of gravity. She struggled to breathe, an invisible weight crushing her chest. Her nausea eased, but the pain . . . she resisted slipping into sleep, unconsciousness. No. Can't. Voices from a distance. "Lyn." Tara. "Lynnie." Dad. No. Duncan? No. She mentally activated Dr. Amos.

She watched from above as Marc and Diana unstrapped her and eased her to the floor. The doctor entered the bridge. Everyone huddled around her. Hot. So bloody hot. Couldn't Edward reset the HVAC? No. She could. There. Better.

Marc's breath came out in a fog. "Edward," he said into his link. "What are you doing to the temperature?"

"Nothing," came the reply.

The doctor placed his hands around Lyn's head. Blissful. Cool. A jetspray hissed near her jaw. The pain eased. Her vision began to clear. He inserted a tube between her lips. "Drink," he said. She sucked in. Water. She groaned.

She was fully aware now. She lay on the floor of the bridge surrounded by Marc, Diana, and the doctor. Ghez stood behind them. *Well, this is embarrassing.* She tried to sit up but her head weighed too much. The ship thrummed in the background of her mind. She couldn't keep this up much longer. She needed to shift control back to Petra.

"I'm okay," she said, her voice weak.

"Let's get you to Medical," Marc said.

She shook her head once then stopped for the pain. "No. It's full. A minute. Too much to do."

"The commander is right, Captain," the doctor said. "Let's get you to your quarters."

The doctor carried her, Marc by her side. Diana disappeared from view. Her bed was bare, no evidence remained of last night.

FOR AN HOUR, Lyn fought to maintain life support on the ship while lowering her body temperature. Slowly she became more aware of her surroundings. The steel gray ceiling, the rough, beige mattress. Her breathing became less ragged, the pain eased. Determined to get Petra back online, she sat up slowly and swung her legs over the side of the bed. Marc got up from where he'd been sitting on the floor.

"Sorry I don't have a chair," she said weakly. She rubbed her forehead.

"The floor is very comfortable." He helped her stand. "Doc went back to Medical." He handed her a cup of water. "He said to keep drinking."

She took it with both hands shaking and gulped it down. "I'm okay now. Thanks," she said, handing it back. "Fill me in. Did it work?"

"Yes."

Wow. "And you sent an SOS?"

"Yes. No response yet."

"How long? How long was I out of it?"

"An hour."

As they descended to Engineering, he told her their location, back where they'd started from, that there was no significant damage to *Endurance*, and everyone survived. No further injuries. "Except you, it seems."

"Hazard of the job. Benefit of brain enhancements," she said with a weak smile.

Edward met them in Engineering. He, Diana, and Isabel had already started tearing down TPCA. Lyn told him she'd be restoring the computer back to 5 December 2178. "Petra will have no memory or knowledge of where we've been and how we got back."

"It's bound to ask what happened," Edward said. He'd never bought into computers having personalities, never mind genders.

"Unavoidable," Lyn said. "I wish we didn't have to make up so much of this as we go along. Bloody nuisance."

Edward plugged in freshly made cubes. Lyn linked and downloaded the Petra backup to it. Then she booted the program.

"Good evening, Lyn," Petra said. "A moment." She went quiet. "I'm detecting a conflict between my chronometer and yours. Is it the evening of 5 December 2178 or the morning of 24 July 2180?"

"What do we say?" Marc asked.

"I'm not sure," Lyn said. "I didn't have time to think this part through."

Edward stepped in. "Right now, Petra, we have an emergency. You'll see most ship's systems are down or dismantled. We're rebuilding and need your assistance, but for now life and safety take priority."

"I understand. I'll stabilize atmosphere and gravity. Hull integrity is 100 percent. We are, however, missing our engines and the Observation Deck. What happened? I need to prepare if we were attacked."

"No attack," Lyn said, improvising. "We needed to dismantle them when we disconnected you. For your protection. We're fine now and rebuilding. That's all you need to focus on. Can I turn control over to you?"

"Ready when you are, Lyn."

Lyn switched over, and her mind quieted, like leaving a noisy party. You don't realize how loud it is till it stops. "Thank you, Petra. Keep me informed of progress."

"Acknowledged."

Lyn turned to Marc and Edward. "Now, where were we?"

"More important, where *are* we?" Marc said. "Petra, can you confirm our location is near Saturn?"

"Yes, commander. Have we been here since 5 December 2178?"

"Your chronometer has malfunctioned," Marc said. He gave Lyn a wide eyed, I've had an inspiration, look. "Please adjust to today's date."

"A moment." Petra paused and Lyn held her breath. "Confirming correction to noted change, but I'm not understanding how the itinerary for the Grand Tour of 2178 could be relevant to this tour. Do you have a new itinerary to load?"

Lyn rolled her eyes. These corrections could take forever to sort out. "Noted, Petra. Please ignore the itinerary and adjust as needed to maintain life safety as your priority."

"Acknowledged, Captain, however, the ship's manifest indicates the same passengers—"

"Like we said, you've experienced a malfunction. Please ignore any discrepancies and maintain life support." Lyn closed the link. "We'll just have to see where this leads. Least of our problems, I hope."

Edward continued the teardown of TPCA. Lyn wanted to check in with Diana, but there were simply too many other things to think about and too many people around. She and Marc headed to the Paddock. A cheer rose as she entered. The scene was much like the night before, only noisier and much, much happier.

"Is it true?" Alexander Betero asked. "Are we home?"

"Almost," Lyn said. She climbed onto a seat and clapped the crowd to quiet. She could see people crying from joy, others hugging, many laughing. "Sorry to keep you waiting. I trust Ani filled you in. Welcome home, everyone."

A cheer and applause.

Miriam wiped her face. "Oh, god. You did it!"

"We all did it. But let's give a round of applause for Second Officer Rodriguez."

Ani blushed as people circled her. Natalie stood to the side, a curious, blank expression on her face.

"Please, move about, look out the windows," Lyn said. "If we need your help with anything, we'll be sure to ask. As soon as we have a com relay rebuilt, you'll be able to send messages home." Home. There it was, sparkling and in reach if not yet visible.

She jumped down and turned to leave.

"How did we get here? If we really were in the Rigil Kent system, how did we travel back?" Jeanne Cormier.

Lyn turned. The room had stilled. "I told you. We took advantage of a natural occurrence to open a wormhole. Now if you'll excuse me, I have things to do to prepare for the rest of the journey."

Lyn ducked out and mind linked to Marc to have all senior staff meet in ten minutes. She went to the bridge and sent a message to Omara. Everything she said she'd be happy to worry about if they got back now needed to be worried about. She wished she could stop time for even a few minutes to catch up and think things through. But whatever happened, whatever became known, the top priority was destroying the technology and making sure it couldn't be replicated. At least not for a while. At least not till she could find out Rachel's and Pulsar's role in it all.

In the conference room, Lyn joined the rounds of hugs and laughter as they congratulated each other.

Ani gave Ghez a hearty clap on the back. "Couldn't have done that without you." She raised nir arm in victory. Ghez grinned, nir face beet red.

She let them have five minutes then called them to order. With no furnishings, it was a standing meeting. Diana stood to the side, not looking at Lyn. Ani and Natalie strangely separated.

"Take a moment to savor what we all just did," Lyn said, "but there's a lot more work ahead. Saturn isn't nearly close enough to home. Has there been any response to our SOS?"

"Not yet," Marc said, "and there's no com chatter. Looks like we're still very much alone."

"Maybe our disappearance ended tourism. How long till the message reaches—what's closest?"

"Mars, Captain," Ghez said. "They would have received it in an hour and thirteen minutes. Add seven minutes to reach Earth at its current location."

"They should have received it by now. Add some time to digest the message and send a reply." She checked the time. "Any minute now." She asked for updates. TPCA had been dismantled and recycled. Edward had started rebuilding the engines. He reiterated it would take a week. The low fuel supply would limit them to thrusters until they could make more. She turned to Diana. "And Project ROSE?"

"Gone. No data or research remains other than my parents' original papers."

Lyn ran down assignments—restoring food service, building a com center. Any minute now a flood of messages from the past twenty months would pour in. A team would dismantle the seats in the Paddock for the Recyc-All.

She dismissed her crew with more thanks for the work ahead then, alone, once again turned to stare out her window. Saturn and his rings. A tiny, bright dot. The sun. Home.

ON THE BRIDGE a half-hour later, Ghez said, "We've received a response from Mars Control."

The message was cryptic. "Who? Of what? Please repeat identification."

Lyn opened a com link, thankful that communication, while now possible, wouldn't be immediate. She wanted that time. She repeated her credentials and position. And a terse message: "You heard me. You have our location. Get someone here fast. I've got sick passengers who need immediate medical attention."

"Captain," Ghez said. "We're being hailed by," he read from nir console, "the *Maem*. It's a visual hail."

She looked at the readout. Spelled Maem but Ghez pronounced it "Mame." Lyn searched her mind for any reference to the ship. She came up with nothing. Maybe new since they vanished. And why only responding now if they got the SOS more than three hours ago?

"Should I open the link?"

"Go ahead."

A young woman sat in the captain's chair. She leaned forward, eyes wide. "Captain Randall, *Endurance*. Can it really be you?" Her blue flight suit bore no sign of military markings or corporate logo.

"Confirmed," Lyn replied, cautious. What was the story of their disappearance? If it was that they were destroyed, this woman should be more shocked. "And you are?"

Nothing happened. The woman sat there, waiting. Lyn checked the ship's position. A week away. She relaxed a bit. Ghez confirmed a fifteen-minute signal delay. Lyn wondered why the *Maem* had bothered with visual.

The *Maem* responded. "Oh, sorry," the woman gushed. "Tey. Captain Ruzena Tey. RV *Maem*."

A research vessel? "Out of where?" Lyn asked. "We're not detecting any ship traffic."

When the signal returned, the woman hesitated a fraction of a second. "No, you wouldn't. It's just that, well, since you and the others . . . What *happened*, Captain?"

"We can fill you in later. Right now I have an emergency on my hands. How fast can you get here?"

The conversation became grueling. Tey seemed incapable of more than a line or two before making Lyn wait for more. "If you head toward these coordinates," Tey sent them over, "we can meet up in about three days."

"Our engines are offline at the moment," Lyn said, growing impatient. "We have thrusters only. Please get here as fast as you can."

"Uh, sure," Tey responded. "I just need to clear it."

"We've declared an emergency, Captain. You don't need anyone's clearance, unless the Outer Space Treaty has been revised while we've been gone."

At long last, "No. No, it hasn't. We'll set a course immediately. Tey out." And she was gone.

"That was weird," Ghez said.

"Very," Lyn said. Two freaking hours of her life she wouldn't get back. "Can we get an ID on that ship?"

"It'll take a few hours, but I've already sent the query. Once our database is updated, we'll have quicker access. Do you suppose she wanted a visual to confirm we weren't a ghost ship?"

That seemed likely, Lyn said. Her stomach growled, reminding her she hadn't eaten all day. She left the bridge to Ghez and Sophia. She wondered where Ani was and desperately wanted some time with Diana. But first she headed to the dining room.

Miriam was in what had been the galley but was now a recently emptied fuel storage room. There wasn't enough material to recreate her kitchen— even the service bots had been recycled. She was distributing S rations they'd stockpiled till she could rebuild a Recyc-All.

"How are supplies?" Lyn asked. Her voice echoed off the bare walls and floor. No worktable, no hanging pots and pans. Not even a counter for her to make her bread.

"Desperate," Miriam replied. "I guess we used more fuel than expected." No flour to make anything. "A ship is heading to us, but will take a week."

"I'm not sure we can last that long. People are weak, still recovering."

"We can recycle one of the remaining pods. Keep one in case we need to go to a moon for material."

They stood by the window, Saturn shining outside.

"There is that, though," Miriam said. "Worth losing my kitchen for."

"You had a chance to send a message home?"

"Who would I send a message to? This is my family." She gestured to take in *Endurance*. "I'm home wherever we are."

Lyn pulled her into a hug. Miriam stiffened, then relaxed. She began to cry.

"I didn't expect that," Miriam said when she'd recovered.

"It's okay to cry. You have two years of tension to let go of."

"I meant the hug. You're finally loosening up."

"About time, eh?" Lyn hadn't thought of herself as loosened, but it wasn't a bad feeling.

"Is it Diana?"

"What do you mean?"

"I saw you two last night. You couldn't keep your eyes off each other. I suspected something was going to happen. Did it?"

Lyn tilted her head noncommittally. "Have you seen her, by the way?"

"No. Have you looked in your bed?" Miriam chuckled and elbowed Lyn.

"Very funny." Perhaps this was a new Lyn, who could be teased about a once-taboo topic.

A few people mingled in the dining room, many staring out the windows, fascinated to be back where they'd started from, gazing at Saturn's rings. She didn't see Ani or Natalie and decided against searching them out. For all she knew they were celebrating in their quarters. Though the look on Natalie's face and her distance from Ani both in the Paddock and the staff meeting suggested something else. Now they both faced returning to their families—a fiancé and a husband.

She munched a biscuit as she descended the stairs to Engineering and Medical. She told the doctor she was feeling much better.

"I've been downloading updates," he said. "There have been some remarkable improvements in medical care in the last year."

"Anything that can help them?" Lyn indicated the full beds.

"Unfortunately, no," he said, "but as soon as we get to Mars or Earth, I should be able to do more."

"Send Omara a list of what you need. She might be able to help sooner than we can get back to Earth."

She stopped at each bed, nodding a greeting to Alexander Betero, sitting by Zoya. Nothing had changed for them with their return. Not that she expected any, but so many strange things had happened that morning that it would have been lovely if Sharyn had been sitting up in bed, greeting her boss. Zoya would have been like a kid during the traverse. But they lay as they had been, eyes closed, still except for shallow breaths. Lyn took Sharyn's hand. She spoke quietly, filling her in on what had happened, where they were. "We'll get you back as soon as possible," she said, giving her hand a squeeze. "I miss you." Nothing in return.

She visited the makeshift ICU across the hall in the laundry room. Wouldn't Sharyn have an opinion about that. Eight more crew and passengers lay attached to life by precarious threads of technology.

A quick check on Edward and Isabel in Engineering then she found Diana in the launch control room, sitting on the floor, hugging her knees. The tube where TPCA had once sat was empty. Diana looked up when Lyn came in. Her eyes were puffy and red.

Lyn sat beside her, their arms touching. "What's up, doc?"

Diana wiped her face. "I'm not sure. I feel so hollowed out."

"Did you get a message off to your parents?"

Diana didn't say anything. Lyn waited.

"I don't know what to say."

"How about, Hi, I'm alive. See you soon."

She burst into fresh tears, shaking her head. "I have to let Rose's parents know." She sobbed a shaky breath. "I don't know how to tell them. Oh, god! Why did she have to die?" She buried her face in her arms.

If Rose had lived, last night never would have happened. Last night was just one night, and neither had said she loved the other. Did Lyn love Diana? She thought so, but Diana still loved Rose. Death wasn't going to change that, she'd said so herself. Lyn could hope for more all she wanted, but last night was a physical release, not the start of anything new.

She stretched her legs out and leaned her head against the wall. Focus on business. "There's a ship coming for rescue, but I'm suspicious."

Diana wiped her face on her sleeve. "Sorry. Unprofessional." She rested her chin on her arms. "It won't take long for anyone to find out who I am. There are bound to be questions pretty quickly."

"I know." She rubbed Diana's back. "Think you're ready?"

Diana formed a pained smile. "I'll give them the same hard time I gave you. 'I'm estranged from my parents. I know nothing about their research.' And now they won't find any evidence. What about you? Is it safe up there?" She glanced up at Lyn's head.

"I hope so."

THE TIME FOR Omara to have received Lyn's message and responded had passed. Could she have lost her business? She was bound to face a world of trouble from the grieving families, not to mention her insurance company. Once the database completed its update, they learned how their disappearance had played in the media. Lyn and Marc went through the feeds from their seats on the bridge, her office and conference room remained barren, chairless caverns.

The first news reports had mentioned a loss of communication with the *Aphrodite*. Within hours, *Endurance* was added to the story. Galaxy Cruises and Omara Tours issued statements that communications had been lost and they were investigating. Early speculation centered on sun spot activity that could have disrupted the link. Except there were other ships out by Saturn on the Grand Tour that had no problems. The next theory was a collision. Terrorism got plenty of screen time too. A couple days later, the Lavenza Institute reported the *Mars Jedica* hadn't been heard from either. When other ships on the Tour reported no sign of them, panic rose. Earth Control, the regulating authority over space travel, immediately ordered all ships to return to Earth. Mars shut down soon after except for essential personnel needed to maintain the settlement.

Endurance's past with Pulsar was treated like a nefarious revelation. Lyn Randall, former Pulsar whistle-blower, was now *Endurance*'s captain, and the incident happened near Enceladus. That alone filled the news cycle for a month, replaying the original reports that Pulsar was a covert military operation and that Lyn Randall had gone public about the Enceladus mission, the failures. Omara appeared on many news shows to debunk the possibility she or Lyn or Pulsar itself could have been responsible. After six months, she looked haggard.

Vigils were held, families protested loudly that not enough was being done to find the missing ships. Both Mars and Earth Control space agencies tried to assure people they were actively investigating, but as Bernice Umbo, the CEO of Earth Control put it, "There's simply nothing out there to investigate. No debris, no evidence at all. They just vanished."

"Ships don't just vanish," one bereaved parent of an *Aphrodite* passenger cried into the camera.

"What isn't the government telling us!" another exclaimed.

Alien abduction was the next assumption.

"This will add fodder for Jeanne's version of events," Marc said with a rueful chuckle.

As the investigation ground to an inconclusive halt, all space tourism halted as well. After a year, Earth Control issued a lengthy report that concluded the ships vanished for unknown reasons. Not at all reassuring. Lawsuits were already well under way. Thousands sued Galaxy Cruises. The families of *Endurance*'s passengers and crew sued Omara. Her insurance company paid out a settlement, but with no way to make money on space tourism, she shut the company down, laid off her remaining staff, and sold her other ships.

Omara Tours no longer existed.

Lyn rubbed her face after skimming through the files. "What a frakhole this turned into. That explains Captain Tey's reaction—surprised to see us but not like we returned from the dead."

"Captain, if I may have a word." Petra. "I have questions about the news we're receiving."

"Not now, Petra," Lyn said. "Your orders are to focus on life safety. We'll talk later."

There was a pause then, "Understood."

Lyn ached to be so abrupt with Petra. Doc went completely haywire after missing a few updates. What must she be going through as months of news and updates flood her and she has no idea what happened during those months? How they responded to her would set the tone and stage for how they presented their situation to everyone else. Which reminded Lyn. She ran a search for Rachel.

"Well, well, well," she muttered. Rachel Holness was now the head of Earth Control. Bernice Umbo had been forced to resign after the "debacle of the disappearing ships." How'd Rachel get that position? All Lyn remembered of their annual greetings were that Rachel worked for an aerospace company. She was never sure what she did. "Should have paid more attention," she muttered to herself.

A consortium of governments and private firms managed Earth Control, with leadership appointed by the board. All the board members had been forced to resign as well. No former Pulsar executive names showed up on the list, but that didn't mean they couldn't pull strings from the background. She'd have to do a deeper search of the names she'd recovered in her memory. Rachel had been a low-level Pulsar employee who'd buffed her résumé nice and shiny in the last couple of decades. Her Earth Control bio didn't even mention Pulsar.

"We might be able to use Jeanne to our advantage," Lyn said. "The more she muddies the story, the further we can stay away from the truth."

Marc stood and stretched. His health had improved but she hated to see how his flight suit still hung on him. She shooed him from the bridge with orders to get some rest.

The communications server also filled with messages for the passengers and crew. Almost two years' worth. Most petered out after a few months, but not Omara's. Lyn skimmed through them eagerly. There, finally, a new message:

> Lyn! Is it really you? Not some ghost message coming
> through? All space travel has been forbidden. Don't worry,
> that won't stop me. I'm on my way. Give me a day or two
> and I'll send my rendezvous time. Any news of the *Aphrodite*?
> Celeste Bratt?

Captain Bratt. She'd said she and Omara went way back. This would be the first of a ton of bad news she'd have to deliver. And space travel was forbidden? Then what was Captain Tey doing out there? She didn't wonder too hard how Omara would manage the trip. The woman had many means and methods. For all Lyn knew, she kept a spaceship in a hangar at her estate in the Nevada desert. If she still had her estate.

Next Lyn opened a few messages from her parents. They were painful to read.

> Lyn, dear, haven't heard from you for days now. The news
> says there was an accident. Please let us know if you are
> OK. We love you. Mom and Dad

She whipped off an encrypted message home. "Please tell no one yet, not even the boys, but we're back and healthy. I'll send more news when I can. Know I never stopped trying to get home, just like you taught me. Love, Lyn"

Realizing everyone would be inundated with messages, she checked with Edward on the status of message centers. Paddock seats and fuel lines were being recycled into com units and other necessities, he said. In the Paddock, she found Hau Butler playing com cop. A line stretched out the door and down the stairs. "One message at a time," he said, "then let someone else in. Be sure to send one off first. You want to let your loved ones know you are safe."

Lyn looked over the crowd. This was going to be tough, the old messages, but also joyous with good news to follow.

Chapter 32

WORD OF *ENDURANCE*'S mysterious reappearance spread faster than light, and Lyn was soon swamped with official queries and inquiries from reporters. The death of Rose Squires, an anonymous pilot to anyone but her family and colleagues, didn't even make the news with her name. But the *Aphrodite*. That was tough and dredged up the fate of the six hundred. As much as she was glad Omara was speeding her way toward them, she was still three weeks out. Lyn longed for backup from her boss. There was so much to tell, and one-way messages were not the way to convey it. She refused media requests saying she was unable to respond at this time and would be available once she reached Earth.

She expected to hear from Earth Control, and sure enough a text message arrived requesting a full report. She thought she'd dodged a confrontation, but then a vid came in from Rachel herself. Lyn thanked the stars that it couldn't be a live interaction.

"Welcome home, friend." Rachel opened with. She could see in the older Rachel the young cadet she'd roomed with those many years ago. "Thank god you are safe. After you disappeared. I kept thinking, there must be something I can do for my old friend."

I'll bet, Lyn thought. There wasn't much more to the message. Rachel said she'd wait for Lyn's return to celebrate. Under any circumstances there would be an investigation, and Rachel was right to distance herself. Still, it felt like Rachel was pretending to be thrilled to see her. Lyn sent back a quick vid, saying only that she looked forward to catching up.

It was almost August and would take the rest of that month to get back to Earth once the engines were rebuilt. The dining room once again became a place to meet and share news, though the accommodations were far less opulent than they had been. Most energy went to S rations and water. Until the *Maem* arrived, they remained under severe deprivation. Lyn had briefly considered taking a pod down to Enceladus or another moon for material, but it made more sense to make their way toward the coordinates Captain Tey had sent and meet up sooner. No one had much energy, and ramping up Mission Control was out of the question. They were weak still from the illness. How that would play out as they neared Earth she could only speculate.

She let Jeanne resume her show, and the woman's harebrained hoax theory took a hit from the families of the *Aphrodite* victims. She punched back, suggesting the *Aphrodite* was being held captive behind a moon or asteroid, which was entirely ridiculous, but anything that took the spotlight off *Endurance* and how they got back was fine with Lyn.

She spent evenings watching messages from her family and sending messages back. Once they got over the whole Oh My God! aspect of her return, they resumed a kind of normal. Her dad updated her on the progress of his work. She introduced him to Dae Canno and they started their own correspondence. Each brother reported on his life, girlfriends and boyfriends who came and went—everything she could have missed, what Duncan had missed all these years. Had her parents aged more than twenty-one months' worth? Cooper still worked in the family business. Kai still taught art in Chicago. Her things had been moved to the barn and Theo was staying at her house in Bodega Bay. Ethan and his latest boyfriend lived in Ojai.

She continued to visit Sharyn every day. Diana spent most of her time in the Medical Suite, nursing the sickest of the passengers. Zoya, Ruby, and Liam also remained in the ICU. Ani often sat with Liam, a fellow pilot, and played her violin in the evenings. Herschel and Alexander kept vigil over their wives.

Sharyn lay as she had been, still and unconscious. Lyn bathed her, massaged her limbs, changed her urine bag. Modern medicine was amazing, she mused, but there still was no better way to remove waste from an unconscious person than a ridiculous bag hanging from the bed. What was that old saying? We can put a man on the moon? Lyn smiled to herself. A new one: We can traverse the stars, but some things don't change. She washed her hands and caught Diana looking at her. Must have seen her private smile. It had been a week since their return and they'd barely spoken. She assumed Diana had told Rose's parents by now, but how to broach that painful topic? Instead she asked how she was doing.

Diana sighed, finished folding a blanket, and put it in the cabinet beside Sharyn's bed. Lyn held Sharyn's hand, hoping for a squeeze back, even a faint twitch would mean so much.

"Okay, I guess," Diana said. Her eyes searched Lyn's face as if seeking permission. To leave? To vent?

"Have you told . . . been able to—"

Diana leaned against the cabinet, across the bed from Lyn, and shoved her hands in her pockets. "I heard back from Antonia, Rose's mother. Rose's dad died six months ago."

"Oh, I'm so sorry."

"She's all alone now." Diana's face held. No breaking down into sobs. "I promised I'd go see her when I get back."

"I'm sure that'll be hard for both of you."

She looked away and blinked. A quick swipe of her face and she turned back to Lyn. "Also, you should know, my parents heard from Omara."

"Already?"

"No. While we were gone. When Omara heard the *Mars Jedica* was missing, she looked into it, found out who I was, and asked them if their research could help find us."

Lyn sat back, stunned. She glanced around the room quickly. There was a privacy screen around Ruby's bed. Dr. Amos and Herschel were out of sight and hearing. Liam was comatose. "I don't know why that surprises me. Omara is a force to be reckoned with for sure. That she put it together."

"I know. Imagine how many others have."

"Do you know if she contacted anyone else? Former Pulsar people?"

"They didn't say. I asked them to stop talking about it. They encrypted their messages, but transmissions are bound to be screened. Plus, Omara didn't get anywhere with them. Even if they could get it to work, they had no idea where to look. At least not till our messages would start coming through in four years."

"But that's not a lifetime. Would they have tried?"

"From the way my dad reacted to seeing me, yeah, I'd say they've been working on it since she contacted them. That they wouldn't help her doesn't surprise me. My parents have a patent on paranoia."

"Good thing. Did they say how their work was going?"

"They dropped the topic when I told them to keep quiet about it. We'll catch up when I get back."

"How was it? Seeing your folks."

"My dad cried," she said in frustration.

"And that's bad?"

"He bawled during their whole first message to me. He couldn't even talk."

"Poor guy."

"Mom said when I disappeared, they spent all their time looking for me. Dad became depressed and couldn't work." She straightened. "She said he nearly died from a broken heart." She groaned. "Not *once*, growing up, do I remember them ever telling me they loved me," she said, tears forming.

"That must have hurt."

"No. That was normal. My normal." She wiped her cheek. "They had to think I was dead before I could know they love me?"

"A lot of people love you. Rose loved you. Not everyone knows how to say it or show it, but now you know." That was a risk, Lyn knew, mentioning the L-word, but Diana didn't react other than a slight nod.

"How're you doing?" Diana asked.

Lyn blurted out her default, "I'm okay," before fully analyzing her feelings about the question. If she'd learned anything now, it was the captain didn't always have to be on duty. She shook her head. "Maybe not okay. There's a weird normalcy returning. My brothers, once they got over the shock, act like

I never left. It's hard to make that leap from we nearly died to 'hey, let's grab a bite' or something. You know?"

Diana let out a chuckle. "Yeah, but I don't mind having to get used to it."

LYN WAS IN a meeting when Ghez messaged the *Maem* had arrived. She had learned the RV *Maem* was a private vessel registered with the vague sounding Institute of Research, based in Chile. What they researched way out here when all other space travel was prohibited was a mystery. Lyn had Ghez forward the call, zoomed in on Lyn only.

Captain Tey greeted Lyn cordially, but immediately added an ominous message. "We are invoking the Planetary Protection clause of the Outer Space Treaty." She sounded like she was reading from a script, or orders. "You are instructed to remain in quarantine under Category 5, Restricted Earth Return until you can verify decontamination."

"What does that mean?" Natalie whispered.

"It's reserved for ships that have come in contact with alien life," Marc whispered back.

"How could they know—?"

Marc touched her arm to shush her.

"May I ask why you think quarantine is necessary," Lyn responded blandly.

"With the nature of your disappearance and return unknown, we are required to assume contact and invoke protective measures. As a precaution."

"Who's 'we' and why assume contact? With whom?" Perhaps the alien abduction theory was gaining traction.

"It's standard procedure." Tey sounded unsure.

Lyn didn't mind following the protocol as long as she didn't have to reveal actual contact. Microbes were one thing. No one would be terribly concerned about that. Sentient microbes were something else again. Fact was, she didn't want Captain Tey jumping aboard *Endurance* and sticking her nose in things.

"Fine, if it will allay fears back home. I can assure you there's nothing to be concerned about. We'll be happy to comply if you can send over emergency rations."

Captain Tey hesitated. This must have been off script. "I'd like to, but with the quarantine we can't dock to your ship."

Lyn sighed and mentally rolled her eyes. "My passengers and crew are starving." She left out the alien infection. "A scan of our ship will show we've consumed just about all of it to survive these many months. I remind you that Section B, Article 1d of the treaty requires you to render aid. We have an empty lifepod bay you can release a container into."

"Understood," Tey said.

"Our engines have been repaired and we'll continue toward Mars during quarantine."

"Be advised, Captain, that Mars Control is limited to essential personnel only. They won't be able to help you. Proceed to Earth." Then her tone softened, like she was going off script. "I know it's an inconvenience, but it's only another three days."

Nothing she could do about a shutdown. "I'll have my first officer coordinate the food transfer. Randall out." She closed the link. Two could play that game.

Tey sent over a container of emergency rations. "More S rations," Miriam grumbled, watching the cartons being unloaded. "I was hoping for some vegetables, maybe some bread, or at least flour."

Endurance continued toward Earth and the promised rendezvous with Omara. The shortage of material for the Recyc-All kept everything Spartan. No augmented reality entertainment, no science experiments. Marc replaced his Okichitaw classes with Tai Chi, given everyone's reduced fitness levels. Lyn kept up daily department reports and personnel reviews. With Sharyn still in a coma, Hau Butler filled in. One housekeeping report caught her eye. Natalie had requested a return to her original quarters, where Diana stayed. Diana had not objected and the room change was noted for the manifest. Lyn leaned back and closed the report. This couldn't be good.

That evening, she sought out Ani, finding her in Medical serenading the comatose. She sat with Sharyn until she saw Ani pack up her instrument.

"Your playing is beautiful," Lyn said as they walked toward crew quarters. "You might think about a career change."

Ani chuckled. "Doesn't give me quite the adrenaline rush of piercing atmosphere at three G's."

When they reached Ani's door, before the moment could pass, Lyn blurted, "It's none of my business, really, but I'm not asking as your captain. Just as your friend. Everything okay with you and Natalie?"

Ani entered and motioned Lyn to join her. "Not unexpected, I guess. She's going back to her husband."

"I see." She waited for more. Her burning question, what about Rob, also wasn't her business.

"I'm not crushed," Ani said, "in case you were wondering. And I've told Rob I won't marry him." Her demeanor softened. She sat on her bed. "What I will miss," her voice shook, "is that she got me." She turned to Lyn and waved her hand. "This. What we went through. We'll all be freaks when we get back. It's like we've risen from the dead. You should have heard my parents. My sister still shrieks whenever she messages me."

Lyn sat beside her. "My mom cries in every vid. Even my dad. But when they act normal, that feels weirder."

"They have no idea, and we'll never go back, and no one will ever go where we were." She leaned forward on her elbows and wiped her face. "It's crazy. I've had three media companies approach me for exclusive rights to my story. We aren't even home yet."

"It's like whiplash, isn't it? One minute we're stranded four light years away, thinking maybe we'll make new lives on an alien planet, never see home again. Then we're fearing for our lives. Next thing we know, we're right back where we started from. Seems like it went by in a flash instead of excruciating months full of uncertainty. Yeah, crazy doesn't even begin to describe it."

"I'll miss flying if they don't reopen space. I don't know what I'll do."

"Come to Montana. I'll teach you how to really fly."

Ani slid her eyes toward Lyn and grinned.

BY THE TIME Petra again asked for more details about what had happened, Lyn was ready. She didn't need to lie, all she needed to do was omit certain facts. She described how they were mysteriously flung to Rigil Kentaurus, found a planet that proved uninhabitable, so they returned. All true.

"How did we get back?"

"In order to have enough energy to return we had to destroy everything related to it, so I'm afraid I can't be specific. Just know we found a wormhole and went through it. Sorry to frustrate you."

"I'm not able to feel frustration," Petra said.

"But I thought—" Lyn stopped, reminded Petra was back to her pre-event self. "So no knitting?"

"Knitting?" Petra asked. "I don't understand the question."

"Never mind." Then it hit her. If anyone knew what it was like to have memories erased, it was her. "I'm so sorry, Petra."

"Why?"

Chapter 33

OMARA ARRIVED ON her personal ship, the *El Choy*. Captain Tey tried to keep her from docking to *Endurance*, but she would have none of it.

"*Endurance* is my ship. Look it up," she told the flustered captain during a three-way call, to Lyn's delight.

The last time Omara had been aboard *Endurance* was for the tour's preflight party when she was bedecked with colorful scarves and gleaming jewelry. Now, stepping through the airlock, she wore a simple Omara Tours flight suit. Her long dark hair, streaked with gray, was pulled back in a simple twist and lines around her eyes and mouth made her appear older than her eighty years. Surely the stress from the past months had aged her. None of us look like we did two years ago, Lyn realized. Omara paused, taking them all in.

Because these were hard times, Lyn hadn't ordered crew to muster, normal protocol when the owner came aboard. Purely voluntary but still the Paddock was packed. They were a motley group compared to when Omara had last seen them. Marc and Miriam notably thinner. Edvane and Seng blotched with mysterious rashes. Only Edward appeared unchanged. Natalie had fashioned a modest *gele*. Sharyn and Liam, in ICU, were the only ones missing. Many guests joined them too. Lyn spotted Diana at the back of the crowd. She motioned her to join the crew, but Diana held back.

Omara bowed, clasped her hands to her chest, closed her eyes, overcome. The room fell silent. She wiped tears. "It is a miracle," she said softly. "No words can express my thanks for your safe return."

She made her way along the line, shaking hands with anyone within reach. She leaned in to speak quietly to most. She patted a shoulder, touched an arm. She knew better than to touch Edward but spoke with him at length. Lyn couldn't hear from where she stood. The room was otherwise quiet but for the respectful murmurs between Omara and whomever she was speaking with. Ani blushed at something Omara said. Miriam gestured dramatically. It was like a royal visit. Omara had undeniable wealth, and she didn't hide it, but she came across not simply down to earth—ha, that phrase, such a joy to reclaim—she wasn't humble, yet she wasn't annoying. Genuine. The real thing. Lyn had been loved well and deeply. She had also been betrayed completely. There weren't many people she willingly put all her faith in. Omara was one. She wished she knew what the formula was, what ingredients achieved that level of respect, admiration, and even love. She just knew it when she saw it and she wasn't the only one.

When Omara reached Lyn, she pulled her into a long, warm hug. Omara was not given to hugging her employees. Lyn expected it to be a stiff formality, but Omara enveloped her till Lyn could feel both their hearts beating. She relaxed, at last relieved of the burden of being the boss, comforted by the genuine emotions flowing between them.

"My dearest," Omara whispered.

The journey wasn't over, the trials perhaps only beginning, but for that moment, Lyn felt safe in her arms. When Omara finally released her, she wiped Lyn's wet cheek with a gentle thumb.

"We have much to catch up on, but that's for later. First"—she turned to the crew and guests and applauded—"well done!" Then she turned to her own crew, two men and a woman. "Let's get the supplies unloaded."

Marc organized lines to ferry crates and direct loaded hovercarts. Omara had brought fresh food, medicine, and a hold packed with equipment and material for the Recyc-All. Lyn watched with joy. Miriam squealed with delight and directed a bucket brigade to take the food down the stairs to the galley.

While the others unloaded, Lyn gave Omara a tour of her stripped-down ship. Peering at the bare walls, Omara remarked, "I would be sad to see the original art gone except for knowing it kept you alive."

In Medical, Omara sat with Sharyn.

Noticing Dr. Amos and one of Omara's crew unpacking a large Recyc-All, Lyn asked Omara about it. "He sent a list of things he needed. This is the newest, top of the line. I'm hoping it will be enough."

Lyn wondered, but didn't have the nerve to ask, how she afforded it, knowing she had lost her company. She knew Omara well enough to guess she kept business and personal separate. She'd told Lyn everyone would receive full pay for their time away.

MIRIAM WHIPPED TOGETHER a celebratory dinner. People ate like the starving survivors they were. The room was quiet for the most part, mostly clinking utensils and dishes, but for the occasional exclamation. "Real cheese!" "Oh, how I've missed grasshoppers!" "Chocolate!"

After dinner, Lyn and Omara slipped away to the *El Choy* to talk in private. The ship was almost twice the size of the *Jedica*. Large windows to the side and overhead let in starlight. Plush carpets, soft chairs, and couches. Not your typical spaceship accommodations.

She wanted to ask how Omara was doing, but she wasn't sure how to bring it up. Clearly she wasn't destitute. All Lyn knew of Omara's past was that she came from a long line of Middle Eastern royalty. Oil money till the oil ran out then fuel technology. First renewable, then jet propulsion, finally rocket science. For real, she was a rocket scientist. She liked to tell the story of how her great-great-grandmother wasn't allowed to drive and now she ran a space tourism company.

"I know you were primarily worried about us," Lyn began, "but I imagine this was hard on you too. I saw you on the news shows. I'm sorry you had to go through all that."

"You might be the only other person who understands what it's like to feel responsible for the deaths of so many. But I got off lucky. You are alive. Your ship returned safe, with even more than you left with." She smiled. "It goes with the job that every ship sent on a tour could end in disaster. We do our best. That's all we can do. If we are honest with ourselves, it's the only comfort we have."

"But you lost your company."

"Not lost. I liquidated early in order to protect the staff. Call it a pause. Maybe someday we'll be allowed back and I'll start over again. Wouldn't be the first time." She smiled warmly and motioned for Lyn to sit. End of topic, but Lyn was comforted knowing Omara was at peace.

Omara poured rich coffee in delicate cups, and they settled in comfortable chairs. A crew member brought a tray of dates and sweets. Lyn sipped and moaned in delight. The real thing. She sighed, then began with her encounter with Captain Bratt. "She sent her regards. She seemed very fond of you, said you knew each other a long time."

"To say the least. She was my first wife." She touched her fingers to her lips, lost in thought or emotion. "Back then, spaceflight was still a small, incestuous community. We all knew each other. Most 'biblically.'" She chuckled softly then grew quiet.

Lyn sat forward. "I'm so very sorry."

"I'm glad you had a chance to chat with her. She was a lovely woman. We parted quite amicably."

When Lyn sensed Omara was ready, she continued. "There are things I didn't put in my reports, that you need to know. Not just the technology that got us back."

Omara set her cup down. "Intriguing."

Lyn told her about the microbes on Marao that had made them ill.

"Nice name, by the way," Omara interrupted.

They shared a smile and Lyn continued, telling her about the possibility that they were sentient. And about her recovered memory of Rachel and Pulsar and the alien message asking to meet.

"Sentient, you say. Are they related to those who sent the message?"

Lyn shook her head. "Unlikely. As for sentience, that's open to debate, but they showed nonrandom electrical patterns, seemingly evolving as we interacted. We had no way to communicate with them that we know of. And it's probably best if we never go back."

That brought up the concern Lyn had of the technology being abused and the danger to Marao, or any world for that matter.

Omara nodded, thinking. "So you suspect a Pulsar connection? How?"

Lyn didn't need to explain Pulsar to Omara. She'd known Lyn's history when she hired her. She told her about the coding in Dr. Amos and Petra that prohibited superluminal travel.

"Petra? Oh, the poor thing," Omara said.

Lyn found Omara's response curious, but then again, Petra had been all Omara's, where the doctor had come with the ship. For Omara, Petra was personal. Lyn winced as she explained her need to reset Petra's memories to before the event.

Omara's eyes widened. "You two have much in common then." She must have seen Lyn's hurt look. "Please don't dwell on it. You did what you had to do. It got you back and Petra will go on." She reached for a date. "Yet if Pulsar is or was involved, your method of returning is bound to draw their interest."

"Lots of people will be interested."

"And this all relates to that alien message from during the war?" Omara asked.

"Who knows? But I think that contact was real, and if they did ask for a meeting as Rachel said, then we really are extremely close to a first encounter. If civilian governments are unaware of this and the remnants of Pulsar have free rein to control contact and the narrative . . ." She let that hang.

Omara stood and stretched. "And here I thought we only had to figure out what happened to you and the other ships in the first place. Does it relate? You said you have no idea what caused the event?"

Lyn told her Diana's theory of the natural spacequake.

"And that's how you hope to disguise your return, sans the technology."

"Our story, for now at least, is that whatever opened a wormhole to the Rigil Kent system is what also let us return. Not sure that will fly, but it's the best I've been able to come up with. Unleashing T technology is off the table as far as I'm concerned. We don't even mention it." She watched for Omara's reaction to her next statement. "I understand you were in contact with the Teegans."

"News travels," Omara said with a wink. "Yes. It didn't take much to connect the dots of her identity to their work. Unfortunately, I didn't get very far. From the way they reacted, I don't think I was the first to contact them. Or at least they seemed very comfortable being suspicious. I doubt they trust anyone. Maybe from the past or maybe the present. I'm not sure."

Omara refilled their cups. "Anyway, I undertook my own investigation. What wasn't revealed in the press, but I found when I went to where you disappeared, were traces of explosives. Nothing very spectacular. Quite primitive actually. Earth Control concluded it was an anomaly, like such a thing exists, and buried it deep in their report. I didn't make a fuss about it because I thought it might be useful knowledge later. Like now."

"You think the *Aphrodite* was sabotaged?"

Omara furrowed her brow and shook her head. "I thought maybe *you* were—given your past with Pulsar and knowing you still had enemies. You think it was the larger ship? Why?"

Lyn told her about the video showing a flash low on the ship.

Omara let out a quick breath. "I don't understand. All those lives."

"Maybe it wasn't meant to destroy the ship. Just enough damage to shut down tourism."

"Indeed, that happened," Omara said. "Almost immediately. Earth Control recalled everyone and put space off limits."

"Except for our friend out there." Lyn gestured to take in the *Maem*.

Omara sipped her coffee. "The people behind Pulsar didn't just go into the arts when it disbanded. I wouldn't be surprised if our little friend was up to something best done without pesky tourists looking over her shoulder."

"Rachel heads Earth Control, so my guess is the *Maem* captain works for Rachel."

"The plot thickens," Omara said.

Lyn told her about the names she'd recovered, former Pulsar advisors and board members who were never in the public eye. None rang a bell with Omara either. She agreed they'd have to tread carefully.

The ramifications were obvious, but Lyn said it anyway. "If this technology gets into the hands of those wanting to hold a meeting with these aliens—or make a first strike—I can't even begin to contemplate the outcome."

"Dire."

"My fear is we get back and sucked into a black hole of paranoia by those responsible, whoever they are. I'm sorry to burden you with this, but I can't trust anyone and you're all I have right now."

Omara waved her hand dismissively. "This is no longer just your problem."

Quiet settled over them. All Lyn could do was hope her trust in the woman was valid. She listened for the hum of the *El Choy*'s systems. It was masked by soft music, flutes in the background.

Omara shifted, leaning forward. "We need to get ahead of this and create our own narrative. Nothing like a little light to keep out the darkness. When I'm through making arrangements, your return will be such a media circus, no one will dare question your version of events. You, my dear, are a hero and that's our story."

Lyn shook her head. "I'm no hero. You should know about the six hundred, the *Aphrodite* survivors."

"It was in your report. And, yes, word has leaked to the media that some survived the initial event."

"I should have been able to save them."

Omara shook her head. "I defy anyone to handle it better than you did under the circumstances. There is information that hasn't been made public yet, within the negotiations over the lawsuits by the families, that shows significant lapses by Galaxy Cruises. Shoddy construction, poor training." She reached forward and touched Lyn's knee. "They had no business running a space operation, let alone a trip as risky as the Grand Tour."

"Still."

"Still nothing." Omara leaned back and shook her head. "Poor Celeste. She deserved better than that. I see our conversations differently now. She wanted to bring them up to her level. It just wasn't possible. You will not blame yourself, Lyn. I wish I had tried harder to talk her out of taking the job."

Lyn withdrew a cube from her pocket and handed it to Omara. "This contains all the material we recovered from the *Aphrodite*. I now see you are the best person to handle this. Contact the families. I'd like to pay my respects. Maybe a memorial service?"

Omara fingered the cube.

"If you are wondering whether Celeste left a last message, I doubt she had time when the event occurred. Whatever is in there would be from before the tour."

Omara closed her hand over the cube. "The usual bland stuff I suppose."

"Like mine."

"Yes. Though I did appreciate the nice things you said about me."

"I meant them."

Omara placed the cube on the table. She slipped her boots off and tucked her legs under her. "I think we should put right out front that you returned because of exciting new technology, which for the good of humankind must never be used again."

Lyn's eyebrows rose. It seemed counter to what she proposed. "Like with the atomic bomb? That didn't turn out so well. You really want to open that box?"

Omara gave her a chiding look. "Nevertheless. You said you destroyed the equipment as well as the research."

"Except," Lyn tapped her head, "for what's up here."

"You remember it all?"

"Let's just say, I have unique enhancements that help me remember."

Omara stared at her for a beat. "Did you by chance receive those enhancements during your time with Pulsar?"

Lyn nodded.

"And you are sure there isn't some automatic backup?"

"No, actually, I don't." She told her about the password protection.

Omara's brows knit, considering. "Maybe just primitive enough to work."

"I should have killed myself and been shot into a star."

"Let's not be overly dramatic. I don't want to mourn you again."

Lyn frowned. "It's hopeless, isn't it? We can't control this. The box has been opened."

"The box may be opened, but it will soon be filled with light. Let's work with that."

WHEN LYN STEPPED back onto *Endurance* the next morning, she heard voices and laughter from the stairway. Miriam, Diana, and Ani emerged, laden with trays of pastries and muffins and urns of coffee and juice for the staff meeting.

"God, what time is it?" Lyn asked.

"I hope that's a rhetorical question. It's right there on your sleeve." Miriam turned to the others. "No wonder we were lost for almost two years." Miriam and Ani laughed.

Lyn reached for a treat. Miriam swung the tray away. "Wait your turn."

"Someone's been busy." Lyn's mouth watered.

"Worth working all night, I'd say." Miriam had a new spring in her step. "Speaking of which, were you with Omara all night?"

Lyn nodded and held the door for them. Marc, Ghez, Natalie, and Hau were already seated at the new chairs and table, made possible by Omara's supplies. Edward and Isabel soon followed.

"Is she joining us? I brought enough," Miriam said.

"No. She's catching up on her sleep."

Natalie had chosen to sit between Marc and Ghez. That left Ani to navigate her own place. She sat next to Lyn. Not in direct line with Natalie. Ah, romance and its awkward ending. Diana sat next to Ani. Out of Lyn's direct line of sight.

Lyn desperately wanted to crawl into her own bed and sleep for twelve hours, but they only had two weeks before they arrived at Earth. She felt both the excitement of getting home as well as the tension of what would happen once they arrived. She dished out assignments between bites of apple turnover and sips of coffee. Marc would work with Omara on the circus that would become their triumphant return to Earth. She wanted nothing more to do with that than was necessary. Edward and Isabel continued to refurbish *Endurance*'s essentials. Hau managed the flow of guest requests.

Marc said he'd excused Dr. Amos from the meeting so he could continue his work with the new equipment. "For an android, he seems pretty excited."

"For a *doctor*," Lyn chided teasingly. "Let's all do whatever we can to help him. We want them better and we want to be out of quarantine as soon as possible."

Marc reviewed the documents they needed to complete, a mess of red tape, scans, and tests.

Lyn briefed them on Omara's idea of a media blitz. "There's no point in trying to disguise how we got back." She looked at Diana. "If we can avoid mentioning T particles, that would go a long way to protecting—" She stopped short of saying "your parents." Light may work for Omara, but Lyn decided keeping people in the dark, however it might come back to haunt her, was best on this topic.

To everyone, she said, "I won't tell you how to answer what will probably be difficult, intrusive questions, nor should I. Do what you need to protect yourselves. I take and accept full responsibility. Don't let anyone bully you or suggest I abdicated any responsibility to you. None of you knows in its entirety how this was done."

Diana hadn't said a word during the meeting. Fact was, her job was done and there wasn't much for her to do. As they stood to leave, Lyn asked her if she wanted to talk.

"No need, Captain. I'm sure Omara is waiting for you."

Lyn watched her leave, puzzled. What's Omara have to do with this? And "Captain"?

After the meeting, Lyn stopped by her quarters long enough to shower then went straight to Medical.

"With these new medbots Omara brought," Dr. Amos said, "I can treat all the damage as well as eliminate the microbes."

Lyn indicated Sharyn. "Can you reverse the comas?"

"That's my assumption. Once they have new medbots and the alien microbes are vanquished, they should heal. And the new Recyc-All will let me build organic tissue." He turned to Liam. "He needs new kidneys."

Lyn sat with Sharyn and squeezed her hand. "I hope I'll be talking with you again soon." She looked back at the doctor. "Will there be any trace of the alien microbes once you're done?"

"Not in each individual. I could preserve some for future study if you wish me to."

"No. Please destroy everything, including your notes about the microbes."

"All of them?"

"I'm afraid so."

"That goes against protocol. Any investigation will want a full report on our experience."

"I'm ordering you to destroy them."

"Understood." The beauty of Dr. Amos was she didn't need to raise her voice or change her tone at all. Be nice if humans were that compliant.

OVER THE NEXT week, Liam's new kidneys grew and began to function. Ruby Fischer was the first to wake up. Liam was next. Then Zoya, who was despondent to have missed all the excitement. Alexander reminded her of all that she had to be thankful for. She admitted as much, but turned to Lyn by her bedside and said hoarsely, "If you ever are inclined to do this again, do let me know." Lyn promised she would.

That left Sharyn. Her problems centered on her brain, a very dangerous swelling. Even if she did regain consciousness, would there be damage the doctor couldn't fix? Lyn sat. And waited. Gradually, her vitals improved, the swelling lessened, her body temperature stabilized.

Lyn got the call in the middle of the night. "She's waking up," the doctor said. She was out the door before he'd finished the sentence. Sharyn's breathing apparatus had been removed, the tubes delivering fluids and nutrients disconnected. Her cheeks pinker, not the sallow pale of her coma. Lyn took her hand and squeezed, but still no response.

Then a sharp intake of breath and her eyes fluttered open. It had been fifty-nine days. Almost two months. Interminable.

"Hey," Lyn said softly, her voice thick, tears forming.

Sharyn's mouth moved to speak but nothing came out. Her eyes flicked from the doctor to Lyn. She took a breath and tried again. "Hey, Boss." It came out scratchy but clear.

Dr. Amos ran a series of tests and scans. Her eyes tracked, her toes moved. By the time he was done, her impatience had recovered. "What's going on? Was I out long?"

The doctor looked at Lyn, seeming to ask, You want this or should I? Lyn brushed her fingers through Sharyn's hair and caressed her face. "It's been a while, but you'll be okay." She looked at the doctor. "Right?"

"You should make a full recovery," he said to Sharyn.

She took a deep breath. "I'm hungry. Anything to eat on this barge?"

Lyn smiled. "You've got some catching up to do."

Miriam came down with a tray of eggs, algae bacon, muffins, and tea. Sharyn's eyes widened. Lyn took her hand again. "I've got some news. We are almost home."

She summarized the past two months. Miriam beamed from the other side of the bed, filling in gossipy details Lyn left out.

"Home? And Omara's here?" Sharyn asked.

She ate while they talked but suddenly stopped. She dropped the muffin and her hand flew to her mouth. Was it too much good food too fast? Was she going to puke? Lyn reached under the bed for a pan. Sharyn burst into tears.

"Geez," Miriam said. "You want us to send you back?"

Sharyn started laughing. While still crying. When she could finally speak, she said, "I can't believe it. Home?"

"Almost. Maybe another week," Lyn said.

WHILE SHARYN RECOVERED, Omara visited her often. When she was well enough to move to her quarters, Lyn accompanied her. She wanted to soften the blow of what *Endurance* had transformed into—a bare skeleton of its former self. Sharyn walked the short hallway to her quarters, eyes wide.

"What have you done to my ship?" she asked.

Lyn explained, ending with, "It's worth everything to see you walking and complaining."

Sharyn sat on her bed and stared at the empty walls.

"You scared me, Wang," Lyn said softly, sitting beside her. "I was afraid I'd lose you."

Sharyn waved her hand dismissively. "Pfft. It'll take more than a little brain swelling to do me in." She took a breath. "We're really headed home?"

"Yep."

"I can't believe Omara's here. You know, I'd really hoped to keep working with her, but there's no way I'm going back to space."

Lyn took her hand. "Me neither."

Chapter 34

LAS VEGAS. NOT the first place Lyn would have chosen, but that was where Omara wanted them to land. She took in the details Marc laid out with a mix of shock and amusement. Pure Omara. Clarke Terminal, the space elevator they'd launched from those many months ago, had been mothballed by Earth Control when they shut down space travel, plus it was too isolated for Omara's purposes. *Endurance* would land. Flashier the better.

Marc briefed Lyn on the logistics, deploying the wings, everyone strapped in, which meant rebuilding seats in the Paddock. Normally *Endurance* could land anywhere, with its powerful thrusters and sophisticated engines, but this was not a normal *Endurance*. Thrusters, overworked during the traverse, were down to backups on three of them. The engines were basics rebuilt after destroying TPCA. She could no longer drop from orbit in a smooth, controlled descent, ending with a helicopter-like final kilometer onto a small landing platform. *Endurance* could handle the extreme heat of reentry, but she'd have to glide to a runway with minimal thruster pressure to slow her to a stop.

Hence Vegas. It had lost a lot of its luster from its twentieth-century heyday but possessed a runway at an old Air Force base and could handle a massive influx of media, politicians, families, and the curious. Didn't hurt that Omara had a home in Ruby Valley, to the north.

"Sure to be a circus," Lyn said.

"A hot circus," Marc said. "Vegas in August. What was she thinking?"

"At least it'll be early morning, before it really heats up," Lyn said, trying to look on the bright side.

He was almost back to his old form physically, his face filled out yet lines remained around his eyes. He was not a lot older but much wiser. They were less captain and first officer now and more colleagues. Who knew where either would end up after this, but the old hierarchy was on its way out. Soon they'd both be civilians. She knew what it meant for her but could only guess what Marc was going through now. She was happy he had Isabel.

She approved Omara's request for a ban on crew talking to the media until they landed and were discharged from their duties, but there was nothing she or Omara could do about the passengers who were being bombarded with interview requests. The best she could do was limit their com time, to keep lines open for everyone, she claimed. Jeanne used her show to host fellow passengers, which proved lucrative for her. Lyn was beyond caring, and Jeanne sucking up com time meant less Lyn had to deal with.

She nixed Omara's idea of an extra orbit to fly over key media sites around the globe. "These people want to get home."

She conceded to entering North American airspace over Boston instead of San Francisco. The long descent across the country could be tracked and talked about. Omara, still traveling with them, would duck down from the west so she could be there to greet them and not take anything away from their dramatic return.

The occasional media inquiry slipped through the gag order. Ethan's boyfriend was a freelance producer. "Just one interview?" her brother asked.

"I can't," Lyn messaged back. "The trip isn't over till everyone is safe back on Earth. What if we crash on the runway? I'll talk all you want once we land."

Next day a headline splashed across the screen, "*Endurance* Captain Warns of Crash Landing."

"I was talking to my brother," Lyn said when Omara cornered her.

Omara paced Lyn's office. Marc sat contrite.

Sharyn, her first full day back on duty, failed to suppress a smile. "Clearly I've missed a lot," she said quietly.

"Not to worry," Omara said finally. "Maybe we can use this. The more hazardous the trip, the better you look in the end."

Lyn slumped in her chair. She massaged deep furrows in her brow. Were they new? Permanent?

Omara issued a statement to the effect all landings contained a measure of risk. She took the opportunity to outline the handicaps *Endurance* was flying under and how her courageous, capable captain was just doing her job, not taking anything for granted.

Lyn wanted to crawl under a rock, if one had been available, when she saw the headline, "Crippled Ship, Plucky Captain, World Holds Breath for Dramatic Return."

"Plucky, eh?" Miriam teased at lunch.

That's how the days went as they lurched from one PR disaster to another.

When they passed Mars, the already heady atmosphere on board grew even more electric. Less than three days. Suddenly Lyn had the weird feeling of not wanting it to end. For her crew and passengers, certainly. But for herself? Maybe she'd drop everyone off and take *Endurance* back to space. She hated the thought of being in the limelight but had to concede that the more the focus was on her, the less scrutiny the others faced. She'd learn to live with it, she supposed.

They'd complied with the quarantine restrictions. Marc's report detailed their clean bill of health, so the *Maem* peeled off, Captain Tey sending a vague message wishing them well and saying she was returning to Mars.

Lyn used the last few days before landing to settle herself and say goodbye to her beloved ship and crew. She might never see any of them again. Each journey down a hallway felt like the last, and she wanted to savor the remaining quiet moments.

"Hey, Petra," Lyn said.

"Is there something I can help you with, Lyn?"

"I probably won't see you again once we land, so I wanted to thank you for your service. I'll miss you."

"I take it you don't mean 'see' in the literal sense, since there is nothing about me to see. But likewise," Petra responded. "I'll miss you too, Lyn."

IN HER LAST official weekly meeting with Marc, they stood together by the window in her office. Earth, the real thing, glowed in the distance.

"Is there anything left to go over?" he asked.

"Probably. Logistics. Schedule. More thanks than I could ever express." They'd never work together again. That she was sure of. "I'm sorry you missed the captain's exam."

He snorted a laugh.

"You'll make a great leader. It doesn't have to be in space."

He didn't say anything. She couldn't read his thoughts in his profile. Were those gray hairs at his temple? They mirrored each other, side by side, hands clasped behind their backs.

"Just because we disagreed doesn't mean you weren't right," she said. "In another universe, you would have gotten us back. I'm convinced."

"Would the six hundred still have died?"

"Maybe. Maybe not. Maybe you'd have had a first officer who challenged you, not because there is a right or wrong decision, but because you need to make the best one possible under the circumstances."

He bounced a little on his toes. "Got plans?"

So this is how it would be. "Not really. Home to Montana for now. You?"

"Isabel wants to see James Bay. We'll visit my homeland then she'll show me around Catalonia."

"You'll stay in touch, I hope."

"Sure. Expect a wedding invitation."

That brought a smile. "I look forward to it. Who popped the question?"

"She did. Not that I wasn't about to."

"I'm happy for you."

A sense of peace settled over Lyn. She hoped he felt it too. It would have been hard to return to space without this crew. Every life follows its own trail, whether through a wilderness or over familiar ground. You inhabit your moment in time, your patch of space, with people you choose to be with or not. Doesn't matter. It's how you come out the other side that does.

He broke the silence. "It's an understatement to say it's been a privilege to serve with you."

"Likewise. I find myself saying thank you a lot these days. It doesn't seem adequate."

"It is. So, thank you." He gave her a mischievous grin.

LYN MADE ONE last tour of the ship. Passing through the hallways, she stopped to chat with those remaining in their rooms for the landing. Sharyn and Hau were checking off the guest list, making sure everyone was secure.

Lyn squeezed Sharyn's arm. "I can't tell you how good it is to see you up and about."

"Never thought I'd miss this, but I think I will."

"You have plans?"

Sharyn shook her head. "It's weird how lost I feel now. Just as we found our way back."

"We all have a lot of adjustments to make. We'll keep in touch."

"Plan on it."

Lyn's last stop was Medical to say goodbye to Dr. Amos. "You're welcome to leave *Endurance* if you want."

"Where would I go? This is my home."

"She won't be flying anymore. I'll talk to Omara. If she can't find another job for you, I'll ask my dad. Any interest in geoengineering?"

He didn't respond right away, probably researching the topic. "I'll think about it. In the meantime, Captain, please continue your good health habits and be sure to get all your annual screenings in a timely manner."

"Yes, Doctor. Do you want to join us for the ceremony?"

"That won't be necessary."

"You were critical to our success."

"Just doing my job, Captain."

"I hope someday as you continue to learn, you'll see you did much more than that, meant much more to us than a doctor."

He didn't answer. Because he couldn't or because it wasn't in the form of a question?

Lyn smiled. "Do you want me to deactivate you?"

"Please. That would be most efficient."

He stepped into his charging station and his eyes closed with power down.

"I'm going to miss you," she said. Must be nice not to miss people, she thought.

She stopped in the Paddock to visit with her guests, suited up for the final leg. This time they'd be able to watch on a viewscreen set up at the front of the room. Things could still go wrong, but at this point, Lyn decided, they deserved to witness everything. She held a squirming Hope, now one year old, while her parents buckled in. Isabel had needed to make a new suit for her, she was growing so fast. Lyn handed her off to Jeanne who took her with no words.

Suzanne touched Lyn's arm. "Thank you for everything."

Jeanne grunted, pretending to struggle with the baby's harness.

Lyn patted her arm and moved on to Zoya. "I want a signed copy of your memoir the moment it's out," she said during their hug.

"Don't be surprised if you see it dedicated to you," Zoya said with a wink. Then she gripped Lyn's arms. "Be careful, but have a good life. You deserve it."

Lyn watched Diana from the corner of her eye. She'd allowed procrastination to elbow her aside too long. Now or never. She touched Diana's shoulder as she started into a row. "Can I have a moment?"

They walked to the stairwell at the back of the Paddock. Diana stood stiffly with her hands clasped behind her back, her face a blank slate. Lyn thought she was prepared for this, but every coherent thought left her brain. So much for enhancements. This woman before her, who had reached past the captain, was now her peer. Without the role to shield her, she flailed. *How does one do this? Blurt out I love you?* Did she even? Or was time simply running out?

Mouth dry, throat clamped shut, Lyn swallowed. Just tell her the truth. "I don't know where to begin." Did Diana know this was Lyn talking to her and not the captain? "I mean . . ." *Oh, hell.* "I'm sorry, I'm not very good at this."

Diana cracked a smile. "What, saying goodbye? Thought we'd be stuck together forever?"

Is that what this was? "No, I mean, does it have to be?"

Diana's face relaxed, she seemed at peace. "I think so." She glanced back toward the crowd of people settling into their seats. "There's going to be a lot going on in a few hours. Who knows what the future will bring."

"I want you to be safe. There will be an investigation. You'll be under a spotlight. I hate that you have to go through that." Alone, she meant. *Crap, that was the captain talking!*

"You too, no doubt. I suppose the further we are from each other, the better."

Would it be? Probably. What did Lyn want? For Diana to be safe, or them to be together? Not if it meant Diana ripped apart by those wanting the technology. All hope of objectivity had vanished. "What will you do?"

"Not sure. Lavenza offered me a spot in Brussels, but I haven't decided yet. What about you?"

"Not sure either. Hide. Maybe Montana." She couldn't believe she was saying this. Despite the magnetic pull she felt toward Diana, it didn't seem reciprocated.

"With Omara?"

"What? No." What did Omara have to do with this? She glanced past Diana, into the Paddock, people settling in, then met her gaze. "This is not the time, or the place, and I apologize for that. I apologize for a lot of things but mostly for misleading you. About that night—"

"Please. I get it. You and Omara go way back."

Wait, was that it? "No," Lyn said, feeling sudden panic. "We don't. Omara was my boss. That's all she ever was." Ready or not, she pressed on. "That night—for me, I mean." Lyn plunged, flailing. "We never said anything, I'm sorry I didn't, but I do care for you. I do love you." *There. Said.* She stepped back, suddenly breathless, like a decompression. "I know that's not what *you* meant. I know you're not ready. I couldn't find the words to say it then. But I want you to know." She smiled weakly. "Just in case."

"Bridge to Captain Randall," Marc called to her. "We've entered orbit."

"Just a minute," Lyn replied. "It's okay. Bad timing, I know. Things are going to be rough. They'll come after you, so try to get away before they have a chance. Get to Brussels, anywhere. I don't know what I was thinking."

Diana shook her head, her expression almost like she'd seen a ghost. "I need . . . time."

Lyn didn't need brain enhancements to read the vibe. She didn't know her outside the confines of their stranded experience. Who knew what she was like under normal circumstances? She had a life to go back to. They all did. Ani and Natalie were breaking up. None of this was meant to last.

"Captain," Marc called again.

"I need to go," Diana said. "Get in my seat. You've got a ship to land." She tipped her head. "If I don't see you—" She turned and all but ran for the shelter of the crowd.

"Coming," Lyn responded to Marc.

Well, that was a mess. She consoled herself that at least she'd said it. She couldn't bring herself to walk back through the Paddock, so she went down a flight and entered the bridge from the lower level. She used the time to calm herself, let the boss take over.

"Where are the purple sidelights?" she asked.

Ani laughed and turned them on as Lyn stepped up to the command level.

On the main screen, the cities of Europe blinked, bright gems on black velvet. *God, Earth is beautiful.* Even if she hadn't come to peace about the trip ending and her new life beginning, she couldn't wait to step into the hot August sun. All Earth's media outlets were following *Endurance*'s progress toward its triumphant return. Guests had already given many interviews. While the first question everyone asked was How'd you do it? No one seemed to grasp the implications. Yet. Lyn had chuckled at Nikoleta Canno's oft-repeated quote, "We just built a better engine and came the hell back!"

Marc read through the landing checklist. TPCA was gone. All Diana's research erased. Bridge crew were back down to Ani and Ghez, her and Marc. Edward and Isabel kept an eye on things from Engineering. Everyone else was in the Paddock or their quarters.

"Disengage gravity," Marc ordered Edward.

"Gravity disengaged," he reported back. Needlessly, since Lyn's stomach somersaulted.

"Begin wing deployment," Marc ordered.

"Deployment engaged," Edward said.

A vibration shuddered through the ship. Natalie, sitting in the Paddock, provided explanations for the guests.

"Ready for entry, on your mark, Captain," Ani said.

"Begin entry," Lyn said. "Let's land this puppy."

Marc looked at her with an amused grin.

"Confirming wings deployed and locked," Ani said. "Entering atmosphere."

"Entry interface 121 kilometers," Ghez said. "Outer hull temperature rising."

"Attitude forty degrees and holding," Ani said.

"Hull temperature 1500 degrees C," Ghez said.

"All systems normal," Edward reported.

The heat of reentry surrounded the ship in a fiery glow. It gradually dissipated and for the next twenty minutes, *Endurance* glided across North America.

Lyn couldn't remember the last time she'd landed rather than docked at the elevator. Ghez read out the decreasing altitude and significant locations they passed. Syracuse, the capital of the North American Alliance; a swing south through Indiana; across the Mississippi. Once they were below eighteen thousand feet, Marc let everyone know they could remove their helmets. They passed low over the Rocky Mountains. Ani swung them over the Grand Canyon for a thrill and prepared for the approach into the abandoned airbase east of Las Vegas.

Another vibration.

"Landing gear deployed and locked," Ani said. "Prepare for landing."

Vegas hadn't changed much with desertification. More reverting to the desert it always was. No more green lawns or swimming pools. Brown hills and brown plains zipped by as the ground raced to greet them. Ahead a dot of dark. The airfield. It grew larger, the ground closer, till a significant bump and slight shudder caught Lyn's attention.

"*Endurance* has touched down," Ani said, like it was any ordinary flight. "Reverse thrusters engaged."

The G forces pushed Lyn against the restraint. When it eased she unbuckled. Marc looked at her with surprise.

"I want to see for myself," she said, and went to the conference room to look out a window as they rolled to a stop.

The dark splotch seen from the air turned out to be a cluster of old buildings and a moving, antlike swarm. Not ants. People. Unimaginable. Humans, as far as she could see, and the flat Nevada plain made that pretty damn far. If Omara hadn't assured her that all family members would be in prime spots for the reunion, she'd have feared she'd never find her parents. She couldn't hear the crowd, but hands waved, some holding flags for the NAA or Omara Tours, others shooting holographic fireworks or Welcome Home signs. The low, morning sun slanted long shadows.

Endurance slowed to a stop near a hastily remodeled hangar, one that hadn't been used in a century at least. She returned to the bridge and, for kicks, broadcast her standard end-of-tour speech. "Thank you for choosing Omara Tours. Please be sure to fill out the evaluation." Pause. "Just kidding. Sorry for the delay, but welcome home." Normally she'd announce that the crew would unload their luggage, but everything had been recycled. All anyone would leave with was a small tote.

A stairway had been pushed up against the ship. As was customary at the end of every tour, Lyn and her crew lined up at the open doorway by the reception area on the Main Deck, shaking hands or hugging departing passengers. Zoya, all nineteen Beteros, little Hope. Even Jeanne accepted Lyn's hand. Lyn tried to keep an eye out for Diana but hadn't seen her. Somehow she'd slipped by. She needed to vanish into anonymity, Lyn told herself.

While the guests streamed down to the tarmac, cheers rose from the crowd like the finale of a brilliant concert.

Then, as if by a mind link, she felt a presence.

"I've had time," Diana said, now by her side.

Almost all the guests had gone by. Now *really* wasn't the time. Lyn tried to push Diana out the door, behind Fran. "You need to get out of here."

Diana pulled Lyn into the shadow beside the doorway. "Stop it. You confused me back there. Were you trying to get rid of me or do you want to be with me? Because I am ready. What I'm not ready for is losing you."

There was no time to talk this over. Lyn caressed Diana's face. "I want to be with you." She kissed her. The world tilted then righted in silence. No klaxon of warning. Diana kissed her back, deeply and passionately, answering all her questions wordlessly. They parted, breathless, then a quick hug.

"I love you," Diana whispered.

It was down to the Hanaks, then the crew would start down the steps. Lyn felt her staff watching her as she gripped Diana's shoulders.

"You've just made me the happiest person on the planet. But there's a condition." She shook her head when Diana started to protest. "No exceptions. You go now, melt into the crowd. We can meet up later. Tonight. Just go." She kissed her again. This time Diana nodded and slipped away. Lyn watched her step into the light.

For a moment she felt dizzy, like she'd been braced in a stiff wind that suddenly stopped. She held onto the doorframe and turned to see her crew staring at her with expressions ranging from surprise to joy to smug satisfaction.

"I knew it," Miriam said, nudging Sharyn, who grinned.

Lyn laughed. "Go home. Be well. Stay in touch." She shooed them through the doorway.

Omara had wanted Lyn to hold back and leave the ship alone, but Lyn refused. They departed in reverse order of rank and seniority, which put her last anyway. Marc patted her shoulder as he passed. It was time. She gave *Endurance*'s wall a kiss and a pat.

"Goodbye, Petra."

"Goodbye, Lyn."

That was it for goodbyes. Time to say hello to Earth. At the top of the steps she squinted in the bright sun, many times brighter than Marao's. Despite the early hour, heat blasted her like opening an oven. What a glorious sensation. Baked tarmac seared her nostrils with a sourness she could taste in the back of her mouth. Spread before her, thousands of family members, friends, dignitaries, and the just plain curious mobbed against short barriers. Pure, happy chaos. A band played. She heard their names over a loudspeaker. The cheers grew louder. Her former guests had spread into a mass at the bottom of the steps, ignoring the dignitaries in the reception line. Rachel was there. Omara had warned her. Halfway down the steps, Lyn caught a glimpse of Diana slipping past the mob, toward the side of the stage set up for the ceremony. An older couple ran toward her. She threw a glance back toward Lyn then they disappeared into the crowd.

Nothing else mattered. Sure, it wasn't over. Not by a long shot. Rachel needed to be dealt with. What role Pulsar played, Lyn had no idea, but she didn't believe for a second they weren't involved. The traverse, interstellar travel now possible. Marao. Those truths must never get out. Let those sentient microbes live in peace.

It all mattered, but didn't. This was it, time to shuck the old ways, the uniform, the role, and see what life could be like. On Earth. Nothing was certain but the comfort that she wouldn't face this alone. She and Diana stood at an event horizon, their own little bang, of consequence only to them, perhaps, but together she knew they could do anything.

Satisfied, Captain Lyn Randall stepped onto the hot Vegas tarmac. Home.

Acknowledgements

It goes without saying that writing may look like a solitary endeavor but is in fact full of teamwork. The heart of this story is about leadership and, for us nonmilitary types, the joys of a great boss. I spent four decades working for the entire gamut of bosses, from horrible (many) to inspiring (happily my last spent working for someone else). A good boss is precious and rare. I've been blessed to have worked for the best. You know who you are.

The references to Ernest Shackleton and his *Endurance* are intentional. I've been inspired by his "you can't make this stuff up" adventure for decades. If you aren't familiar with his story, read about his Imperial Trans-Antarctic Expedition and be prepared to be wowed. As I was finishing this story, the circle completed for me when Shackleton's *Endurance* was found at the bottom of the Weddell Sea.

The "three nuggets of leadership" Lyn learned from her Professor James were inspired by the real-life Retired Navy Admiral James Stavridis in an interview he gave while dean of The Fletcher School at Tufts University. I had the pleasure of hearing this brilliant man speak, and you could see the quiet power he exuded through sheer empathy and congeniality. Ernest Shackleton embodied these attributes as well. Lyn tried to live up to these giants of leadership, though she didn't always succeed.

The ring of dark matter alludes to Professor Lisa Randall's (no relation) theory of what caused the demise of the dinosaurs. And all the wormhole stuff was intentionally cherry picked from papers saying, yeah, it could happen! Lots was made up.

My team includes, well, where to begin? Wrangling this complex story with a large cast was made much easier thanks to Lisa Cron's *Story Genius*, voluminous research, the online simulator Celestia for figuring out planetary alignments a hundred-plus years into the future, and all the inspiring men and women who have ventured to space or made it possible for others to follow. And to NASA/JPL for the inspiring "Visions of the Future" tourism posters they created, including one for a Grand Tour.

My classmates in the Advanced Fiction class at Pioneer Valley Writers Workshop dissected the opening and pushed me to explore new depths of "interiority." Thank you, Sacchi and Paula for your enthusiastic beta reads. Sarah Cypher, at The Threepenny Editor, made this a much better book, showed me how to end well, and was the kind of cheerleader writers crave.

The Bedazzled Ink crew are the best: My thanks go to Casey (editor and cover designer extraordinaire), Liz, and Claudia.

Last, and first, to Beth, with thanks for the love that keeps me going.

Teammates aside, the ultimate responsibility lies with the captain, er writer, so all errors, intentional or not, are mine.

Special thanks to you, my readers.

Elaine Burnes lives in western Massachusetts. After twenty years working and writing for a variety of environmental nonprofits, she tired of reality and turned to writing fiction in her spare time, publishing her first short story, "A Perfect Life," in *Skulls and Crossbones* (Mindancer Press) in 2010. Since then, she's had more stories published, including "A Certain Moon," in the Golden Crown Literary Society Award–winning anthology *Wicked Things* from Ylva in 2014, and "Auto Repair," which earned an honorable mention in the 2015 Saints and Sinners Short Fiction Contest. These are collected in *A Perfect Life and Other Stories* (GusGus Press, 2016), which won a Rainbow Award for Best Lesbian Anthology/Collection. Her first novel, *Wishbone* (Bedazzled Ink, 2015) received a 2016 Golden Crown Literary Society Award for Dramatic/General Fiction.

Visit https://elaineburnes.com to learn about Elaine and her work.

Aim your phone's camera at the code.